W9-AUY-699

BLIND SPOT

THE SPENSER NOVELS

THE JESSE STONE NOVELS

Robert B. Parker's
Damned If You Do
(by Michael Brandman)

Robert B. Parker's
Fool Me Twice
(by Michael Brandman)

Robert B. Parker's
Killing the Blues
(by Michael Brandman)

Split Image
Night and Day
Stranger in Paradise
High Profile
Sea Change
Stone Cold
Death in Paradise
Trouble in Paradise
Night Passage

THE SUNNY RANDALL NOVELS

Spare Change
Blue Screen
Melancholy Baby
Shrink Rap
Perish Twice
Family Honor

THE COLE/HITCH WESTERNS

Robert B. Parker's
Bull River
(by Robert Knott)

Robert B. Parker's
Ironhorse
(by Robert Knott)

Blue-Eyed Devil
Brimstone
Resolution
Appaloosa

ALSO BY ROBERT B. PARKER

Double Play
Gunman's Rhapsody
All Our Yesterdays
A Year at the Races
(with Joan H. Parker)

Perchance to Dream
Poodle Springs
(with Raymond Chandler)

Love and Glory
Wilderness
Three Weeks in Spring
(with Joan H. Parker)

Training with Weights
(with John R. Marsh)

THE JESSE STONE
NOVELS

Robert B. Parker's
Damned if You Do
by Michael Brandman

Robert B. Parker's
Fool Me Twice
by Michael Brandman

Robert B. Parker's
Killing the Blues
by Michael Brandman

Split Image
Night and Day
Stranger in Paradise
High Profile
Sea Change
Stone Cold
Death in Paradise
Trouble in Paradise
Night Passage

THE SUNNY RANDALL
NOVELS

Spare Change
Blue Screen
Melancholy Baby
Shrink Rap
Perish Twice
Family Honor

THE COLE/HITCH
WESTERNS

Robert B. Parker's
Bull River
by Robert Knott

Robert B. Parker's
Ironhorse
by Robert Knott

Blue-Eyed Devil
Brimstone
Resolution
Appaloosa

ALSO BY
ROBERT B. PARKER

Double Play
Gunman's Rhapsody
All Our Yesterdays
A Year at the Races
(with Joan H. Parker)
Perchance to Dream
Poodle Springs
(with Raymond Chandler)
Love and Glory
Wilderness
Three Weeks in Spring
(with Joan H. Parker)
Training with Weights
(with John R. Marsh)

ROBERT B. PARKER'S
BLIND SPOT

A Jesse Stone Novel

REED FARREL COLEMAN

G. P. PUTNAM'S SONS

NEW YORK

DOUBLEDAY LARGE PRINT HOME LIBRARY EDITION

G. P. PUTNAM'S SONS • *Publishers Since 1838*
Published by the Penguin Group • Penguin Group (USA) LLC
375 Hudson Street, New York, New York 10014

USA • Canada • UK • Ireland • Australia
New Zealand • India • South Africa • China

A Penguin Random House Company

Printed in the United States of America

ISBN 978-1-62953-113-7

Book design by Amanda Dewey

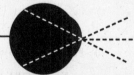

**This Large Print Book carries the
Seal of Approval of N.A.V.H**

For Bob and Joan Parker

BLIND
SPOT

There was no taking it back now, no do-overs. Never. He had said yes, so he was going. There were storm clouds over Paradise as Jesse Stone looked out at the Atlantic and remembered his last night in L.A., staring out into that other ocean. What Jesse thought was that water color in sunlight was beside the point. At night, all oceans were black. He understood that a lot of people, maybe most, believed the ocean symbolized endless possibility, better days, bright futures. Jesse knew better. He took a sip of his Black Label and soda. He was alone, with only the ocean and his regrets for company. You can gaze at the road ahead of you all you want, but your future is in your rearview mirror.

"Jesse...Chief Stone," a busboy called to him.

Jesse was too busy time-traveling there on the dock behind the restaurant to hear.

"Excuse me, Chief Stone," the kid tried again.

This time Jesse heard him and turned. He nodded at the kid.

"The boss, he wants you to stop by the office before you leave."

"I'll be right in."

It was the usual kind of thing in a small town. Dan Castro, chef and owner of the Lobster Claw, was a squat man with sad brown eyes and the weight of the world pressing down on him. The place had been up and running for only two months and Dan had discovered why it was easier to want to own a restaurant than to actually own one. He wanted to know if Jesse could talk to the health inspector. Jesse was the police chief, so he must have a lot of pull with the selectmen, the Health Department, the dogcatcher. Jesse tried listening, without much success. Stared at Dan's moving lips, watched his gestures, but Jesse wasn't exactly in the moment. He was thinking about tomorrow's drive down to New York City, about the reunion. He had been thinking about it on and off for the last six weeks, ever since he'd gotten the invitation from Vic Prado and sent back the little RSVP card with a check in the yes box. As the date got closer, it was all he could think about. He said something reassuring to Dan and left. It must have been good, because Castro's eyes weren't quite so sad, nor did he seem as much a victim of gravity.

As Jesse drove back home through the streets of Paradise, he tried to recall exactly what he had said to the restaurant owner. For the life of him, he couldn't remember. That's how distracted he was by what lay ahead of him over the next few days. The scotch hadn't helped with his memory and this reunion hadn't helped with the scotch. Jesse's tug-of-war with booze no longer held any romance for him, nor anyone else. He had a problem with drinking. It was like a given in a geometry equation. When he realized his words to Dan Castro were lost to him, Jesse shrugged and moved on. He remembered he was a cop, the top cop in a town fifteen miles outside of Boston. A million miles from L.A.

The rain came in a light spray not even heavy enough for Jesse to use the wipers. He studied the streets. He had settled into the rhythms of town life, but thought that only someone who didn't know him would describe Paradise as his adopted hometown. He'd grown up in Tucson, lived in L.A., and now Paradise. Were any of them really home? That was for someone else to ponder. For the moment Jesse Stone was running through his checklist for tomorrow, making sure everything was set before he went down to New York. As he turned for home, the skies opened up, the rain falling in sheets so thick that he could no longer make out the streets of Paradise. He was no longer paying much mind to the rain or the streets. Distracted again, Jesse Stone was caught in a rundown between his past and New York City.

2

The Salters' place was a red brick Victorian nestled on an ocean bluff just north of the yacht club. As Victorian houses went, it was more reserved than most, smaller than the sprawling manses that dotted cities and towns throughout New England and points south. There was one spire, two chimneys, a widow's walk. No gazebo, no wraparound porch, no whimsical paint job, no whimsy at all. It stood solid and restrained as Harlan Salter, the dry-goods magnate who had commissioned it in 1888. The Salters still owned the place, but these days most of them split their time between Boston and the Vineyard.

Mostly it just sat up there on the bluff and reminded Paradise of a faded past.

There was one light on in a small bedroom on the second floor.

"This place is so freakin' creepy and so cool, Ben," said Martina Penworth.

Benjamin Salter made a face. "We only

use this place in the summer, and then not always."

"Any ghosts?"

"No. Plenty of spiders, though."

She slapped his biceps. "I hate spiders."

"Don't worry. I'll protect you."

"Mmm," she said and stepped closer to him. "I just bet you will."

She angled her head up to his and planted her lips on Ben's. He returned the favor and it didn't take long for them to advance beyond kissing. When they came up for air, Ben grabbed the bottle of Pappy Van Winkle and took a swallow.

"Hey," she said, grabbing at the bottle, "what about me?"

Ben smiled, yanking the bottle out of her reach. "Patience, baby, patience."

He took another swig but was careful not to swallow. He winked at Martina, pressed his mouth hard against hers. She parted her lips just enough so that the warm amber fluid drained slowly into her mouth from his. When she'd taken it all in and swallowed, she sighed, and her body shuddered involuntarily. Ben reached for the hem of her T-shirt and lifted it over her head. She did the same for him and she kissed his chest, brushing her hand across his nipples. As Ben fingered the clasp of her bra, Martina pushed him away. She strolled around to the opposite side of the big cherrywood bed and swayed while she unhinged the silvery silken bra. She swung it over her head and threw it at him.

He snatched it out of the air, took in her scent, and stared at her pert breasts. Her nipples were red, erect, perfect, and he said so. There wasn't much about Martina Penworth that wasn't perfect. She had that sun-streaked blond hair other girls spent hundreds to imitate but could never quite pull off. Her eyes were a shade of deep blue that he hadn't seen before. Her lips, her nose...they were all amazing. Nor did it hurt that Martina had the body of a cheerleader and the brain of a professor. He didn't much care about the latter at the moment. He knew he was lucky to have her. He wasn't bad-looking. He had been with plenty of girls before, but not girls like Martina. That was why he had brought her here. No dorm room beds or cheap Boston motels for her.

Just as Martina unbuttoned her jeans and began wriggling out of them, she thought she heard something coming from downstairs. Ben saw the look on her face.

"It's an old house and it's storming like crazy. Don't worry about it." He half smiled. "Maybe it's a ghost. Like I said, I'll protect you."

"That was from spiders."

"Spiders and ghosts."

He walked around to her. He had waited long enough. They fell into bed together.

When they were done, she lay with her head on his hairless chest. They were silent. First times, even at their best, come with a certain amount of awkwardness. Besides, wanting and having are two very different things. Then the silence was broken, but not by either Ben or Martina.

The bedroom door flew back so hard that the old hinges nearly pulled away from the oak frame. As it was, the brass doorknob had made an oval dent in the plaster and lath. A tall man dressed in matte black military-style garb strode into the room. He wore a black balaclava over his head and face. Only his shark eyes and crooked mouth were visible. In his right hand he held a black sidearm with a sound suppressor extending from the barrel. He turned to face the two nude college freshmen, pointing the tip of the suppressor at them. Martina wanted to scream, but her fear swallowed it up. Instead, she dug her nails into Ben's biceps. He didn't feel it, not even when he bled.

"Look, mister, my parents have a lot of money," Ben said, his voice cracking. "They'll pay you anything you want."

The gunman shook his head.

Ben realized this guy might be here for Martina. She was so hot, so perfect. Here she was for him, undressed and vulnerable.

"Don't even think about touching her," Ben warned. This time his voice was strong and steady.

"She's not as good as you'd think," he said, because he couldn't think of what else to say. "She—"

The gunman stifled a little laugh and put his left index finger across his lips to shush the boy. The boy shushed. The gunman waved the tip of the suppressor at Ben, gesturing him away from Martina. When the kid hesitated, the gunman put a round in the wall above the headboard. Ben got out of the bed, shaking. The gunman motioned for Ben to get on his knees at the side of the bed. Ben got on his knees.

"Don't worry, baby," Ben reassured Martina. "He wants me, not you. Isn't that right, mister? You want me."

The gunman nodded, stepped close to Ben. Now there was something in the gunman's left hand. Before Ben could figure out what it was, he pressed it to Ben's neck and stunned the kid. Ben Salter collapsed to the floor, his convulsing body thumping against the bare wood. Tears streamed down Martina's face as the gunman turned the tip of the suppressor in her direction. The gun barked twice and Martina Penworth stopped crying forever.

3

Jesse Stone stared at himself in the full-length mirror as he adjusted his bow tie. He had always looked good in uniform— Albuquerque Dukes, USMC, L.A.P.D., or Paradise PD dress blues, it didn't matter. A tuxedo, he thought, was just another kind of uniform. He had been away from baseball for many years now, but he kept in good shape. He was no more than five pounds heavier than when he was a soft-handed shortstop prospect in the Dodgers' organization. While he hadn't been a five-tool phenom, he had the requisite skills to make it to the bigs: great glove, cannon arm, quick pivot, adequate speed, average bat, less-than-average power. What he lacked in natural physical skills he compensated for with what sports types called intangibles. He rarely made mental errors. Bonehead plays were what other guys made. He was like a manager on the field, mentally tough. That much hadn't changed. When some wiseass pitcher tried backing him away from the plate with a little chin music, Jesse dusted himself off, and stood a few inches closer to the plate for the next pitch. As one scout wrote, "Stone always seems to be in the right place at the right time." Not always.

It was precisely because he had been in the wrong place at the wrong time that he was forced to trade in his baseball uniform for all the others. Now the closest he was ever going to get to the infield dirt at Dodger Stadium was the softball fields of Paradise, Mass. He was the terror of the team, playing for the police department slo-pitch squad. His less-than-average power in pro baseball made him the Hank Aaron of the softball diamond, but that wasn't much compensation for a man who was once a phone call away from the Dodgers. He made one last adjustment to his tie before heading downstairs. Time to face the music.

Jesse Stone wasn't big on irony, but even he couldn't ignore the fact that there was almost nothing standard about The Standard, High Line. The angular glass, steel, and concrete beast straddled the elevated High Line park that ran along the west side of Manhattan from the Meatpacking District to West 30th Street. He couldn't decide whether he liked the exterior of the building or not. It was like both something out of the 1960s and a sci-fi movie. Not that he had seen many sci-fi movies. He didn't much care for movies, except Westerns and they didn't make many Westerns anymore. The interior was just weird, provocative for provocative's sake. Until he arrived and read up on the place, Jesse hadn't been aware of the least standard thing about The Standard: its reputation. The Standard was infamous for couples renting rooms, pulling back their curtains, and having sex in front of the floor-to-ceiling windows for people strolling the High Line to see. The Standard had always seemed like an odd choice for a reunion of a minor-league baseball team from Albuquerque, New Mexico. Now that Jesse had seen it, knew its rep, the place seemed an even less likely choice. He shook his head.

At the elevator, he fidgeted with his tie some more. When the elevator door opened, Jesse got his first gut punch of the evening. He had anticipated taking some blows, but not this one, not so soon. Inside the elevator was a dazzling woman with yellow-green eyes and jet-black hair cut in a perfect wedge. The hair that fell over the light mocha skin of her left cheek made a crisp angular line from her delicate cleft chin to her bare collarbone. Her plush red mouth neither smiled nor frowned at the man getting into the elevator with her, though her nose twitched ever so slightly. She wore a tight, satiny champagne-colored gown that made her look like she was moving in the wind even as she stood motionless. There was a rope of diamonds around her long, tanned neck. Sprinkled in among the diamonds were blood rubies, emeralds, and sapphires.

"Kayla," Jesse said as the door closed behind him. "You look lovely." He bent and gave her an awkward kiss on the cheek.

"Jess." She touched his cheek once and then quickly put her hand down by her side. "You keep a portrait in your attic? You haven't aged a day."

"Thanks. No portrait. Vic?"

She let out an exasperated sigh. "He's down at the bar already with the boys."

They rode the remainder of the way to the bar level in uncomfortable silence. Their story was an old one. Jesse had been dating Kayla for a few weeks after getting the bump up to the Dodgers' triple-A team. She was a beautiful girl even then, if not the finely polished trophy she was now. They weren't too serious, but the sex had been ferocious and Jesse thought there might be a future for them together. That lasted only until a slow ground ball was hit in the right-side hole and was smothered by Jesse Stone's roommate, Vic Prado. Instead of getting the sure out at first, Prado got to his knees at the edge of the outfield grass and threw across his body to Jesse, who was just coming across second base. The runner went hard into Jesse, trying to take him out and prevent an accurate throw to first. Mission accomplished. He took Jesse out, all right: right out of a career. Jesse's throw was legless and awkward. He had no balance and crash-landed on the hard infield with the point of his right shoulder. Jesse's initial thought: **Did I get the runner at first?** His second: **I'm screwed.** By the time he came back from the hospital in L.A., post-surgery, Kayla had switched roommates from the one whose future had recently passed to the one scheduled for a September call-up to the big club.

When the elevator car came to a halt, Jesse gestured for Kayla to exit first. As she did, she said, "I still think about you, Jess," and left. He stood in place. Almost from the moment he had checked the yes box on the RSVP card and mailed it back, Jesse Stone had wanted to undo it, but he also knew he had demons in him that needed to be exorcised. Now he had a better idea of just how many there were to deal with and how difficult a deal it might be. When the elevator door began to close again, Jesse stuck out his right arm to stop it. He stepped out of the car, finally, and headed for the bar and into his past.

4

The first thing Ben Salter sensed was the vague odor of car exhaust. Then there was the pain. He felt as if he'd been rolled down an endless flight of stairs. He was conscious of the full-body soreness even before he opened his eyes and realized the hurt meant he was still alive. **Martina! Where was Martina? Was she safe? Was she—** The car hit a bump and he thought his head would split open. He howled in agony and from the suffocating fear—fear for himself, but especially for Martina. He tried remembering what had happened, tried piecing it together, but after he'd knelt down at the side of the bed, it was all a jumble.

Blinding tears poured out of his eyes. He tried moving his hands to hold his head, to wipe away the tears, but he might as well have tried wishing himself to Oz. His hands were cuffed behind his back, the metal bracelets too tight, cutting into

ROBERT B. PARKER'S BLIND SPOT   19

the skin of his wrists. It didn't help that his
ankles were bound with rope and that the
rope was looped around the handcuffs.
When he pulled his legs down to gauge if
there was any slack in the rope, he felt like
his wrists would snap off, and the cuffs
chewed more deeply into his flesh. It
was no good. Another pothole. For a brief
second Ben Salter was weightless. Then
he fell to earth, his head smacking down
on the cold metal of the carpetless trunk.
His body stiffened and he was completely
consumed by pain.

When the jolt of it eased, the fear
returned, the fear for himself and the panic
over Martina. She had to be all right.
Obviously, the guy in black had come for
him. He really hadn't seemed interested
in Martina at all. Maybe he'd tied her up
as he was tied up. Sure, that was it. He'd
tied her up and shoved her under the bed
or put her into a closet. She'd be a little
worse for wear, but someone would find
her soon enough. Ben's dad and uncle
kept the property impeccably maintained.
Gardeners and handymen were stopping

by all the time. **She'd be okay. She'd be okay. She'd be okay.** He kept silently repeating it as if it was a prayer. Maybe it was.

At least he hadn't been gagged. He took a deep gulp of air and screamed, "Help me!" Only it wasn't much of a scream. His throat was so dry with panic that it came out flat and brittle, barely loud enough to hear above the road and engine noise. It also sent a fresh wave of pain through his head. He weathered the pain. Forced himself to relax, willing his mouth to moisten, letting some saliva drip down to lubricate his throat. He tried it again. "Help me! Somebody help me." Better. He collected himself again. "Help me! Help, some nut's got me trapped in here. Help!" Better, much better. He repeated the process over and over again until there was nothing left of his voice and the pain in his head demanded he stop. He was spent and felt himself slipping into unconsciousness.

As his eyes were fluttering shut, the car jerked to a stop. Ben's panic was reborn and the shelter of unconsciousness was suddenly lost to him. Panic seemed to be the only thing in his universe of which there was an infinite supply. The trunk latch released with a telltale click. The trunk lid popped open a few inches and night rushed in. With it came the strong salt smell of the sea and a final acrid whiff of tailpipe fumes. The car swayed on its suspension. A car door slammed. Footsteps came his way. The trunk lid was raised up. The shark-eyed gunman loomed above Ben.

"Where's Martina? Is she safe?" Ben asked, his voice a dry, cracked whisper.

The gunman's mouth formed itself into a cruel half-smile. He slowly shook his head from side to side as he placed the stun gun to Ben's neck once again. Ben Salter understood his captor's silent message. Ben's silent prayer would go unanswered. Martina was dead. With the fervor of a martyr, Ben retreated into a netherworld of muscle spasms and guilt.

5

Malo Enriquez was the first to say something as Jesse Stone walked into the bar.

"Hey, look, boys, it's the commish, man," he shouted in an over-the-top Chicano accent. Malo was a left-handed reliever for the Dukes at the very end of his career, just hanging on for a paycheck and one last shot at the majors when Jesse was promoted from double A to triple A. Malo had been the oldest member of the team. The guys had called him Viejo, old man, out of respect. After all, Malo had been in the bigs, on and off, for more than a decade. He had been to baseball's Promised Land, a land of significant meal money, plane travel, smooth infields, and three-tiered stadiums. He was more than ten years older than most of his former teammates. The age difference hadn't been as noticeable back then. It was now. His once-purple-black hair was gray and thinning. His waistline was moving in the opposite direction. He was thick around the middle, but Malo looked happy in a way Jesse could never quite imagine himself looking.

"Chief of police, Viejo," Jesse Stone said, clasping Malo's meaty right hand in his. Jesse felt an odd rush of respect and jealousy for Malo. Was it because Malo had made it to the top of the mountain or because the old reliever was happy? Both seemed like perfectly adequate reasons.

Only sixteen of the men who had played with Jesse were in attendance. A few had simply turned down the offer of an all-expenses-paid trip to New York City. Some men just didn't like looking behind them. Jesse thought there was something to be said for that. A couple had fallen through the cracks, beyond even Vic Prado's considerable reach. Two were dead: Paulie Hamacher in a car crash, Johnny Wheeler by a self-inflicted gunshot wound. Jesse knew about Paul and John, but he hadn't paid attention to the e-mail updates concerning the reunion Vic had sent along every week leading up to the event.

Jesse knew each of the men in attendance by face and by name in spite of the
fact that he hadn't seen or spoken with
any of them since the day he packed his
duffel bag and left Albuquerque. And as
he went teammate to teammate, shaking
hands, Jesse read their life stories on their
faces. Not much got past Jesse Stone.
Not then. Not now. Julio Blanco, the
catcher, was still a cold, pock-faced
bastard with a handshake like a vise. Rob-
bie Townes, the first baseman, had the
beatific smile of a man who had found
God. Good thing, too, because he had
never found a way to hit a curveball. Cal
Manley, the right fielder, had the restless
look of a man in two places at once.

"Cal," Jesse said, shaking the outfield-
er's hand.

Cal's unfocused eyes looked past Jesse.
"Stoney."

Neither man was much of a talker, but
just the distracted way Cal spoke Jesse's
name told Stone that Cal was in a bad
place.

One look at Jimmy Neidermeyer, the

Dukes' old third baseman, told Jesse that Jimmy had probably been up to no good. He had a prison physique: all upper body, no legs. He also had the bloated look of a juicer: acne, thinning hair, the feral eyes of a man spoiling for a fight.

The other guys, the guys who had had at least a cup of coffee in the majors, all seemed to be in better places. Not that they had made fortunes in real estate, restaurants, and venture capital like Vic or even that they had achieved a level of status equal to Jesse's. In fact, Jesse was doing better than most of them. By some measures, he had gotten further in life than anyone except Vic Prado. That's not how Jesse saw it. What Jesse saw was a runner barreling into him at second base. Moses had nothing on Jesse Stone. Neither had made it to the Promised Land.

Vic Prado, the man behind this whole affair, seemed to be purposely hanging back. It was like opening-day festivities when the team is introduced to the crowd, called out one by one, then waits along the first or third base line. Each player pops out of the dugout and shakes the hand of all the guys introduced before him. And there was Vic, waiting at the end of the line for Jesse. He looked like a million bucks, tens of millions. Everything from the manicured hands and the straight white teeth to the perfectly tailored tux- edo and the Patek Philippe on his wrist spoke of pampered wealth. It didn't hurt that Vic was still a handsome son of a bitch.

"What'll you have, old buddy?" asked Prado, squeezing Jesse's hand.

"Black Label and soda. Tall glass."

"Good taste in scotch for a shortstop, but don't be shy, Jesse. Have a Macallan or a Blue Label. It's on me. Think of it as helping me with my taxes."

"Cop," Jesse said, correcting his former double-play partner and taking back his hand. "Black Label suits me."

"Black Label and soda, tall glass, for my friend here," Prado shouted to the barman.

The word **friend** stuck in Jesse's craw. They weren't friends. They had been roommates once for a few months, and a very good combination on the field. Friends? Not that he was aware of. Over Vic's right shoulder, Jesse spotted Kayla talking to another woman. The woman was spectacular-looking, if in a blond kind of way. He turned his attention back to Prado.

"Skip's not here," Jesse said.

Vic stared directly at Jesse. "No skipper. No coaches or organization people, either. Just us."

Us? Jesse got a weird vibe. Vic was talking about the players from the team, but it felt like he was being even more selective than that. He sensed that Vic was talking about just the two of them. Jesse knew that couldn't be the case. No one would go to such elaborate lengths just to celebrate with a guy he had shared a room with half a lifetime ago. Not even a man as flush as Vic Prado.

Prado stepped away from Jesse, raising his glass. "To the Dukes," he called out in his rich baritone. Then, looking back at Jesse, "To us." They drank. Vic clinked Jesse's glass. "Okay, guys, the limos are out front. We'll be heading down to the steakhouse now."

Vic walked out first. Jesse stayed back to finish his drink. He had the feeling the limos weren't going anywhere without him. He didn't know why he should think that, but he did. And if he was wrong, so what? He'd walk.

"Hello, Jess." It was Kayla, the blonde at her side. "This is my friend Dee Harrington."

Dee was quite a friend, and on closer inspection, **spectacular** didn't quite do her justice. She was otherworldly. More striking even than Jenn, Jesse's ex-wife. She was a few years Kayla's junior and had the fire in her eyes that Kayla no longer seemed to possess. Dee looped her arm through Jesse's.

"Do you mind," she said. "I feel like a spare wheel. I'm here to keep Kayla company, but I've got no one to keep me company."

"Sure." Jesse put his empty glass on the bar. When he turned back to Dee, he noticed Kayla's eyes. The fire was back.

Jesse held out his other arm for her.

She took it and put her lips very near to his ear. "We need to talk, Jess. But not here and not now."

Jesse nodded and the three of them made their way out of the bar.

6

After stashing the kid, Joe Breen had showered and swapped out his matte black outfit for a green-and-white Celtics warm-up suit. He'd stopped by his local for a few pints of Harpoon while he chowed down on hard-boiled eggs and hot mustard. Doing violence always put him in the mood for hard-boiled eggs and hot mustard. It also put him in the mood for comfort, to hold someone in his arms and to please them. He liked that best of all, pleasing his lover. He was particularly fond of art-school girls, all pale-skinned and deep. They could be so very lonely, not unlike himself. But he dared not scratch that itch until he had gone to see the boss. And it was at Mike Frazetta's front door that he found himself.

Mike's wife answered the door. She was dressed in a long T-shirt and fuzzy pink slippers. She had her bottle-black hair pulled tightly back behind her head, but she hadn't yet removed her makeup. Joe didn't get the attraction. He guessed Lorraine was pretty enough, but, Jesus, she was a pushy broad. And that voice of hers...it grated on you like the constant buzzing of mosquito wings. Given the chance, he'd have liked to take his uncle's hurley stick to her or to have used his fists to shut her up. Breen was certain she'd be easier for Mike to replace than himself, and he smiled at the thought. He didn't always enjoy killing, but there were times he took a religious joy in it. So it would have been with Lorraine Frazetta.

Lorraine was no happier to see Breen than he was to see her. And being the boss's wife, she had no compunction about showing her displeasure. She rolled her eyes at him.

"You!" She packed a lot of contempt into one syllable. "Ever hear of this thing called a phone? Even you could learn to use it because the numbers are all single digits from zero to nine and you only have to use one finger. If you called ahead, I'd know you were coming and I could have someone else answer the door."

"You know he doesn't favor me using the phone," Breen said, stepping inside. "And you did buzz me through the gate."

"No one else is around." Lorraine nodded to her right. "He's in there."

Mike Frazetta was seated on a long black leather-and-steel couch opposite a flat TV screen that dominated an entire wall of his office. Frazetta was watching **Unforgiven**, the Clint Eastwood Western, and he was reciting the dialogue along with Eastwood's character, Bill Munny, when Joe Breen came through the door.

"Funny thing, killin' a man. You take away everything he's got and everything he's gonna have."

What a load a shite, Breen thought. Philosophical killers were crap. You think about it, you're lost. "Boss!" Joe screamed above the movie.

Frazetta muted the sound and turned to face Breen. Mike Frazetta was a lean man of six feet, with vulpine eyes and thin lips. He had dark brown hair, slicked back and sprayed into place. He wore an expensive gray sweater that hung loose over his thin frame and black wool pants.

"The kid?" he asked Breen, getting up and moving to the bar.

"Stashed. His head will be aching for some time to come, but he won't be a bother."

Frazetta poured himself a Chopin vodka on the rocks, threw in a wedge of lime. He didn't offer one to Breen. "Any problems?"

"A bit. He had a girl with him. A shame, really. Pretty slip of a thing."

"Did you have to do her?"

"What was I supposed to do, send her to summer camp?"

Frazetta shrugged. "You know best. Anyways, the kid's father as good as condemned her when he wouldn't listen to reason. This way maybe he'll take us a little more serious that we're not jerking around here."

"About the father...you want me to—"

"Nah, let that WASPy bastard sweat a little bit. Let him come to us. Where's Vic, just in case the father gets nervous quicker than I expect?"

"In New York."

Frazetta shook his head. "That fucking little-league reunion."

"Why'd you say yes to that, Boss?"

Frazetta shrugged. "You gotta let the man have his fun. Even marionettes need to think they got some control of things sometimes. Besides, Vic's our shiny side. We need him to look good to the world. When everyone in this town whispers my name the way they used to whisper Whitey Bulger's, it'll be worth it. We're gonna show people some old-time religion like they ain't seen in years. Now get outta here. See you at the office in the morning."

As he headed out the front door, past the gate and the surveillance cameras, Joe Breen noticed that itch had gotten considerably stronger. Now there was nothing standing between him and getting it scratched, and scratched good.

7

The steakhouse was all dark wood paneling, red leather banquettes, and testosterone. The testosterone level went up a few notches after the old Albuquerque Dukes strode through the place and into the private dining room at the back. That's what steakhouses are really about, red meat and testosterone. In the private room, two walls of the dark paneling had been supplanted by clear glass. On the opposite side of the glass were wooden racks filled with hundreds of bottles of wine. The other two walls were bare red brick, chipped and pitted with age and a hundred years of construction. There were two long tables set close together, with ten seats each, running lengthwise in the dining room. Jesse sat at the end of one table, with Julio Blanco to his left. An empty seat next to his least favorite ex-teammate was his reward for getting there late in the last limo. At least Dee had taken the seat directly across from Jesse. Her beautiful face was almost compensation enough for Blanco's presence. Almost.

Vic and Kayla were at the head of the other table. Vic was in his glory. This was his show. As he got up to speak, Jesse noticed that there were two guys in attendance whom he'd spotted back at the hotel bar but hadn't connected to the reunion. They were both ten years younger than the youngest member of the old Dukes, and neither of them looked like baseball players. Football, maybe. Not baseball, not built the way they were: thick necks, thick arms, tree-trunk legs. Jesse knew the type. They were security. Muscle, probably ex-bouncers with a few ounces of smarts between them. They reminded Jesse of Jo Jo Genest, the musclehead rapist and murderer who'd been part of his unwelcome wagon to Paradise. He hadn't thought of Jo Jo in years and he didn't like that these two guys brought Jo Jo to mind. What, he wondered, was a man like Vic Prado doing with clowns like these two? If Vic could afford to foot the bill for this entire gig, he could afford the real thing, lethal Blackwater types you'd never see coming at you. Another thing Jesse noticed was that the two trees in suits hovered very close to Vic, paying more attention to him than to potential danger. They seemed more like keepers than protectors.

Jesse leaned across to Dee. "Who are those bookends up there with Vic?"

"You mean Tweedle Dumb and Tweedle Dumbbell?"

"Uh-huh."

"Security, I guess," she said, flashing a neon white smile at Jesse. "They drive Kayla crazy. They're like annoying relatives who never leave."

He raised his drink to her. She returned the gesture. He liked her smile. There wasn't much about her not to like. Before they could continue the conversation, Vic started up, making a nice little speech about how, regardless of his years in the bigs, it was the guys here with him tonight who he would remember and treasure.

That was why he'd paid to bring them here to be together.

"I made three all-star teams," he said. "I rubbed elbows with some of the greatest players to ever grace a baseball field. I've met Ted Williams, Stan Musial, Willie Mays, Sandy Koufax, and many other hall-of-famers. I played against Wade Boggs, Mo Vaughn, Barry Bonds, Doc Gooden, but it's you guys that have meant the most to me."

Everyone applauded but Julio Blanco. All Julio did was grunt. It was an eloquent grunt that said more than all of Vic's lofty words. If Jesse hadn't happened to catch a glimpse of Kayla at that moment, he might not have taken the bait. But the dejection and defeat on her face pushed Jesse to say something to Blanco.

"Okay," Jesse said, "I'll bite. What was the grunt for?"

"Vic, he loves us like brothers, huh? Funny how I never heard a word from him until six weeks ago. You?"

"Nothing since I left Albuquerque. Never heard from you or any of these guys, either."

"True that." Blanco nodded. "And the guy says in his speech it's all about us, but he does everything but mention his lifetime batting average and on-base percentage."

"It's his party."

Blanco's smile was cold enough to chill the wine. "He fucked you like he fucked you and you still defend him. I don't get it."

"Say what you have to say, Julio."

"That play, the play in Pueblo when you got taken out..."

"What about it?"

"Think about it, **jefe**. It's an exhibition game against a bunch of fuckin' college kids and indie minor-leaguers on a shitty field in Pueblo, Colorado. All Vic has to do is toss the ball to first on that play and it's you up there making the speeches about all the all-star games you been in instead of him."

"It was instinct to go for the double play."

"I call bullshit on that. You forget, I was watching the play as I'm coming up the first-base line to back up. It was a tough

play Vic made, sure, but the kid running
from first to second got a bad break on
the ball. He had to hold up so the grounder
wouldn't hit him. When Vic got to his
knees, he hesitated."

"Hesitated?"

"Yeah, until the kid was almost on you.
Then he threw to you."

"You were always a miserable SOB,
Julio."

"Maybe, Stoney, but that don't make me
no liar."

Before Jesse could say anything else,
the waiter came over and took their orders. After ordering the rib steak, Jesse
shook his empty glass at the waiter.

"Black Label and soda, right, sir?" the
waiter said.

"Half right. Black Label, rocks. A double."

"Very good, sir."

Only it wasn't very good. None of it.
Jesse half ate his steak. He supposed it
tasted all right, but he wouldn't have been
able to swear to it. Dee was making pleasant conversation, asking him about his life
and about the things Kayla had told her

about him.

"She warned me you weren't much of a conversationalist," Dee said, after Jesse gave her another one-word answer to a question he forgot as soon as she asked it.

Jesse put down his silverware, the steak and the scotch turning foul and bitter in his mouth. "You want to get out of here?"

Dee smiled her neon smile. "I was hoping you'd get around to asking that." She was already standing up as she spoke.

Jesse Stone stood, too. Julio Blanco turned, smiling up at him, but the message in his smile was as subtle as a slide trombone. Jesse gave Blanco the dead-eyed cop stare. Blanco wasn't buying it. He'd gotten into Jesse's head and they both knew it.

On the way out, Vic Prado grabbed Jesse's forearm. "Hey, where you going?"

"Out."

Vic was on his feet now. He made a show of looking happy. He leaned in close to Jesse's ear. "We need to talk."

Jesse could tell by Vic's tone that he

didn't want the world to hear their conversation. "Breakfast tomorrow...early," he whispered back.

"Okay, you guys have a good time. You need a ride to or from anywhere, I'll send a limo." Prado wasn't whispering now.

"We're all growed up," Dee said. "We'll survive in the big city."

When they were at the door, Jesse turned back for one last glimpse at all of them and saw the look on Kayla's face. The defeat and dejection were even more profound than they'd been only a few minutes earlier.

She mouthed, "We need to talk."

He nodded, Dee pulling at his wrist. Everyone needed to talk to Jesse Stone. Talking was the last thing he was in the mood for.

8

Ethan Farley looked like an escapee from **American Gothic**. He was bald-headed, sported wire-rimmed glasses, and wore denim bib overalls. All he needed was a pitchfork and a drab wife by his side. Emily, his drab wife, was dead seven years now, and there wasn't much need of a pitchfork in Paradise. Farley's family went back as far as the Salter family, and their relationship to the Salters had remained pretty constant over the last century. Plus, the Salters were rich and the Farleys worked for them. Until the boys returned from WWII, the Farleys worked both inside and outside the Salter family houses in Paradise, Boston, and on Martha's Vineyard. But come the late forties, the Salters realized they were nearly halfway through the new century and that they ought to begin acting like the Gilded Age had actually come to an end. Ethan's folks and his uncle Harold and his aunt

Ruella were the last Farleys to work as
house servants for the Salters. Good
thing, too, as far as Ethan was concerned.
He had never wanted to wear a fancy suit
a day in his life and was happy to grow
things and fix others. Dirty hands and a
wet brow were the measures of a good
man.

He hadn't planned on checking on the
Paradise house that day, but the storm
had lasted for nearly thirty-six hours.
Farley wasn't worried about the brick
structure of the old place. It was as solid
a house as had ever been built, but the
stone foundation did spring the occasional leak in bad weather and parts of
the roof were susceptible to powerful
gusts. He'd found over the years that
water damage was best dealt with quickly.
All those solid wood floors and all that
plaster and lath were bad news to deal
with when water got in and was left to its
own devices.

As Ethan drove up to the noble brick
house on the bluff, he got a bad feeling in
the marrow of his old bones. You work on

a house long enough, you get connected to it. You can read it, feel its distress like a father feels his child's pain. And something was definitely amiss. Christ, he hoped it wasn't anything major. With the way the Salters had shifted their focus away from Paradise, he feared they might just sell the place if the damage was too bad. He wasn't in fear of his livelihood. No, the Salters were good that way. He had been well compensated for his loyalty to the family and wouldn't want for much as long as he kept it simple. Simple was all he knew. What he worried about was keeping busy if the Salters sold the old house.

Then he spotted the bright red Toyota Scion FR-S parked in the drive and smiled. He didn't know the Salter kids the way he used to, but Ethan would have laid odds that the little Japanese sports car belonged to Harlan IV's youngest, Ben. Ethan liked Ben. A college student down in Boston, he was a polite boy, not as full of himself and his money as his two older brothers. Good or not, boys would be boys, Ethan thought. He had witnessed generations of Salter men bringing their women to the house in the off-season for a bit of privacy. Ethan parked his Ford F-150 right behind the kid's red machine and walked the perimeter of the house. It didn't look worse for wear, but morning was just now breaking and the light wasn't the best. Still, experience had taught him that things could look fine from the outside and be pretty bad on the inside.

Ethan didn't want to walk in on the kid, so he stood on his pickup's horn and gave two long warning blasts to Ben that he and his female companion were no longer alone. After the second blast, he gave the lovers a few more minutes to get some clothes on. It wasn't until Ethan placed his hand on the brass thumb latch on the big front door that his smile ran away from his face. The door was unlocked. As he opened the door and walked into the front hallway, he called the kid's name. The echo of his own voice was Ethan's only answer. As he climbed the stairs, he detected a faint, unwelcome odor. At the top of the stairs, the odor was stronger, and he noticed a light coming from one of the small second-floor bedrooms. He called Ben's name again. No reply. As he approached the bedroom, Ethan saw that the door was nearly off its hinges and that the odor was definitely coming from that room.

When he stepped into the bedroom and saw Martina Penworth's nude, dead body sprawled face-first on the floor beside the bed, it was all he could do not to heave up his breakfast. He didn't make it very far out of the bedroom before he did. It was only several minutes later that he had collected himself enough to call the police.

9

Jesse Stone hadn't dreamed about Pueblo or Vic Prado or Julio Blanco. He hadn't dreamed about Ozzie Smith, the Wizard of Oz. He hadn't dreamed. Given the prodigious amount of scotch he had consumed after leaving the reunion dinner, he wasn't sure he'd had enough functioning brain cells to conjure up a dream. His mouth was as dry as a kiln, and though he couldn't actually see it, he was certain there was a long, sharp object embedded in his head somewhere. He was impressed. A man who drank as regularly as he did had to work pretty hard to whip up a hangover like the one he was suffering from. It wasn't all bad, because Dee really was in bed next to him, naked as the day she was born, but looking like a goddess. He hadn't blacked out, nor had he imagined how intense the sex had been. Jesse hadn't forgotten the sounds Dee had made, the way her body had shuddered. He had been with many women in his lifetime, and not many were a match for Dee.

It was still dark when Jesse cranked open his eyes and wrestled himself out of bed and into the bathroom. He found a glass somewhere and drank what felt like a gallon of tap water. It was no myth, New York City tap water did taste good. He dug a fistful of aspirins out of his bag and swallowed some more water. He brushed his teeth and showered as quietly as he could, which, given the design of the room, was no mean feat. He couldn't manage to shave for the throbbing in his head. Before stepping back by the bed, he fantasized about waking Dee up in a way that might inspire another bout like last night's, but his head was killing him. The fantasy he settled on was a few more hours of sleep. Neither fantasy was going to come true.

Dee was up, and though she smiled as she passed him, some of the glimmer was out of her neon. She'd had a fair amount to drink as well. And the sun was now coming up.

"Listen," he said, "I promised to meet Vic for an early breakfast."

"Ooh, can I tag along? I think I need to put some nourishment into my body that wasn't distilled in the Scottish Highlands."

"I don't think so. Vic seemed to have something important to say to me in private."

"Sounds mysterious. Any ideas?"

"None," he said. "How are you feeling?"

"About you, pretty fantastic. About my hangover, not so much. Can I see you again later?"

"I'd like that, a lot. After breakfast I'm going to come back and get some more sleep. We can talk after that."

"I'm heading down to my room," she said, emerging from the bathroom and slipping into her dress. She put her hand on Jesse's cheek and rubbed her thumb across his lips. "Are all cops so amazing in the sack?"

"How else do you think I made chief?"

"Don't make me laugh. It hurts too

much." Dee bundled up her underthings, tucked them beneath her arm, and hooked her shoes on her fingers. "Later, darlin'." She kissed Jesse's cheek and left.

He called the hotel operator and asked for Vic's room. Vic seemed to be waiting by the phone and picked up on the first ring.

"The lobby in five minutes," Jesse said and hung up.

Though the sharp object in his head had softened around the edges and the pain was duller in kind, Jesse knew he looked like crap. Vic, on the other hand, looked like he got up this early every morning and had a team of valets to put him together. But Jesse saw some cracks in his old double-play partner's veneer. Vic was on edge, pacing, his head on a swivel, making sure the Tweedle Dumbbell boys weren't around. When Jesse walked up to him, Vic placed a cup of takeout coffee in his hand.

"I hope you like milk and sugar in your coffee," he said, urging Jesse toward the front door.

"Fine with me." At that point, Jesse would have accepted anything that mildly resembled coffee. He took a long swallow and followed Vic out of the hotel onto the street. Even at that hour a fleet of yellow cabs prowled the avenues and traffic was building. Jesse took notice, and Vic noticed Jesse notice.

"God love this town," Vic said. "When we used to come in to play the Mets—"

Jesse wasn't in the mood, especially with a hangover, especially after what Julio Blanco had had to say. "You didn't drag me down here to talk about playing at Shea, Vic. It's gone now, anyway."

"Yeah, you're looking a little green around the gills. So tell me, how was she? I mean, sometimes it's all I can do not to put the moves on Dee myself."

"And you didn't meet me down here at this hour to question me about something I would never talk to you about."

"You used to tell me all about you and Kayla," Vic said.

"That was then."

"You mean before she—"

"Yes, I mean before all of it. That was a long time ago, Vic. A lot has changed."

"I saw you were sitting next to Blanco last night. What garbage did that miserable prick—"

Jesse's temporary reprieve from the headache was over. He took another sip of the coffee and said, "Forget Julio Blanco. Forget Kayla and Dee. What am I doing here, standing on the street with you at—"

Jesse Stone never finished the question. His cell phone buzzed in his pocket. Vic's cell phone went off as well. Only his ringtone was "Take Me Out to the Ball Game." Neither man seemed pleased by their respective calls. It was too early for peanuts and Cracker Jacks.

Jesse saw that the call was from the Paradise PD. He excused himself and stepped away from Prado. "This is Chief Stone."

"Jesse?" It was Molly Crane, and he didn't like the tone of her voice.

"What's up?"

"Nothing good. You better get back

here. The Salter family handyman just found a murdered girl at the old house on the bluff."

"Murdered how? When?"

"We just got the call. I'm headed out there now."

"I'm on my way. And call Healy."

Jesse looked back at Vic Prado, who appeared worse than he had only a few minutes earlier. Prado was still on the phone and he didn't seem happy with the party on the other end of the line. But that wasn't Jesse's problem. He walked back into the hotel and through the lobby. As he hurried to catch the elevator, he saw Vic's pair of muscleheads rushing to the hotel door.

10

Vic Prado turned and saw Jesse retreating into the hotel. **Fuck!** The whole point of this stupid reunion was to get with Jesse. Months of planning, of playing Mike Frazetta, all for nothing. Jesse Stone was going to be his way to get out from under, and now it was all slipping away. But Vic hadn't put up with all the shit he had had to endure in the minors, the long bus rides, horrible food, and inept coaching, without learning to cope. The only way to survive long enough in the boonies so that you could thrive on the big stage is to be adaptable, and Vic Prado was nothing else if not adaptable.

"Yeah, I see 'em," he said to Joe Breen as the two pet gorillas emerged from the hotel. "They're coming out the door right now."

"What the fuck were you doing talking to that cop without my boys around?"

Vic had come to understand that he

could sometimes manipulate Mike Frazetta, but that his charms were lost on Breen. Frazetta was susceptible for the same reasons the marks were: They were in awe of professional athletes. They had all dreamed the dream. Had all played Little League ball and imitated their favorite player's rituals: the way Nomar used to adjust his gloves, tug his jersey, tap his toes; the way Ichiro held the bat straight at the pitcher, tugged the right shoulder of his jersey, and seemed to rest his chin on that shoulder. It was that dream that Vic used against the men who ran the asset-management firms they had targeted. Even the most intelligent men he'd met got completely stupid around him. It was the same way men reacted to a gorgeous woman in the room. He had seen men of all stripes melt in the presence of Kayla. Hadn't he? Hadn't he ached to find a way to have her? And now it was Dee who made men stupid.

"What did you want me to do, Joe? The guy was my roommate, for crissakes! I married the woman he was dating when he got injured. It would have seemed very odd for us not to have talked in private, to clear the air. I mean, I haven't talked to the guy in forever."

Breen was a cold one. "I don't care for it."

"Well, you don't have to worry about it now. Because of you, he's heading back to Paradise. Did you have to do that, kill a girl? You and Mike promised—"

"I promised you nothing, Prado. And it wasn't me that killed the girl. It was you. You picked these guys as targets. You said they would be no problem. If you had been right, the Salter kid would be waking up with the girl right now."

"Fuck you, Joe."

But Breen didn't get angry. He just laughed into the phone and said, "Enjoy the rest of the day with your old mates, Vic. I have the sense Mike will want you to contact the father again soon."

Back in his flat, Breen pressed the hang-up button on his phone, let himself out of the bathroom, and tiptoed around the kitchen. He hit the brew button on the coffeemaker and then headed back into the bedroom. There he crawled in bed next to Moira, a girl from the old country and a student at the School of the Museum of Fine Arts. Moira was still asleep. Joe Breen got a strange feeling in his gut as he watched Moira. Come the morning after, Joe, having satisfied his need for comfort and for comforting, would usually send the girls on their way, sometimes with a few extra twenties stashed in their pockets or their backpacks. He knew student life was a struggle. But this morning, Joe Breen didn't want to send Moira on her way. He wanted her to stay as long as the girl cared to.

11

Dee had taken three ibuprofen and treated herself to all the ridiculously priced bottled water the room had to offer. She kept her head under the shower for a long time after cleaning the scotch-scented sweat off her body. She was much less anxious to scrub away the remnants of Jesse Stone. Before she had met Jesse, she knew it was possible, even likely, that they would wind up together, but she hadn't expected to want to be with him so badly. Whether she had compromised herself by not keeping him at arm's length was a question for later, for post-hangover self-assessments. Stepping out of the shower, all she wanted to do was dry off and dive feetfirst into the well of sleep.

She nestled in bed, the cool top sheet and soft quilt molding over her body like a downy cast. It didn't take but a second for her eyes to flutter shut and for her to begin to drift away. At the same time, the feel of Jesse's lips against hers, the power of his arms around her, came rushing back. She was going to enjoy this sleep.

No, she wasn't.

There was a loud, persistent banging at the room door. She had sunk so quickly and so deeply into sleep that it took a few seconds for Dee to make sense of it. Hadn't she hung the privacy notice on the door? She had. The banging got louder, more persistent.

"Open the door, Dee!"

It was Kayla.

Annoyed, her headache reasserting itself, Dee scrambled out of bed and went to the door. She didn't bother covering up. She knew that her body sometimes made Kayla jealous, and at the moment, that was just fine with her.

"What?" she said, pulling back the door.

Kayla didn't hesitate, walking into the room past Dee. Dee shut the door.

"And good morning to you, darlin'," she said, her voice thick with sarcasm.

The sarcasm was lost on Kayla, but Kayla's appearance wasn't lost on Dee.

The woman was a mess, and looked as if she hadn't slept. Her face was free of makeup and her hair was all over the place. In the year since she had insinuated herself into Kayla and Vic's circle of friends, Dee had only once seen Kayla in such a state. That time, too, she had showed up at Dee's doorstep early in the morning, in tears.

"How could you do that?" Kayla was shouting.

"Do what?" Dee said, though she knew that Kayla was talking about Jesse.

"Don't play the dumb blonde with me, Dee. You're as smart a person as I've ever known. You know about me and Jess."

"Okay, Kayla," Dee said, now putting on a robe. "You don't act dumb with me, either. Don't you think I realize you and Vic invited me along for two reasons only? One was to hang out with you while Vic rekindled his youth. The other was to entertain Jesse. For some reason, it seemed important to both of you to keep Jesse happy."

"But—"

"No buts, Kay, sorry. You guys made me feel like an expensive escort, a party favor for Jesse Stone, if he were so inclined. Well, as it turned out, I was so inclined."

Kayla had no answer for that but tears.

12

Jesse had driven past the Salter house before but hadn't spent a lot of time in that
part of Paradise. With the Atlantic, the
lighthouse, Paradise Neck, and Stiles Island spreading out below, the view was
breathtaking, and it was easy to understand why the wealthy had once made the
bluffs their own. It was also easy for people
to forget that attitudes toward the sea had
changed over the last hundred and fifty
years. Once upon a time, men understood
their insignificance in relationship to the
ocean. They respected its might and its
bounty. They weren't so cocky as to think
of the ocean as something the Lord had
put there as a means for their leisure. In
the past, the wealthy built their houses by
the sea not so they might play in it, but that
they might revere it.

His first reaction after getting the call
from Molly about the murder was to fly
back, but Jesse realized that between the

New York traffic, the potential delays at LaGuardia, and traffic on the other end, he might as well drive. And it would save him the trouble of having to get his car back to Paradise from New York. Once he got out of New York City, past New Rochelle and into Connecticut, the drive hadn't been too bad, and there were the memories of his time with Dee to keep him company. He'd left a note for her at the desk. It wasn't poetry. Hard to write poetry when you know someone's just killed a girl in your town. Hard for Jesse to write poetry, period. The note explained the essentials and he hoped Dee could understand why he'd left without saying good-bye. If she couldn't, he wasn't sure he'd want to see her again, anyway.

Jesse was okay until his Dee fantasies had run their course. By then the aspirins were losing ground to his headache. The headache wasn't the only thing making a comeback. With the pain came Julio Blanco's voice. Jesse wished he had pressed Molly for some details, any details, or had stopped to call back for an update. At least then he could begin thinking the basics of the case through instead of hearing Blanco's indictment of Vic Prado over and over again in his head. Blanco's voice was bad enough, but now Jesse kept rerunning the play in his head, trying to view it from the catcher's perspective. He scoured his own memory for any hints he might have suppressed, for any sense that Vic had held on to the ball too long before throwing the ball. It was no good. Jesse had and would only ever have the memory of the play he had carried with him since the night of the game. Except now he carried it with doubt.

One of the things, maybe the only thing, that had let Jesse move on with his life after his shoulder was torn apart was the belief that what had happened was fate. It wasn't preordained or anything, but things played out as they'd had to: because the ball was hit as slowly as it was, because of where it was hit, because of the speed of the runner, because Vic had better range to his left than to his right, because Vic had to throw from his knees across his body, because Vic was such an instinctive fielder, because the runner was trying to impress the scouts, because the infield was so hard, because, because, because...Now there was a different because, one that had nothing to do with bad luck or unfortunate, immutable events. This new because was tainted with all the worst aspects of human weakness.

Jesse pulled over at the next-to-last rest stop in Connecticut. He let out some of that gallon of water he'd had earlier, bought a liter bottle to put back in, swallowed another fistful of aspirins. Once he felt the aspirins taking effect, he called Molly.

"Any details?"

"God, Jesse," Molly said. "She was eighteen."

Jesse Stone let Molly have a minute. She was a good cop, a tough cop. Unlike some of the other cops on the Paradise PD, she would have done okay for herself on the L.A.P.D. or any other big-city PD. Guys like Suit Simpson, as good and loyal as he was, were better off in Paradise. Jesse understood that his demeanor at crime scenes sometimes led his cops to believe he thought that one corpse was like the next, that one murder victim was like any other. He supposed that it was okay for them to believe that. He also supposed it was true, if not completely. Every murder victim deserved justice, needed an advocate. Just as every living citizen was entitled to equal protection under the law, so, too, were the murdered entitled. Yet some victims were more equal than others. Maybe that wasn't fair or right, but it was human, and cops were owed that much leeway.

"Name?" Jesse said.

"California driver's license says Martina M. Penworth. She's—was a student at Tufts. Same school as Ben Salter, one of the sons."

"How? Where?"

"Handyman came to check out the house after the storm. Found the Salter boy's car out front and the front door unlocked. He discovered the body in a small second-floor bedroom. Two bullets in her, probably nine-millimeter. One in the heart.

One in the head. Close range, but the entry wounds weren't contact wounds. There was another round put into the wall above the headboard. There was evidence of sexual activity."

"Rape?"

"Hard to tell, but I don't think so. Just a used condom. ME will be able to tell you more."

"TOD?"

"Last night, around ten."

"The Salter kid?"

"No sign of him," Molly said.

"Any ideas?"

"I guess the kid could have done it, panicked, and took off. But it doesn't explain the car and it doesn't explain the damage to the bedroom door. Door seems like it was kicked in."

"The girl's parents been notified?" There was silence from the other end of the phone, which Jesse understood perfectly. "I'll do it," he said. "It's my job. How about the Salters?"

"The father, Harlan IV, is on his way from the Vineyard. No doubt he'll have a Boston lawyer in tow."

Jesse agreed. "No doubt."

"Healy?"

"Should be here any minute."

"Okay, Molly, I shouldn't be too much longer. I want to drive by the scene first, then I'll come into the office. I'll want to talk to the handyman."

"Ethan Farley."

"What about him?"

"He's worked for the family forever and his family has worked for the Salters going back generations. He's not our man," Molly said.

"Anything else comes up, call me."

Jesse got back into his car, his headache ebbing away. Before pulling out of the parking spot, he bent his right arm at the elbow and touched his hand to his shoulder. It didn't hurt, not in a conventional way. It was more of a phantom pain, one that spoke of what could have been. Right now, finding Martina Penworth's killer was more important than all the coulda-beens and shoulda-beens in Jesse Stone's life.

13

Monty Bernstein hated his name. It was absurd, nearly as absurd as the reasoning behind it. The least his mom could have done was lie to him about why she'd hung Monty on him, told him she'd had a fierce crush on the young Montgomery Clift or that she had greatly admired the WWII British field marshal Sir Bernard Law Montgomery. But no, she felt compelled to tell him the truth: "I loved to watch **Let's Make a Deal**, and I thought Monty Hall was handsome." He supposed it really didn't matter, that when your last name was Bernstein, Monty fit just as well as anything else. He also knew that the name worked for him. No one forgot his name once they heard it, even if it did elicit sneers and whispers at the country club. Harlan Salter IV had remembered it. And even though the WASPy prick had counted his fingers after shaking Monty's hand for the first time, Monty didn't care.

Bernstein knew that among Salter's army of attorneys and legal advisers, he was more stray dog than top dog. It didn't matter. Salter paid him a nice retainer, and when Harlan called he needed the kinds of services only Monty could deliver. One high-end corporate lawyer was much like the next. What did it matter if one was a member of the Harvard Club or the Cornell Club? That wasn't the case when it came to criminal defense attorneys. The majority of criminal defense lawyers began their careers as prosecutors, so they understood the hunt from both the cheetah's and gazelle's perspectives. They knew which judges could be played and how to play them. They knew who among their former colleagues were hardasses or soft touches. They knew which cops had weaknesses and how to exploit those weaknesses. Most important, there was one other resource criminal defense lawyers had at their disposal that the Skull and Bones boys didn't: bad people, very bad people.

For the bulk of his ten years under Harlan

Salter IV's retainer, Monty Bernstein hadn't had to dip into that exclusive well. He'd had to ask a favor from a former lover to get the oldest Salter son, Micah, out of an assault charge stemming from a bar fight near Boston College. He'd acted as a go-between for Harlan with a narcotics detective who'd caught the middle Salter son, Elijah, buying coke in Roxbury. But until now, Monty hadn't had to do anything for the youngest son, Ben. He was the good kid, the one who followed the rules and kept his nose clean. The problem with life was that even if you didn't go looking for trouble, trouble sometimes came looking for you. From what Harlan had told Monty on the phone, it seemed that the worst kind of trouble had found Ben.

Monty stepped out of his offices and into the backseat of the black Lincoln Navigator. Harlan's driver closed the door behind him. Salter was in the backseat as well, staring out the window, smoking his pipe. The earthy, sweet cherry aroma of the smoke overwhelmed the lawyer. Monty should have been used to the aroma of

Harlan's pipe by now, but it was always a shock to him. He couldn't think of another person he knew who smoked a pipe. Salter didn't acknowledge Monty until the large SUV began moving. Even then, he didn't look at the lawyer.

"You've spoken to your friends about how to proceed?" Harlan said, his voice cool and firm.

"I have."

Harlan clicked the stem of the pipe against his teeth. "And their advice?"

"Get the kid back first."

That got Salter's attention, and he deigned to look at Bernstein, pointing the pipe at him. "Your friends have a flair for the self-evident and a gift for the obvious. I hope they prove to be more helpful than this as matters progress."

Monty was unfazed. "Get Ben back any way you can. Promise them anything. Sign anything you have to. Promise them money or the moon...whatever. We have a pretty good idea of who snatched him, right? So we don't have to draw attention to you by churning up any soil. Once we get Ben back, my friends will handle things."

"Once we get my son back safely, I want that girl's murder avenged. I want it done in a way that sends a clear message to the people who perpetrated these acts. I want people to suffer and I want to watch."

"As your attorney, I have to advise against—"

Harlan Salter interrupted, sticking the tip of his pipe into the lapel of Monty Bernstein's gray Armani suit. "I want people to suffer and I want to witness their suffering. Do we understand one another, Monty?"

"Perfectly, Harlan," he said, wiping a drop of saliva off his lapel.

"And the police in Paradise, will they be an issue?" Salter returned his gaze outside the Lincoln.

"The chief's ex–L.A.P.D. Homicide. He's no dope. Ben will be their first suspect, but let's see what they have in terms of evidence. One way or the other, we'll get around the cops. Just please let me do most of the talking, Harlan."

Harlan Salter IV seemed to take his lawyer's last piece of advice immediately to heart and didn't say another word all the way to Paradise.

14

heart and didn't say another word all the

There were no right words, no magical
phrases, and it never got easier. Jesse
Stone had just hung up with Martina Penworth's parents and he needed a drink.
Notifying next of kin was the worst part of
the job. Notifying parents of a child's murder was the worst of the worst. And doing
it over the phone was the worst way to do
it. There was the initial disbelief, the silent
denial. Then the gut-wrenching shriek or
the breathless repetition: **Oh my God. Oh
my God. Oh my God...**There was often
anger, lashing-out, the cursing. Then,
whether there was any justification for it
or not, inevitable guilt. Guilt at both ends
of the phone. It was at times like these
that Jesse Stone was most relieved he
and Jenn had never had children.

When Jesse looked up, Captain Healy,
Homicide commander from the state police, was standing directly in front of his
desk. Healy was dressed pretty much the

way he was dressed the first time they'd met, the year Jesse had been hired as chief. He had on a worn gray suit, a blue oxford shirt, a patriotic tie, and polished black shoes. His hair was the same shade as his suit. He was about Jesse's size, but thinner. He was older and had the flat stare of a man who took it all in and gave nothing away.

Jesse liked Healy, and that made for a good relationship. Jesse respected Healy's mettle and abilities as a detective. But they shared something else beyond respect. Healy had been a minor-league ballplayer, a pitcher in the Phillies organization. Vietnam and marriage, not a hard slide at second, had gotten in the way of Healy's baseball career.

"A tough one," Healy said. "You look like crap."

"I feel worse than I look. That was the parents. They're flying in tonight."

"It never gets any easier, does it?"

"Drink?"

"Sure."

Jesse took a bottle of scotch out of his

drawer and put two plastic cups on his desk. Sometimes it was scotch in the drawer. Sometimes it was Irish whiskey. Sometimes there was no bottle. He poured a few fingers in each cup, screwed the cap back on the bottle, but didn't put it away. Healy took one of the cups and sat down across from Stone. Neither man toasted. This was the kind of drink that didn't call for one. They halfheartedly raised their cups to each other and drank in silence.

"Suit told me you were down in New York at a reunion of your old team. You were teammates with Vic Prado?"

"Uh-huh."

"Did you know he was going to be a star back then?"

"He was good," Jesse said, then changed the subject. "You been to the scene? Seen the body?"

"Both. Pretty girl."

"Not anymore." Jesse poured himself a little more scotch. "You like the Salter kid for it?"

"I suppose he might have done it, but

who kicked in the door? There's also a broken window on the first floor."

"The storm." Jesse waved the bottle at Healy. Healy shook his head no. The bottle went back into the drawer.

Healy gave a skeptical shrug. "Maybe."

Jesse said, "I can make a case for it. The kid brings the girl up to his fancy house to impress her. He gets drunk, gets her drunk, but she decides she's not so impressed by the Salter kid, the booze, or his house. He doesn't take no for an answer. Forces himself on her. Molly tells me there was blood and tissue under the nails on the vic's left hand. He goes to wash up, but she locks him out. The kid goes nuts, kicks in the door, and shoots her. Then, realizing what he's done, he freaks and runs."

"And leaves his car, the body, and all the evidence except the murder weapon? I don't like it."

"I don't like it, either, but what's the alternate theory, Healy?"

"Abduction. Somebody comes for the kid and the girl's in the way. Easier to kill her than to tie her up or take her along. Guy didn't want a witness. She was collateral damage."

Jesse Stone got a sick look on his face. "Maybe. Either way, we have to find Ben Salter. I'm heading home to shower and shave before Harlan Salter gets here. You going to stick around?"

"Tomorrow for the autopsy."

"Tomorrow, then."

When Healy left, Jesse took out the bottle and had another drink. It didn't make anything better.

15

There was a knock at Vic Prado's door.

"Just a second," he said, pouring out two glasses of the Malbec he'd ordered up.

He surveyed the room, making sure everything was just so. He wasn't sure why he was acting like a dumb schoolkid on a first date, but it had been a long time since he had been with another woman. During his playing days, he had had all the women he could handle on the road, and then he'd come home to Kayla. There were no kids. Vic and Kayla knew they were both too selfish to have kids. They were nearly too selfish to have each other.

Satisfied things were right, Vic moved to the door. He'd given Kayla and Dee permission to go on a shopping spree. Easy to do with Mike Frazetta's money. Neither woman had seemed thrilled at the prospect. They went just the same. Dee was disappointed because Jesse Stone was gone with the wind. Kayla was just disappointed. The reasons didn't matter. Disappointment was her natural state of being, her default setting. Even if they came back early, Carlo and Geno would run interference. At least those two assholes served some purpose other than breathing down his neck. He needed only an hour or two with the escort. The girl's murder had wound him up and there was only one way to relieve that kind of tension. An hour on the hotel treadmill hadn't done the trick.

Vic reached out to open the door and he noticed his hand was trembling. He wondered if he was simply out of practice or if it was that he had ordered up a woman who fit Dee's description. For almost a year now, he had lusted after her. Wouldn't any man? It wasn't like she hadn't encouraged him, flirted with him just out of Kayla's line of sight. She'd let him kiss her once, let him slip his hand under her tennis skirt, but that was as far as it had got. They'd gone shooting to-gether at the Scottsdale Gun Club, played golf together. Always going for a drink together afterward. Sometimes Kayla would meet them. Mostly not. Maybe it was that Vic had shut her out of his business. Dee had seemed keen to put some of her inheritance in Vic's hands, but he'd had to say no. That was one of Mike Frazetta's ground rules. No friends. No family. Only the customers that were already serviced by the management firms, and not all of them, either. Frazetta was a dick, but in this he was smart, and Vic knew it. Though Prado was tempted on more than one occasion to break the rule if he was sure Dee would have let him have her.

There was a second knock.

"Okay, baby. I'm here."

When he pulled back the door, the person on the other side of the threshold didn't resemble Dee Harrington. Joe Breen pushed into the room past Prado and slammed the door shut behind him.

"What the fuck?" Vic said.

"Ah, lovely of you to pour me some wine, but I don't favor the stuff."

"Get out of here, Joe. I got a—"

"Nah, sorry to disappoint you, Vic, but the young lady's been sent on her way. She wasn't pleased at all. Apparently she had making a bit of cash in mind. And what is it with you? Paying for skirt has no appeal to me. But those in the know say Kayla's quite the piece of ass. And that friend of hers...why have you not laid her down if you want to stray?"

Strange that Joe Breen should have thought the same thing as Vic Prado himself.

"What are you doing here, Joe?"

"Message for you, special delivery directly from Boston."

"Deliver it."

"I don't care for your tone, Vic. I don't care for you. Never have. Never have understood what the boss sees in you."

"You're nothing but muscle, Joe. Don't overthink it or you'll hurt whatever brains you've got."

Joe Breen's nasty, gloating smile turned angry and cold. "Fuck you, Vic. You never could stand that I could always see through your blarney and your charm. Mike is a real person. All you ever was was a nice smile and a baseball glove. I been onto you forever."

Now it was Vic's smile that turned nasty. "The asshole doth protest too much."

"Watch your mouth, Vic," Breen said, but Vic had hit a sore spot. Joe felt naked and utterly exposed. When they were all kids together, Joe had a kind of friend crush on Mike, something more like hero worship than anything else. While it was true that the enforcer had outgrown his boyhood worship of Mike Frazetta, it had morphed, over the years, into a loyal and enduring attachment that Joe Breen was unable and unwilling to break. Joe let his anger go. He dare not show Prado, the preening, egotistical prick, that he'd pushed a button. That was not to say that Breen wouldn't have wanted to shove his nine-millimeter Beretta into Vic's mouth and feed him the clip, one round at a time.

"You're to finish up your little party here and then head up to Paradise tomorrow with a stop to see Mike in Boston. The

boss says your negotiating skills will be
needed. Thinks your old pal Mr. Salter
won't be in the mood to talk with anyone
else."

"Did you really have to kill that girl?"

That was it. Breen had had it. Before Vic
could react, Joe Breen shoved the Beretta
into the soft, tanned flesh under Vic's chin.
"You ask me that question again, Prado,
boss's orders be damned, I'll murder you
slow and make your wife watch it. After
that, I'll kill her."

But instead of feeling the weakness that
came in the wake of fear, Vic Prado felt
almost giddy. It seemed Jesse Stone
might still be in play as Vic's way out from
under the thumb of Mike Frazetta. He
toasted himself with both glasses of
Malbec after Breen had gone.

16

Jesse Stone didn't miss the cat for a moment. The fact was that he was too much of a cat himself, too solitary, too self-contained. Men don't like to think of themselves in terms of cats. Lone wolf was okay, even admirable, but not lone cat. Female. Feline. Could it be that simple? If it was, it was stupid. What creature was more fierce or intimidating than a male lion? Whichever, lone wolf or lone lion, it was beside the point. In the end, it was the lone part that mattered. For all the women he had been with, from Jenn, Abby, Marcy, and Sunny Randall to Dee Harrington, he was alone. A cat in his house wasn't going to change that. He supposed she'd been as good a cat as any and he was glad that he'd found a place for Mildred where she could be properly appreciated. Fran Marcum, who ran the group home on Scrimshaw Street, said that Mildred had brought a new

measure of joy to the residents. **Joy**—
now, there was a word Jesse didn't usually associate with his gestures.

The hot shower felt good, and the steam
helped drive away the last remnants of the
hangover headache. The steam and a few
more aspirin. He shaved and spent a long
time staring at himself in the bathroom
mirror. For some reason he was thinking
not about his shoulder but about the long
bus rides he'd taken between towns when
he was in the minors. He'd hated those
trips. Sure, the first few were interesting
because the scenery going by out the
window was new to you and you were a
kid and what did you know about anything? But they got old fast, those long
trips. Then he remembered that the only
thing that made those damned trips bear-
able was the company of his teammates.
Even the company of miserable pricks like
Julio Blanco. He remembered that it was
those rides more than all the meetings
and practices that bonded them together
into a team. He realized that the play in
Pueblo had robbed him of much more

than a chance at the majors. It had robbed him of a way of life. One day he was part of a team of men and the next day he was alone. He guessed he'd been trying to find another team of men ever since, but mostly he'd just been alone.

He made himself some eggs and thought about having one drink before heading back into the station. He decided against it. There was a dead girl who needed his full attention and he knew dealing with the Salter kid's dad was bound to be difficult. He was going to have to try to finesse his way around declaring Benjamin Salter a suspect. He was going to want the father's cooperation. It had been Jesse's experience that poking someone in the eye with a sharp stick wasn't the best way to gain his trust or to get him to cooperate. There was no denying that calling a man's son a suspected murderer was a pretty sharp stick.

Jesse looked at Ozzie Smith in his white, red, and yellow Cardinals uniform. As good a gloveman as Jesse had been, he would have been no match in the hands department for the Wizard of Oz. But Jesse had once possessed what several scouts had called the best infield arm they had ever seen. That rocket arm had allowed Jesse to play deeper than most shortstops. Deeper meant he could cover more ground, meant he had more time to react, meant he could throw runners out on balls deeper in the hole than other shortstops could ever dream of. That was the beauty of baseball: There was more than one way to be great at any position. Sometimes Jesse imagined himself squaring off against Smith, the two of them at high noon on the field at Busch or Dodger Stadium.

Baseball was a game of subtleties and opposites. At bat, the greatest players failed seventy percent of the time. In the field, if you were anything short of near perfection, you were considered a failure. Homicide investigation could be like that, too, like fielding. You had to be nearly perfect. Martina Penworth's parents weren't going to accept anything less, and Jesse was determined that they wouldn't have to.

17

Molly Crane stopped Jesse Stone in his tracks. She nodded at his pebbled-glass office door.

"Salter and his lawyer are waiting for you inside. I figured it was just easier all around if they waited in there."

"How long?"

"Five, ten minutes, tops," she said.

"Thanks for the heads-up. What do you think?"

"The father is calm. A cold fish, that one. The lawyer is cute."

Jesse smiled at Molly.

"What are you smiling at?"

"You're a married woman with a houseful of children," he said.

"Married, not dead."

"But he's a lawyer."

"There's that strike against him, I'll admit," Molly said. "Didn't stop you from being with Abby."

"Old news."

She shook head. "Men!"

He looked at the Seth Thomas wall clock behind her. "It's been a long day. Go home. I need you to pick up the Penworths at Logan in the morning."

Molly was a pro, but she got a sad look on her face. "You want me to be with them when they identify the—"

He put his hand on Molly's shoulder. "No, I'll meet you there. That's my job."

"Okay, Jesse. What should I tell them?"

"As little as possible. Tell them that I'll fill them in."

She took a few steps, stopped, turned around. Her expression now a mixture of anger and pain. "I've got girls at home. I don't like young girls murdered in my hometown, Jesse."

"I don't like it in anybody's town, but we're not solving it tonight. See you in the morning at the ME's."

She opened her mouth to say something and thought better of it. Molly turned and walked away. Jesse called after her and she about-faced.

"What is it, Jesse?"

"It may not be my hometown, but it's my home. Remember that."

When Jesse walked into his office, he didn't need a scorecard to distinguish Salter from his lawyer. Salter was a tall, gaunt man. He was clean-shaven and rather plain-faced, with a head full of wispy silver hair to which not much attention had lately been paid. He wore a deceptively expensive navy blue suit—unremarkable, but it fit him like a second skin. All of his accessories—the light blue silk tie and matching pocket square, the custom-made white shirt with French cuffs, the gold cuff links, the black, English-made wing-tip shoes—were just so: understated, but of superb quality. He smelled of too-sweet Clubman aftershave and cherry pipe tobacco. And though he smelled like someone's dear old grandfather, there was something menacing about him. Maybe it was his piercing gray eyes or high forehead. Maybe it was the way he held his unlit pipe like a switchblade. Or maybe it was simply that he carried himself as if he was always the most important man in the room, no matter the room or the other men in it.

The lawyer was something else altogether. While not exactly out of central casting, he was close. Forty, maybe a little younger, athletic, handsome, with black hair and perfect white teeth, he was all the things Harlan Salter IV wasn't and probably all the things his client despised. From the light gray Armani suit to the fat Rolex to the tan, he was a flashy SOB. Jesse knew the type from L.A. Probably drove a cherry-red BMW 635 and played tennis with his dentist's wife. While the lawyer didn't think he was the most important man in the room, he thought he was the smartest.

"Gentlemen," Jesse said, retreating behind his desk but keeping his feet. "I'm Chief Stone."

The lawyer stepped forward, right hand extended. "I'm Monty Bernstein, and this is my client, Harlan Salter the Fourth. That's my card on your desk there."

Jesse shook the lawyer's hand. Nice firm handshake. Salter didn't seem interested in hand shaking, so Jesse sat down. Bernstein sat opposite Jesse. Salter wasn't in the mood for sitting, either. He just stared out the window. Jesse looked at Bernstein's card, waiting for the lawyer to speak again. He didn't have long to wait.

"Chief Stone, my client is well aware of the tragic circumstances surrounding the death of Martina Penworth."

Jesse said, "Is he?"

"Yes."

"Then perhaps he can save us all a lot of trouble."

Bernstein was skeptical. "And how can Mr. Salter do that?"

"By telling me where his son Ben is."

"Chief Stone—"

"Jesse."

The lawyer cocked his head. "What?"

"That's my name...Jesse," he said. "Makes it easier than starting all your sentences with 'Chief Stone.'"

His information on Stone was spot-on, Monty Bernstein thought. The chief was no idiot. He'd have to be careful with this cop.

"Jesse, I can assure you that my client has no idea of the whereabouts of his son. It is precisely out of concern for Ben's safety that Mr. Salter has come here to offer his full cooperation to your department. We are particularly concerned that Ben not be considered a suspect and that you are careful not to endanger his life if you should locate him."

Jesse ignored that last part. Waved the lawyer's card between his fingers. "If Mr. Salter is so interested in cooperating, why did he feel the need to bring a criminal defense attorney with him?" Jesse didn't let the lawyer answer and spoke directly to Harlan Salter. "Is that correct, sir, you've come to offer your help?"

"Please direct your questions to me, Chief Stone," Bernstein said, emphasizing **Chief Stone**.

Jesse could tell that Harlan Salter was losing patience. Salter's mouth was clenched and there was a tightening of the muscles around his jaw. The veins in his neck were emerging. That all suited

Jesse just fine. He thought with just one more little push, he could get the investigation started in earnest, so he pushed.

"Look behind you, Mr. Bernstein."

"What?"

"Read what it says on the glass there," Jesse said.

"What?"

"Let me help you. It says 'Chief.' This is my office in my station in my town."

"I don't know what you're playing at, Chief Stone, but I—"

"Enough!" Harlan Salter had been sufficiently pushed. "Enough. My son is missing, Chief Stone, and I want him back safely. As Mr. Bernstein has stated, I fear your department may consider my son a suspect in that poor girl's murder and that you or your subordinates might shoot first and ask questions later. If my answering your questions will assist you in apprehending the man actually responsible for this heinous act, I will answer them to the best of my ability. But first, if you'll indulge me, you must answer a question for me." He pointed the stem of his pipe at Jesse.

"Ask your question."

"Is my son Ben a suspect in the homicide of Martina Penworth?"

"The truth?"

"Always, sir."

"Yes, your son is a suspect," Jesse said.

"Thank you for that, but I detect some hesitancy on your part, Chief."

"Do you?"

Salter pressed. "I do. I wonder why that is?"

"I answered your question, Mr. Salter, and you've promised to cooperate."

Harlan Salter IV was a man who didn't like being told what to do. "Ask your questions, Chief Stone."

Twenty-five minutes later, Harlan Salter IV and Monty Bernstein walked out of Jesse Stone's office. Jesse accompanied them. Luther "Suitcase" Simpson watched the procession from the front desk. To his eye, none of them looked pleased. He guessed that made sense. When the station door closed behind Salter and the lawyer, Jesse stopped to talk to Simpson. Simpson was a big man with a round face who would always look years younger than he actually was.

"You play basketball, Suit?"

"You know football was my game, Jesse. Why?"

"You ever hear of the four corners offense?"

"Only four corners I know about is that Indian reservation where Utah, Arizona, Colorado, and New Mexico meet. I guess it doesn't have anything to do with that."

"No, Suit, it doesn't. The old University of North Carolina basketball coach, Dean Smith—"

"I heard of him."

Jesse smiled. "In a time before college basketball had a shot clock, Coach Smith devised the four corners offense. It was a way for his team to waste time and run out the clock when they had a lead. It was boring but effective."

"Sorry, Jesse, but is there something I'm missing here?"

"Funny thing, Suit, that's what I keep asking myself. Feels to me like those two are just playing out the clock."

"Huh?"

"Never mind. The father says the kid doesn't know how to shoot. Never even owned a BB rifle. Check it out."

Jesse Stone walked back into his office and closed the door. He still didn't like Ben Salter as a suspect. What he couldn't get a grip on was the father's priorities. If the kid hadn't killed the girl and he hadn't run, he'd probably been abducted. But all the father seemed concerned about was that a cop not shoot his son. Jesse got that Harlan Salter was about as warm and fuzzy as a metal casket, but according to Ethan Farley, the Salters' handyman, Harlan loved Ben to a fault. He was the good son, the one who was doted on. It just didn't feel right, not any of it. Jesse knew better than most that there wasn't anything about the murder of an eighteen-year-old girl that was right or would ever be right.

18

The woman the folks in Scottsdale knew
as Dee Harrington stared long and hard in
the mirror. She understood that her reflection was pleasing, that any modesty
about her appearance would be false.
And while she wouldn't say that her beauty
was a curse, it hadn't always been a blessing, either, especially not at the Bureau.
Men and women alike were always eager
to take her, but never took her seriously.
They were always willing to pay her attention, but never heed. As she tried to look
through her own naked reflection to what
lay beneath, she wondered if that's what
this had all been about: the need to be
taken seriously. When she began this so-
journ fourteen months ago, she didn't
think so. Then it felt like it was about getting the bad guys, about getting justice
even if everyone else looked away. Now
that her resources were nearly depleted
and she'd only scratched the surface of

Vic Prado's criminal enterprise, an enterprise her supervisors at the FBI dismissed as fantasy or stupidity, she wasn't so sure it had been worth the risk. More and more she felt like the desperate gambler who had gone all in with only a pair of deuces to play. At the moment, she was questioning every decision she'd made, from taking medical leave to sleeping with Jesse Stone.

She liked Jesse well enough. He was certainly a good-looking man, and while no one would ever confuse his dinner repartee for Churchill's, he had an edge and a vulnerability about him she couldn't quite make sense of. The sex had been mind-blowing, but had she slept with him purely out of desire or because she hoped Jesse might finally be her way to get to Vic Prado? Had she slept with him as a kind of fuck-you to the Prados? Or was sleeping with Jesse a wave of the white flag? Did she just want to grab a little bit of joy for herself before surrendering, before going back home to D.C. and trying to rebuild her life? She just wasn't sure of anything anymore. What she knew was that she'd been invited along to New York to keep Kayla company and to entertain Jesse. For reasons she only vaguely understood, it seemed that Jesse Stone's pleasure was of paramount importance to both Vic and Kayla. Both spouses had separate agendas, and both prominently featured Jesse Stone. Now, because he'd been called back to Paradise on what his note had called police business, even Jesse Stone was a dead end. One of a hundred dead ends she'd steered down since she began tilting at this particular windmill.

With Jesse gone and last hopes gone with him, she'd feigned illness, opting out of another night of hand-holding with Kayla while Vic acted the part of grand pooh-bah to his minor-league baseball buddies. She supposed she could have dealt with Kayla. She sometimes enjoyed her company. Apart from her vague melancholy, Kayla could be fun. Kayla understood better than most what it felt like not to be taken seriously. There was one night back in Scottsdale, when they'd both had a little too much tequila, that she'd almost confessed to Kayla about coming after Vic. That what galled her more than anything else was that her female bosses had been the most dismissive of her. But the words never made it past the tip of her tongue. Had their paths crossed by chance rather than by plan, she and Kayla might have been friends. **No.** She shook her head at the mirror and watched her blond hair sweep back and forth over the tanned skin of her bare shoulders. Not only wouldn't she and Kayla have moved in the same orbits, they wouldn't have even moved in the same galaxy. Who was she fooling?

She knew she was fooling no one, especially not herself, not any longer. Although it felt as if she had pushed all her chips to the center of the table with a fatally weak hand, she knew she had one last chip in reserve. She could finally give Vic the only thing he really wanted: her. She had toyed with the idea for the last month or two as her money ran low and time grew short. Once that barrier had been crossed, she was sure he would tell her things. Nothing else had worked. No matter how she had coaxed or cajoled, flirted or badgered, he had refused to let her invest money with one of the firms she was sure he was fronting for. It would have been so easy. Her money would have been like a dye marker in the blood. She had downloaded everything off the hard drive of Vic's home PC, off Kayla's laptop. She had asked Kayla a thousand different questions in a thousand different ways. She had talked to all of Vic's closest friends in Scottsdale. All it got her was eyestrain and a few lurid propositions. At least Vic hadn't been crude about it. He had made his desires known to her, but without pretense, without pushing. She had to give him that. There was that one time six months ago when they were going to play tennis. A storm blew up and they wound up drinking instead. He had kissed her, slipped his hand under her skirt before she pulled away. Now she wished she hadn't. She wished she had just got it over with. Now it was way beyond wishes. It would be about desperation.

She noticed tears in the mirror and turned away. She had played the part of Dee Harrington for so long, she wasn't sure of who she really was anymore. She threw on a robe and reached for her phone to call Abe, the only person at the Bureau who knew what she was doing during her medical leave. But before she could dial, the phone rang in her hand. She recognized Kayla's ringtone, saw Kayla's sad and lovely face on the screen. She thought about not answering, but Dee Harrington was feeling so empty at the moment, she picked up.

"Dee! Dee!" Kayla said, nearly breathless. There was a lot of background noise, as if she was calling from a bar. "Vic says he's got to go to Boston and then to Paradise. Wanna come?"

Dee couldn't answer for the sense of relief she felt. Then, almost immediately, the relief was replaced by the memory of Jesse Stone's touch. "Just try and stop me, darlin'."

19

You're never as tough as other people believe you are. That's what Jesse Stone was thinking when he spotted Molly's unit pulling into a lined spot outside the morgue. He got a sick feeling in the pit of his belly and reminded himself that these were the moments when a cop earned his pay. There were a lot of things about the job the public considered hard that weren't nearly as difficult as this was likely to be. Not by a long shot. Back in L.A., where he'd been a Homicide detective, he had done this gut-wrenching Kabuki dozens of times. Unfortunately, he hadn't left that aspect of the job behind him and had been forced to do it several times since becoming chief of police in Paradise. It was, in its way, very much like a dance: The steps were the same, but because the partners changed, it was a different experience each time. Never a pleasant one.

Jesse went outside to greet the parents. He wanted to establish some rapport before they stepped inside. It was his experience that once they got inside the building, the parents would be beyond his reach. He couldn't let that happen. He needed to say some things to them that they would need to hear. He stood on the curb, watching Molly open the rear door for the Penworths. He watched the parents force themselves out of the car. **There it was,** Jesse thought, **that expression on their faces.** He'd seen it before, a jumbled look of intense denial, of desperate hope, of shock. A look that would vanish soon enough in favor of something much, much worse.

Forty-five, tanned, and fit, with wide, deep blue eyes, the father stood about six feet tall, maybe six-one. His posture was unnaturally stiff as he tried to hold himself together and keep strong for his wife. His wife had blond hair just like her daughter's. She was already falling apart, fiercely clutching at her husband's right arm. Without him to hold her up, it seemed she might collapse and disintegrate into a wet stain there on the pavement. Jesse didn't blame her. This was another one of those times he was thankful he didn't have kids. Mrs. Penworth's eyes were so bloodshot that Jesse couldn't make out their color. Her grief was so palpable that it was difficult for Jesse to judge her height or her appearance for the pain. Molly, stoic, also stiff, stood next to the wife. This was hard for Molly, too. She had kids at home and knew better than most how dangerous the world could be. Paradise or Boston, it didn't matter. Danger could find you anywhere. They stepped up onto the sidewalk, where Jesse waited for them.

Molly said, "Chief, these are Martina's parents, Jim and Jan Penworth."

Jesse had sent Molly to get the Penworths precisely because she was good at understanding how to handle difficult situations. She knew to refer to the dead girl by her name in front of the parents. He recalled the times in L.A. when his partner or another cop would refer to the deceased as the vic, or the victim, or the dead kid, or the body in front of the relative who'd come to make the ID. It wasn't out of malice or callousness. Jesse knew that. It's just what the job did to you. You had to self-protect, to create a little distance between yourself and the victims, or you couldn't do your job with a clear head. But Jesse was always careful with the families. He shook the father's hand and then placed his left hand on Jan Penworth's shoulder. He remained silent. The last thing he wanted to do was say something patronizing or hurtful.

Then, after a moment, he said, "A hard day."

Jan Penworth took a deep breath but didn't say anything.

Jim Penworth smiled a wounded smile at Jesse and said, "Hardest day of our lives. Martina's an only child...was an—she—" He stopped talking.

"It's going to get harder. I want you to understand that there's no way for me or Molly to make this part any easier on you. We wish we could, but I won't lie to you. I won't ever lie to you."

"Thank you," Jan Penworth said, her voice barely audible.

"Would you like for Molly to come inside with us?"

Jan Penworth nodded. Jim Penworth smiled again. He started to speak, but the words caught in his throat and he, too, began to crumble. Molly spotted it and propped him up. The will and strength the Penworths had summoned to make the trip was at an end. So, too, was the unreality of the situation. Denial and hope can take a person only so far. This far.

Jesse took a minute to explain the procedure and to prepare them for the shock of how Martina might look.

"You only need to look at her as long as it takes for you to be certain it's her. You can spend a few minutes with her after that. Do you understand?"

"We do," said Jim.

Jesse knew at least one of them would say that, but the truth was there was no understanding what they were about to go through. As many times as he had been a part of this process, Jesse still wasn't sure he understood it. He stepped forward, and the automatic door pulled back. He took measured steps as he entered the building, Molly and the Penworths following slowly behind.

20

Monty Bernstein wasn't looking his bright, chipper self as he walked into the dining room of the bed-and-breakfast. The lawyer had been chauffeured back to his Boston town house after the meeting with the chief of police and had driven himself back in time to meet Harlan Salter IV for breakfast. He hadn't had more than two hours of sleep. Instead, Monty had been a busy boy, spending most of his time on the phone. But there was some business to be done that people felt uncomfortable doing over the phone, the kind of business that required words spoken in dimly lit rooms between men of less- than-honorable intention. Words spoken so that there could be no misunderstandings and from which there could be no safe retreats. Words sealed with cold stares and rough handshakes held a beat too long. Words sealed with cash and dark promises.

Monty wasn't so tired or distracted that he didn't take in his surroundings. Quaint seaside inns weren't his thing. Monty was all about elliptical machines, a golf course, spas with mud facials and four kinds of massages, and tai chi classes. His taste ran to boutique hotels with Michelin-rated restaurants and rooftop bars that had lists of fine ports and sherries as long as the Old Testament. Places like the Osprey Inn Bed and Breakfast, with its heavy burgundy velvet drapes, oak paneling, pendulous hanging fixtures, and cranky staircases reminded him of his grandma Hanna's apartment. The air in the Osprey was a clash of unpleasant and opposing scents. There was the predominance of lavender and orange-rind potpourri, pounds of which seemed to fill bowls on every flat surface in the lobby. But just beneath the floral and citric assault came the even less appealing grace notes of camphor and mildew. For crissakes, Monty thought, if the cook had been stewing some stuffed cabbage, the place would have smelled like Grandma

Hanna's apartment.

Salter was sitting alone at a small round table for two, his unlit pipe resting on the fussy lace tablecloth. Dressed in a suit and a tie, he was reading **The Wall Street Journal**, which was folded up and over into a neat rectangle. Monty checked his watch and couldn't believe that Salter was dressed in a suit and tie. Paradise wasn't a suit-and-tie kind of town, and no one else in the Osprey was dressed in anything more formal than a sweater and khakis. Then again, Monty couldn't recall ever seeing Harlan when he wasn't dressed in a suit and a tie. He probably slept that way. Also had an iron rod permanently stuck up his ass.

"Good morning, Harlan," Monty said, pulling out a chair and sitting down opposite his client.

Salter didn't acknowledge Monty's arrival. He kept on reading. Monty flagged down the waitress and made the universal sign for coffee.

"Is it done?" Salter said, finally conceding he was no longer alone, but without moving the paper away from his face.

"The meeting went well."

"It could scarcely have gone worse than your meeting with the chief last evening."

"I told you in the car on the way up here that Stone was no fool," Monty said in his own defense. "I wish you wouldn't have let him bait you like that."

The coffee arrived. The waitress asked Monty if he would like something to eat. Before the lawyer could answer, Harlan Salter made a choked kind of bark that passed for a laugh.

"Mr. Bernstein will have fresh berries and yogurt," Salter said to the waitress and then turned to his lawyer. "They don't serve the usual compost you put in your body here. No golden beet, alfalfa, and carrot concoctions today, I'm afraid."

"That's fine," Monty said to the waitress, and she left.

"From where I stood, it was you who looked like a fool. Stone was goading you."

"He was goading me, but it was to get to you. Please, Harlan, from now on, let me be the one to handle the chief.

Besides, I don't think the chief will be an issue much longer."

That got Salter to finally put the paper down. "Meaning?"

Monty said, "I got a call last night. Blocked number. A voice I didn't recognize. Sounded Southie with a vague hint of Dublin."

"And..."

"And the voice said that the next time you're made a generous offer and you refuse it, it won't be a poor girl who loses her life. That Ben would be returned to you after you'd had some time to reflect upon how you—he emphasized **you**—were responsible for an innocent girl's murder."

"What else?"

"He said that we'd be contacted in very short order by a party familiar to you and that you'd be wise to quickly agree to the now-somewhat-less-generous terms."

Salter's jaw clenched again; a vein pulsed in his neck. His pale face turning an angry shade of red. "Did he say how we'd be contacted? Did you inquire?"

"It wasn't a conversation, Harlan. He spoke and I listened. But at least we know who has Ben and that he's safe. It's just as we suspected."

"Why do I find no comfort in that?"

"Because he's your son and you love him and you won't feel better about any of it until you have him back."

"Stick to what you know best, Monty. Don't discuss my feelings as if you had any notion or concept of what they might be," Salter said, a sneer on his face. "Are the arrangements in place?"

"Things have been set in motion."

Salter picked up his pipe, leaned across the table, and poked the tip of the stem into the lawyer's chest. "Not until I have Ben back. Is that understood?"

"I made that clear to them, Harlan. Nothing is going to happen until I give the green light."

Salter sat back, pulled the paper in front of his face, and didn't say another word.

21

The phone vibrated and rang on the blond-wood table an arm's length away from her bed. It took her so long to wake up and answer it that the phone had nearly danced its way over the edge. Still only semiconscious, she grabbed the phone and put it in bed next to her. While she didn't have a hangover like she had when she'd woken up in Jesse's bed the previous morning, she was still a little high. Kayla had come back from the stupid farewell dinner and the two of them had gone out drinking to celebrate their coming adventure in Boston and Paradise. They'd talked about getting away from Vic and his ridiculous reunion. **Have you ever met a less interesting group of men? They make all the men back in Scottsdale look like Einstein and da Vinci.** Kayla and Dee talked about Jesse Stone, Kayla giving a friendly warning.

"If he will, I will, Dee. I made a wrong

turn back then, and seeing him again..."

"Don't worry about it, Kay. I can stand the competition." She didn't mean it for a second, but couldn't afford to alienate Kayla, not now, not with some air back in her balloon.

The more interesting part of the conversation had come during their cab ride back to the Standard. Kayla was pretty drunk by then, and the veil of melancholy, which had lifted for most of their bar hopping, was settling back down around her.

"Something's up with Vic," Kayla said, resting her spinning head on Dee's shoulder in the backseat of the cab.

"By **up**, do you mean wrong?"

"I guess. He's worried."

"About what? He didn't seem worried when I saw him today. He just seemed like Vic."

"You guys may be tennis and gun buddies, Dee, but you don't know my husband. He's worried about something. When I got back to the hotel this afternoon, he was in the room, drinking by himself. In all the years we've been together, I've only seen him do that a few times—drink by himself, I mean. When he knew he didn't have it anymore and had to retire. And when the economy went to shit. He did it every day there for a little while."

"This time do you think it's got to do with our trip to Paradise?"

"Probably...maybe. I don't know. I don't know why I should care. I don't even know why I mentioned it," Kayla said, her words slurring into one another.

But she had mentioned it and Dee had hardly been able to get to bed thinking about it.

That was hours ago. Now Dee finally put the phone to her ear without checking the screen. "What?" she said, yawning, stretching her muscles. The sun streaming through her windows.

"Hey, Diana, you called me last night, remember?"

"Abe Rosen?"

"You know anyone else stupid enough to risk his job the way I am?"

"Me."

"You don't count. Me, I'm taking a risk for a friend. What you're doing is professional suicide."

"Then it's an assisted suicide."

"Don't remind me," he said.

"What time is it?"

"Nine-forty-seven, sleepyhead."

"Anything?"

"Yes, as a matter of fact. You're either second-sighted or you got a tip. There was a homicide in Paradise, Massachusetts, two days ago."

She sat up in bed, her head clearing as if by magic. "Victim?"

"Martina Mary Penworth of Huntington Beach, California. Female. Caucasian. Eighteen years of age. Freshman at Tufts. Two gunshot wounds. Probably nine-millimeters. One to the heart, one head shot."

"What was she doing in Paradise?"

"That's the interesting part," Rosen said. "The prime suspect, the only suspect, is another Tufts freshman named Benjamin Holden Salter. Rich kid. Scene of the homicide was the family homestead in Paradise."

"What's so interesting about that?"

"Kid's still at large, but left his car at the scene."

"So what? The kid killed the girl, panicked, and ran. Not exactly a unique scenario," she said, her enthusiasm fading.

"Maybe, maybe not, but the kid's not really the part that will interest you."

"Abe!"

"It's the kid's father, Harlan Salter IV. The father and his brother Owen are the majority partners in the Coastline Consultants Group, a small but very profitable asset-management concern out of Boston."

"Holy shit."

"Holy shit indeed, Batgirl."

"Thanks, Abe."

"I'm not sure you should thank me, Diana. Before you, I didn't understand what an enabler was."

"Don't worry, when this whole thing blows up, I'll make sure you get some roses tossed your way."

"Keep the flowers and watch your ass." He hung up.

Diana pumped her fist and jumped out of bed. Then, when she realized her joy had come at the cost of murder, she crossed herself and showered in silence.

22

Lorraine Frazetta lit up like a road flare at the sight of Vic Prado at her door. Lorraine, Vic, and Mike went back a long way, all the way to Lowell. Joe Breen, too, but Lorraine didn't want to think about that asshole, not with Vic standing in front of her. Vic had always been the golden boy, and for a long time everyone just assumed Lorraine would be the golden boy's dark angel. They had dated all through high school and it seemed predestined that they would marry after Vic got drafted, but nothing is really predestined. If Lorraine or Vic or Mike had once believed in fate, as it was easy for high-schoolers to believe, they didn't anymore. Lorraine guessed she had landed on her feet in the end and that she had it pretty good with Mike. He loved her, had been a good enough husband. He was pretty good-looking. Was good enough in bed. But for Lorraine good enough wasn't ever going to be good enough, because Mike Frazetta, as rich and feared and powerful as he was, wasn't Vic Prado.

Vic got her juices going at the mention of his name. Now, with him standing so close to her...forget it. She loved the way he had aged, the way he smelled, the athletic, confident way he carried himself. It had always been so, and she guessed it would always be so. And yet she'd been the one to throw her golden boy away. Lorraine wasn't a regretter by nature, but losing Vic was the big regret at the center of her life. One stupid night of jealousy and revenge during their senior year had changed her universe forever, and all because she had overheard Vic telling Mike how hot he thought Fatima Borrego looked in her sparkly magenta majorette outfit. Fatima fucking Borrego, Lorraine thought, who was now as big as a house and lived on food stamps and welfare back in Lowell. That night, the night she heard Vic confide his teenage lust for Fatima, Lorraine seduced Mike in the backseat of his car. It wasn't much of a seduction, really. Mike had never been very good at hiding his crush on her. Problem with revenge sex is that it too often bites the wrong party in the ass, and in Lorraine's case, the bite was deep and particularly brutal. Two weeks before baseball's amateur draft, when Vic found out about what had happened between Lorraine and Mike, he broke up with her and stopped talking to Mike. A month later, Lorraine found out she was pregnant by Mike. She married Mike, and when Lorraine miscarried only a few weeks later, it was already too late. She didn't think about it much. As her mom used to say, "You can't uncook the ziti if you leave it in the water too long." But when she saw Vic, when he was standing so close to her, it was impossible not to beat herself up for what she had done.

She asked, "Where's Kayla?" What she wanted to ask was where is that sad, stuck-up bitch wife of yours?

"Not here," he said, winking at Lorraine.

Vic smiled, remembering how she had

been his first. He wondered if she realized that her screwing Mike all those years ago had made his life a whole lot simpler. He had planned on dumping Lorraine anyway. She was fine for a Lowell girl, but he was going to be a star. He was going to play in the bigs, make wads of money. He wasn't going to be one of those dopes who would be saddled to his high school sweetheart his whole life. Vic thought about all the guys he had met during his time in the minor leagues, either the guys who pined away for girls back home or the dumber ones who schlepped their girlfriends with them.

Standing there next to Lorraine, it was clear to Vic that she still had it bad for him, even after all these years. She made that painfully obvious to him every time he saw her. The thing was, he'd never given Lorraine a second thought. Getting girls, then women, had always been easy for Vic. Then, when he met Kayla, a rich college girl who was rebelling against her folks, he was smitten. He had to have her one way or the other, Jesse Stone or no

Jesse Stone. She was everything the girls he had known back home in Lowell were not. Not only was she drop-dead beautiful, but she was classy. She knew about art and music and poetry and had eaten things beyond chorizo and red sauce. She had been around the world. Before he made it to the minors, Providence had been the far point of Vic Prado's travels. They'd been happy for a while, Kayla and him. He couldn't quite recall when Kayla's sadness had set in. Nor could he point to the date when Kayla had made her feelings evident about having married beneath her station.

He looked at Lorraine, really looked at her for the first time since they were high school seniors. She had aged fairly well, but she looked the part of the mobster's wife in her expensive, gaudy jewelry and clothing. Her features had hardened and the jet-black dye job on her hair was a joke. Still, since he'd found out that Joe had killed an innocent girl and that Mike Frazetta couldn't have cared less, Vic had been thinking about sleeping with

Lorraine again. It was a coward's revenge, but it was revenge. And he wanted to sleep with a woman who wanted him back, not because he was rich or famous or because it was part of the bargain.

"Where's Mike?" he said.

The smile vanished from her face. "In there with Joe."

He hesitated, put his lips close to Lorraine's left ear. "I want you." Then he turned and walked toward Mike's TV room. When he looked behind him, Lorraine was a road flare once again.

23

Jesse Stone figured the back deck of the Lobster Claw was a better place to speak to Jim Penworth about Martina than his office at the station. Grief was as personal as DNA, and experience had taught Jesse that some people, especially men, didn't quite know what to do with it. Penworth seemed relieved, if not glad exactly, to have a beer in his hand. And Jesse wasn't exactly complaining about drinking a Black Label and soda in a tall glass.

"Your wife back at the hotel?" he asked.

"She is. The doctor Officer Crane recommended gave her something. Thank her for that. Jan needed to get some rest."

Jesse took a sip of his drink. "Did you make arrangements to bring your girl home?"

"All taken care of. They're re-...leasing her to-...tomorrow." Jim Penworth's words stuck in his throat as they had that morning. "Sorry."

"Don't be."

"I just don't know what to do with my-self, Chief Stone. One minute I want to fall apart. The next minute I want to go to the morgue and just be with her even though I know she's not there, not really. Then I lose my patience with Jan. That's the worst, my anger. Why would I be angry at Jan? You prepare yourself for all sorts of things in life, you know? You plan for all contingencies, but...not all, I guess."

"Call me Jesse. Paradise is a first-name police department. Don't beat yourself up, Jim. No way for a man to prepare for this. No parent should have to. There's no instruction booklet for bringing them into the world, and there's none for when they leave."

"You have kids?"

Jesse shook his head, noticed that Jim Penworth needed another beer, and signaled to the waiter. "No. Never been that lucky."

"But it seems like you really get it."

"I was a Homicide detective in L.A. for almost ten years. I'm sorry to say that I get it because I've been through this too many times."

"Does it get easier, Jesse?"

"For me, no. For you, I hope it will with time. Someday you'll stop thinking of Martina as a murdered girl who was stolen from you. Someday you'll just remember that you and your wife made a great kid and you'll miss her."

Penworth smiled at that but changed subjects. "L.A., huh? I knew you weren't from here. Born there?"

"Tucson."

"I like Tucson," Jim Penworth said in that grief-distracted way, looking out at the Atlantic. "Weird ocean, the Atlantic. So cold. I used to surf professionally. Now I sit at a computer all day long. I used to hope that Martina would take up surfing. I wanted to teach her, to share that with her. I used to nag her about trying it. I used to—"

Jim Penworth was sobbing, head bent, arms folded across his abdomen. The waiter bringing his beer stopped in his tracks at the sight of the crying man. Jesse waved him to come ahead. The waiter put the bottle of Sam Adams lager on the table and fairly ran away.

Jesse held up his scotch. "To Martina."

Penworth grabbed the beer and raised it. "To my best girl." He took a long drink.

"I spoke with Captain Healy, the state investigator, a little while ago," Jesse said. "He was down at Tufts today, interviewing your daughter's roommates and friends. He tells me Martina had only just started dating Ben Salter. Did she mention him to you guys?"

"She did. She liked him a lot. Too much, according to my wife. Jan was afraid Martina might not let herself get the full college experience if she got hooked up with a guy too soon."

"Makes sense, but what did she tell you and your wife about Ben?"

Penworth shrugged. "That she really liked him and that he was cute and gentle and rich."

"In that order?" Jesse said.

"In that order. Do you think he murd— Do you think he did this?"

"I don't know, Jim."

"But what do you think?" Then, before Jesse could answer, Penworth said, "Remember, you promised not to lie to us."

"Right now, he's our only suspect, but I don't think he did it, no."

"Why not?"

"Just my sense of things, but I've been wrong before. Don't worry. I don't investigate things based solely on hunches. We'll follow the evidence, no matter where it leads. Your daughter's life is worth more than my pride. And Healy cares even less about my hunches. He's been at this a long time. We're going to try our best to find out what happened and why."

"Jan wants me to stick around until you find the boy," he said.

"Go home, Jim. Bury your girl. I'll call and keep you posted. When we track the guy down, you and your wife can come back for the trial."

Jim Penworth looked at his watch with a kind of dread. "I better get back to the hotel to be with Jan. I don't want her waking up in an empty room."

Jesse stood, reaching for his wallet. "Let me take care of this and I'll give you a lift back."

"No! Sorry, Jesse, but I want to walk. I need some space."

"Sure. You know the way?"

"I do, but I wouldn't mind getting lost." He extended his right hand to Jesse. "Thank you for this. It helped a little bit."

Jesse shook his hand and watched Jim Penworth leave. He sat back down and finished his drink.

24

Vic Prado walked into Mike Frazetta's TV room the way he walked into every room, like he owned it. **The Outlaw Josey Wales** was playing on the huge screen and Mike, as always, was mouthing the words with Clint Eastwood's Josey Wales: **"To hell with them fellas. Buzzards gotta eat, same as worms."** Vic stood there, shaking his head at his childhood friend. Some men grow old, he thought, but never grow up. Still, Mike Frazetta had gotten pretty far in life for a poor Italian kid from Lowell with a jones for Clint Eastwood Westerns. One thing Mike had always had was a steely determination. He tended to get what he wanted regardless of how he got it. If Mike had to pay for it, that was fine. But if someone else had to pay the price, that was even better. Mike owned a lot of things. A big heart wasn't among them. One of the things he did own was Vic Prado—lock, stock, and barrel.

Mike was still busy watching the screen, waiting for Clint's next line, but Joe Breen had spotted Vic the moment he walked in. Joe had just sat there in the dark, staring at Prado. Eventually, Vic felt the chill of Joe's icy stare and turned to see Breen's familiar and unwelcome silhouette. Vic and Joe had known each other since Joe's mother had sent her son away from Boston to live with her brother in Lowell. "Maybe your uncle Declan can knock some sense into that thick skull of yours, boy" were his mother's parting words. Joe's uncle Dec, a tough Irishman from the other side with a brogue as thick as road tar, lived two doors down from the Prados and around the corner from the Frazettas. The boys had become a trio from early on, but there had always been something cold and menacing about Joe. It bothered Vic. It still bothered Vic. It never bothered Mike.

When he was sure he had unnerved Vic, Joe said, "Look who's graced us with his presence, Boss. It's the utility infielder from the Kansas City Royals."

Vic cringed. Mike Frazetta wasn't the only man in the room who hadn't grown up. Vic had played fourteen years in the majors, but should have played only eleven. Toward the end of his career, with his knees failing and his bat slowing down, he'd leapt at a free-agent offer from the then-lowly Royals. It hadn't worked out for either party. Switching leagues and having to learn a whole new set of opposing pitchers was tough. And adjusting to the designated-hitter rule drove him mad. For the last two years of his time in the bigs, Vic had been relegated to occasional pinch-hitting duty and playing once every two weeks, usually out of position. He was once a borderline hall-of-famer, but his time in KC had driven a stake through the heart of his chances for Cooperstown. He barely hit his weight, and his range in the field was very limited.

"Yo, Vic," Mike said, clicking off the TV. He jumped off the couch and turned up the room lights. He put his hands on Vic's biceps. "You look like a million fucking bucks, like always."

Mike may have owned Vic, but he still admired him. It was like a hardwired dynamic. He couldn't help himself. Although he was a few months older than Prado, was vastly better off and more powerful, he would always feel like Vic's little brother.

"Thanks, Mike. I'm okay." He looked over and saw Joe Breen smirking at him.

"'Okay'? I hear you had a good time in New York on my dime, Vic."

"Yeah, thanks for that. That was good of you to let me have the reunion."

"Nah, forget about it," Mike said, not meaning a word. "Where are Geno and Carlo?"

"Parked on the street. About them, Mike..."

"What about them?"

Vic said, "Can't take them with me in Paradise. No way. They'll stick out there and call attention to our business. A man like Harlan Salter will run in the other direction if he sees your boys with me."

Mike turned red. "Harlan fucking Salter will do whatever the fuck I want as long as I got his son."

"I admit you have leverage, Mike, but it's limited. You kill the son and Salter will run to the cops and he'll blow up the whole network. We got a scheme here that Madoff would be proud of. As long as we keep adding new firms to our group and use some of their assets to pay off the investors from the other groups, we got it made."

"He'll blow you up, Vic," Breen said. "Salter doesn't know Mike. He doesn't know me. He knows you. See, that's what a front is all about. And you aren't likely to speak if you should be arrested, are you now?"

"Fuck you, Joe. I don't need your implied threats. If you hadn't killed that girl, we wouldn't be in this mess."

"Not for nothing, Vic," Mike Frazetta said, "but if you had chosen more wisely in terms of asset-management firms, the girl would still be breathing. It was your mistake that killed the girl as much as Joe. So don't be pushing back so hard."

Vic knew Mike was right, but it wasn't supposed to happen this way. Vic picked

Coastline Consultants Group precisely because he knew Harlan Salter IV would resist his overtures and because the Salter family was based in Paradise. He had timed everything just right. Had got Mike to let him have the reunion and got Jesse Stone to come. Maybe the girl's murder would help him when it was all said and done, but it ate at him.

"Okay, Mike, I'm sorry, but I can't have your guys around me. And I could tell Jesse Stone was already suspicious of them in New York. If I show up in some bullshit little town with bodyguards, he's going to—"

Frazetta held up his palms. "You made your point."

"Good." Vic smiled with relief, but his win was short-lived.

"Geno and Carlo are out, but Joe will go instead. Before you say anything, listen. He'll just hang around at the fringes. He won't be with you. He'll just be keeping an eye on things, watching my back and yours at the same time."

Vic knew better than to argue. This was

as much of a concession as he was likely to get from Frazetta. "Whatever you say, Mike."

"That's better." He went over to a desk, pulled out a file, and handed it over to Vic. "These are the new contract terms. Salter agrees and signs, he gets the kid back the following day. He don't sign...well, he better sign."

Meanwhile, Joe Breen slumped back in his chair. He had planned on spending the next few days at home in bed with Moira. He'd done all sorts of shopping to please the lass, bought a few bottles of expensive champagne. Now he'd have to babysit Vic Prado. One day, Joe promised himself, he would have that pebble out of his shoe once and for all.

25

He kept his cars like his appearance, innocuous and unthreatening. It was always best for them not to see you coming. This way you were on them before they could react. And it made the pain that much sweeter when they realized who it was killing them by the inch. Today his car was a white Nissan Sentra. Plain even by his standards, nearly invisible. Just the same, he hung back, keeping several cars between the Nissan and the limo. It never did well to be overconfident. Experience had schooled him that even the terminally oblivious sometimes checked their blind spots. That's where he lived, where he made his living, in people's blind spots.

It had been an uneventful trip, the limo driver finding a comfortable slot in the middle lane and doing a steady sixty from Boston up to Paradise. **Paradise! How ridiculous,** he thought. He wondered what got into people sometimes. Talk about tempting fate. Why not just name the place Heaven or Nirvana or Valhalla or Eden? It so cut against his instinct for invisibility that he couldn't wait to poke his finger in the eyes of the town fathers. Everything about this job—the intense beauty of the victim; the client's desire for a slow, painful revenge; an audience; even the name of the town—made him pray for the green light. He hated it when clients got weak-kneed and backed off. Sure, he got half his fee that way, without having to do the deed and risking capture, but he didn't do what he did for the money, not exclusively. He did it for the rush, for the surprise in the victims' eyes, for the joy of the pain.

The limo turned off the highway and onto the two-lane state road. He knew he could have easily kept going to the next exit and come into Paradise from the opposite end of town, but he got the sense that he should follow his first impulse and continue to trail the limo. Fortunately, enough cars exited the highway so that his white Sentra didn't emerge from the scenery. Still, he slowed down and followed from even farther back than he had during the trip up from Boston. That, too, proved to be a wise decision as the cars between himself and the limo peeled away one by one until only the Sentra and the limo were left heading directly into town.

The town seemed like many other New England towns, places caught between their pasts and their futures, their myths and their mysteries. He shook his head at the quaint shops with harpoons above their doors and other whaling paraphernalia in their windows or used as signage. What was the deal with this whaling fixation? It seemed to him that every coastal town from Long Island to Maine wanted to lay claim to a whaling tradition. **How odd,** he thought. Did the towns in the Plains States want to brag about nearly killing off the bison? He wondered if the women in the limo were taking notice of the shops. He wondered what they were thinking. It's what a good hunter did, tried getting into the minds of his prey. And he was a very good hunter.

The limo slowed. He slowed. He scanned the street to see if there was a hotel or inn on the block. There was none. The limo stopped. He stopped. Except he had stopped his Sentra in front of a donut shop. The limo had stopped in front of the police station. He was right to have followed the limo instead of coming into town from the other direction. Maybe this was going to be more of a challenge than he had anticipated. That was just fine with him.

26

Healy was sipping his coffee, sitting across from Jesse Stone. Jesse had his feet up on his desk. He'd finished his coffee and wasn't ready to get up for a second cup quite yet. These were men comfortable with each other, men who could sit quietly together and think.

Healy said, "So the tissue and blood under the vic's fingernails are a match for the kid's."

"Uh-huh."

"That's not good for him. He forces himself on her. She defends herself, digging her nails into him, draws blood."

"That's possible, but there was another set of footprints on the porch of the Salter place."

"Size-twelve men's Adidas basketball shoes," Healy said. "It's all there. Too big for the Salter kid. Didn't belong to the vic. And the handyman, Farley, he doesn't strike me as an Adidas-wearing kind of guy. Also found a partial shoe imprint in the mud below the broken window that's a match for the porch print."

"That works against the kid killing the girl," Jesse said.

"Would seem so."

"And the slugs were nine-millimeters, like we thought. Also seems that the father was telling the truth about the kid not owning firearms. I had Suit check it out."

They sat in silence again.

"Well," Healy said, "if the kid didn't do it, what have we got?"

"What we've got is one definite homicide that now may be two. At the very least we've got an abduction in addition to the homicide."

Healy screwed his face up as if the coffee had turned bitter in his mouth. "Where's the ransom note?"

"Sometimes the family gets the note and they don't get the cops. You know, 'Don't involve the police or else.' Harlan Salter the Fourth strikes me as the kind of man who likes to handle things his way and on his own. He could barely tolerate his own lawyer."

"You think he'd risk his kid's life that way, by not involving the police? Doesn't make a lot of sense to me."

"Healy, there's nothing about this case that feels right to me. Everything feels just a little off."

"You going to put a man on the father?"

"Maybe, but it's not like I've got the resources of the L.A.P.D. at my disposal," Jesse said. "I've got a twelve-person department."

"You never told me about your reunion with Vic Prado. Guy could play him some second base."

Jesse thought about it for a moment before answering. He hadn't really given Vic or the reunion much thought since he'd got back to Paradise. Murdered girls trumped Julio Blanco, Vic Prado, slow-hit grounders, and late throws. Well, there was one aspect of his brief time in New York City he had given some thought to: Dee Harrington. It was hard to escape thinking of her. Jesse considered several answers to Healy's inquiry, but all he said was, "Better to leave the past where it belongs."

Healy raised his eyebrows and left it at that. "I'm out of here. Anything comes up, I'll let you know."

"Same here."

Jesse waited until he was sure Healy had left the station and then asked Molly Crane to come into his office.

"What's up, Jesse?" she said.

"Who would you trust to tail someone without getting made within the first five minutes?"

"Suit. Me. You."

Jesse shook his head. "Anyone else?"

"Buddy, maybe," she said. "Gabriel."

"The new guy?"

"New to us," Molly said, "but he had a few years on the job in Boston."

"Is Gabe on shift now?"

"Yeah."

"Call him back here. I need to speak to him in person."

"Care to enlighten me?"

"I want someone to keep an eye on

Harlan Salter," he said.

She frowned. "I can do it."

"No, sorry. I need you for other things, and Salter's seen Suit."

"What's going on, Jesse? You don't think the father knows where the kid is, do you?"

"Not yet. I just have a feeling about this."

"You're going to leave us a man short based on a feeling?" she said.

"I get to do things like that because—"

"I know, Jesse. Because you're the chief of police."

"You're catching on, Crane. Maybe I'll keep you around."

"Or promote me?"

He smiled at her. "Not likely, Crane."

Molly smiled back. "Screw you, Jesse."

Almost as soon as she closed the office door behind her, there was a knock on the pebbled glass. Molly stuck her head back into Jesse's office.

He said, "You here to curse at your chief again?"

"I wish. There are two women here to see you, Jesse. And..."

"And what?"

"And they both make your ex-wife look like the ugly girl at the school dance. I don't know what it is they all see in you."

"Would you like to find out?"

She shook her head. "I don't need a promotion that badly."

"Maybe it's my wit," he said.

"No, Jesse, I can pretty much guarantee you it's not that."

"Send them in."

"And when Gabe gets here?"

"Tell him to wait," Jesse said.

When the door pulled back, Kayla Prado and Dee Harrington walked into Jesse Stone's office.

27

Joe Breen preferred his old beat-up '68 GTO to Mike Frazetta's pearl-white Caddy CTS Coupe. The ride was velvety yet responsive. And sure, the Caddy had a ridiculous glut of horsepower, but the engine hummed, dosing out the muscle so smoothly that you hardly had a sense of speed. It was like sitting in first class on a jetliner. You knew you were going more than five hundred miles an hour, but it felt like you were on your living room sofa. Joe liked to feel the shifts, liked the strain of the engine, enjoyed the roar of it. Humming was for birds, not for engines. But he couldn't argue with Mike. It would have been too risky to drive the GTO back into Paradise this soon after he'd killed the girl and snatched the boy. He usually wasn't big on regret, but he hated imagining Moira's reaction if she ever found out what a monster her lover could be. Moira was such a gentle and cultured girl. Just thinking about the sadness in the lass's eyes when he told her he'd have to be away for a few days nearly broke what little heart Joe Breen had remaining in his chest.

Joe had no such heartbreak when it came to the man seated to his right. Vic Prado was a smug bastard, a smarmy shite, his uncle Declan might have said. Joe shook his head as he thought about Vic. What, he wondered, did everyone see in this guy? Vic's charms had forever escaped Joe. Even as kids, when Mike and the other boys in the neighborhood followed Vic about as if he was the Pied Piper, Joe was at a loss to comprehend it. Was it that Vic was always the best athlete among the boys? Joe knew that sports was a measure by which most boys found their place in the world, but so was toughness. And by that measure, Joe should have had as big a following as Vic. Not one of the boys could touch Joe's willingness to fight older boys. Not one of them matched Joe's determination. It was true that Mike Frazetta had always admired

Joe for that.

"How do you do it, Breen?" Mike had once asked after Joe had kicked the shit out of Chicky Giardo, a guy five years older and half a foot taller.

"You're going to get hit, Mike, and it's going to hurt. The trick is not caring that it hurts. The trick is making sure he knows that no matter how bad he hurts you, you're willing to hurt him worse, much worse. You hurt a few guys bad enough, no one wants a piece of you anymore."

It was something Mike never forgot, and when he followed his dad into the family business, he took Joe along with him. That was another thing about Vic, he was a one-way kind of guy. His loyalty was to himself alone. The minute he knew he was getting out of Lowell, he dropped his old friends and never looked back. Joe detested Lorraine, and yeah, she had cheated on Vic with Mike, but Joe wasn't fooled. He knew that Vic was going to scrape Lorraine away like shit off his shoe whether she had been faithful or not. She had just made it easier for Vic to do the inevitable.

Everybody made it easy for Vic until all of his investments went south and he showed up on Mike's doorstep with his hand out and an idea.

It still burned Joe's ass that Mike hadn't made Vic crawl. If it had been up to Joe, he would have made Vic Prado beg and give his paw before he would have given the bastard a penny. But Mike had never got over his boyhood admiration for Vic, nor had he got past the guilt he felt for what had happened between himself and Lorraine that night all those years ago. Vic was a lot of things. Stupid wasn't one of them. Joe had to give Vic that much. Joe sat there and watched Vic use Mike's guilt to manipulate him into fronting him the money for his scheme. Yeah, the scheme had worked like a charm, at least until now, and everybody, including Joe Breen, had made a lot of money from it. Even the firms that had reluctantly got into bed with Vic's front company had profited like mad. Yet Joe had foreseen trouble from the moment Mike shook hands on the deal with Vic, and he had warned Mike about it from time to time.

"It's just a fancy Ponzi scheme, Boss. Sooner or later Vic's going to run out of these asset firms and then it's going to blow up in everybody's faces. Once you don't have one more Peter to pay the next Paul, the whole thing falls to shite."

Mike would just laugh and pat Joe on the cheek. "You worry about me, Joe. That's great, but don't lose no sleep over it. Everything got a shelf life. The only stupid person is the one who don't know that and don't plan for it. I know it and I got a plan for it."

Joe wasn't buying it. There was too much money being made, and Joe had seen what greed did to men. They didn't like giving up the nipple if they didn't have to. Maybe the girl hadn't died for nothing, Joe thought, as he turned off the state road into Paradise. Maybe his killing her would wake Mike up, maybe get him to realize the shelf life on this scam was almost up. **Yeah,** Joe thought. Maybe she hadn't died for nothing.

"What are you smiling at, Joey," Vic said,

noticing the cracked and cruel look on Breen's face.

"Mind your own affairs. Forget it."

"Try me."

"I don't think so, Vic."

"Whatever. Just drop me off anywhere along here. I have to make the call to set up the meeting for tomorrow."

"I should come in with you to the meeting," Joe said.

"No, you heard Mike. We can't spook this guy and we can't get Jesse Stone suspicious. That's why Geno and Carlo are back in Boston. You just leave me here. I'll call you afterwards and let you know where the meeting is. Once I get the papers signed, we can kick the kid loose and get back to business."

"Where are you staying?" Joe said.

"Not where Salter is staying."

"That's not an answer, Vic."

"It's the only one you're going to get. I'll call you about the meeting. Pull over."

"I don't like it."

"Have you ever liked anything in your life, Joe?"

"Nah, Vic, for me it's always been a choice between things I don't like and things I hate. You care to guess where you fit in on that scale?"

Vic Prado just flashed his expensive smile at Joe and blew him a kiss. He got out of the Caddy, not looking back to see Joe Breen make a gun of his right thumb and forefinger. Joe aimed the finger pistol square at the back of Vic's head and pulled the trigger.

28

The three of them sat at a table at the Gray Gull. Jesse had thought about taking them to the Lobster Claw, but didn't want to press his luck. He'd managed to elude Dan Castro while he'd been there with Jim Penworth and didn't think he would be able to avoid him on a second visit, especially not with Kayla and Dee in tow. This wasn't L.A., a place where beautiful women seemed to sprout from the soil. Jesse had often wondered what the experience was like for the women who flocked to Hollywood—the ones who had been the prettiest girls in their high schools, the ones who had won every local beauty pageant, the ones who had turned heads back home—when they came to the realization that every waitress and hostess they encountered in L.A. had been the prettiest or hottest or most talented girl in their towns. L.A. was a town that chewed up beautiful women, spit them out, and made no apologies. Jesse had tried discussing it with Jenn, his ex, but as stunning as she looked, she was so insecure about her own career and appearance that it was impossible to scratch the surface. He wondered if it was the same as it had been for him when he showed up in class-A ball and every guy on the field had been all-city, all-county, all-state. Now, suddenly, you were just another guy who had to prove himself all over again.

Because this wasn't Hollywood, Jesse knew that word of his companions would soon spread from the front of the house to the back and that within ten minutes, every male employee would be out to have a look for himself. He was right. By the time they had finished toasting, the entire kitchen staff had been out at the bar asking for a Coke or glass of juice. Each one of them then taking a circle route back to the kitchen that included a close pass by the chief's table and a quick hello.

"You're the most popular cop I've ever met, Jess," said Kayla.

Dee agreed. "Very popular with the kitchen help, I see."

"Uh-huh. Usually they stop to kiss my ring." He sipped his Black Label and soda. "So what is it exactly that you two are doing in my town?"

"Doesn't everyone want to see Paradise someday?" Dee said, smiling. The neon was on full power tonight.

Kayla leaned in very close to him. "Vic said he was disappointed that you had to leave so suddenly. He had some business in Boston and figured he'd come up and visit with you when he was done. He sent us ahead."

Jesse liked the way Kayla looked tonight, the way her perfume smelled on her skin of musk and fresh-cut grass. She seemed alive, untamed, more like the woman he had dated in Albuquerque than the vaguely sad woman he'd just seen in New York. All his life he had been partial to blondes, the one big exception being Kayla. She was so intelligent, so well bred, yet almost feral when they were alone together. Jesse had never forgotten that part of his past life. He had got over the sting of losing Kayla to Vic a long time ago. The sting of losing his career as a major-league shortstop always overwhelmed everything else. Still, he remembered being with Kayla, and, right or wrong, if he harbored any lingering resentment, it was for Vic, not Kayla.

Dee noticed Jesse's interest in Kayla and broke the spell. "We're kind of like advance scouts."

"Advance scouts," he said. "Planning an invasion?"

Dee arched an eyebrow. "Of sorts. We were hoping you'd give us a tour of Paradise."

Jesse frowned. Caught himself. Undid it, but not fast enough.

Kayla said, "What's the matter, Jess? Something's wrong."

"There's been a murder in town. A college girl."

Kayla put her hand to her mouth. The light dimmed in her eyes. "That's why you had to rush back from the reunion."

"Uh-huh."

Dee asked a question she already knew the answer to. "Do you know who did it?"

"We have a suspect we're looking for."

"Not what I asked," Dee said and then immediately regretted saying it. She was letting her training show.

But all Jesse Stone said was, "No, it's not."

"Sorry, Jess," Kayla said, placing her hand on Jesse's. She tried staring into his eyes, but he was somewhere else.

He turned his hand over to clasp hers and he brought his other hand over to cover hers. "Thanks. Things are still raw around here." Then he let her hand go. "But I can give you two a quick ride-along."

Dee winked. "**Mmm,** a ride-along. Sounds like fun."

Kayla slapped Dee's wrist only half playfully. "Take a cold shower, Dee. He means we can do a short tour of the town in his police car."

Dee's eyes got big. "Can we use the siren and flash the lights?"

Jesse shook his head and smiled. "Let

me go settle the bill. I'll meet you out front."

As Jesse watched Kayla and Dee head for the exit, he got a funny feeling. He didn't believe in coincidences, and as stimulating as it was to see Kayla and Dee, he didn't much care for the timing of their visit. He hadn't seen Kayla or Vic in forever and now here they were showing up on his doorstep two days removed from seeing them in New York. And there was something else, something about Dee that had gotten his attention. Something that had nothing to do with her looks, but he couldn't quite put his finger on it. Not yet.

29

Jesse was having a scotch with his favorite but least talkative drinking companion, Ozzie Smith. Ozzie existed in suspended animation, his body parallel to the infield as he dived to snatch a line drive out of midair. The poster of Ozzie frozen in time and space had survived many moves with Jesse, though Jesse had never given a lot of thought to why he dragged the Wizard of Oz around with him from house to house. Sure, Jesse liked to talk to Ozzie occasionally, raise his glass to him. Jesse would sometimes brag about his arm to Ozzie. **I would never have had your range, but I had a better arm, Oz. I had a monster arm, a cannon.** Sometimes Jesse thought Ozzie understood him better than anyone. Better than Dix or Sunny or even Molly. Certainly better than Jenn. Better than himself.

When he went to pour himself another, he realized that between his time with Jim

Penworth and Kayla and Dee, and now
here, he'd had quite a bit to drink. Jesse
had stopped beating himself up over his
drinking, but he hadn't stopped keeping
track of it. There was one time a few years
back when he'd just lost it one day and
drank himself into oblivion. The next morning, he was still so many sheets to the
wind that he'd been forced to blow off
work. Molly and Suit covered for him and
there had been no fallout over it. Yet that
day stuck in his head like the point of a
thumbtack. Two mobbed-up guys had
been murdered in Paradise, so it was
about the worst possible time for Jesse to
go off the deep end. The thing was, it
wasn't the killings that set Jesse off. It was
about two beautiful women, twins, Ro-
berta and Rebecca Bangston. They had
triggered Jesse's meltdown.

As he held the rectangular bottle of
Black Label in his right hand, contem-
plating his next drink, he thought about
Kayla and Dee. Jesse put the bottle down.
One more drink and clear thought would
be lost to him. He wanted to think clearly,

needed to. What were Kayla and Dee doing here, really? Mostly he wanted to know about what they were doing here now. And what was it about Dee, who had been a nearly perfect companion during his brief time in New York City, that now seemed a bit off? He turned back to Ozzie and asked him. "So Oz, you got any ideas about Dee?" Ozzie gave the same answer he always gave: silence. "Come on, Oz, even Dix gave me feedback every once in a while." But Ozzie was nothing if not consistent, in the field and in his Zen-like silence. As it happened, Ozzie wouldn't have got the chance to change his ways, had he been so inclined.

First there were the dancing shadows cast by headlights against the walls of Jesse's house. Then came the telltale grousing and ripples of tires against the rough road surface outside his house. A car door slammed. Shoes, women's shoes, clickety-clacked along the walk. A bell rang. A hand rapped the wooden door. Jesse pulled back the door.

He bowed his head slightly. "Dee."

"Aren't you going to invite me in?"

"Give me a minute to think about it."

She punched Jesse in the right arm. "Time's up, darlin'."

"Then I guess I better invite you in."

Dee stepped close to him, stood on her toes and kissed him softly on the lips. She kicked off her gray slingbacks and strolled past him. She was dressed in tight jeans, but not the kind they sold at Old Navy. These were expensive jeans that showed off what you had and hid what you didn't. That second benefit was wasted on Dee. There wasn't much she didn't have. She wore a lightweight periwinkle sweater that made her eyes almost glow blue. The sweater's neckline plunged just enough to show off the tanned and slightly freckled skin of her upper breasts and the cleavage between them. She smelled great, too. Her perfume was more peppery than Kayla's and was put on with a gentler hand.

"Make yourself at home," Jesse said, though it seemed a moot point. She'd already walked past him and found the bar.

"You mind if I make myself a drink?"

"No."

"Want one?"

"Sorry, I've passed my limit," he said.

"But you're the chief of police and this is your house."

"A short one, then. Plenty of ice and soda."

Dee poured two drinks. They clinked glasses. And sipped.

"So," Jesse said, "how'd you find this place?"

"Magic." She laughed and drank some more. "I wanted to see you by myself. When we were together in New York... Well, I kinda felt cheated when you left so suddenly."

"Murder trumps sex," he said, "even incredible sex."

She smiled that neon smile and then turned it off. "I know I sound selfish and that you're in the middle of this horrible thing, but I haven't enjoyed being with a man like that in a very long time." She drank a little more and came very close to him.

With his face cool and serious, he said,

"You mean I wasn't your first?" Then the corners of his mouth curled up slightly. Suddenly, with her standing so near, the questions he had about her seemed to vanish.

She nestled her head against his chest. "If it makes you feel more special, you were my first chief of police."

"That works for me."

He put his drink down, lifted her face by the chin, and kissed her hard on the mouth. At first she just let him kiss and then kissed him back with equal verve. When they stopped, they were both breathing heavily. They stared into each other's eyes for a few seconds. Jesse wasn't sure about what she had seen in his eyes, and he was even less sure about what he had seen in hers. It was strange, he knew, but he felt as if he could only see so far into her. That at some point, the blueness of her eyes became an opaque barrier. **You may see into me just so far, Jesse Stone, and not an inch more.** There were those questions again, only they didn't matter at that moment.

"Show me around the rest of your place," she said.

"Where would you like me to start?"

She kissed him softly again. "Your bedroom seems like an awfully good place to begin the tour."

He grabbed her hand. "It's a big house," he said.

"Don't worry, darlin'. We can get up early in the morning and finish the tour."

Jesse led her to the bedroom.

30

They were to meet at Burt's All-Star Grill, a drab little restaurant in the equally drab little town of Helton, Mass. Helton was about forty miles due west of Paradise. Unlike Paradise, Helton fell beyond the sway of Boston. It had once been the kind of place that employed thousands of people who manufactured this or that, and probably both. These days all it manufactured was future candidates for unemployment insurance. Its old red brick factory buildings stood soot-covered and disused, the habit of persistence being about the only thing preventing their imminent collapse.

Dawn was still a faint promise when the black Navigator stopped in front of Burt's. Monty Bernstein laughed to himself when he emerged from the SUV and walked into the restaurant. **What a dump,** he thought, but at least Burt had had a sense of irony when he named the joint. Monty almost shared his observation with his client, then reconsidered. Even if they hadn't gone there to negotiate Ben Salter's release, Harlan Salter IV wasn't a man prone to casual laughter. He wasn't a man prone to casual anything. As they'd been instructed, Monty and Salter sat at the last booth on the right. Their suits seemed to stick to the red vinyl as they slid into the booth. The cushions themselves were more springs than padding. The vinyl was scarred and patched with copious amounts of duct tape. The plastic-covered menus and Formica tabletop were coated in a thin layer of yellowed grime that smelled vaguely of ancient cigarette smoke and cooking oil. Both men brushed their palms together as they waited for the other party to show. Monty waved a waitress over and ordered two cups of coffee.

After the waitress left, Salter made a face. "I wouldn't use the commode in this establishment, let alone drink coffee from one of its cups."

"Toilet's probably cleaner," Monty said,

"but we had to order something."

Around the corner from Burt's, Joe Breen pulled Mike Frazetta's Caddy to the curb to drop off Vic Prado.

"How will you get back?" Joe asked.

"I'll get a cab or something."

"Seems wasteful to me."

"I'm sure it does."

"I don't trust these fellas. I should be there in case—"

"Enough, Joe," Vic said. "We've been over this like three times already. You have Salter's son and they know you're just as likely to kill him as let him go. You proved that by murdering the girl. They're going to do as they are told. Papers will be signed. After it's done, I will call you. Then you can let the kid go."

"I'll not let the lad go until Mike gives me the say-so."

"Fine. Fine. Whatever," Vic said. He slammed the Caddy's door shut and walked quickly around the corner.

Through Burt's glass front, Monty Bernstein spotted Vic Prado. He had never met

Prado before. Harlan's previous dealings with Prado either had been just between the two of them or had been done in the presence of one of Salter's corporate attorneys. Now that things had moved from the business suite to the sewer, Monty was on hand. Monty, a pretty fair high school pitcher himself, was a little embarrassed by the fanboy jolt he got at seeing Prado. He hoped it didn't show.

But Salter had noticed something as he tapped his unlit pipe against the table. "What's the matter with you?"

"This coffee," Monty said. "You were right. It's terrible."

Harlan opened his mouth to speak again, but was interrupted by Vic Prado.

"Gentlemen," Prado said. He held his right hand out.

Monty took it. "Monty Bernstein."

"Vic Prado," he said, his handshake firm. "You're the lawyer, right?"

"I am."

Prado wasn't foolish enough to offer his hand to Harlan Salter.

"Sit down," Salter said to Prado,

pointing at the empty spot next to Monty. "Let's get this distasteful business over with so I can get my son back and we can move on. As little time as I have to spend in your odious presence, the better."

"Look, Harlan, I understand your being upset, but I want you to know I had nothing to do with that ugliness. If it had been up to me—"

"Ugliness!" Salter slammed his pipe down on the table. "Your associates murdered a young girl in cold blood and have done God knows what to my son."

Vic smiled across at Harlan. "Trust me, your boy is fine."

"Of what value are your assurances?" Salter said.

Vic shrugged. "Look, Harlan—"

"I would caution you to never refer to me that way again, you murderous coward."

Prado turned red with anger. He pulled a thick white envelope from his jacket pocket and tossed it into Monty Bernstein's lap. "That's fine with me, you self-righteous prick," he said to Salter. "From now on I'll just refer to you as **partner**. Everything you need to sign is in that envelope. Our stuff is already executed and notarized. When we get what we need back from you, you'll get your kid. But only then." He stood and leaned his face close to Harlan Salter's. "And if you want to lay the blame for the girl, partner, look in the mirror. You could have prevented that just as easily as anyone else." He turned back to Monty. "A pleasure to meet you, Mr. Bernstein. The quicker we get those papers back, the quicker he gets his kid back."

Harlan Salter's face was still a twisted red mask thirty seconds after Prado had left Burt's. It was another thirty seconds until he could speak. And when he spoke, he said, "Him, too, Bernstein. I want him to watch and then I want him to suffer."

"I figured you might feel that way. It's already been seen to."

"Well done, but not until—"

"I understand," Monty said. "Not until your son is safe." He held the envelope up. "And speaking of that, we better get these documents fixed up and delivered.

Then you can have your son back and get some satisfaction."

Monty threw a ten-dollar bill on the table and followed Harlan Salter out of Burt's All-Star Grill.

31

Gabriel Weathers sat in his wife's beat-up Honda Civic, wishing he'd stopped for coffee before heading back over to the Osprey Inn to keep an eye on Harlan Salter IV. He hadn't got much sleep to begin with because he'd waited until midnight before going home and because he was so pumped about getting this assignment from the chief. The adrenaline kept his eyelids rolled up and he'd mostly just laid in bed, listening to Laura snore. Although Gabriel had put in five years on the Boston PD, he was still the new guy on the Paradise PD, and no one likes being the new guy. Everyone's watching your every move, waiting for you to screw up. Funny thing was, he had more street experience than anyone in the department except for the chief.

Turned out that his sleeplessness had worked to his advantage. At about four he just gave up, rolled out of bed, showered, shaved, then set off for the Osprey. Good thing, too, because about fifteen minutes after he got there, Salter's black Navigator showed up at the little inn's door and out came Salter with his lawyer in tow. Now he was parked across the street from some joint called Burt's that gave greasy spoons a bad name, in a decrepit little town he'd never even heard of. The chief hadn't told him to take photos, but Gabriel figured it couldn't hurt to have a camera on hand. That also turned out to be a good decision because a few minutes after Salter and his lawyer sat down, another guy strolled into Burt's and slid into the same booth. Gabriel thought the guy looked familiar—an actor, maybe— but he couldn't place him. Whoever he was, Salter didn't seem pleased.

Then there was the pearl-white Caddy that circled past Burt's three times before parking down the block on the opposite side of the street. He'd made sure to get plenty of pics of both the Caddy and the actor. The Caddy stuck out in a town like Helton. Not a whole lot of Caddys, Jags, and Beemers that Gabriel could see. He'd jotted down the Caddy's tag number and decided to call the desk at the Paradise PD to have the tag run through the system. But before he could dial, the actor guy stood up from the booth, leaned over, and wagged his finger in Salter's face. When the actor came out the front door, he turned to his right, walked about twenty paces toward where the Caddy was parked, and then came to an abrupt stop. He shook his head, about-faced, crossed the street, walked right past Gabriel, and disappeared around the corner. Just as the actor turned the corner, a plain white Sentra, parked about five cars ahead of his Civic, pulled away from the curb. Gabriel almost ignored it. Almost. He took a shot of it anyway. When he saw the mousy guy at the wheel of the Sentra, Gabriel laughed at himself for taking the bother. **A real killer, that guy. Probably an accountant.**

He was loving this. Gabriel had liked his time on the job in Boston, but the thing about big-city police work was that you were just a cog in the machine. You were another badge number and nothing you were likely to do would matter. In a small department, you could make a difference. He ached to make a difference. He also wanted a quieter life for himself and his family. So when he got wind of the job opening in Paradise, he'd jumped at the chance. He didn't mind sacrificing some pay and status. So far it was working out pretty well. He liked the chief a lot, though he couldn't get used to calling him Jesse. In Boston, you didn't address your COs by their first names. Molly Crane was cool. He thought Suit was a big doofus, but he would want him on his side in a fight. Everyone else had been okay.

At that moment, he wasn't thinking about any of that. He was focused on Salter and the lawyer getting back into the black Navigator and pulling away from Burt's All-Star Grill. He counted to ten—one Mississippi, two Mississippi, three Mississippi—then yanked his wheel right and gave the Civic some gas. Gabriel's full attention was on keeping the black

Navigator in his sights and not getting spotted while doing so. His focus on Salter was so intense that Gabriel was completely oblivious to everything in his rearview mirror. Everything, including the white Nissan Sentra that had circled the block and the mousy guy in the driver's seat.

32

Jesse was almost drunk at the smell of sex in his bedroom. As much as he liked Johnnie Walker Black, he thought this was a better high. Way better. And getting to this point hadn't been too shabby, either. He had always enjoyed sex, but sometimes, with some women, it was nearly an out-of-body experience. It was that way with Dee. There was a kind of desperation and ferocity in her that made her seem more naked than any woman he'd ever been with. Strange, he thought, that she should seem so naked although he was sure she was hiding something, something big.

The sun was just up, and when he rolled over to her side of the bed, she was gone. But the sheet was still warm. He rolled back over and closed his eyes, remembering how they'd exhausted themselves, almost challenging each other to go again. When he opened his eyes, Dee was coming out of the bathroom. She wore one of his old uniform shirts as a robe, her water-darkened blond hair falling over the collar. She came over to the bed and kissed him lightly on the lips.

"Sorry," she said. "I didn't mean to wake you. I was trying to be quiet."

"You didn't wake me." He reached out and pulled her onto him. He didn't kiss her quite so lightly as he ran his fingers through her wet hair. "You look sexy in that cop shirt," he said.

"Can't resist a girl in uniform, huh?"

He winked at her. "Don't be silly. I bet there are at least a hundred women in the world I wouldn't find sexy in a cop shirt."

"Good to know I made the final cut. Me and about three billion other women." She pushed him away, smiling. "Jerk."

"That's Chief of Police Jerk to you."

He pulled her close and didn't let go until they were both perspired and dazed yet again.

"We keep this up," he said, "and they're going to find us both dead in here."

"**Mmm.** I can think of worse ways to

go."

"Much worse," he said, kicking his legs over the side of the bed. "Got to start getting ready for work."

"I'm going to make us some breakfast. That okay with you, Jesse?"

"The kitchen's yours. Impress me."

"If I haven't already done that, darlin', there's nothing I'm going to do in your kitchen that will help my cause."

They both laughed at that.

Dee was wrong, because the cheddar-cheese-and-spinach omelets she whipped up impressed the hell out of Jesse. They were creamy and fluffy, but still firm and cooked through.

Jesse looked up from his plate. "Now that we have graduate degrees from the school of carnal knowledge, how about telling me who you really are?"

Dee nearly choked on her omelet before she realized the question was probably a more innocent one than she might have assumed. She knew enough not to give too many details. Too many details and it sounds like you're reciting a cover story. If

Jesse wanted details, she had those, too, but she would wait for him to ask.

"Not much to tell," she said. "Grew up rich in northern Georgia. Went to school in Maryland. Kicked around the world for a time. Inherited some money and settled in Scottsdale. That's where I met the Prados."

Jesse sipped his coffee and thought about asking a follow-up question when the doorbell rang. He didn't like it. Someone at the door at this hour of the morning without a call first usually meant bad news. At the moment, he had all the bad news he cared to handle at any one time. He was no closer to finding out who had killed Martina Penworth than he was two days ago and he still had no clue where Ben Salter was or if he was still alive. He got up from the table and went to the door. When he pulled it back, the bad news waiting there wasn't the kind he expected.

Kayla Prado stood just outside the door, dressed not unlike Dee had been dressed the previous evening when she, too, showed up unexpectedly. Kayla might have even been wearing the same brand of jeans as Dee. Her shoes were black pumps, but she wasn't wearing a sweater underneath her black leather jacket. She was wearing a gauzy white blouse that didn't leave much to Jesse's imagination.

"I had to see you," she said.

"How did you find this address?"

"It's not exactly a state secret. Kid at the rental counter told me. I guess I sort of tricked him into it."

Jesse shook his head. "Tricked or flirted?"

"I prefer **charmed** to **flirted**." She smiled at him in a way that reminded Jesse of why he had been so disappointed to lose her all those years ago. "Please don't be mad at me, Jess. I just had to see you alone. Vic's been gone since before I got up and I wanted to get over here before Dee could get her hooks into you again."

"But—"

Kayla laid her finger across Jesse's lips. "**Shhhhh.** Don't talk." She pressed herself against him and kissed him on the mouth. Then she stepped back. "Remember how it used to be between us?"

"Be hard to forget," he said, his head filling up with her grassy, musky perfume.

Kayla noticed the odd expression on Jesse's face.

"What's wrong, Jess? Is it Vic? Don't worry about Vic. I lost track of how many other women he's been—"

"It's not Vic, Kayla," Jesse said. "You better come in."

He walked into the dining room, Kayla at his heels. Dee was at the table, still dressed only in Jesse's old uniform shirt. Her hair drying but still damp.

"Morning, Kay," Dee said with no gloat in her voice. "Want an omelet?"

Kayla got a sick look on her face but quickly pulled herself together. "No, thanks, Dee. The coffee smells good, though."

Dee stood up and walked into the kitchen, her lean, muscular legs pulsing with each step. Kayla took off her jacket, threw it over the back of a chair, and sat down as if this was the sort of thing that happened to her every day. Jesse realized that this was your basic lose-lose situation and that getting into work early had never seemed like such a good idea. He was about to say something about going to work when his cell phone rang.

He looked at the unfamiliar number and said, "Chief Stone."

"Chief, this is Rob Mackey of the Helton Fire Department."

"Helton?"

Mackey heard the question in Jesse's voice. "Helton, Mass," he said. "We're about forty miles west of you there in Paradise. We've had an accident here just outside of town involving one of your officers. I think you might want to get over here ASAP."

"Bad?"

"Possibly very bad."

With that, Jesse headed out the door. Dee and Kayla's competition for his affections had just plummeted to the bottom of Jesse's list of priorities.

33

By the time Jesse got close to the scene of the accident, Weathers had been taken to the regional medical center. But Gabe's wife's Honda was still upside down, the roof smashed where it had slammed into the concrete median. Although a fair amount of time had passed since the accident itself, traffic was still moving slowly on both sides of the road and a big crowd of gawkers had gathered along the shoulder. Jesse parked on the shoulder and had to work his way through the gawkers.

He flashed his badge at the cop in charge of the scene and explained who he was. "What happened here?"

"From what witnesses have said, it seems that your man's right rear tire blew out. He lost control of the car, slid to the right, hit the rear of another car, flipped twice, and landed on the median there."

"How is he?"

"Lucky and alive," said the cop.

"Lucky how?"

"There was a trauma-room doctor about fifty yards behind your guy's car when it flipped and two state troopers were headed to work going in the other direction. They were the first at the scene. Probably saved your guy's life."

"You're right," Jesse said. "He was lucky. Injuries?"

"He was unconscious when they pried him out of there. There were definitely some broken bones."

"By the look of his car, there would be broken bones. Where are the guys who helped? I'd like to thank them and then get over to the hospital."

"Sure. The doc went with him in the ambulance, but the troopers are over there by the fire truck with Mackey."

"Good. Mackey's the guy who called me to come down."

Jesse walked over to the group of men seated on the rear step of a fire truck and introduced himself. He shook all of their hands and thanked them for saving Weathers. They looked spent, their eyes unfocused. Jesse had been in their shoes. Saving lives, dealing with emergencies was part of the job. It gave you a big rush, but there was no such thing as a rush without a crash. They all said they were just doing their jobs and were happy to help save one of their own. That's what you said. Jesse had said it himself, many times.

Mackey was a short man with a blotchy red complexion, arms like telephone poles and a neck to match. "So, Chief, what was your man doing around here at the crack of dawn?"

Jesse shrugged. "Why?"

"The cops aren't going to find any drugs or alcohol in his blood, are they?"

Jesse understood Mackey was doing him a professional courtesy. "I doubt it. He was Boston PD for five years, but still in his probationary period with us."

"Just asking, you know, just in case..." Mackey said.

The younger trooper, Kirkpatrick, still in his twenties, stood from the rear of the fire truck and stretched, looking out at the crowd of onlookers. "Fucking parasites."

"Comes with the territory, kid," said the older trooper, Williams. "People look because it's exciting, but also because they know the body or the guy being pulled out of the wreck could be them. It's a natural thing. You'll get used to it."

"Yeah, maybe," Kirkpatrick said. "But what about that guy we caught sniffing around the vehicle after we pulled the chief's man outta there? Nothing natural about that."

That got Jesse's attention. "What guy?"

"It was nothing," Williams said. "Some little guy got too curious and carried away."

The younger trooper disagreed. "Bullshit! That creepy little bastard was trying to take a souvenir or something. People are sick."

"What did he look like?" Jesse said.

Williams tilted his head at Jesse as if Jesse was speaking a foreign language. "Who, the little guy? What does it matter? He was just some freak."

"He was...You know, Chief, I don't know," said Kirkpatrick. "He was little. He had glasses, I think."

"No, he didn't have glasses," Williams

said. "He had brown hair."

Kirkpatrick shook his head. "Gray hair."

"What was he wearing?" Jesse said.

"Forgive us, Chief, but we were a little busy trying to save your guy's life," said Williams, frustration in his voice. "We shooed the guy away from the car and that was that."

Jesse let it go. "You're right. Sorry, gentlemen. I better get over to the medical center to check on Gabe. Thanks again. Any of you ever in Paradise, I owe you dinner."

He walked away from the fire truck and crossed the road. As he crossed, he held his palm up to stop a car inching past the accident scene. The driver in the white Sentra waited patiently for Jesse to cross. When Jesse got to the shoulder, the Sentra sped on. Jesse waded into the crowd of onlookers to get back to his car. As he walked through them, Jesse studied the gawkers, looking for the little man who may or may not have worn glasses and had either brown or gray hair. It was no use.

34

Molly knocked on Jesse's door and entered. Jesse was staring out the window, slamming a baseball into the pocket of his old Rawlings glove. She winced at the pop the ball made as it hit the leather. She could only imagine how strong Jesse's arm must have been when he was a player. She thought that her boss had been through a lot as chief in Paradise and she'd been through a lot with him. There had been homicides, too many homicides, some higher-profile ones than Martina Penworth's. And cops had been hurt on his watch before, but that came with the territory. Two of Paradise's finest had been killed when the bridge to Stiles Island was blown up during the big heist. But for some reason, it seemed to Molly, things were weighing especially heavily on Jesse today. She guessed she knew Jesse Stone better than most, probably better than his ex-wife—or anyone else, for that matter. Funny thing was, she didn't feel like she really knew him at all, not really.

"Penny for your thoughts," Molly said.

"You'd be overpaying. What's up?" He folded the glove over the ball and put it on his desk.

"Just wanted to let you know the update from the hospital."

"Good news?" he said.

"Pretty much. Gabe's coming out of it. He's in a lot of pain and he's still pretty confused."

"Concussion, broken pelvis, and a dislocated shoulder will do that to you."

"I don't ever want to find out," she said. "Dislocated shoulder is bad enough."

"That what happened to you, Jesse?"

"The dislocation was the easy part. I got a three-for-one package deal. Dislocated my shoulder, tore my rotator cuff, and broke the tip of my humerus bone off where it inserts into the shoulder."

Molly clenched. "Ouch!"

"Beautifully put, Crane. You should have been a poet. So, is Gabe's wife fixed up

with a room in the hotel across the street
from the medical center? Someone
watching out for their kids?"

"It's all taken care of. She's got everything she needs, and she knows all she
has to do is call if she needs anything
else."

"Good."

"The selectmen are going to turn green
when they get the bill," she said.

"Green is their best color."

"You don't really care, do you, Jesse?"

"Not much, no. He was hurt doing his
job for this town."

"Speaking of that...What do you think
Gabe was doing in Helton in the first
place?"

"Wrong question, Molly. I know what
Gabe was doing there. He was tailing
Harlan Salter."

"Then what's the right question?"

"What was Harlan Salter the Fourth
doing in a place like Helton so early in the
morning?"

"Point taken. Helton isn't the kind of
place that fits a pipe-smoking guy who

probably wears a three-piece suit to bed. You going to check it out?"

"Is the Pope Catholic?"

"I'll take that as a yes," she said. "Oh, I almost forgot. Don't worry, I've spoken to the rest of the department. There'll be one of us or one of our spouses at the hospital twenty-four-seven for Gabe."

He said, "Anyone ever tell you you were good?"

"Everyone." She winked at him.

"Bragging again?"

"It ain't bragging when you can back it up."

"Want to let me be the judge of that?"

"I'm taken."

"I guess you neglected to tell that to Crow?" he said.

"Old news. The answer is still no." Molly shook her head. "Besides, you don't look like you've gotten much sleep since the dynamic duo of babes arrived in town."

"Long story."

"No doubt. But there's something else going on with you, Jesse. What is it?"

"The Penworths flew home with their

girl last night. It doesn't feel right to let her go back home without being spoken for," he said.

"Is that how you saw it when you worked Robbery Homicide in L.A.?"

"Not always. It was one thing when two gangstas shot it out and one of them ended up dead, but when some little girl caught a stray bullet in a drive-by, that was something else. I needed to stand up for her, for all of us. This is like that."

"I want this guy, Jesse. Do you think we'll get him?" Molly said.

"Maybe. If wanting somebody bad enough mattered, we'd get him. But wanting doesn't usually account for much."

"Then I hope we get the bastard."

"Hoping is kind of like wanting, but, for what it's worth, I hope we nail the bastard, too."

Molly smiled at Jesse and closed the office door behind her.

35

Ben Salter's voice was gone. He had spent the better part of two days—no, three, or was it four?—screaming his lungs out. He'd lost track of the days. It had been impossible to have a sense of time in the windowless, barely lit little room that defined his universe. It never brightened. It never darkened. There was just the one bulb. The plastic chair. The mattress. The box of packaged foods. The bottled water. The concrete floor. The concrete walls. The steel door. The five-gallon bucket.

There had been long hours when he felt he was now beyond fear, whole stretches of time when he thought he might never be afraid again. It was a game of rationalization he played with himself to occupy his time as he waited and waited and waited. **If he wanted to kill me, he would have done it already. If he wanted to kill me, why would he have left me with**

food and water? If...If...If... And then, just as he was sure he was impervious to fear, he would think of Martina. He could almost feel himself inside of her, almost taste the smoky perfume of bourbon on her hot breath as they kissed, almost hear her sigh, feel her muscles contract. Then it all turned to dust and the panic would wash over him so that it nearly choked the air out of his lungs. Martina was dead, and the thought of it made him want to rip his heart out. At first he had tried convincing himself that the guy in the black fatigues was just toying with him, that Ethan Farley or one of the other handymen had found her and that Martina was okay, a little traumatized, for sure, but safe. Maybe back home in California with her parents, on the beach near her house, watching her dad surf. No, that fantasy had vanished the first day. He had cried over it for a long time. But his tears, like his voice, were gone.

For however long he'd been there, the only sounds he'd had for company were the sounds of the ocean. He never wanted to hear the sound of waves again. He was sick to death of waves. He was sick to death of the sound of his own internal voice. He was working himself up again into one of the fits of anger that had come over him during his time in captivity. Fits that had possessed him to bruise both of his hands and break a toe pounding at the steel door. Ben had done far more damage to himself than his captor had done to him. Then, as the anger was building up in him, he thought he heard something just beneath the swoosh and roar of the waves. He held his breath and funneled every ounce of energy he had left into his hearing. **Wait,** he thought, **there it was again.** A car. He heard tires on the road. He hadn't heard that sound in days, and hearing it could only mean one thing: They were coming for him.

Ben Salter did not hesitate. He centered the chair directly beneath the bare bulb. Not high enough. Even if he stood on tippy toes and stretched his arm as far as he could, he wouldn't be able to reach the bulb. He surveyed the room, though he already knew he had only one option. He took the five-gallon bucket, his ersatz toilet, made sure the lid was closed, and placed it on the seat of the chair. The bucket's flat round bottom did not conform comfortably to the molded plastic of the chair, but Ben had no choice. He needed a weapon and he had long ago decided that a broken bulb was the best he could do. He climbed up the chair and balanced himself atop the bucket lid. The bucket teetered as he reached. The hot bulb burned the skin of his fingers. "Shit!" he said in a whisper, blowing on his hand. He realized too late that he should have ripped some fabric off the mattress before trying this. Now he didn't have time for that. He cursed himself for not having gotten the bulb earlier, but he had balked at that idea. The thought of sitting there nude, alone, in total darkness for days or weeks on end wasn't an option he had been willing to entertain. He took a deep breath and girded himself against the searing pain he knew was coming. He clutched the bulb, unscrewing it even as the smell of his burning skin nauseated him.

He had the bulb. Unfortunately, the little room was now totally dark and he could not see. As he tried to work his way down off the bucket, it and the chair went sideways. He jumped off, his ankle twisting in a way that it wasn't designed to twist as it hit the floor. Ben winced and writhed in pain but forced himself not to scream. He crawled to the wall, leaned against it, and worked his way upright. He gently broke the bulb against the wall as if he were cracking an eggshell, careful not to damage the yolk. The glass broke in a few shards, one about three inches long and very sharp. He felt his face work itself into a smile. It was good to smile again, even at the thought of revenge.

Ben heard footsteps on the floor above him. Footsteps on a creaking staircase. Keys jangled. A key slid into a lock. The lock clicked. A bolt pulled back. Ben held his breath. The door pushed in, a swath of light rushing in with it. The man in black stepped halfway into the room but stopped when the tip of the door hit the toppled chair. He immediately stopped pushing the door. A gloved hand came up, and in it was a familiar black automatic with a sound suppressor at the end of the barrel.

Ben exploded, screaming and slashing at the hand. The sharp edge of the glass ripped through the glove material and gashed the skin beneath it. The glove soaked through with blood and the gun fell to the floor with a dull clink. Then Ben slashed at the mask, cutting into the gunman's face.

"Ya bastard!"

The now-gunless hand swung out at Ben, but Ben was like a wild man. He slashed at the man's neck, the shard catching in the flesh of his body between the neck and shoulder. As Ben tugged on the glass to free it, it snapped off in his hand. The remainder of the brittle glass crumbled. Ben reared back and jumped at his captor, but it was no good. That second of hesitation it took for him to rear back was enough time for his captor to regain his wits. The man in black stepped fully into the room and unleashed a vicious elbow to Ben's nose. Ben's world went foggy and filled with pain the likes of which he'd never before experienced. Tears and blood came pouring out of him, filling his eyes, nose, and mouth, but before he could even collapse, a hard fist connected square with his jaw. He was down now: disoriented, choking on his blood and mucus. Then he felt something against the skin of his neck and his world went away. In its place, only blackness.

36

Vic Prado lay in bed, his head at an angle
so that he could see the mirror on the wall
in the alcove near the bathroom. In the
mirror, he watched Lorraine Frazetta hook
up her black La Perla bra and wriggle
into her matching thong. It didn't seem
like she was conscious that he was watching her. He didn't like that. He wanted her
to know he was watching her. He snapped
his fingers. And when he snapped them,
Lorraine looked up and noticed Vic in the
mirror, staring at her. She turned around
and smiled at him, her concentration
ruined.

"Get over here," he said.

"But—"

"Get over here."

She walked over to the bed.

"Take those off...slowly. Panties first.
Then put them on again and face me when
you do it."

As she clipped her thumbs under the

string waistband of the thong, Lorraine felt the heat rise beneath her skin again. Being with Vic, even in a cheap motel room halfway between Boston and Paradise, was everything she hoped it would be.

Vic smiled back as she bent over, sliding the panties down the smooth, shiny skin of her legs. His smile was for show. His snapping his fingers at her. His making her strip and redress in front of him. It was all a show. Lorraine had certainly been eager and accommodating, but she was a disappointment to him. She was a mature woman now and she kept her body in great shape, but beneath it all she was still just a poor Lowell girl in expensive underthings. She still made love the same way she had in high school. It was all very sweaty and conventional. He guessed it made sense. She had been with only Mike for these many years. Mike, who, for all of his money and power, was just another tough guy with some brains and balls. Mike and Lorraine were a matched set. Vic and Kayla were no such thing, not even close. Vic had had women in every major-league city. All kinds of women: white, black, Hispanic, Asian, older, younger, two at a time, three at a time...For all her sexual enthusiasm, Lorraine wouldn't have made it to the instructional league. She probably fancied herself a real hellion in bed when all she really was was somebody's wife.

Disappointed or not, Vic realized he might need Lorraine. He might need every ally he could get. If it came to a choice between him and Mike, and it might, he needed to put on the full-court press.

When she had done as he asked, she stood once again naked before him. "Time's almost up and I've gotta get back home. Can I finish getting dressed now?"

Vic snapped out his right arm, grabbed her by her bare waist, and pulled her down onto the bed. He rolled over on top of her. Her damp hair darkening the top sheet. Her breathing was rapid and Vic could see yearning in her eyes. **Good,** he thought. **Perfect.**

"You didn't say please," he said into

her ear.

She screwed up her face. "What?"

"You didn't say, 'Can I finish getting dressed now, please.'"

"Can I finish getting dressed now, please," she said, nearly breathless.

"You don't mean it, do you, Lorraine?"

"No. I want you again."

He rolled off her. "You can finish getting dressed now, but only if you promise we can do this again and soon."

She took in big gulps of air and slowly calmed her breathing. "How about tomorrow?" she said, raising herself up on her elbow.

"We'll see."

Vic made sure to watch her get dressed because he knew she would expect it. As he watched, he could feel himself getting angrier and angrier. Not that Lorraine was unpleasant to look at, although her hair was just a little too black. Not that she wasn't getting dressed in a way that was, in fact, more stimulating than her actual sexual technique. His anger was only obliquely about Lorraine. No, it was mostly about Joe Breen. The way Vic figured it, if that thug hadn't killed the girl, he could be well out of it by now. This charade with Lorraine would not have been necessary. Vic would have had his talk with Jesse. Arrangements would have been made and Vic would have been in the warm bosom of witness protection. He had been so careful, skimming just enough money not to get noticed and sending it offshore. He'd done his research and figured he'd have to testify a few times, might get a year or two in federal prison, max. Then he'd make a settlement with Kayla, move to the Dominican Republic, maybe invest in a baseball academy down there. But no, the girl's murder had complicated everything. He needed to stall for time and to find a way to distance himself from the murder. He'd have a few days once the Salter kid was released. That knowledge eased his anger enough so he could manage a smile for Lorraine.

She turned to him just as she finished putting on her lipstick. "Okay, Vic, I gotta go."

But as she was walking past him, he jumped off the mattress and blocked her path. "You're not going anywhere."

It had taken a few hours, but Jesse had
finally made his way to Burt's All-Star Grill.
After some nosing around on his own,
he'd gone to talk to Mackey at the fire-
house. Mackey explained that unless one
of the parties owned a home in Helton,
there weren't many places where people
could meet early in the morning.

"Not likely this bunch owned property
around here," Jesse said.

"Collars not blue enough, huh? Too
good for drug dens and overcrowded
union halls?"

"Too rich, not too good."

"I ain't come across many rich types in
Helton," said Mackey. "But from where I
sit, the rich seem to think rich equals
good."

"Uh-huh."

"They got some funny ideas about the
world, rich people."

Jesse shook his head. "**Funny** isn't the

word I'd use."

"Still, I'd like to try rich on for size someday."

"Let me know how it fits."

Mackey had given Jesse a list of five places: three illegal after-hours joints, a donut shop, and the grill. One of the after-hours joints was in what looked to be someone's house. No one came to the door when Jesse rang. The other two after-hours clubs ran out of legit day businesses, and everyone who would speak to Jesse seemed to have two things in common: ignorance and amnesia. As Tony Dolce, an infield instructor Jesse had in class-A ball, used to say, "Nobody knows nothin' about nothin'."

He parked out in front of Burt's All-Star Grill in almost the exact spot Harlan Salter IV's driver had parked the black Navigator. And Jesse, too, shook his head at the name of the place. He couldn't help but wonder what Burt was thinking when he gave the joint its name.

"Seat yourself," the waitress said, looking up from a glossy magazine. "Anywhere is good."

Jesse doubted that. Since he wanted to
talk to the waitress, he took a seat close
to her. He thought she must have been
pretty once, but had succumbed to cigarettes, alcohol, and gravity. She had that
odd kind of look in that she couldn't have
weighed more than a hundred and ten
pounds in a suit of armor, yet was puffy
and bloated. She had hurt blue eyes, eyes
that had seen way too much and not much
of it good. Her amber hair was especially
sad, as it was still quite lush and beautiful,
though it could have done with a better
cut.

"What can I get ya?" she said, a practiced smile on her face.

"Will the eggs kill me in this place?"

"No, but the coffee might put you on the
disabled list."

That caught Jesse off guard. "Why did
you say that?"

"Say what?"

"That thing about the disabled list?" he
said.

"I always say that. You know, the

All-Star Grill and all. It's a joke. A little joke, I know, but—"

"Never mind. I'll have some scrambled eggs, whole-wheat toast, fries."

"I was only joking about the coffee," she said. "It's pretty good."

"Coffee, too."

She disappeared into the kitchen. Jesse could hear her shouting the order to the cook in Spanish. She reappeared with a glass of water in one hand and a coffee-pot in the other. She put the water glass down, flipped up the coffee cup in front of Jesse, and poured from the pot.

"Cream's on the table. You need any-thing, just let me know."

"Maybe you can help me with some-thing," he said. "Have you worked the early-morning shifts here all week?"

She didn't answer directly. "Cop?"

He showed her his Paradise chief's shield.

"Chief? I must be moving up in the world. I met a lot a cops in my time, fucked more than a few of 'em, too, but never a chief."

He thought of Dee and smiled to

himself. "I'm honored to be your first..."

"Sharon," she said.

"I'm honored, Sharon."

This time her smile was genuine. "Yeah, I been here all week. Not much action. Me, Hector in the kitchen, roaches..."

"Where's Burt?"

"Dead for like twenty years," she said, but didn't feel obliged to give more details.

Jesse pulled out a photograph of Harlan Salter IV he'd downloaded off Coastline Consultants' website. "Was this guy in here?"

"He was. He had a slick operator with him, handsome."

"Lawyer," Jesse said.

"I fucked a few of them, too."

Before Sharon could say another word, a Harley roared up out front of Burt's. The waitress's face took a sour turn. Jesse noticed her hands shaking. A bell rang and a disembodied voice with a Hispanic accent called out, "Order up!"

The waitress raced over to the pickup window and delivered Jesse's eggs.

"You okay?" he said.

But before she could answer, the front door swung open and in stepped a big biker dude who looked like a summa cum laude graduate of Scumbag U. He was big as in mountain big and bald, with the kind of neck that bunched up in back. He wore a sleeveless black leather vest. The words **Satan's Whores, Helton** were written out on the back of the vest, the words framing a devil's head atop the pinup body of a nude woman. There was a bulge under the vest above the guy's right hip, a big bulge. Probably something showy, Jesse thought, maybe a Desert Eagle or a Colt Python. Whatever it was, Jesse was pretty sure the biker didn't have a carry permit for it. A dirty red bandanna was sticking out the back pocket of his shiny worn jeans. And the boots he was wearing would have given Frankenstein's monster a run for his money. The guy's arms and neck were covered in tats. Some of the tats were colorful and skillfully done, especially the skulls and swastikas. Some not so much.

Prison tats weren't usually prized for their beauty or intricate design. Jesse knew all about the Whores. Every cop in New England did. They were responsible for most of the meth trafficking in this part of the country. Jesse ate his eggs and watched.

"Hey, Spider," said Sharon as she leaned over and kissed him.

Spider grabbed her by the hair hard enough to make her gasp.

"Where the fuck were you last night, bitch?" he said, still pulling her hair.

"I told you I couldn't get nobody to watch my kids. I can't just—"

"I don't give a fuck about your little retarded bastards, bitch. They ain't mine. In the wild, you know what the new male in the pride does to the cubs? He murders the little bastards. Just be happy I don't do the same to your little mixed-breed mongrels."

Spider felt a tap on his shoulder and turned around, Sharon's hair still tight in his hand. He smiled a big gap-toothed smile at the sight of Jesse Stone standing next to him.

"What, you gonna be a hero?" he said to Jesse. "Go sit down before somebody gets hurt."

"Somebody's going to get hurt, all right."

Spider was no longer smiling. He let go of Sharon's hair and the waitress collapsed to the gritty tile floor of the restaurant.

"When they're picking pieces of you outta the ceiling fan, don't say I didn't warn you, mister."

Sharon spoke up. "Spider, don't, he's a—"

"Shut up, bitch! I'll deal with you after I'm done with—"

Spider didn't get to finish his sentence because Jesse Stone was busy burying his right foot into Spider's groin. Spider didn't go down immediately, but he did go down. When he went down, Jesse got Spider in an armbar and applied enough pressure to where bones would soon start to break.

"You hurt this woman again, you so much as breathe on her too hard, I'll do this to you again, but I'll do it in front of your gang brothers. In fact, I'll beat you down so bad in front of them that they'll take that pretty vest away from you and you'll be a novice all over again. Now, when you can get up, get up, apologize to Sharon, and get the hell out of my sight."

Jesse let go. He reached under Spider's vest and pulled out the hunk of shiny metal that was lodged between the biker's body and waist of his jeans.

"My guess is you don't have a permit for this ridiculous thing," Jesse said, ejecting a thumb-sized fifty-caliber bullet from the chamber of the Desert Eagle. He ejected the clip, caught it, and flicked the seven rounds out of the clip, one by one. When he was done, he put the empty clip on the floor and stomped it. He broke down the handgun, putting the barrel and slide in his pocket. He tossed the rest of it on the floor.

It took Spider a few minutes to get his wind back and to get up. When he did, he did exactly as he was told. Both Jesse and Sharon watched as Spider drove away, but Sharon looked more scared than pleased. Jesse gave her his card and wrote his cell number on the back.

"What I told him, I was serious," he said.

Sharon took the card, and she did seem to relax slightly. "About the other morning, there—"

Jesse held up his hand and grabbed his cell. He recognized the number. "What's up, Molly?"

"Get back here, Jesse. We found the Salter kid alive."

Jesse hung up, threw a twenty on the table, and said, "I mean it. He hurts you again, call."

With that, he was out the door.

38

When Jesse stepped through the emergency room doors at Paradise General, he spotted Harlan Salter IV pacing a bare spot in the green carpeting of the waiting area. To Salter's left sat Monty Bernstein on an orange fabric sofa that looked like it was from **The Jetsons**. Smartphone in hand, he seemed oblivious of his employer as he scrolled through his messages. Suitcase Simpson was leaning against a nearby wall, inhaling a donut and sipping coffee out of a foam cup. It was an odd picture of three men all there for the same reason, but with different levels of investment in that reason. Jesse ducked behind a corner, waiting for Suit to look up from his coffee. When he did, Jesse waved to get his attention, gesturing for Suit to come over to where he was standing.

"Hey, Jesse," said Suit, a relieved smile on his face. "Molly told me you were heading this way."

"What happened?"

"An anonymous tip came in to the desk about ninety minutes ago that we should send a car over to Kennedy Memorial Park. Male voice, Molly says, with an odd kind of accent."

"Odd how?" Jesse said.

"'Odd' is what she said." Suit shrugged his broad shoulders. "Guess you'd need to ask her."

"Anything else?"

"Molly was going to ignore it, but about five minutes later she got a nine-one-one from a jogger in Kennedy Memorial, screaming about coming across some drunk college kid, nude and passed out on the side of the Whale Bone Trail. You know that trail, Jesse?"

"The one that winds through the woods up to Humpback Hill."

"That's the one. Molly sent me over to have a look and I found the Salter kid semiconscious, just off the trail."

"What's his medical condition?"

"Badly broken nose. Broken ankle.

Possible broken jaw. Cuts, bruises, a broken toe. Looks like he's been zapped with a Taser-like weapon more than a few times."

"He say anything to you?"

"He was pretty out of it, Jesse. He was mumbling about the Penworth girl, asking if she was alive."

"What did you say?"

"Told him to keep calm and that there was an ambulance coming for him. That we would have a chance to talk after the doctors looked him over."

"Anything else?" Jesse said.

"I asked him who did this to him."

"And?"

Suit screwed up his round face. "All he kept saying was that it was a different trunk."

"A different trunk?"

"That's what it sounded like to me, Jesse. A different trunk."

"You did good, Suit. Go get another cup of coffee. I want to talk to the father and the lawyer. When you get back, I want you to stay here with them. Don't crowd them, but keep your eyes open.

You understand?"

"I understand. You want something, Jesse? Coffee?"

"No, thanks. Go ahead. Don't take too long. I have a feeling the father won't be very talkative."

Suit nodded and headed for the cafeteria. Jesse walked over to the waiting area.

"Mr. Salter, Mr. Bernstein," Jesse said, "I hear Ben is here."

Salter was terse. "No thanks to your department."

Monty Bernstein rolled his eyes for Jesse to see. "Obviously, Chief Stone, my client is in an agitated state because of the condition Ben was found in. I'm sure you understand."

"I do. Sounds like he had it pretty rough. Other than his nose, jaw, and ankle, have the doctors updated you?"

Salter was certainly agitated. "They beat and tortured my son! They shocked him, for goodness sakes."

That got Jesse's attention. **"They?"**

Salter was confused. "What?"

"You said **they** beat and tortured your

son. Who is **they**, Mr. Salter?"

Bernstein answered for his client. "It's a figure of speech, Chief Stone."

"Jesse."

"Jesse," the lawyer said. "Paradise is a first-name department. I forgot. In any case, I don't think my client was referring to anyone or any group specifically, but rather to the man or men who might have held Ben captive these last few days."

"Did the doctors give you any indication of when he might be able to speak?"

Salter glared at his lawyer.

"I am not sure my client is willing to risk traumatizing his son any further at this point, Jesse. Ben's obviously been through a lot and I'm not even sure he's aware of Miss Penworth's death."

"I can understand your client's position, but a murder was committed here. An eighteen-year-old college freshman lost her life here, probably because she was with your client's son," Jesse said, for Harlan Salter's benefit. "And I'm sorry about Ben's condition, but as soon as he can talk, I'm going to talk to him."

Salter exploded, bumping his chest into Jesse. "No, you most certainly are not. You're not going to say a word to my son and my son will not speak to you. Is that clear?" Salter poked Jesse with the stem of his ever-present pipe. "The minute he is well enough to travel, I am having him transferred to Tufts Medical—"

"Mr. Bernstein, did your client just assault an officer of the law?"

That stopped Salter mid-sentence.

"I don't believe that would constitute assault," Bernstein said, stepping between Stone and Salter. "As I stated, Jesse, my client is understandably upset over the condition of his son."

"Fair enough, Counselor. But I am putting you both on notice that if you attempt to move Ben Salter out of my jurisdiction before I have a chance to interview him, I will arrest everyone involved, including your client's son. Remember, injuries or no injuries, Ben Salter is still the prime suspect in a homicide investigation. He is, at minimum, a material witness."

Monty Bernstein felt Harlan Salter

surging forward to get at Jesse. The lawyer turned and shepherded his client a few paces toward the rear of the waiting area. As he did, he leaned in close to Salter's ear. "Relax, Harlan. Relax. He's goading you and you're taking the bait. He senses that you know more than you're saying. Stop acting as if he's right, that you have something to hide. We'll deal with his talking to Ben when the time comes. I will demand to be present and will make sure Ben can't say anything that will complicate things. Now, please, walk away or at least sit down and let me handle this."

Salter smirked at his lawyer. "We'll just see about that," he said, sitting down on the chair closest to him. "We'll see."

Bernstein walked back to where Jesse Stone was standing.

"Okay, Jesse, my client has agreed to let you talk to his son when the doctors say that he is well enough to do so and that it will not cause him any further damage. Mr. Salter also wants me to be present during the interview to act on his son's behalf."

"Fine."

They shook hands. Jesse nodded at Harlan Salter and took a few steps to leave. He stopped. About-faced.

"One more thing, gentlemen," Jesse said. "When you're sure Ben is okay and he is moved up to a room, I'd like it if you could stop by my office. Tomorrow would be fine."

Monty Bernstein tilted his head at Jesse and squinted his eyes. "For what possible purpose could you want us to come in to your office?"

"For a chat."

Bernstein said, "An official chat?"

"That depends, Counselor."

"On what?"

"On your opinion of the food and service at Burt's All-Star Grill in Helton."

With that, Jesse Stone turned and left.

39

Suitcase Simpson came around the corner carrying a cardboard cup holder with three coffees in it and a few donuts stacked up in the empty corner of the cup holder. He didn't figure he would be able to establish any kind of rapport with Harlan Salter. That man, it seemed to Suit, was as empty of human warmth as a shark's eye, but Monty Bernstein was friendly enough…for a lawyer. Suit thought that maybe he could get Bernstein to drop his guard a little. Suit knew that because he was a big guy, an ex-jock, with a kindly face that people often underestimated him. They assumed he wasn't the sharpest tool in the shed. Maybe he wasn't, but he had learned a lot from Jesse in the years they'd worked together. Just as he came around the corner, Suit heard Salter's voice. He wasn't exactly screaming at his lawyer. It was more of an angry growl. So Suit stopped in his tracks and retreated back around the corner.

"How the hell did he know about the meeting?" Salter said.

"I told you Stone was no idiot."

"That's not an answer."

"I'm not sure he actually knows about the meeting," Bernstein said. "If he knew, he wouldn't have used it as a parting shot. He has one piece of information that he threw out there. He's shrewd. Tomorrow, when we go see him, we'll see just how much he does know. It's not as if you were engaged in any illegal activity. You simply exchanged documents with another party with whom you are doing business. You are under no obligation to discuss any of it, so don't. You were in Helton at the request of a business associate. You need say nothing more. You don't even need to say that much."

Suit wished he could see the expressions on their faces. It was one thing to overhear a conversation. Faces told you a lot. Jesse had taught him that.

"You make sense," Salter said, his voice calmer now.

"That's what you pay me for."

"No, Bernstein, it is not. I pay all my other attorneys for that. I pay you for a very specific purpose."

"Whatever you say, Harlan."

"And speaking of that..."

"You want me to give the go-ahead, don't you?"

"Immediately and with extreme prejudice."

"It would be better to wait, but—"

"But nothing."

"Okay, Harlan, you just got done telling me you have me on retainer for a specific purpose. Well, then you need to listen to me. It's better to let things calm down first, to let everyone get back to their business before—"

That was the last thing of the exchange between Salter and his lawyer Suit overheard, because an announcement concerning an incoming ambulance blared over the loudspeaker that was situated right above his head. By the time the announcement was over, Salter and Bernstein seemed to have finished their talk. When Suit reappeared in the waiting area, Salter barely acknowledged him.

"One of those for me?" Bernstein said, pointing at the coffees.

Suit handed him a coffee. "Sure. Donut?"

Bernstein patted his abs. "No, thanks."

Suit was happy about that. He didn't care about the coffees. He'd had enough coffee, but there was no such thing as enough donuts.

40

Jesse Stone drove by Burt's All-Star Grill on his way to visit Gabriel Weathers at the medical center outside of Helton. He wanted to check to make sure Sharon, the waitress, was okay and that Spider hadn't doubled back to displace some of his anger and embarrassment. Jesse had run across a lot of Spiders in his lifetime. Bullies came in all shapes and sizes, but inside they were all about the same: weak, brittle, frightened, self-loathing, predatory. Sometimes one kick in the crotch was all it took to warn them off. Jesse hoped that would be the case with Spider. He couldn't be sure, because sometimes that first kick just made them want to strike out, not strike back. They usually didn't have the sand to come back at Jesse directly. No, they had to find a weaker, more vulnerable target. In this case, he thought, that would be Sharon or maybe her kids. Jesse also had his own selfish reasons for wanting to see Sharon. Spider's interruption and the call about Ben Salter had prevented Jesse from getting the full story about what Harlan Salter IV and his lawyer were doing in a place like Helton.

Before heading to Helton, Jesse had gone over to Kennedy Memorial Park to meet up with Healy and to see what the forensics unit had to say about where Ben Salter was discovered. Not that Jesse was a clotheshorse, but he swore Healy had only two suits and they were already old when they'd first met. That was more than a decade ago. He didn't say anything about it to Healy, though Jesse couldn't help smiling about it.

Healy noticed. "What are you smiling about?"

Jesse didn't answer the question. "Anything worthwhile here?"

"Nothing to write home about. We're pretty sure the kid was driven up here via the maintenance access road and dumped. The gate's open and the lock's been cut."

"Tread prints?"

"Access road is gravel, so we're shit out of luck there." Healy pointed to a patch of ground between two pine trees about fifteen feet to his left. "That's where your man found the kid. There's a fair amount of blood, but it's probably all the kid's from the broken beak. You ever break your nose?"

Jesse tapped his nose. "This perfect specimen? Never."

"It is a beaut. I broke mine once. And that's not just an expression. I mean I broke it!"

"How'd you manage that?"

"High school ball. We were down a run late in the game and the eighth-place batter got a seeing-eye single through the hole on the left side. Coach was gonna pinch-hit for me, but because there were no outs, he decided to let me sacrifice and not waste a position player. First pitch is a high fastball, tough to get on top of with the bat. I tried to bunt it anyway. Ball caromed off the bat and hit me square in the honker. The sound of my nose breaking made the catcher puke his guts up. Either that or all the blood that came gushing out of me."

"Maybe both," Jesse said.

"I was in no position to judge. Hurt like a bastard, but it added a lot of character to my face. Don't you think?"

"Character...is that what they call it?"

"Fuck you, Jesse."

"If you find anything out here, let me know."

Jesse fought the urge to stop for a drink during the entire ride to Helton. With the turmoil over the murder and Gabe's accident, he had pretty much put the reunion and the baggage that came with it out of his mind. Even Kayla and Dee hadn't brought it back to him, though he guessed their showing up in town and then on his doorstep unexpectedly probably should have. But Healy telling him that story of breaking his nose in high school had brought it all back in a rush. Suddenly, no matter how loud he turned up the radio, he couldn't block Julio Blanco's voice out of his head. Over and over again he heard

Blanco describing how Vic Prado had caused the injury that ruined Jesse's baseball career forever.

Jesse pictured Dix smiling at this turn of events. It was Dix who had helped him come to see that his drinking was part of a series of unsuccessful mechanisms Jesse had set up to help him control the world around him. Of course, any such system was doomed to fail. Jesse saw that now, but knowing it and changing lifelong patterns were two very different animals. He got the sense that Dix took a kind of perverse pleasure in it when the universe would throw Jesse unexpected curveballs. Dix would claim otherwise. He would say that these unexpected turns of events were great opportunities for insight. Maybe Dix was right, because never in a million years could Jesse have predicted that Healy's story would set him off the way it had. Now it was Dix's voice, not Julio Blanco's, he heard in his head. **Unresolved feelings don't resolve themselves. Just because you shove unwanted things into the attic doesn't**

mean they aren't still there. Man, he especially hated those rare occasions when
Dix would get folksy or metaphorical.

He never supposed he would be pleased
to see Burt's All-Star Grill again, but he
was. Jesse realized that if he was half as
good at life as he was at police work, he'd
be in great shape. Jesse got out of the
car, leaving Blanco and Dix behind.

Burt's was empty but for some flies, and
they weren't ordering off the menu. Jesse
didn't have time to wait for someone to
appear, so he walked up to the pass-
through window where the cook put up
the finished orders. On the other side of
the window sat a young brown-skinned
man in his twenties, dressed in grease-
smeared kitchen whites. He wore a silly
paper cap on his head. He was reading a
Spanish-language newspaper.

"Hector, right?" Jesse said.

Hector startled a bit, then collected
himself. He stood and came to the window. His expression was practiced and
blank. Jesse knew the look, the look of
invisibility. Illegals learned to wear that

expression from the second they crossed the border. It was pretty common in L.A. and now it was pretty common in these parts, too. Concerns over immigration policy were way above Jesse's pay grade, and the way he figured it, people who came here and worked hard to improve their lives should be welcomed, not punished. As Hector approached the window, his face broke into a broad smile.

"You the cop protect Sharon from Spider, **ese chingazo de pendejo**," said the cook, who feigned spitting on the floor.

"You're right, Spider is a fucking idiot."

Hector was impressed. "You speak Spanish?"

"Some. Curses, mostly. I worked L.A.P.D. for ten years."

Hector smiled. It was a nice, kindly smile.

"Let me make you something," he said to Jesse. "Huevos rancheros?"

"That's okay. I'm not hungry. Is Sharon around?"

He waved his hand. "She go."

"Did Spider come back?"

"No, but she is thinking he will, so she

get her kids and go someplace safer."

There was a look in Hector's eyes Jesse couldn't quite read.

"Safer? Safer where?"

"Is okay," Hector said.

Now Jesse understood. "She's with you?"

Hector didn't answer.

"She has my card," Jesse said. "Tell her to give me a call when she gets a chance."

He winked. "If I see her."

When Jesse got back into his car, it seemed Julio Blanco and Dix had taken their voices and gone elsewhere.

41

Kayla Prado slid her Louis Vuitton suitcase into the trunk of the rental car. She thought she'd feel different when she actually left Vic. She had anticipated tears, terror, anger, but there was none of that. She had cried a million tears in the last several years over the state of her marriage. She had cried even more of them when she got back to the hotel. She thought she might die of embarrassment after walking in on Dee and Jess. Desperation was never pretty, no matter how much mascara and lipstick you covered it in. And there was no denying her pursuit of Jess after all these years smacked of lonely desperation.

Was she scared of leaving behind the comfortable, if unhappy, life she had with Vic? Of course she was. She had defined herself by Vic for two decades, had basked in the warmth of his fame and charm and money. She supposed she still might even love him, but without some distance, it would be impossible to tell. She had lost so much of herself in the process that she had almost forgotten who she was. She had once been the wild child: fiercely independent, clever, beautiful. Now she felt like nothing so much as a line drawing: a hollow outline of someone who might or might not be there. The time had finally come for her to redefine herself and to be more than an adjunct on Vic Prado's Wikipedia page. And if there was any anger, it was aimed more at herself than at Vic. She had been complicit, looking the other way all these years as her husband bed-surfed his way first through the major leagues and then through Scottsdale. She had played a fair amount of musical beds herself.

"Come on, Kay, darlin', don't do this," Dee said even as she brought out Kayla's matching Gladstone bag to the car. "The thing with Jesse...I'm sorry about—"

"Don't be sorry," she said, taking the brown leather satchel from Dee's hand and placing it in the trunk next to the suitcase. "I'm happy for you. Jess is a great guy. He deserves someone like you. I guess I half hoped you two might wind up together. Turning up at his house with you there was good for me. Maybe it was the best thing. It showed me how low I'd gotten, how I was looking to be rescued. I'm the only one who can do that. I see that now, and I can't do it around Vic."

"Where are you going?"

"To my folks' house in Taos for a little while. Then..." She shrugged. "I've got a flight to Albuquerque out of Logan later today. I'm going to sightsee a little in Boston first."

"Call me when you get to Taos, please," Dee said. "I want to know you're all right."

"Sure." She wrapped her arms around Dee and kissed her softly on the lips. "You've been a good friend to me. You've been the only real friend I've had for a long time."

"What should I tell Vic?"

"I left him a long letter, but please don't tell him where I went. I'll deal with him directly, but I need some time. You understand."

"I do, darlin'. I do."

"Thanks."

When they let go of each other, Dee called after Kayla, "Don't forget to phone."

Kayla blew a kiss, got into the car, and was gone.

Dee wasn't exactly racked with guilt, but she wasn't feeling very good about herself at that moment. The most obvious reasons being she wasn't real and she wasn't really a friend, in spite of how much she had grown to care for Kayla. And with Kayla gone, Vic would be particularly vulnerable to her. Dee was sure if she gave in to Vic's advances now, she could cull the intel she'd been looking for all these months. The intel that would finally bring Vic's sham empire down. The thing was, she hadn't counted on falling so hard for Jesse Stone. She knew enough of their history from Kayla and had seen enough of the dynamic between Jesse and Vic to know that if Jesse ever found out she had slept with Vic, there would be no second chances. Suddenly everything in her life was at risk and in play. She had staked her savings and her career on a wild gamble. Now she had to figure the odds of that gamble against losing a man she might actually want to fall in love with. Dee was so absorbed with her own troubles that she didn't notice the white Sentra take off after Kayla's rental car.

42

When Jesse Stone came out of the elevator on the third floor, Monty Bernstein was there to greet him. They shook hands. He didn't trust the lawyer as far as he could throw him, but Bernstein was more pleasant than most. As a cop, Jesse understood that pleasant didn't mean incompetent, nor did it mean impotent. Criminal lawyers usually knew the wrong kinds of people. They were sort of like cops in that way. Jesse sure knew his share of bad guys and wasn't above rubbing elbows with them if it meant getting to the bottom of a nasty case. There had been that whole thing with Crow a few years back, and more recently, he'd had occasion to make an ally of Fat Boy Nelly, a Boston-area pimp who was taking the business of prostitution digital. That was another way cops and lawyers were alike: The bad guys with whom they crossed paths often owed them favors.

And Jesse knew if he was willing to call in those favors, so, too, would a guy like Monty Bernstein. That made him potentially dangerous, even if he was more pleasant than most.

"Ben's in room 312," said the lawyer as they moved down the hall.

"Where's Harlan Salter?"

"You seem to have a knack for getting under Harlan's skin. Let's just say that after our first few meetings with you, it was easy for me to convince my client not to be here."

"Your client doesn't seem easy to convince under any circumstances," Jesse said.

"Tell me about it, but he pays well."

"I figured."

Jesse left it at that. This was his second hospital-room visit of the day. He hoped it would be more productive than the one he'd had with Gabe Weathers. Gabe was communicative up to a point, but between the pain from his concussion and his broken pelvis and the medication, he wasn't making much sense. It was clear that the concussion had pretty much wiped out Gabe's memory of the entire morning of the accident. He couldn't recall the accident at all. He remembered that he'd been assigned to keep an eye on someone. He just couldn't remember who or why. Then he got frustrated at trying to remember. Jesse assured him that it was okay and that everyone was looking forward to his return to duty. The doctors told Jesse that return wouldn't be for quite a few months, but that he could probably be transferred to Paradise General in a few days.

"Here we are," Monty said. "Listen, Jesse, I think we understand each other and we're all anxious for the man or men who did this to Ben and Miss Penworth to be brought to justice—"

"But..."

"But if I sense your questions are either straying into areas I feel are unrelated to the case or get Ben agitated, I am going to call an immediate end to the interview."

"Fair enough."

"I was wondering if I might have a moment alone with Ben before you begin the interview."

Jesse nodded. The lawyer knocked and entered Ben Salter's room. Good to his word, Bernstein called for Jesse Stone not two minutes after that.

Jesse introduced himself and explained what he was doing there. The kid's entire face was black-and-blue. His nose and jaw were swollen. His eyes were slits. One of his ankles was in a cast. Jesse asked how he was feeling. The kid said he was glad that his jaw was only bruised and that he guessed he would be okay. Jesse smiled at that.

"Martina's dead, isn't she? No one will tell me anything."

Jesse added to the kid's frustration. "Why do you think she's dead?"

Ben Salter described how he and Martina had just finished having sex for the first time when the guy in black burst into the room.

"He didn't say anything. He shot into the wall above the headboard to show us he was serious. He just kept pointing with his gun and silencer. He motioned for me to get out of the bed and get on my knees. He zapped me with something and...after that I can't remember much. I thought I remembered a shot, but I wasn't sure if I was confusing things. Then, when he got me out of the trunk of his car...I don't know. The way he smiled at me and shook his head when I asked about Martina...I felt like he killed her."

"She's dead, Ben. I'm sorry," Jesse said, finally ending the kid's torment. "Her parents came and took her home."

Ben Salter was sobbing, chest heaving. Jesse asked if he wanted to postpone the talk.

"Fuck no! I want to get the guy that did this to us. It should be me who's dead, not Martina. He was after me. She was just there."

"Why do you think that?" Jesse said.

"It's pretty obvious. He kept me for a few days. I guess Martina was just in his way. Maybe he hadn't counted on her being there."

"Can you think of why he took you?"

"For ransom, maybe? I don't know. He didn't say."

"Can you think of a reason he let you go?"

"I don't know."

Although Jesse was mostly looking at the kid, he glanced at the lawyer out of the corner of his eye during these last two questions. But if he thought they would get a rise out of Bernstein, he was wrong. Monty just sat there calmly, listening.

Ben described in great detail the room in which he had been held captive. He described how he had attacked his captor with the broken lightbulb.

"That was a pretty brave thing to do," Jesse said.

"I wanted to kill that guy."

"I would have wanted to kill him, too, but now my job is bringing him to justice. Did the guy speak at all?"

"When I was cutting him he said something like, 'Ya bastard,' I think, but not exactly that."

Jesse cocked his head. "What do you

mean, not exactly?"

"It sounded funny, like he was sort of Irish, but not really. I guess it was a kind of Boston accent. I don't know. It was two words, and I was half crazy trying to kill the guy."

"Good."

"Does that mean something?" Ben said, sitting up a little straighter in bed.

"Maybe. We'll definitely check it out. One more thing. My officer, Luther Simpson, the guy who found you, he says you kept repeating something about a different trunk. What did you mean by that?"

"The first night when—" Ben stopped himself, remembering Martina. "Anyway, after he took me, I woke up...hog-tied, I guess you'd call it, in the trunk of a car. It was an older car. There was a big spare tire underneath me and no carpeting or anything in the trunk. It was really loud, like it had a big-assed engine and the trunk really smelled of exhaust fumes. This time, when he got me, the trunk was fully carpeted and it was pretty quiet. It smelled like a pretty new car, and it was a big car, I think."

They talked for a few more minutes. Jesse promised to come back and check up on Ben. He also said he might be back if he needed something clarified. Ben said he was willing to do anything to help get the guy who had killed Martina. As Jesse turned to leave, the kid called after him.

"It wasn't great...the sex, I mean," Ben said.

Jesse nodded. "Most first times aren't."

"It was good, you know? But we weren't used to each other. I wanted to do it again. I wanted it to be special for her. She was the most special girl I ever met. Now..."

Jesse wanted to say something to make the kid feel better, but words had never been his thing. Besides, he doubted that even Shakespeare could have come up with the words to ease the kid's pain. Monty Bernstein stayed behind in the room when Jesse left, but he caught up to Jesse at the elevator.

"Thanks, Jesse, you were good with him."

"He's been through a lot."

"Did it help?"

"It's not much. It gives us a place to start. But you already knew that," Jesse said as the elevator door opened and they stepped inside.

"I asked out of habit. Lawyers are always asking questions we know the answers to." Monty then waited for the door to close on them. "About having Harlan come in to your office tomorrow..."

"What about it?"

"Let me save all of us some time and bother."

Jesse said, "I'm listening."

"Mr. Salter was in Helton to exchange some paperwork with a minor business associate. I can assure you that Burt's All-Star Grill was the other party's choice of eateries and not Harlan's."

"I figured. Care to share the name of the other party?"

"Jesse, I'd say that question goes well beyond the scope of your investigation into this case. We weren't obliged to tell you anything at all, but my client felt that any energy you spent tracing false leads or tangentially related issues would only hinder your investigation into the murder and Ben's abduction."

"Thank your client for me."

"So can I tell Harlan that you've changed your mind about having him come in to your office?"

"No," Jesse said. "But you can tell him that the visit is bound to be shorter now that you've shared this information with me."

The elevator door opened. Jesse stepped out. Monty Bernstein did not. Jesse turned back, using his arm to prevent the elevator door from closing.

"Looking forward to seeing you and Mr. Salter in my office. If you come early enough, coffee and donuts are on me."

Jesse removed his arm and let the door slide closed.

43

Lorraine Frazetta nearly lost it at the sight of Vic Prado walking through her front door. Geno, one of the Tweedle Dumb-bells, had buzzed him into the house just as Lorraine was coming down the stairs. When Vic caught sight of her, he smiled and winked. Lorraine flushed, a now-familiar heat rising inside her. She was dressed in a black silk robe, hair up, her too-heavy makeup already on.

"Getting ready to go out for the evening?" Vic said to her.

"Mike's taking me out for a late dinner in a little while." Her voice cracked. She cleared her throat. "Geno, do me a favor. Go get me a bottled water from the fridge."

He stayed put. "Boss says I'm supposed to watch the door."

Lorraine wasn't in the mood to debate. "Get me a fucking bottle of water, Geno."

"Hey, baby," Vic said when the muscle was gone. "You're looking fine."

"You, too. What are you doing here?"

He nodded toward Mike's study. "I was hoping to see you, and I was summoned."

"I need to be with you again."

"Soon, baby. I'm heading to Paradise to see an old friend. I'll call and we can set something up."

"Here's your water!" Geno said, thrusting out a hand so big it nearly covered the entire bottle.

Vic shook his head. "Manners, Geno, manners. This is the boss's wife you're talking to."

Unfazed, Geno gave Lorraine the bottle and turned to Vic. "He's waiting for you inside."

"Nice to see you, Lorraine," Vic said. "Have a pleasant dinner."

Lorraine nodded and started back upstairs, knees weak. When Vic headed to Mike's room, Geno flipped him the bird.

Vic knew it was trouble when he saw that the huge TV was black and Mike was pacing back and forth in front of it. If that didn't spook him enough, Mike's face didn't light up the way it usually did when Vic walked into the room. All sorts of bad thoughts swelled in Vic's head. Had Mike found out about him and Lorraine? Vic's heartbeat quickened even as he told himself that there was no way Mike could know about what had happened between him and Lorraine the previous day. Vic had been very careful. He had instructed Lorraine to leave her cell phone at home, so that it couldn't be used to track her. He had arranged for a cab to pick her up from where he'd had her park. He'd even followed the cab in his rental to make sure the cab wasn't being followed. He'd made sure to meet Lorraine on a day when he knew Joe Breen was too busy doing other work for Mike to be following him around. Vic's equilibrium didn't improve any when he saw Joe Breen was seated in his usual chair, a sullen scowl on his face. Breen was looking worse for wear, much worse. There were bandages on his left cheek and along the left side of his neck.

"Jesus, what the hell happened to you?" Mike Frazetta answered the question.

"That's why I called you."

"I'm not following you, Mike," Vic said. "What's Joe's face got to do with why I'm here?"

Breen spoke up. "That fucking little shite near killed me. Slashed my face and neck with glass. Missed me jugular by an inch."

"Joe and the kid bled all over my Caddy. Car'll never be the same."

On the one hand, Vic was relieved this meeting wasn't about his tryst with Lorraine. At the same time, he got a sick feeling in his belly. "You didn't kill the kid, did you? Jesus, tell me you didn't—"

"Hell, no," Mike said. "But Joe did have to protect himself, and he roughed the Salter kid up pretty good."

Vic was curious. "How good?"

"Broke the little bastard's nose. Maybe his jaw, and I suppose I juiced him one or two times extra."

Vic slammed his palms together. "Shit! We didn't need this."

"What's with the 'we' shit, Vic?" Mike said. "Where's the risk for you? It ain't your ass hanging out there. You're out front, smiling, shaking hands, and busy being famous. What was Joe supposed to do? You do dirty work and sometimes everyone gets dirty. All Joe was doing was going to free the kid, for crissakes."

Joe Breen fought the urge to smile. For the first time in all the years they had known each other, Mike was taking his side against Vic—and strongly, too. It was almost worth the stitches and the blood.

"Okay, you're right. I'm sorry, Joe. I guess you had no choice," Vic said. "So where does that leave us?"

Mike didn't answer right away. He rubbed his cheeks with his right hand, twisted up his mouth.

"You know, Vic, we've done good together since you came to me with this scheme. And because we've done so good, I didn't object too loud when you came to me with the idea of going after Coastline, but I never really liked the deal. The other companies we bought pieces of, they were already pretty compromised, you know? We knew they were working some pretty shady deals and had no choice but to give in when we made offers. Hell, most of them were kinda grateful to share in the wealth. But it was risky with Coastline. The stuff we had on them was minor shit. It was enough to get their attention, not enough to really push them to give us a piece of their pie. But, hey, like I said, we had done so well I was willing to give it a shot."

"I feel a **but** coming on," Vic said.

Mike nodded. "You was always smart that way, Vic. You're right. So here's what's what. I decided that we're going to walk away from this Coastline Consultants thing. It just doesn't feel right to me. It didn't to begin with, and the thing with the girl," he said, crossing himself, "and now this with the kid. Too much trouble."

Vic could feel beads of sweat rolling down his back, gluing his shirt to his skin.

"But we got the papers. We're right there, Mike."

"Funny, it don't feel that way to me, Vic. It still feels like a reach even though we got the papers in hand. And all this blood... I don't like it."

"Far back as I remember, you never minded a little blood. For crissakes, Mike, this whole ball started rolling only after Joe took care of the guy from the SEC." Vic pointed at Breen. "And he for sure never minded blood, no matter how much or how little."

"Innocent blood is different. The girl, the kid, they were civilians," Mike said. "And besides, it was you who suggested we use the kid for leverage. Seems to me your fingertips are a little red themselves, no?"

"I didn't tell him to murder some poor girl or to beat the shit out of the kid. That's not what I meant by leverage, Mike, and you know it."

"Like I said, when you do dirty work, the dirt tends to get spread around."

"But—"

Mike held up his right palm to Vic. "My mind's made up, Vic. You had your say. You don't like it. I get that. Too bad. Time to cut our losses."

"So what are we going to do?"

Breen's mouth took on a cruel aspect

and he made a kind of chuffing, self-satisfied noise.

"We?" Mike said. "We aren't going to do anything, but you're going to make with the carrot and the stick. You're going to make a gesture by giving him the paperwork back and telling him Coastline is all his and his brother's. You're going to tell him that you and your backers regret how things came about. You're going to express our condolences and tell him that it ends here."

Vic laughed a laugh as disconnected from joy as a pulled tooth. "You think Harlan Salter is just going to take the papers and thank me for the gesture?"

Mike shook his head. "That's where the stick part comes in. You tell that dried-up WASPy prick that if he takes one step in the direction of the cop house or drops a dime or whispers in the wrong ear, that what just happened to the girl and his kid will seem like a free weekend at Epcot. Tell him we'll dismantle his family fucking tree one son and daughter-in-law at a time. Then we'll start on the grandkids."

"Mike, c'mon. I'm not going—"

"Yes you are, Vic," Mike said. He turned to Joe Breen. "Give Vic the envelope with the papers. I'm going out to dinner now and I don't wanna hear any more about this shit." He walked out of the room.

Joe Breen got out of his chair and handed Vic Prado a thick white envelope. He made that chuffing sound again and followed his boss out of the room.

44

For the first time in many years she felt like she could breathe. And though her eyes were closed and she was aware of her semiconsciousness, Kayla could swear she was flying. Vic had been reduced to a tiny black bruise in the vast, aqua-watered ocean over which she soared. His transgressions had been packed and bundled, left at the curbside to be hauled away with the trash or washed down the sewer by the next rain. What remained of him was the excitement of that first kiss. It had been innocent enough to begin with, part of comforting each other over Jess's injury. The innocence hadn't lasted very long, but that was all behind her now. She laughed silently to herself over her silly attempt to reignite the flame with Jess that she herself had blown out so long ago.

God, she thought, **was this happiness?** The sun felt like the warm brush of silk across her cheeks and the breeze made her skin electric. It smelled of the sea. In it, she detected the delicate tang of salt. She breathed in other scents, too: crushed rose petals, sage grass, fire-roasted chilies. Scents of home, scents that didn't belong to the sea, but that somehow made perfect sense. Beneath her shadow, a pod of dolphins rocketed through waves green as old bank glass, some of them hurling themselves out of the water in graceful, desperate leaps to fly like the woman soaring above them.

Then a gnawing discomfort imposed itself. Her soaring was suddenly not so effortless. Her shadow on the water dis-assembling. The dolphins getting closer and closer to her with each leap. They did not seem so peaceful or playful, these dolphins. She became aware of their teeth, of them baring their teeth. She wanted it to stop now. The sun was no longer silk on her skin but a rasp, and she was overheating. Perspiration poured out of her so that she thought she might drown in it. She wanted to wake up. She willed herself to wake up, to open her eyes as the dolphins nipped at her. She longed for a drink, for something cool against her skin. Tears. Now there were tears racing down her cheeks from the corners of eyes that stubbornly refused to open.

She pleaded for her eyes to open, begged them. And then...a flutter. The coolness she longed for overwhelmed her. She was cold, ice cold, shivering. She was naked. She didn't have to see to know it. She felt it, felt the stainless steel against the wet skin of her back. Her eyes were open now, unfocused but open. Her instinct was to run. Wherever she was, she knew she had to get out of there. But she could not move, not her arms or legs, not even her fingers. She could not turn her head from side to side. A nauseating wave of panic rolled through her. She was paralyzed. Wait, that didn't make sense. If she was paralyzed, she wouldn't be able to feel things against her skin, right? Maybe not. What did she know about being paralyzed?

Then she felt something, a leather cuff,

being slipped around her right ankle and pulled tight. Then her left ankle. A shadowy figure passed just at the edge of her view. Her right arm was yanked above her head, a leather cuff slipped over her wrist. Then her left arm. She was so consumed by fear now that she thought she might explode. Then the shadowy figure came back into view. She tried desperately to make her eyes focus. The shadow took on more of a human shape, but it was no good.

"You're sweating," a voice said as if from another room.

It was a man's voice, nasal and slightly high-pitched. The voice had a vague familiarity to it, but she was sure she didn't know who it belonged to. She felt terry cloth on her abdomen. A towel. The shadow was moving around her, the towel wiping away her perspiration.

"It's the drugs," he said. "They do that to you. An unfortunate side effect of my little proprietary concoction."

She tried to talk, but her vocal cords were as useless as her arms and legs.

She could only manage weak, choked noises barely louder than a whisper.

"Relax," the shadow said, stroking her hair. "The drugs will wear off in a little while. When they do, we'll hydrate you. Then I will answer your questions. I'm sure you're full of questions. Be back in a jiff."

As he spoke, Kayla searched her mind. **Who is he? Who is he?** And then it came back to her. She'd been walking down a lovely cobbled street in Boston, admiring how the town houses were so neatly shouldered together. A mousy little man in a drab blue polyester suit was walking toward her when he tripped and fell. He had asked her to help him up. When she did, he thanked her. She'd felt a prick in the skin of her neck. That was the last thing she remembered before the dolphins.

The shadow came back into view. She felt his breath on her neck.

"Don't worry," he said. "Nothing will happen to you until your husband gets here. For now, we wait."

45

When he heard from Monty Bernstein that Harlan Salter IV had less than graciously declined the offer of free donuts and coffee and wouldn't be in until sometime that afternoon, Jesse called Dix's office to see if the shrink had an open spot in his schedule. Jesse had a familiar rush of mixed feelings when he was told that there'd been a cancellation and an appointment was available.

"This a Jesse Stone session or a Paradise PD session?" Dix said.

"Mixed."

"You usually are."

"Funny man."

Dix tapped his watch crystal. "Tick... tick...tick."

"I met a woman a few days ago and I already feel I'm in deep."

"That a problem?"

"Might be. She's gorgeous. Incredible in bed. Rich. Intelligent. Understanding."

"Yes, I can see how that would worry you."

"Are you being sarcastic?"

Dix nodded slightly, a vague smile on his lips.

"Okay, I can see how that might sound crazy. That Dee is perfect and I'm complaining about her."

Dix said, "Is that what you're doing, complaining?"

"No. It's just that I get the sense that there's more going on behind who she presents herself to be."

"More than the rest of us?"

"Yes."

"Is it something you sense that might fade with time as you two would get more comfortable together?"

"No."

"Have you asked her about it?"

"Not yet," Jesse said.

"Why not?"

"The timing hasn't seemed right."

Dix nodded. "What would determine the right time?"

"I don't know."

"Yes, you do. Let me repeat my question: Why haven't you asked her about it?"

"Maybe I don't want to know the answer."

"Maybe?"

"I'm afraid of the answer."

"Answer for her," Dix said. "What would she say if you questioned her?"

"That she's hiding something. Something big."

"Are you afraid of the answer because it's what you don't want to hear or because it's exactly what you want to hear?"

"I don't get you."

"Yes, you do. Should I repeat the question?"

"No need, but I'm still not sure I get you."

"Describe Dee to me."

"Physically?"

Dix nodded.

"About five-foot-eight. Fairly long blond hair. Deep blue eyes. Very curvy..." Jesse stopped and then said, "Jenn."

"What about your ex?"

"Dee and Jenn have roughly the same physical description, though they don't really look alike."

"But you have been with more than one woman who meets Jenn's basic physical description. Some, according to you, whom you prefer sexually to Jenn. So what about Dee that is Jenn-like to you worries you?"

"Inaccessibility."

Dix smiled that smile. "What about it?"

"I'm not sure if I'm afraid of her being inaccessible or if it's what I'm finding so attractive."

"Makes sense. Your mutual inaccessibility kept you and Jenn bound together for many years."

"There's something else."

"If you're human, there usually is."

"It's where I met Dee," Jesse said. "It was at the reunion."

"Ah," Dix said, "the reunion. I was wondering when you'd get around to that."

"Dee was there with Vic and Kayla Prado. She and Kayla are close friends. After I had to leave the reunion early to come back for a case, they showed up in Paradise together."

"Isn't Kayla the woman who left you for Vic Prado after you were injured?"

"Uh-huh."

Dix remained silent. Jesse, too, for several minutes.

"Detectives learn early on to be quiet, to give suspects empty space to fill," Jesse said. "But you know that."

"Learned it on the job and in shrink school. Except I'm not a suspect and I won't fill the empty space."

"You think I slept with Dee to punish Kayla."

"Not important what I think."

"Then why do I pay you?"

"Good question. Why?"

"Kayla came to my house essentially to offer herself to me and Dee was there."

"How did it make you feel?" Dix said.

Jesse shrugged.

"Eloquent." Dix looked at his watch. "We'll have to pick it up next time and maybe talk about the case you wished to discuss with me."

"Uh-huh."

"Before you leave, there's something I

want to say to you, Jesse."

"I'm listening."

"I have no doubt you have concerns about Dee and that there must be a very interesting dynamic between Dee, Kayla, and you. But I suspect there's something or someone that motivated you to call for an appointment today. Think about that for our next session."

Jesse didn't have to think about it. It was all about the reunion and the reunion was all about Vic Prado. Julio Blanco's voice kept Jesse company on the way back to the station.

46

Molly Crane showed Harlan Salter and Monty Bernstein into Jesse Stone's office. Jesse was at it again, standing back to the door, pounding a ball into the pocket of his old Rawlings glove. Sometimes he did the ball-and-glove ritual, like praying the rosary, to calm his mind, to help him think. Sometimes it was purely distraction, a way to occupy himself and not to give in to his desire to drink. Sometimes, like that day, it was both. He was frustrated at his lack of progress in the investigation. The Salter kid was in bad shape, but he would survive. It was Martina Penworth that concerned Jesse. If he was to speak for her, so far he hadn't given her much of a voice.

Voice. That was the problem. He couldn't get straight answers. People, often innocent people, gave slightly crooked answers or, as Yogi Berra might have said, they talked out of both sides of their faces.

It was natural for people to put themselves
in the best light even in bad situations.
Good cops understood as much and
corrected accordingly. This was different.
Salter and his lawyer made the right noises
about wanting to help catch the killer, but
that's all it felt like to Jesse: noise. From
the start, Salter and Bernstein seemed
reluctant at best. They parsed their words
with great care and hid behind straw walls
of worry and concern for Martina and the
younger Salter. There was something else
going on here that he just couldn't see.
Frustrated as he was by that, it wasn't
what was making him thirsty for the bottle
in his desk drawer.

He had almost fooled himself that he
had moved beyond his minor-league days
and the haunting ifs and should-have-
beens in his life. At least he thought he
had come to some kind of peace about it,
but the invitation to that damned reunion
had put the lie to that bit of self-deception.
Jesse discovered the hard way that he
was no more at peace with that play at
second base than he had been the night

it happened. He supposed he always drank a little more than he should have, even before that stupid exhibition game in Pueblo. Still, he could draw a crooked line back in time that would connect that aborted double play to the beginning of his losing battle with alcohol. And when his marriage fell to pieces, it totally set him off. His marriage to Jenn had been yet another serious long-term commitment that, just like baseball, had crashed and burned. Dix might say that Jesse had let the alcohol ruin his L.A.P.D. career before it too came tumbling down due to something coming at him out of a blind spot. **Laymen see alcohol as a means to lose control. For you, Jesse, it was a way to exert control. Still is.** God, he wanted a drink, and the internal tape loop of Julio Blanco's voice wasn't helping any.

"Jesse," Molly said. "Jesse."

But he didn't acknowledge her, continuing to pound the ball into the glove.

Monty Bernstein tapped Molly on the shoulder and smiled at her. He pointed his chin at Jesse. "Was he a ballplayer?"

Molly felt a tiny flutter at the lawyer's touch, but she hid her reaction well. She had had her one fling with Crow years back and that was an itch she never intended to scratch again. Though she supposed if she thought about it, at least Monty Bernstein wasn't the stone killer she knew Crow to be. Then again, as handsome and charming as the lawyer was, he wasn't a full-blooded Apache warrior.

"Shortstop with a lot of promise," she said. "It's a long story, and it's not mine to tell." Molly turned to Jesse and put her hand on his back. "Jesse, Mr. Salter and his lawyer are here to see you."

"Thanks, Molly," Jesse said, but he didn't turn around to face them. Even after Molly had closed the door behind her, Jesse remained with his back to Salter and Bernstein.

Harlan Salter was not pleased. "Chief Stone, you forced us to come in here for no good reason. The least you could do is show us the courtesy of—"

"You know what's been bothering me?"

Jesse said, interrupting Salter.

Bernstein spoke up. "No, Jesse, what's been bothering you?"

"A girl was murdered in my town and your client's son was kidnapped, but no one seems to know why. I can almost understand Martina's murder if she got in the way of your son being kidnapped. It's awful to think about, a girl getting killed because she was an inconvenience, but it makes a twisted kind of logic. What doesn't make much sense to me, no matter how I look at it, is why your son was kidnapped in the first place."

"C'mon, Jesse. You were a big-city Homicide detective. I've been a prosecutor and a criminal defense lawyer for a long time," said Bernstein. "Murder, crime ...sometimes there is no sense to it."

Jesse turned around and placed his glove on the desk, ball buried in the pocket. "You're right, Monty. Sometimes there is no sense to it." He sat down. He gestured for Salter and his lawyer to sit as well. When they were seated, he said, "But I'll tell you the part in all this that makes the least amount of sense to me."

Salter rapped his pipe against the side of his chair. "Please do, Chief Stone. I would like to get through this inconvenience and go visit my son."

"Why would someone murder Martina, abduct your son, and then, for no apparent reason, release him? I can't work that out. Any ideas?"

Salter's face grew taut with anger, the veins in his neck pulsing through his pale and papery skin. Jesse noticed. Monty noticed Jesse notice.

"I'm not sure what you're implying, Jesse," Bernstein said.

"I'm not implying anything."

Salter was losing patience. "Then what are we doing here?"

"Helping me think."

Salter stood and thrust his pipe stem at Jesse. "I've had quite enough of this. I am leaving now. Whatever you have to discuss, you can discuss with Mr. Bernstein. I am going to see my son. Good day, Chief Stone."

When the door to the office closed,

Monty shrugged.

"Now that he's gone, you want to tell me what's really going on, Jesse?"

"Sure. How about a drink, since it's only the two of us?"

Monty nodded. Jesse pulled a bottle and two plastic cups out of his desk drawer. He poured a few fingers of scotch for the both of them. They raised their cups to each other and drank.

"So, Jesse, you were about to tell me what's really going on."

"Fair enough." Jesse stood, came around the desk, and sat on the edge so that he loomed over the lawyer. "What I think is that you and your client are full of shit. That your client knows exactly why his son was kidnapped and then released. And if Martina Penworth hadn't been collateral damage, I wouldn't care. But she **was** killed. She was killed in my town and that means I care. I care a lot. It also means I'm putting you and your client on notice."

But Monty was cool. "Good to know where we stand. Thank you for that."

"I'll ask you directly: What were you and Salter doing in Helton the other day and did it have anything to do with getting the kid released?"

"You'll understand if I refuse to comment."

"I'll understand it," Jesse said. "I won't like it."

The lawyer held up his empty cup. "Can a guy get a refill around here?"

Jesse obliged and poured himself another as well.

"You were a ballplayer?" Monty said.

"Dodgers triple-A affiliate in Albuquerque. Next stop Dodger Stadium."

"What happened?"

Jesse's eyes got a distant look in them. "I used to think I knew. Now I'm not so sure anymore."

Monty was about to ask Jesse to explain, but there was a knock on the pebbled glass and Molly stuck her head in. She noticed the bottle on Jesse's desk and the plastic cups in their hands.

"I take it the official proceedings have drawn to a close," she said.

"You should be a detective."

"I would be if my damned boss would go to bat for me."

Monty Bernstein smiled at her. "You could bring suit. I know some very good labor lawyers. I could pretty much guarantee a large cash settlement and that detective's shield. I'm afraid that your boss would probably lose his job in the process."

"Let me think about it," she said, staring directly at Jesse.

"Maybe we can discuss it over a drink."

"Relax, Counselor," Jesse said. "You two want to flirt and plan my demise, don't do it in my office. Molly, you're here because..."

"Because there's someone else here to see you."

"Male or female?"

"Male," she said.

"Mr. Bernstein was just leaving."

Jesse stood and shook the lawyer's hand.

"I'm going to find out what's going on," he said. "Tell your client that."

"I figure you to try, Jesse."

Bernstein turned to go, but before he got two steps toward the office door, another man walked past Molly, through the door.

Annoyed, Molly said, "Excuse me, sir. You'll have to—"

Jesse held up his hand. "Don't bother. This is no 'sir,' Molly. This is Vic Prado."

Monty Bernstein didn't wait around to be introduced.

47

Twenty minutes later Jesse walked out of his office with his former teammate at his side. Vic Prado slapped Jesse on the back, smiled his million-dollar smile at Molly, and left.

"So that's Vic Prado," Molly said. "He always make an entrance like that?"

"If he could have trumpets do a fanfare, he would. He likes to plant his flag wherever he goes. Only he's claiming the territory for himself."

"Doesn't sound like you two had much of a love affair."

"Long story."

"I've got time."

"No, you don't."

Molly stood and put her hands on her hips. "Says who?"

"Your chief."

"Pulling rank again?"

"It has its privileges," he said and turned.

"Jesse," Molly called after him.

He stopped, looked back over his shoulder. "Uh-huh."

"When Vic Prado first came in, Harlan Salter was on his way out."

"So?"

"I don't know...the way they looked at each other...I don't know."

"What don't you know?" Jesse said.

"You know how it is when you run into somebody like an old lover or rival that you don't expect to see in a place you don't expect to see them?"

"Awkward."

"Exactly. I think Prado and Salter know each other."

Jesse walked back toward Molly. "Vic Prado is a famous ballplayer. I'm not surprised Salter would recognize him."

"No, Jesse, it was more than that. The look went both ways."

"How do you mean?"

"Salter scowled at Prado," she said.

"That's his default setting. He would scowl at a basket of mewing kittens and downy yellow ducklings."

Molly laughed. "I guess he would. That

man could probably turn flesh into rock with his looks. But this was different. There was recognition in Prado's eyes, too. And it was pretty uncomfortable."

"You're sure?"

"As I can be."

Jesse tilted his head at her. "Women's intuition?"

"Chauvinist. Cop's instincts."

"Funny."

"What is?" Molly said.

"I got the same sense about Monty and Vic. Felt like it wasn't the first time they had shared the same space."

"Men's intuition?"

"Something like that."

Molly nodded. "Monty did leave in a hurry, didn't he?"

"Bet that didn't please you. If I knew where Crow was, I'd—"

"Fuck you!"

"Excuse me."

"Sorry. Fuck you, Chief."

"That's better, but next time, salute when you say it."

She saluted his back with the middle

finger of her right hand as he retreated to his office.

"And Molly..." he said, sticking his head through his office door.

"What?"

"Good work. Thanks."

48

Dee turned right onto Boylston, left onto Yawkey Way, right onto Lansdowne, and waited. The bus ride from Paradise to Boston was okay as bus rides went. Not that she had taken a bus ride since college. For all the fuss, she should have just rented a car, but money was getting tight and she wanted time to think without having to pay attention to driving.

She wasn't pleased about having to turn down Jesse Stone's dinner invitation. She thought she could get used to living in Paradise as long as Jesse was part of the deal. There was just something about him beyond the fierce sex and the good looks. He was so self-contained, so sure of himself. Yet there was a kind of melancholy in him, a promise unfulfilled, that sang to her. She wondered if he was even aware of it. Why was it that wounded men appealed to women? She couldn't explain it. But who was she fooling? She had been living behind a veil of lies for so long she had actually started believing them herself. There was no future for her in Paradise. Jesse would find out she'd been lying to him soon enough and then their cozy little romance of omelets and old uniform shirts would collapse under its own weight. She could tell Jesse was no saint, but he was not a man to be lied to. That much was evident. What more, she thought, could sleeping with Vic cost her than the price she was already bound to pay?

Jesse and Vic would have to wait. For the moment, she was more concerned with the cryptic message she'd received from Abe Rosen. She'd also been a little worried about Kayla and her failure to text or call as she had promised, but her worries about Kayla didn't run deep. As composed as Kayla had seemed when she drove away from the hotel, it couldn't have been that easy for her to leave Vic. Regardless of the damage each had done to the other, they had spent twenty years together. You don't just turn your back on that as if walking out on a bad movie. Our worst habits are the hardest to break. So she guessed she understood how calling could have slipped Kayla's mind.

She felt a strong hand on her shoulder and recognized Abraham Rosen's touch. They had been close and, on more than one occasion, come close to crossing the line, but Abe had stopped them from making that mistake. They had been each other's only ally back at the Bureau, and an office affair would have complicated that, if not ruined it altogether. But that was before Diana had, to Rosen's way of thinking, gone mad and set out on her single-minded quest. She was as good as lost to him now.

"Hello, Diana."

Abe Rosen looked the part. He was square-jawed, broad-shouldered, clean-shaven, and wore his wavy black hair cropped close to his head. He had hazel eyes that ran to green and a neutral mouth. Even dressed casually as he was in a navy blue blazer, khaki pants, a yellow golf shirt, and deck shoes, he looked like a government agent. He had come to the Bureau the old-fashioned way, out of law school. He had done his time in the field and made some big white-collar cases in Phoenix before getting transferred to headquarters. He had always dreamed of making it to D.C. Since then he had been more judicious in his dreams.

Diana folded herself into Abe's arms and sobbed. She had been on an island by herself for so many months that just being next to him overwhelmed her. He let her cry, stroking her hair, but he was careful not to say that everything would be all right. He didn't believe in lying to friends.

"Come on, let's get a drink."

They found a bar a few blocks from Fenway. It wasn't very crowded, as it was a travel day for the Sox. They slid into a back booth and ordered a couple beers.

"So what are you doing here?" Diana said, taking a sip of her IPA.

"I took a few days. Figured I'd come see the sights, catch a Sox game."

"Bullshit! You grew up a Yankees fan

and the Sox are on the road. In any case, you aren't the type to just take a few days off impulsively."

He took a gulp of his lager. "I came to ask you to come back to work, Di. The bosses are getting antsy and I've heard rumblings that they're going to start looking into your leave situation. If they—"

"No. Not now. I'm close. I can feel it."

"You said that eight months ago. Then you said it five months ago and last month. This is crazy," he said.

She slid out of the booth and stood over Abe. "I love you for doing this, but I'm not coming back now."

"If you won't do it for yourself, Di, do it for me."

She leaned over and kissed him on the forehead. "I would do almost anything for you, Abe. There was a time I would have done anything for you."

He curled up the corners of his lips. "I figured you'd say no. Come on, sit back down. Talk to me for five more minutes. I did come all this way to see you."

When she did as he asked, Abe reached

into his jacket pocket, pulled out a folded brown envelope, and slid it across the table.

"What's this?" she said.

"Probably a mistake."

"Abe!"

"Open it up. It's some eyes-on stuff from the Boston PD you might find interesting."

He sipped his beer as Diana studied the surveillance photos inside the envelope. Her eyes were blank as she scanned the first few photos.

"So who are these people?" she asked.

"Keep going."

"Holy shit! That's—"

"Vic Prado," he said.

"Who are these other people?"

"Here." He gestured for the photos, which she slid across the tabletop to him. He pointed. "This guy is Mike Frazetta. He's Boston Mob. Started out in Lowell. Worked his way up. He's an up-and-comer, but kicks upstairs to Gino Fish. Mostly runs book, some drugs, loan sharking, money laundering."

Diana smiled. "Lowell!"

"That's right." Abe nodded. "Lowell, just like Vic Prado."

"So that's Mike. Vic and Kayla sometimes talked about a guy Vic knew named Mike. Kayla hated it when his name came up, but she wouldn't talk about it. And this guy?"

"That's Joe Breen. He's a bad boy, Joe. Frazetta's enforcer. Lots of arrests. Done some time. One long bid for assault. Want to guess where he's from?"

"Lowell."

"Bingo!"

"And the woman?" Diana said.

"The wife. Lorraine Frazetta."

"Lowell, too, I suppose."

"Apparently, they've all known each other since they were kids."

"Where'd you get this stuff, Abe?"

"I told you, Boston PD. Guy in the OC division owed me a few favors."

"But why now?" she said. "Why haven't we known about the connection between Frazetta and Vic Prado before this?"

"Because he hasn't shown up at

Frazetta's house until now. Twice in the last several days, apparently."

"Why does the Boston PD have Frazetta under surveillance?"

Abe shrugged. "Could be a million reasons. A CI whispered in somebody's ear. Something Frazetta did tripped a red flag. Who knows?"

"And why did this friend in the Boston PD give this to you?"

"For crissakes, Di, stop asking dumb questions." He finished his beer. "I'm trying to help you here."

She smiled at him. "Watch out, Abe, your New York is showing."

He laughed. It didn't last.

"What do you think it means, Vic showing up at Frazetta's house like this?" she said.

"I don't know. Maybe nothing."

She stared at the photos some more, an angry expression on her face.

"What's with the face?" he said.

"If they had only let me follow my gut on Prado. Let me do some digital surveillance on the guy. If they—"

"But they didn't, Di!" Abe stood up. "They didn't, and now you've fucked up your career. For what?"

She waved the photos at him. "For what's right, Abe. For the truth."

"Truth! Whose truth? What truth? Those photos don't mean anything. They're evidence of a guy visiting an old friend. I knew this was a mistake."

"Then why'd you come?" she said.

"If you have to ask that question, then I really am wasting my time."

She tried handing the surveillance photos back to him.

"Keep them," he said. "Consider them my contribution to your obsession. Use them to build an altar to the guy. Burn some candles at his shrine."

"I'm going to get him, Abe. You'll see."

"Maybe you will, Di, but it won't end well."

"What's that supposed to mean?"

"Ahab found Moby-Dick. Look how that wound up. Good-bye, Diana."

He leaned over and kissed her hard on the mouth. He was gone by the time

she could make any sense of things. Then
she checked her phone. Still no call from
Kayla.

49

When Jesse heard the knock on his door, he checked his watch. It was pretty late for a social call. He hoped that Dee had changed her mind or that her plans had fallen through. There had been many women in his life before, during, and after Jenn. He had enjoyed his time with most of them, but there were very few that stayed with him throughout his day the way Dee did. He hated to admit to himself that Jenn had been the only woman to ever occupy his mind in an all-consuming way, and she hadn't been in his life for years. Before Dee, no one had even been in Jenn's league.

If it was Dee, Jesse decided, he'd have that talk with her about what he felt she was hiding from him. He would do it if for no other reason than to get Dix's voice out of his head. Sometimes, Jesse thought, Dix's purpose in life was to be an irritant. To be that grain of sand in his oyster.

Whatever Dix's intentions, his methods worked. Then, as he put his hand on the doorknob, another less appealing thought crossed his mind. What if it wasn't Dee? What if it was Kayla again? Although they had all managed to get through the other morning like reasonable adults, Jesse wasn't up for a repeat. His sleeping with Kayla would probably get to Vic like nothing else could, but using a woman, even one who had dumped him the way Kayla had, wasn't Jesse's style. He believed in dealing with things man-to-man and had little respect for people who slinked around in the shadows. He took a deep breath and opened the door.

Though Jesse was slow to react to the punch out of confusion at seeing Vic Prado on the other side of his threshold, he jerked his head quickly enough to the left so that Vic's haymaker didn't connect squarely. Instead, it was more of a glancing blow to Jesse's right cheek, a knuckle barely grazing the corner of his eye. The shot stung and the vision in his eye blurred. Unless you've ever been hit in the face, you can't appreciate how painful a blow, even a glancing one, can be. Jesse could deal with the pain. He was more concerned about his eyesight. He wasn't staggered by the punch, but he retreated a few steps to create some space between himself and Vic, to give himself a chance to regroup. As he moved farther into his house, Jesse used the heel of his right palm to rub the blurriness out of his eye and to wipe away the reflexive tears.

His retreat barely bought him enough time. Vic launched himself at Jesse through the open door, bulling his way, head down, as he went. That was a mistake. Jesse sidestepped to his left and unleashed a short, chopping left hand across his body that caught Vic flush on the jaw. Prado went sprawling forward, crashing shoulder first into the wall. But if Jesse thought it was going to end there, he was wrong. Vic may have been many years retired, but he kept in shape. He still possessed the gifts—great hand-eye coordination, resilience, strength, determination—that had made him an all-star second baseman. As Jesse approached him, Vic pushed himself away from the wall and got to his feet. He assumed a boxer's stance and Jesse did the same.

"Where is she?" Vic said, his voice almost feral.

Before Jesse could ask who **she** was, Vic moved in, bobbing and weaving as he came forward. He feigned throwing a left jab and threw a right hook to Jesse's ribs instead. This time Vic's punch hit with full force. Jesse winced in pain, struggling to keep his dinner down. He decided he'd had enough. Jesse moved a step back, inviting Vic to come at him again. Vic took the bait. This time Vic threw that left jab as he came. Jesse swatted it away with his right forearm and, in one deft motion, spun on his heel and buried his right elbow in Vic's solar plexus. The wind came out of Prado in a sickening rush. Jesse raised up his right arm and, using the back of his fist, smacked Prado right in the nose. Vic collapsed to his knees, struggling for breath and bleeding all over the hardwood floor. With the sound of Julio Blanco's voice ringing in his ears, Jesse was tempted to deliver a finishing blow that would either have dislocated Vic's jaw or broken a few of his ribs. Instead, he laid Prado on his back, stretched out his legs.

"Lay there and take it easy," Jesse said. "I'm going to get us both some ice."

Jesse returned, carrying two evidence bags full of ice and several dish towels. "What the hell was that about?"

"When I got to the hotel today after I came in to see you, Kayla had checked out. There was a letter waiting for me at the desk. She's gone."

"What do you mean, she's gone?"

"She left me."

"You probably deserved it. Here." Jesse handed him the towels and an ice bag. "What made you think she would come here?"

"I'm not blind. I saw the way she was looking at you in New York. You're her big-fish story."

Jesse pressed the other ice bag to the right side of his face. "Huh?"

"You're the one that got away," Vic said.

"That's not how I remember it. I seem to recall that when I got back to Albuquerque, my girlfriend and my roommate were shacked up."

"We didn't mean for it to happen, Jesse."

"Sure."

"Anyways, it did happen. So you've always been the big 'what if' in Kayla's life. What if Jesse hadn't gotten hurt? What if I had stayed with him? What if he still wants me?"

"She's not here," Jesse said. "Go check under the mattresses."

"No, that's okay. You going to arrest me or what?"

"Assaulting a police officer is serious. Assaulting the chief...that's a hanging offense."

"But you're not going to arrest me?"

Jesse took the ice bag away from his face and shook his head. "Not unless you want to go another round."

"No, thanks. Your shoulder may be

fucked up, but there's nothing wrong with the rest of you."

Vic Prado's nose had since stopped
bleeding, though it was already swollen
and bruised. The right side of Jesse's face
wasn't as bad, but he'd have some
explaining to do for a few days to come.
They were both working on their second
ice bags and second glasses of scotch as
they settled into the Adirondack chairs on
Jesse's deck. It was a comfortable night,
early enough in spring so that insects
weren't an issue. Late enough in the
season so that jackets weren't required.

"Nice out here," Vic said just to say
something.

"I like it."

A few minutes of uneasy silence
followed. Uneasy for Vic, not for Jesse.
Jesse was good with silence. There were
many months, especially after his
marriage had fallen apart and his L.A.P.D.
career was going down the tubes, when
silence had been his only friend. He

thought back to that long drive from L.A. to Paradise when the only words he'd spoken were to gas station attendants and truck stop waitresses.

"I guess I knew she was going to leave me someday," Vic said, "but you never think the day it happens is that someday."

"Sounds about right."

"She's been so unhappy for so long. Maybe if we had had some kids... who knows? But neither one of us was unselfish enough for kids."

Jesse said, "Probably better you didn't have any. My job, I deal with the kids people had for the wrong reasons or for no reasons at all. Those kids grow up, sometimes into very bad people."

"You were right before. I deserved it. I've never been able to keep it in my pants. I had women in every major-league city, different ones on every road trip."

"I wouldn't know about that. I never got the chance to find out."

"What, I'm supposed to feel sorry for you? I'm the one whose wife just left him."

Jesse kept quiet for several more minutes after that.

"All right, Jesse. Okay. You're right. You got hurt. I got Kayla. I got to go to the show, but it's not like you've had a bad life. I mean, did you see those other guys we played with? Losers, cons, and holy rollers. You got a good gig here."

"It isn't Dodger Stadium."

Vic downed his drink and reached for the bottle on the deck between their chairs. He thought about pouring himself another, but didn't, not immediately.

"I saw that Ozzie Smith poster you got inside there. What the fuck is that all about? You were good, Jesse, maybe the most talented shortstop I ever played with. You definitely had the best arm, but the bigs ain't like you think."

"Same answer as before, Vic. I wouldn't know."

Now Vic was agitated. He turned in his chair to face Jesse. "But I do know," he said, pounding his chest. "I know. You're in the minors, you think just getting to the bigs is the end, the goal. Nah. It's the beginning. Every day all you're thinking about is how you got to do something, anything, to stay there. You never want to get back on those damned buses or stay in another cheap motel room or rented apartment in some guy's basement. It eats at you, the nerves, the insecurity. You don't know how hard that is, and it never goes away. Never. Every slump you go in, every error you make...it all feels like it's going to disappear."

"I would have liked to have found out."

"Yeah, I can understand that, but that poster in there, that's nuts. What do you do, drink with the Wizard of Oz and tell him how good you would have been?"

"Sometimes."

"Getting hurt was a gift."

"How do you figure that?" Jesse said.

"Because you could drink with Oz and tell him how great everything would have been and how you would've been the greatest shortstop ever, but you never really had to test that out, did you? You never had to get in the box against Maddux or Randy Johnson. You never had to play short on the crappy infield at County Stadium in Milwaukee in April with frozen hands. Getting hurt saved you from having to prove yourself every day. This way, Jesse, you'll always be the golden boy. You're like James Dean."

"How do you mean?"

"Your career died young and pretty. Your baseball career will always be full of promise and potential. Your skills will never diminish. You'll always bat a thousand and never make an error. I saw the glove on your desk. You're still living the dream."

"Have another drink, Vic. I like it when you talk crazy. All those women, all those guaranteed contracts, all the adulation, all those all-star games…man, must've been rough on you."

"Fuck you, Stoney."

Jesse poured himself another Black Label. He drank it all in a single gulp. "Did you do it on purpose?"

"Do what on purpose?"

"In Pueblo, when you fielded that ball in the hole, did you hesitate? Did you wait for the runner to get on me before you threw the ball?"

"Now who's talking crazy?" Vic said. He wasn't smiling.

"Not much of an answer."

"Who put that thought in your head? Blanco? I bet it was Blanco, that miserable prick. Was it Julio?"

"Not much of an answer."

"Yeah, Jesse, you said that."

"I can keep saying it. Your choice."

Vic finished his drink and poured himself another. "You want the truth?"

"It'd be nice for a change. You don't hear a lot of truth in my line of work."

"Truth is, Jesse, I don't know if I hesitated or not. If I did, it wasn't because I was trying to get you hurt. It was more likely that I was admiring the fact that I got to the ball at all on that shitty infield. Did I want Kayla? You bet your ass. Every straight guy with a pulse in Albuquerque wanted her. But even if I was the most calculating bastard on earth, how could I know that a takeout slide would ruin your career? In all the years I played ball, I've seen plenty of guys get hurt making the pivot and relay throw to first on a double play. I saw guys get wiped out twice as bad as you. I seen guys land on their heads, get spiked, get their ACLs and MCLs ripped up, but I never saw a guy land on his shoulder and get ruined the way you got ruined. Not before. Not since."

Jesse just nodded. What else was there for him to do?

"How are you and Dee doing?" Vic said, happy to change the subject. "You two seemed to hit it off."

"So far, so good. How did you guys meet her?"

Vic tilted his head in surprise. "She hasn't told you?"

"We've been too busy with other things."

"I just bet you have. God, is she not gorgeous?"

"How'd you meet?"

"You are a persistent bastard. She moved into our gated community in Scottsdale about a year ago. Kayla and her hit it off immediately, but I think she spends more time with me. She's a tennis nut and can shoot."

That made Jesse sit up a little straighter. "She shoots?"

"Like an assassin. You should see her with a sidearm, any sidearm. I'm good. She's great. Good thing I'm better at tennis."

"She tell you her story?" Jesse said.

"Poor little rich girl. Inherited some money, I think. Something like that."

Jesse hoped Vic might shed a little more light on the subject, but he didn't seem so inclined. He poured them both a little more scotch. Neither bothered to lift their glasses to the other. They were way past that, twenty years past. Jesse stood, sat on the railing to face Vic. Prado didn't know it yet, but their conversation was about to move away from the personal to the professional.

"Today when you came to the station," Jesse said, "why did you disrespect Officer Crane like you did by barging into my office?"

"Officer Crane's pretty hot for a woman her age."

"She'll be thrilled to hear it, but—"

"I wanted to surprise you," Vic said. "Nothing more than that. Please send her my apologies."

"Funny you should say the word **surprise**."

"How's that?"

"Because it seemed to Molly—Officer Crane—and me that I was the least surprised person in the room."

"I'm not getting you, Jesse. Is there something I'm missing here?"

"Did you know the man who was in the office with me when you came in?"

"No, should I have? Who is he?"

"He's a lawyer named Monty Bernstein."

Vic laughed. "There's a name for you. Sorry, never met him."

"How about the older gentleman you passed on your way into the station?"

"The nasty-looking guy with the pipe clenched in his teeth?"

Jesse nodded.

"Nope," Vic said. "Sorry. Who's he, another lawyer?"

"Bernstein's client. A rich guy from an

old local family named Harlan Salter the Fourth."

"Don't know him. I hope the first three Harlan Salters were cheerier than number four."

"Probably not. I don't think cheery is in their DNA sequence, but he's got good reason to be miserable. His son's girl-friend was murdered recently and his son abducted. The kid was released, but he's in the hospital."

"That's rough. Will the kid be okay?"

"You're a cop long enough, Vic, you learn that **okay** is a relative term. He'll recover from his injuries. Whether he'll get over the guilt about his girlfriend and the trauma of being held captive is something else."

Prado shrugged. "He's young yet. He'll have time to heal."

"So you're sure you don't know either Bernstein or Salter?"

"Look, Jesse, I'm famous. I'm not com-plaining. Fame certainly has its perks. It opens up all kinds of doors, if you know what I mean. Fame is like a drug to people who don't have it. Fame makes you more charming, better-looking, wiser. Men want to be your friend. They want to buy you drinks and dinners. They want to give you stock tips and take you golfing. Women... they just want you. But it's also weird. People recognize me all the time or think they might recognize me. They can act strange when it happens. I'm pretty used to it. So why the third degree? Would it matter if I knew those guys?"

"Guess not. Just curious."

They drank some more, so much so that the air on the deck smelled of stale breath and scotch. They were slurring their words now, no longer finishing their sentences. As they got drunker, their silences got less uncomfortable. Jesse was looking out at the water. It wasn't Dodger Stadium, he thought, but it **was** pretty damned good.

"You know, Vic, I never got to ask you what that reunion was really for."

Vic didn't answer. Jesse waited. Then asked again. Vic still didn't answer. When Jesse turned around, Vic Prado was passed out in his chair.

51

Vic Prado woke up to the tune of "Take Me Out to the Ball Game" coming from his iPhone. God, how he had come to hate that song, yet it played into his image. Everybody, but most particularly the starstruck investors, loved it when his phone went off in their presence. There were times he had arranged for someone to call him in the middle of a meeting to remind the people of just who he was: Vic Prado, former all-star second baseman for the Dodgers. If he survived his wicked hangover headache, he swore to change the ringtone to anything else. He didn't bother checking the incoming number. Part of him hoped it was Kayla and, given the pounding in his head, he didn't want to be disappointed.

"Vic here."

"You sound horrible."

"Kay?"

"No, Vic, it's Dee."

"Dee!"

He sat up too quickly in bed and a jolt of pain shot through him. Worse, he got dizzy and nauseated.

"Hold on a minute," he said.

He put the phone down and scrambled through Jesse's house to find a bathroom. About three minutes later, he found his way back to the guest bedroom and the phone he'd left on the floor beside the bed.

"Dee, you still there?" His voice was shaky. He was shaky.

"I'm here. Are you all right?"

"She left me, Dee. Kayla—"

"I know, Vic."

"You knew about this and you didn't say anything to me?"

"I found out as she was packing her car to go. I don't think this was a big plan or anything."

"But why yesterday of all days? I mean, I didn't even see her for a few days."

Dee said, "I don't think it was about you as much as it was about her."

She liked that. It was one of those lines that sounded deep and significant, but actually meant very little.

"I guess. She said stuff about how unhappy she was with herself in the letter she left me. Do you know where she went?"

Dee lied. "No clue. Have you heard from her? Did she call or text you or anything?"

"No. Why, was she supposed to?"

"She promised to call me when she got to where she was going, but I haven't heard from her."

"That's not like her," Vic said. "Then again, I'm not sure what's like her anymore. Leaving me the way she did isn't like her, either."

"Are you okay?"

"I'm pretty hungover."

"Where are you?" Dee said, feigning concern. "I can come get you."

"Stoney's house."

"Stoney?"

"Jesse's. It's a long story. Listen, Dee, I got to take something for my headache and get water in me. What are you calling for, anyway?"

Holding the photos Abe had given her in

her hand, she said, "I need to see you."

That got Vic's full attention. Also got his hopes up. He'd always wanted Dee, but now that she was Jesse's, he wanted her even more.

"Maybe later. I'm wrecked."

"Call me when you're feeling better. I really need to see you," she said, stressing the word **need**.

He noticed, but hung up without committing to a time. As much as he wanted to console himself with Dee, he had more pressing business. As he walked slowly around Jesse's house, looking for aspirin, he thought back to the previous evening. The fight was nothing. Guys, even guys their age, found a certain comfort in mild forms of violence. Men were always testing themselves, testing one another. He remembered that his mom used to say that men got older but they never grew up. Vic smiled, thinking about that and remembering his mom. Then the smile vanished as he remembered other parts of his time with Jesse. Why did Jesse have to bring up Bernstein and Salter? Why'd he have to bring up the dead girl and the Salter kid?

Fuck! It had all gone so wrong. He had so carefully manipulated everything and everyone and it had all blown up because of that idiot Joe Breen. Thinking about Breen frustrated Vic at the best of times, now it was making his headache even worse. He found a Costco-sized bottle of aspirin under the bathroom sink and swallowed a handful. He took another bunch and shoved them in his pocket. He went to the kitchen, drank the town reservoir half dry, and made an ice bag for his head. He found a note from Jesse on the counter. **Too late,** Vic thought, he'd already found the aspirin and he was in no mood for food. As he waited for the aspirin to take hold, he walked past the poster of Ozzie Smith and made a face at it. **Did I hesitate on that throw to Jesse? Did I want Kayla so bad that I tried to get Jesse hurt?** It was impossible to know anymore.

A half-hour later, he dialed Harlan Salter's phone number.

52

Joe Breen rolled over to the opposite side of the bed and was immediately aware that Moira was gone. His heart sank and there was the briefest moment of panic. The snap of fingers lasted longer. Still, he thought, if this was love, he wasn't sure he wanted any part of it. The ache he felt during that finger snap in time cut a jagged fist of a hole right through him. It hurt worse than any punch that had ever landed on him, worse than even the deepest, most ragged stab wound that had ripped into him, worse than the two gunshot wounds he had absorbed.

What he couldn't fathom was why Moira. Over the years he'd had many of these art-school girls warm one side of his bed and many of them a fair bit better-looking than Moira. Could it be that he felt connected to her because she came from Ireland? That her accent, unlike his uncle's, was sweetly lilting and fell like music on his ears. Could it really be that simple?

She was paler than most of the other girls, and that was a bold statement, given how little of the sun most of these girls seemed to expose themselves to. And thin! Goodness, the girl looked as if she barely ate at all. Her teeth were a bit crooked and her wispy light brown hair fell off her head as if each strand had a will of its own. But there was no denying her eyes were rare gems. They were deep blue crystals, flecked with black and gold. When he looked into them, damn him if his knees didn't weaken. The thing that scared Joe was what followed in the wake of the knee-weakening rush: the over-whelming panic at the thought that she wouldn't always be in his life or that some-one like himself could cut her out of his life. And that was followed by something even more foreign to him than love: regret. He couldn't get the image of the lifeless nude body of Martina Penworth out of his mind. He shook his head as if trying to shed the image. For fuck's sake, he thought, next thing he knew he'd be praying for his deeds to be undone.

His momentary panic was erased by the aromas wafting into his bedroom from the kitchen and the padding of Moira's feet heading his way. Before she got to the bedroom door, Joe's mouth was watering. The sweet and smoky scents of crisp fried bacon and breakfast sausages were so strong he swore he could already taste them. There were eggs, too, and maybe toast. There were other scents as well, not as familiar. Moira came through the door, a breakfast tray in her arms. A mock frown on her face.

"I'd hoped ya'd still be asleep, Joe. Now ya've gone and spoiled me surprise." When she saw that he had taken her joke to heart, she said, "Don't be daft, Joe. I was only havin' a piss with ya."

Joe smiled at her and stared at the tray in Moira's hands. Lorraine Frazetta had bought the tray for him when he moved into the house as a kind of nasty joke. Lorraine could never imagine anyone who would want to share Joe's bed. Could never imagine anyone whom the heartless bastard would ever bother serving breakfast in bed to. Could never imagine anyone caring enough about Joe to serve him.

"What's this?" he said as Moira placed the legged tray over Joe's lap.

"Have ya never had a good Irish fry? It's a breakfast that'll last ya the day. Fried eggs, bacon, sausages, toast, black pudding, strong Irish tea—"

"Black pudding?"

"Don't ask, Joe, just eat." She bent over and kissed his forehead.

"Aren't you going to have any?"

"I've eaten mine. I used to think my ma was mad when she said she just enjoyed watchin' Da eat her cookin'. Now I know. I just wanted to watch you enjoy."

Joe wasn't a man who needed to be told twice. He dug into the food with the same gusto as when he made love to Moira. He wanted to please her in all ways. But as he ate, Martina Penworth haunted him.

"Is it not to yer likin', Joe?"

"I love it. Just work stuff getting to me." He pulled her close and kissed her hard on the mouth. "I love it and I love you."

His heart stopped. He closed his eyes. He had never uttered those three words before, and the panic returned. When he opened his eyes, Moira was smiling at him. But before she could speak, the doorbell rang and there was a fierce knocking at Joe's door. Joe's face went ice cold. His voice colder.

"Stay here."

He closed the bedroom door behind him. He went into his hall closet, pulled out the third shoe box stacked on the floor, opened the lid, and grabbed the loaded .45. He didn't prefer the .45, but he didn't want to grab the nine-millimeter he kept near the bed in front of Moira. He racked the slide to chamber a bullet and went to answer the door. He stood to the inside of the door opposite the knob so that if anyone shot through the door he would be safe. He aimed the .45 at where a six-foot-tall man's torso would be.

"Yeah, who is it."

"Open this fucking door right now. I don't have time for this crap." It was Mike Frazetta.

Joe opened the door, putting the .45 in the drawer of a cabinet in the hallway. Joe wasn't alarmed by his boss showing up at his door because Mike hated using the phone unless he absolutely had to. It was the one thing he was paranoid about. When Mike came in, Joe put his left index finger across his lips and nodded at the bedroom door. Mike understood and smiled.

"I got you," he said, his voice just above a whisper.

"What is it?"

"I want you to keep an eye on Vic. I think he might run, maybe even skip out on us before he delivers the envelope to Salter." Mike handed Joe a slip of paper with the address of Vic's hotel in Paradise.

"What do you want me to do if he runs."

Mike slapped Joe playfully on the cheek. "Do what you do best."

Mike winked and walked out the way he came in. Joe smiled as he went back to breakfast. Then he thought about Martina again and Moira standing on the other side of the bedroom door. He stopped smiling.

53

Jesse came into the station carrying a dozen donuts and wearing his baseball-style Paradise PD hat pulled down low. Suit Simpson was at the desk, talking to Molly Crane. All Suit noticed was the box of donuts. Not Molly, but she didn't say anything in front of Suit. When Suit, donuts in hand, headed back out on patrol, Molly went to talk to Jesse.

"What happened to you?" she said.

He shook his head, thinking of repeating the battered-wife lies he'd heard a hundred times and never believed. **I banged into a cabinet. I fell down a few stairs.** Instead, he repeated another pat line he had used before.

"You should've seen the other guy."

She walked right up to him, placed her hand gently under his chin, and turned his head so that she could get a good look at the right side of his face.

"Don't see many black eyes on the

outside of the eye. Your cheek's a little swollen, too. Does it hurt?"

"Only my pride," he said.

"You're just full of clichés today."

"I could've said 'Only when I laugh.'"

"You could have, but that would only have made you seem like an even bigger ass."

He wagged his finger at her. "Rank, Crane! Rank."

"That would have made you seem like an even bigger ass, Chief."

"Better."

But Molly wasn't smiling. "Enough, Jesse. What really happened?"

"The guys on the softball team were reenacting the Battle of Hastings."

Her face clenched. "I don't know why I bother."

"Because you love me," Jesse said.

"Love means straight answers."

"Vic Prado's wife left him and he had to take his frustration out on somebody. And before you ask, yes, he looks much worse."

"Thank you for telling me the truth."

"He also confided to me that he thought

you were pretty hot."

Molly tried unsuccessfully not to smile.

She said, "What are you going to tell the rest of the department?"

"Nothing. I'm the boss of them."

"What do you want me to tell them? Because you know they're going to come to me."

"I'm sure you'll think of something. Be creative, just not too creative."

She was smiling broadly when she went back to her desk, but it wasn't long before she was on the intercom.

"You miss me already, Crane?"

"Dream on, Boss. It's the chief of the Helton PD for you, line one."

Jesse pressed line one and picked up. "Jesse Stone."

"Morning, Chief Stone. Ralph Carney here, chief of the Helton PD."

"Too many chiefs. Let's go with Ralph and Jesse. Okay with you, Ralph?"

"Works for me."

"What can I do for you, Ralph?"

"Wanted to let you know that the accident investigation has been completed on the incident involving your Officer Weathers. How's he doing, by the way?"

"He's smashed up pretty bad, but the good news is he'll recover. He'll be getting transferred over to Paradise General soon as his concussion symptoms have cleared. Thanks for asking."

"Not at all. Miracle he survived at all, given the severity of the accident. Also wanted to tell you that the blood analysis showed no alcohol in his system, so he's clear. And you can send someone to come pick up your guy's personal effects."

Alarms were going off in Jesse's head.

"Ralph, what's up? I appreciate the courtesy of your call, but chiefs don't usually call other chiefs about a simple car accident."

Chief Carney said, "What if it wasn't simple or an accident?"

"If you wanted my full attention, you just got it. Want to explain?"

"I think maybe it would be better if you came over to Helton sometime today so we could have a private chat and I could show you Weathers's car."

"Okay, give me a few hours to clear some of my work. I'll call ahead to give you a heads-up."

"Sounds like a plan."

Jesse stared at his phone for several seconds after he hung up. He wasn't sure what to make of the conversation he'd just had. That was okay, he would have his curiosity satisfied when he got to Helton. Without thinking, he reached for his glove and ball, which were still sitting on his desk from the previous evening. He stopped himself. A lot of what Vic had said to him while they were drinking was bullshit, but not all of it. Jesse thought that maybe it was time to stop looking at his poster of Ozzie Smith and time to take a good long look in the mirror.

54

This time they didn't meet at Burt's All-Star Grill in Helton but at a rest stop on the interstate between Paradise and Boston. Harlan Salter IV was equally out of place at the rest stop as he was at Burt's. He wasn't a man who frequented grills or rest stops or did the kinds of things most people did. He made money and liked to sail. He tolerated his older boys and his wife. He enjoyed a bowl of good pipe tobacco, savored a glass of aged single-malt scotch, liked to fantasize about women he would consider cheap. He detested Vic Prado. Monty Bernstein's eyes got wide as Prado approached their table.

"Did the person whom you procured do that to him?" Salter said to his lawyer.

"I don't think so. His reputation is that when he does a job, the victim no longer moves among the living. Vic Prado must have other enemies."

"No doubt a lengthy and comprehensive list."

Prado came to their table. As wrecked as he had looked from across the food court, he looked even worse up close. His face was swollen and bruised, though not quite as badly as Ben Salter's. There were heavy purple bags under his eyes that blended into the bruising from his nose. He reeked of sweat and whiskey. His jacket sleeve was torn and the rest of his clothes looked as if he had slept in them. For the first time since Prado had approached Harlan Salter at a hedge fund managers' meeting in Chicago the year before, Salter took some pleasure at the sight of this man he hated.

Prado, a large to-go cup of coffee in his shaky right hand, slid in across from Bernstein and Salter.

Monty couldn't contain himself. "What the hell happened to you?"

"I pinched a nun's ass and God hit me with a lightning bolt," Prado said. "Does it matter?"

For some reason it mattered to Harlan

Salter IV. "Yes, it does. If you don't want us to walk out of this meeting, please answer Mr. Bernstein's question."

Under any other set of circumstances, Vic would have told the prune-faced Brahmin to go shove it. But he was still fairly nauseated and his headache was in crescendo. He just wanted to get it over with.

"Jesse Stone," he said. "We got into it last night."

Monty had liked and respected Jesse Stone from the first. Vic's face reinforced Monty's faith as a judge of character. Salter gloated quietly.

"You summoned us here," Monty said. "I'm not sure I see the point, given—"

"Please, Counselor, enough," Vic said, reaching into his jacket for the envelope Mike Frazetta had given him.

"My client isn't signing anything else. We did as you asked. And Mr. Salter's son has been—"

"For crissakes, Bernstein, shut up!" Vic said too loudly. People at surrounding tables turned to stare at him. When they turned back, he lowered his voice to a whisper. "Consider this a gesture of apology from me and my partners." He opened the envelope and showed the papers to the men across the table from him. He then proceeded to rip the papers into confetti. "Our partnership is dissolved."

Monty was skeptical. "Just like that?"

"Just like that." Prado brushed his palms together twice. "Coastline Consultants can go back to doing business as usual. You have my word that we won't disclose any information we have about your prior questionable practices. We are sorry about the girl and your son. Believe me when I tell you that we didn't mean for anything to play out this way."

"Believe me when I tell you to go fuck yourself," Salter said, his voice an angry growl. He was shoving the stem of his pipe into Vic Prado's chest. He was nearly as shocked by his words and actions as Prado and Bernstein. "My son was nearly beaten to death and an eighteen-year-old girl was murdered in cold blood and I am supposed to simply say thank you and smile and move on? Unlikely, sir. Very unlikely indeed."

Now it was Vic's turn to make some threats. He leaned across the table. "Listen to me, Salter. You do anything **but** say thank you, smile, and move on, and what happened to your son and that girl will look like a sunny Sunday at the state fair. To paraphrase one of my partners, we'll dismantle the Salter family tree one branch at a time. And since Ben is already damaged, we'll start with him and work our way through the rest of you. Believe me when I tell you this isn't an idle threat. It ends here or it's an end to you and your whole fuckin' clan. Consider yourself warned. Your choice."

Prado slid himself away from the table and left.

In the car on the way back into Paradise, Monty Bernstein decided his client had sufficiently calmed down to have a rational conversation.

"Do you want me to call off the hounds now that you're out of it," he said.

Salter stared at his lawyer as if he had just

sprouted a second head. "Are you mad? Of course not. I spit on their gesture."

"Why borrow trouble? You have your company back. Your son is safe and he will recover in time."

"Because, Mr. Bernstein," he said, holding the bowl of his lit pipe and pointing the stem at Monty, smoke leaking upward out of the tip, "there is a price to be paid."

"Yes, I know. The girl, but—"

"It's not about the girl. What do I care about some girl? No, balance needs to be restored. A bill is due and someone must pay with their blood. I want it to be Prado's blood and I want to be there to see the remittance."

"Harlan, I need to advise against this. You heard Prado, his partners will—"

"You may be very good at your job, Monty. In fact, I've no doubt of it, but I am very good at mine, too. That Prado was forced by his partners to come crawling to me to beg forgiveness should tell you something."

"What's that?"

Salter drew in a lungful of smoke and let

it escape slowly from between his thin, crooked lips. A damp, smoked-cherry aroma filled the air. "They will be as happy to see Prado gone as I will. They won't lift a finger against me. I wouldn't be surprised if they sent me a bouquet and a thank-you card for having him excised."

"Still, Harlan, I have to advise against it. Innocent people are going to get hurt here. Why put yourself in danger of the blowback?"

"The innocence threshold has already been crossed. Loss of innocence is often the price of doing business."

"It's a dirty business."

"Something you know intimately, Mr. Bernstein, dirty business." Salter smiled an icy smile at his attorney. "As I recall, it was you who knew how to contact this man who would collect the debt, not me."

"That may be true, Harlan. But I'm asking you to please reconsider."

But Harlan Salter was no longer listening to Monty. He was staring out the Navigator's back window, imagining Vic Prado's screams of agony.

55

Like hardware stores and sporting-goods shops, garages were places in which men seemed genetically predestined to feel at ease. Whether they knew a lug wrench from a pipe wrench, football cleats from a hammer claw, or a fuel injector from a smoke detector was beside the point. Jesse was no exception to the rule. A kind of beatific smile flashed across his face as he stepped into the Helton Police Department Garage and Motor Pool. If asked, he couldn't have said what it was exactly that triggered his involuntary smile. Maybe it was the smell of the place: the metallic tang of glowing hot welds, the earthy scent of used motor oil, the distinct odor of new tires, the cloying chemical aroma of fresh paint. Maybe it was the sights of the garage: cars up on hydraulic lifts, engines suspended in midair on chain hoists, men in dirty coveralls wiping sweat from their brows with grease-blackened sleeves. Or maybe the sounds: the snap and crackling of sparks from the welders, the insistent drone and chatter of pneumatic tools, the **thump thump thump** of tires bounced against the concrete floor. Whatever the reason, Jesse felt a level of comfort, a kind of mindless ease he seldom experienced anymore.

The garage was on Park Place around the back of police headquarters. Chief Ralph Carney, decked out in full dress blues, shiny black shoes, and a classic cop hat. His hat had more cabbage on it than a local farm. It was a match for General MacArthur's, and that was saying something. At least Carney had forgone the white gloves. Jesse felt like a slob next to his Helton counterpart. After shaking hands, Carney asked Jesse about the bruises.

"What happened to you? Nice shiner you're working on."

"Long story not worth the time. In any case, Ralph, how could you even notice my face with all those shiny brass buttons on that uniform. What do you wear when

ROBERT B. PARKER'S BLIND SPOT

the governor passes through town, one of Liberace's capes?"

"I knew you were gonna say something. Don't get bigheaded. This getup isn't for you. I had to give a speech over at the high school and the town requires me to do the fancy-Dan routine when I make official public appearances."

"Paradise is a little more relaxed about my dress code, but I have to get on the blues once in a while myself. Ralph, somehow I don't figure you called me down here just to see you in your dress blues, as sharp as you look in them."

"Nope. C'mon with me."

Jesse followed Chief Carney through the garage, past the paint booth, to a separate area. It was a much quieter space, full of mostly wrecked vehicles. Some with evident splotches of dried blood on their cracked windshields and side windows. Jesse spotted Gabe Weathers's smashed-up Honda Civic almost immediately. Standing next to Gabe's car was a large, officious-looking man wearing safety glasses and a Helton

PD windbreaker. When Jesse and Chief Carney came into view, the man in the windbreaker grabbed a flat and ripped tire out from behind the Civic. He rested the tire against his leg and waited.

"That's Paul Bynam, our lead accident investigation guy," said Carney.

Jesse was impressed. "We've only got one person who does accident investigation."

"So do we." Carney laughed, covering his mouth with his hand. "You know how some people just got to have a title and their own little kingdom?"

"I do."

"Then you understand Paul. Don't get me wrong, Jesse. He's very good at his job. Got all kinds of awards and certificates. He'll explain it all to you."

Carney made the introductions. Jesse waited.

"Okay, Paul," Carney said. "Walk Chief Stone through it."

Bynam said, "When there's an accident in this jurisdiction on a municipal thoroughfare or a section of state road that—"

"Cut to the chase, Paul. Jesse is a chief of police. He doesn't need the pre- requisites."

"Understood, Chief," Bynam said and then turned to Jesse. "When we first got your officer's vehicle in here, our working theory about the cause of the accident was that he was traveling at a high rate of speed and had a blowout. This caused him to lose control of the vehicle, resulting in the vehicle hitting the median and flipping over."

Chief Carney rolled his hands, motion- ing for Bynam to speed it up.

"However, when I got around to exam- ining the rubber on your guy's vehicle, I noticed that the tires were not only of high quality, but basically brand-new. I found a receipt in the glove box for the tires that indicated the rubber had less than two thousand miles' wear on them. I checked the data on blowouts on these tires and discovered that they almost never occurred. So I immediately began to search the blown tire for indications of penetration by a foreign body."

"Road debris," Jesse said. "A nail, glass, something like that."

Bynam's face lit up. "Exactly. We removed the tire from the rim."

Chief Carney prompted his man. "And..."

"Right, Chief. And we found this." Bynam handed Jesse a sealed evidence bag with a small piece of metal inside.

Jesse's expression took a serious turn. "Is this what I think it is?"

"Ballistics tells me it's a twenty-two," said Carney. "It's been distorted by the rim."

"Someone shot out my man's tire."

Carney nodded. "Looks that way, Jesse." He turned to Bynam. "That'll be all, Paul. Great work, but I need a minute with Chief Stone, if you don't mind."

"Yes," Jesse said, "you did good here. Thank you."

Bynam bowed slightly, leaned the tire back against the car, retreated to a small office, and closed the door.

"You see why I called you down here now, right, Jesse?"

"Absolutely. This is no longer a simple accident, but possibly attempted murder."

"So you see where I'm going with this?" Carney said.

"You're going to launch a full criminal investigation."

"Already launched." He handed Jesse a business card. "Detective Lino Basquet, silent **t**, is in charge. He'll be in touch."

"He'll want to know what Gabe was doing here in the first place. Whether it was official business," Jesse said, frowning.

"Problem?"

Jesse shrugged. "Maybe. I can tell you it was official. He was doing surveillance on a subject who is related to an ongoing homicide investigation."

Carney nodded. "The girl?"

"Uh-huh."

"Terrible thing. I read up on what was going on in Paradise when Bynam came to me about the twenty-two slug in your man's tire. Any progress on the case?"

"We got the kid back, but we've hit a

dead end on the murder. I've got a theory about it, but that's all it is at the moment."

"The guy Weathers was tailing...he a suspect?" Carney said.

"No, but—"

"But you don't want him to know he was being tailed."

Jesse smiled. "No wonder they made you chief and gave you that natty uniform."

Carney understood Jesse's predicament. "I'll talk to Lino and explain the situation. I don't think it will be a problem. Probably road rage. Your guy cut somebody off because he wanted to keep up with the subject car and some nut took offense."

"Probably," Jesse said, but didn't quite believe it. Too convenient. Jesse believed in convenience about as much as he believed in coincidence.

He thanked the Helton chief for all the help. Before they parted ways, Carney reminded Jesse to stop off at the evidence desk and collect Gabe Weathers's personal items. When Jesse walked back through the police garage and motor pool, he was no longer at ease and he was no longer smiling.

56

The aspirins had helped a little to begin with, but they had become decreasingly effective as the day wore on. So in addition to the pounding headache, nausea, and full-body weakness, his stomach was killing him. His early rest-stop meeting with Salter and his lawyer hadn't done much to improve his condition. There was no way he was going to see Dee today. He didn't have the energy or the desire. Although he had lusted after her for so long and here she was demanding to see him, it was a no-go. Even picturing her tanned nude body, muscles twitching in anticipation, and fantasizing about her begging him to take her in that sexy, vaguely Southern accent of hers couldn't do the trick. So he texted her and told her the rendezvous would have to wait another day. She'd tried calling a few times, but he refused to answer and let her calls go to voice mail. He texted her again, explaining that he was honestly quite sick, and asked her to give him a day. The calls stopped after that.

Dressed in the same rumpled, sweaty clothes he'd slept in, he'd fallen into bed. He'd spent most of the day in that half-conscious, half-asleep state that only hangovers and certain drugs can induce. At about three in the afternoon, after Dee's calls had stopped and he felt a bit more human, he got up, took a long shower, and shaved. His hair still wet, he fell back into bed and finally into a deep sleep. It didn't last, and that was a shame. He was dreaming of Kayla, not Dee. They were young again, impulsive, and stupid in love. They were on a beach somewhere, naked, just holding each other. Kayla was laughing. Even in the dream he realized Kayla's laugh was something he hadn't heard for years. It was one of those paradoxical things about dreaming, how you could be a part of it and be apart from it and that the contradiction didn't matter. Then a weird image attached itself to the dream. He looked away from Kayla to an impos-

sible tree rising out of the sand.
On a thick branch above their heads, a
stunning, black-feathered bird was
singing, but without sound. It wasn't that
Vic couldn't hear. He heard the roar of the
waves. He heard Kayla's laugh. It was that
he knew the bird's voice had been taken
from it. He heard the phone, too. And that
was not part of the dream.

He grabbed the phone and checked the
number to make sure it wasn't Dee again.

"Lorraine, hi," he said, still groggy.

"Umm. Your voice is all sleepy and sexy."

"Sleepy, yes. Sexy, no."

"What's the matter? What's wrong?"

"Nothing. I got into a fight with an old
friend and then we got drunk together.
Now I'm just trying to get some sleep and
recover."

"Poor baby," she said without a hint of
sarcasm. "I can come over and make it
better."

"A long sleep is the only thing that will
make this better. Why are you calling?"

"I have a surprise for you."

"Really? What kind of surprise?"

"I told Mike that I was going back to Lowell to visit my aunt Maria."

"I'm not getting you," Vic said.

"I'm here, Vic."

"Here? Here where?"

"In Paradise."

Vic sat up in bed as if he were spring-loaded. That undid all the good the sleep had done him.

"Vic! Vic," she said when he didn't respond.

"Yeah, Lorraine. Sorry, I'm still waking up. That's great."

"You know what's even better?" Her voice crackled with excitement. "I'm in the hotel lobby."

Vic fell silent again. A spectrum of emotions went through him that began in anger but ended in a kind of serenity. Serenity because Lorraine had helped push him to make up his mind. He was going to run and though he hadn't yet figured out just how, he thought that maybe Lorraine could help him.

"Well, then," he said, "if you're in the lobby, you better come on up."

57

Jesse and Dee were to meet at the Lobster Claw for dinner. Jesse sat out on the back deck, waiting for Dee to arrive. He had chosen the Lobster Claw because it was only a few months old and was a Jenn-free zone. For many years, the Gray Gull had been his go-to restaurant, but so much of the drama with Jenn had played out there. It never got public or ugly. There were no screaming fights or nasty scenes. That's not what Jesse and Jenn were about. Yet so much of their relationship was spent in a constant push/pull: one step forward, half a step back, living together, living apart, dating each other, and dating others. Jesse shook his head just thinking about how much time and energy they had both invested in a long-drawn-out dance that, in the end, came to so much smoke. Although it had been years since they had been together in any real sense of the word, he guessed he was still attached to Jenn. He didn't need Dix to tell him it was time to move on. He wanted to move on. Dee made him want to move on.

He was already at the table, sipping a beer. Beer was sometimes part of a game he played with himself about his drinking. There was a hierarchy on the Jesse Stone alcohol scale that ran from water to beer to wine to scotch and soda to scotch to martinis. Beer was one step up from soda or sparkling water and several steps removed from martinis. He had a number value system as well that he used in conjunction with his alcohol scale. Two beers were equal to one scotch and soda. Two scotches were equal to one and a half martinis, and so on. Of course it was all nonsense: Alcohol was alcohol. Any cop or bartender knows that there's roughly the same amount of alcohol in one beer as in one glass of wine as in one shot of eighty-proof liquor. But drinkers feed their habits with these games, and Jesse was an experienced player.

Dee came out on the deck in tight white

slacks, red deck shoes, and a beige sweater under a perfectly faded denim jacket. Dee was smart about how she dressed. She didn't always play up her beauty, but she always let it shine through. She had on some makeup, but an appropriate amount for a spring dinner with the chief of police at a place called the Lobster Claw in a town called Paradise. She always smelled great. Jesse lit up at the sight of her. She smiled that neon smile back at him, but he detected a note of seriousness in her he hadn't seen before. He wasn't sure what it was, but he knew it was something. Dee noticed him notice. She also noticed the slight swelling and bruising on the outside of Jesse's right eye. She leaned over and kissed him not so softly on the lips. When she pulled back, Dee stroked her fingers along his bruises. She ordered a martini, dry, three olives, from the waitress standing at her shoulder. She sat down and turned her attention back to Jesse.

"What happened to you, darlin'?"

"You first," he said.

"What do you mean?"

"I saw it on your face."

She thought about saying something witty to deflect him but couldn't think of anything witty. Then she remembered about the call that never came.

"It's Kayla," she said.

"I know."

Dee's eyes got wide. "What do you know?"

"She left Vic."

"But how—"

Jesse pointed at his eye. "Vic told me while he was trying to break my cheekbone."

"You two got into it?"

"We did."

"Bad?"

"Not for me," Jesse said, the corners of his mouth turning up.

Dee understood. "Men! What did you do to him that he came after you?"

"He thought Kayla had left him for me."

She shook her head and smiled.

"I'm wounded," Jesse said.

"No, darlin', it's not that I don't think

Kayla or any other woman wouldn't run in your direction at the drop of a hat. I sure would. It's just that I know where Kay went."

"Where?"

She winked at him. "I'm sworn to secrecy."

"But I'm the chief of police," he said, a broad smile on his face.

"You going to take me back to the station and beat it out of me?"

"Beating isn't what I had in mind."

It was her turn to smile. The waitress delivered Dee's martini. She stirred the drink with the speared olives, raised the glass, and said, "To thorough interrogations."

He raised his nearly empty beer glass. "Uh-huh."

Dee ordered a field-greens salad with goat cheese and walnuts and a lobster roll. Jesse ordered a shrimp cocktail, extra cocktail sauce, a burger, and another beer. They ate mostly in silence, both taking time to look out at the Atlantic. They were thinking about very different subjects as they stared out at the water. Jesse was trying to find the words to ask about the big thing he was certain Dee was hiding from him. He was also worried that asking might ruin it. He could hear Dix in his head, chiding him about his desire to control everything, even things completely beyond his control. Dee was breathing a sigh of relief that Vic had told her the truth about not being in any shape to meet with her and that he wasn't just avoiding her. She was also thinking that she didn't want this night to end.

The waitress broke the spell. "Coffee? Dessert?"

They ordered coffee.

Jesse waited for the waitress to leave. "Are you going to tell me where Kayla went?"

Dee made an exaggerated frown. "I was kind of looking forward to that thorough interrogation you'd mentioned."

"I'll come up with a new question you can refuse to answer."

She looked around as if to make sure no one was listening. "You can't tell Vic."

"Word of honor."

"She went back home."

"Scottsdale?"

"New Mexico. She's going to spend some time in Taos with her folks and try to figure out what to do with her life."

"Good for her."

"But didn't she really hurt you?"

"Long time ago."

"That's a very enlightened lie," she said. "You forget, I saw the look on your face in New York when Kayla was around."

He shrugged.

"That's it, a shrug? You can do better than that, darlin'."

"Probably."

"Jesse Stone, are you always this effusive?"

He didn't answer.

The waitress delivering their coffees saved Jesse from further questioning. The waitress also put two snifters of amber liquor down on the table next to their coffees. The intense smell of alcohol and the tang of concentrated orange rose up from the fancy glassware, blending with the salt smell of the sea and the earthy fragrance of coffee. She placed the check on the table as well.

"The Grand Marniers are compliments of the owner," the waitress said. "Dan wants you to stop by on the way out. I'll take the check when you're ready."

Jesse thought back to the night he'd stood alone on this very deck, drinking his Black Label and thinking about his transition from one ocean to another. Dan Castro had wanted to speak to him that night, too. Less than a week had passed, but it felt like a distant memory. Lots had changed in the last several turns of the earth. Mostly he thought about the murdered girl. The last time he'd stood on the Lobster Claw's deck, Martina Penworth's life stretched out before her like a long, dimly lit road full of potholes and promise. Now that road was forever closed, promise forever unfulfilled.

"What's wrong, Jesse?"

"I was thinking about the dead girl."

"Any progress?"

"None."

They sipped their orange-infused brandies. Dee liked it. Jesse didn't. He wasn't a Grand Marnier type of guy.

"I don't want to add to your worries," Dee said.

"But..."

"But Kayla was supposed to let me know she arrived safely in New Mexico."

Jesse said, "She hasn't called?"

"Not a peep."

"Have you tried calling her?"

"About twenty times. The first calls went straight to voice mail. Then the voice-mail box filled up."

"Do you know her parents' number?"

"We're friends, but we're not that close, darlin'."

Jesse said, "She probably just wants some solitude. But I'll get hold of her folks tomorrow morning."

"That makes me feel better."

"While we're on the subject of making you feel better, how about we head back to my place and get that interrogation started?"

"What about speaking to the boss? He

did buy us drinks."

"You want to bribe the chief, you've got to do better than a round of drinks."

Jesse put three twenties on the table and took Dee by the hand.

"This way," he said, "through the parking lot."

58

When Jesse walked through the front door of the Paradise police headquarters, he once again came bearing donuts. This time because he was a little late for work. As chief, he didn't need to answer to anyone if he took an hour here or there, but that wasn't his way. Though he had no experience at being a chief when he got the position and had walked into the middle of a shit storm from his first day on the job as chief, there were lessons he had learned in the Marines and as a ballplayer that applied. One was to never expect more from the people who work for you than you expect from yourself. Good leaders lead by example. So Jesse had tried, for the most part successfully, to be in early and get the lay of the land. On those rare occasions when he fell down, he had Molly Crane to protect him. He loved Molly for her loyalty and for a hundred other reasons. Problem was, Molly liked to gloat about having to save her boss's behind. And when he walked in late that morning, he knew Molly would be all over him. But Molly was too busy to bust on her boss for being late. She was taking a report from a neatly dressed young man who sat across from her. Jesse walked directly into his office without even saying hello.

He sat at his desk, pulled a jelly out of the box of a dozen, and sipped at the extra-large milk-and-sugar coffee he'd bought at the donut shop. Some days, the stationhouse coffee sufficed. Some days not. He was in the midst of a sex hangover—weak-kneed, lightheaded, and dreamy—and that required copious amounts of good coffee and as many bad carbs as he could stuff into his body in a brief period of time. He took a bite of the donut and remembered the lesson his training officer had given him his first day on the job in uniform in L.A. During a break, they drove to Randy's Donuts, that place near LAX with the giant stucco donut on the roof. His TO, Rodriguez, was a tough guy built like a pit bull, only not as pleasant. He was the type of guy who told rookies not to speak unless he gave them permission to speak and then only if they had an intelligent question to ask. Rodriguez bought three different kinds of jelly donuts, moved away from the cashier, and placed them in a row on the counter.

"First and most important test, rookie," Rodriguez said. "I'll know all I need to know about you when we're done. You gonna be a good cop. You gonna be a bag of leaves. I'll know after this."

Jesse had no idea what was going on but went along with it. As a Marine and as a ballplayer, he was used to all the weird, often inexplicable hazing rituals the new guys had to endure.

"Okay, rookie. Here we got a jelly donut covered in powdered sugar. Here we got a jelly donut covered in colored sprinkles. Here we got a jelly donut covered in granulated sugar." Rodriguez pointed as he spoke. "Which one you going to eat?"

"Granulated sugar," Jesse said.

"Why's that, rookie?"

"Our uniforms are black, sir," Jesse said.

"You get any powdered sugar on your uniform and wiping it will only spread it around. Sprinkles are better, but in hot or wet weather, you can have the same trouble as with the powdered sugar. Worse, because the stains will be colored. Granulated sugar you can brush off."

Rodriguez smiled at Jesse. "Outstanding, rookie. You're going to make detective someday."

Jesse was smiling about that memory when Molly came through his office door.

"Donut?" He hoped she'd be distracted.

It was a waste of time.

"You forget to change your clocks in March?" she said.

"Go away, Crane. That's an order."

Not only didn't she leave, she stepped closer to Jesse's desk and leaned in to take a close look at him.

"The swelling's gone down on the side of your face, but you're looking like you spent the night with other body parts—"

"Molly Crane! You're a good Irish Catholic girl. You are not supposed to know about such things."

"That's the great paradox of my faith. We learn about such things so we know what not to do."

"You've got me there."

"But I'm not here about your persistent debauchery," she said. "I've got Ron Pearl from Mayflower Rental out front."

"They rent pilgrims?"

"Stick to police work, Jesse. Your stand-up is weak. They rent cars."

"And..."

"One's missing."

"And..."

"It was rented by a woman named Kayla Dante Prado."

"Send him in."

Ron Pearl was an athletic, good-looking kid who couldn't have been two years out of college. He had the well-scrubbed, go-getter glint in his eyes. He wore a black golf shirt over blacker slacks and black loafers. Emblazoned on the chest of his shirt, over his heart, was an embroidered facsimile of the Mayflower done in brown and ivory thread. The words **Mayflower**

Rentals showed above the masts of the ship. Beneath the keel the company motto—**The gift of thrift**—was done in red. Jesse gestured for Ron to sit in a chair facing the desk. The kid sat.

"Molly tells me you've got a missing car?"

"Yes, sir. A brand-new Chevy Malibu sedan, plate number—"

"First thing, Ron, call me Jesse. Second thing is that I'm sure you've given all the car details to Officer Crane. Is that right?"

"I did, Jesse."

"Good. I'm more interested in how you know the car is missing."

"It was an eight-hour rental. That's a service we offer that our larger competitors don't offer," Ron said, his voice full of pride. "It was also supposed to be dropped off at our Logan Airport location. We understand that there are times people keep the cars longer than they've contracted for, and we write a clause into the rental contract—"

"Interesting, but let's stick to the program. Okay?"

"Sorry. In any case, a red flag comes up on our daily reports if the car hasn't been returned within a twenty-four-hour period."

Jesse nodded. "What if a renter were to return the car, but to a location different than the one specified? Let's say she drove it to Hartford Airport and returned it there?"

"The red flag would still come up. But I checked with all of our destinations and with those companies with which we have reciprocity agreements."

"No luck?"

"Sorry, Chief—Jesse. The car isn't anywhere in our system. Company policy requires me to report the car as stolen in the jurisdiction in which it was rented."

"That would be Paradise?"

"It would. It's a shame, too," said the kid.

"How so?"

"I was the agent who rented her the car. She was beautiful, but there was something about her."

That piqued Jesse's curiosity. "Something?"

"A kind of sadness. Also, I think she'd been crying. Her eyes were all red. I hope she didn't..." He stopped himself from saying it out loud.

"You think she might have harmed herself?"

The kid shrugged. "I was a business administration major, not a psych major. I don't know. She just seemed so sad."

Jesse stood and held out his hand to the kid and they shook.

"Thanks for coming in and for talking with me, Ron. If there's anything else you remember, anything at all, please call—"

"Wait! There is something. She asked me for a map of downtown Boston. She had me point out some of the popular sightseeing spots. I don't know if that helps."

"No, Ron, that's great. Thanks."

Jesse watched the kid leave his office and thought about their conversation. He thought back to what Dee had said the night before about her concern that Kayla hadn't called. He walked out to talk to Molly. She was on the phone and looked behind her as Jesse walked toward her. She clicked the hold button.

Jesse nodded at the phone. "Important?"

"Just one of my kids. It can wait. The woman who rented the car was here the other day, wasn't she?"

"The black-haired one. Vic Prado's wife. But you knew that. That's why you sent the kid in to talk to me."

Molly nodded and said, "You look worried."

"Concerned."

"Okay, concerned. What's up?"

"Call Boston PD and give them the details on the missing car. Tell them we're pretty sure it's parked near one of the big draws."

"Are we sure?"

"Not sure, but it's a good guess. Also, you can't tell BPD that it's a guess. And tell them the woman who rented the car might be missing and is a potential suicide candidate."

Molly wanted to ask how Jesse knew all of this, but the look on his face told her to just do as he said.

"After that, check with the airlines to see if they had a no-show for a flight to Albuquerque in the last forty-eight hours under the name Kayla Prado or Kayla Dante Prado. Then get a Taos listing for the Dante family. I think the dad's name is William."

"When I get the number, do you want me to call?"

"I'll do that."

As he answered, the cell phone buzzed in his pocket.

"Jesse Stone," he said, putting the phone to his ear and walking back into his office.

"You told me to call you if he showed up again, and he did and he beat the shit out of—" The woman on the line was beside herself, breathless and nearly hysterical.

"Okay, okay, calm down. Who is this?"

"Sharon."

Jesse searched his memory, but the woman on the other end of the phone couldn't wait.

"Sharon, from Burt's All-Star—"

"The waitress."

"Right."

"You told me to call you if Spider came back and made trouble for me," she said.

"Since you're calling, I assume he came back."

"He beat the shit out of Hector!" She was screaming into the phone. "He came into Burt's and shoved me aside, then he walked into the kitchen and just started beating on Hector. My God, his face is all fucked up and it's all because he was good to me and my kids."

"Where's Hector?"

"I took him to the ER. Then I split and got my kids."

"I'll call the Helton PD. I know some people over—"

"No! You said to call you. That you'd take care of it. Anyways, the Helton cops don't do shit about Satan's Whores. You think Spider ain't done something like this before?"

"Where are you now?"

She gave him the address.

"I'll be there as soon as I can."

Jesse checked his .38 and headed out of his office.

"Where are you going?" Molly said.

"To Helton."

"For what?"

"To keep my word," he said and then left.

59

Vic had to admit that Lorraine had been great. After reassuring him that visiting her aunt was a regular occurrence and that Mike never got suspicious of her—**I've never given him a reason to be suspicious...until now**—Vic relaxed. Although she came to Paradise with only one thing on her mind—a repeat performance of their tryst at the motel—she'd put her desires on hold and took good care of him. She'd cradled his head in her lap as he slept. She'd gone to the Chinese takeout place on Schooner Avenue and got him two quarts of hot chicken broth. She'd forced him to drink a liter bottle of water. She'd given him something for his headache that didn't do any further damage to his stomach. Her patience ran out at about one in the morning and, feeling human again, Vic didn't see how he could say no.

When they woke at seven the next

morning, Vic was feeling almost himself again and he'd figured out how to use Lorraine to help him get away, but he knew he had to be circumspect about how he broached the subject to her. He had no thought of actually telling her the truth, only enough of it so that what she told Mike would give him cover. First, though, he had to get her in a cooperative spirit. He kissed her on the neck, and she shuddered from the chills.

"How do you do that to me?" she said. "Even in school you could do that to me. I think you're still the only man who could do that to me."

He pulled her by the hair. "Get into the shower. Now!"

This time her shudder was more pronounced and it came with a not-so-soft sigh.

"Come in with me, please," she said, her voice a little breathless.

"You first. I'll be right in."

Lorraine got out of bed and walked unsteadily into the bathroom.

Perfect! She would do exactly what he

wanted and would provide the misinformation to Mike.

When he heard the spray of the shower, Vic texted a coded message to his lawyer. His lawyer would set it all in motion: the crossing into Canada, the cruise down to the Caymans, the new identity, and everything else he had so meticulously planned. Vic knew that only idiots went through life without a plan B, and he was no idiot. Anticipation and adaptation was a big part of being a good ballplayer. Knowing what might go wrong and what to do if it did was more important in life than on the field. So Vic understood from the outset that even if everything had gone according to spec, he might have to run. Good thing. The reunion had gone terribly in terms of Jesse Stone, and that damned Joe Breen had to go and kill the girl. Every time he thought about that aspect of it, he shook his head.

He turned for the bathroom and put the phone down on the nightstand. As soon as he did, "Take Me Out to the Ball Game" began playing. He recognized Dee's number. He wanted to let it go to voice mail but figured he should pick it up. He couldn't afford Dee showing up at his hotel door with Lorraine Frazetta there. Whether he wound up boinking Dee or not wasn't the point. It was that he couldn't afford a scene and he couldn't risk Lorraine's ill will.

"Yeah, Dee, what's up?"

"Can I come over now?"

"Not now," he said a little too loudly. "I need to wake up and shower and all. Then I want to get some breakfast in me."

"I can come over to see you afterwards?"

"Why don't I come over to your room?" he said. "It's just easier, okay?"

"I need to see you, Vic. Please."

"Okay, by noon. I promise."

"Have you heard from Kayla?"

"I'm the last person she'd call. I've got to go."

He hung up, put the phone down, and went into the bathroom. Lorraine was in the shower, waiting for him.

60

Jesse never gave his word casually, and he never second-guessed himself about giving it. Sometimes he paid a price for it, but it was usually a price he was willing to pay. Today it had been the price of a motel room the next town over from Helton. It wasn't a no-tell motel, but it wasn't exactly the Four Seasons, either. Fifty bucks for the room and another fifty in cash for food was worth the few hours of security it bought for Sharon and her kids. He didn't think taking care of Spider was going to be an all-day project and that Sharon could probably take her kids home in a couple hours.

Now Jesse was standing at the door for 221B Locust Street in what looked to be the most run-down section of Helton. The area was largely made up of old squat concrete-block buildings with flat, tarred roofs and loading docks. These buildings looked like they had once been used as machine shops, for light manufacturing or warehousing. These were not the big, forlorn dinosaur factories Jesse had seen driving through the other side of town, but they were equally desolate. The door at 221B Locust Street was a battered, gray steel door with a peephole. Written on the door in red spray paint was a warning:

SATAN'S WHORES

STAY THE FUCK OUT!

On the rolled-down corrugated-steel door by the loading dock was the gang's pinup girl/devil's head logo. There was a line of seven motorcycles on the pitted cobblestone street parked at an angle to the curb. Most of the bikes were Harley derivatives, black and muscular but without the affectations of the weekend rider. No fancy saddlebags or radios or polished chrome doohickeys. Recognizing Spider's bike was easy. It had black widows painted in bright red on either side of its gas tank. **Good,** he thought. **Better to deal with**

Spider directly and get it over with. He had a contingency plan to deal with Spider if the coward wasn't around, but it was a bit more complicated and involved another member of Satan's Whores. That contingency would almost surely have guaranteed a premature death for Spider and a burial at the bottom of a quarry lake without gang honors.

Jesse took out his badge, held it up to the peephole, and kicked the door three times. The door creaked open and a guy who made Spider look puny filled the doorway. He was dressed in dusty black leathers, a gang vest over a faded and torn black-and-orange Harley T-shirt, and every inch of his exposed skin was tattooed. He stank of sweat and stale marijuana smoke. Jesse could easily imagine that every inch of his skin, exposed or not, was similarly adorned. He was mostly bald, but had a long, gray, braided ponytail that hung over his left shoulder down along his chest. He had a gray Fu Manchu mustache with a long soul patch that was braided and hung off his chin like a thin rope. His lips were wrecked and some of his teeth were missing. The ones that were still in his mouth were stained yellow.

"I don't know you, pig."

"That makes us even."

"Funny man."

"I have my moments," Jesse said. "Can Spider come out and play?"

"You got a warrant for Spider or a warrant to search the place, we'll talk."

"You don't look like a lawyer."

"Get the fuck outta here. You don't want me to call Carney on you, do you, asshole?"

"I'm not local. Call Carney. Call anybody you want, but just get Spider out here."

The big man shook his head and said, "Fuck off!" He started to turn his back on Jesse.

"I asked politely. Now I'm done asking and done being polite."

Jesse unholstered his snub-nose .38 and shot out the front tire of Spider's bike.

"Wait a fuckin'—"

Jesse shot out the back tire of Spider's

bike.

"The next one's in the engine block," he said. "The one after that's in you. Now get him out here. Now! Ten...nine...eight... seven..."

"Spider! Get out here. Some pig's messing with your hog," the big man said.

Spider came running out the door, face distorted in rage, but some of it went out of him when he saw it was Jesse. His groin had only just fully recovered from Jesse's kick, and he remembered the threat Jesse had made the other day at Burt's.

"Hello, Spider," Jesse said, his voice calm. "I told you what would happen to you if you bothered Sharon again."

"I didn't touch her. I beat down that rice-and-beans-eatin' little weasel that—"

Jesse fired two shots into Spider's engine block.

"Motherfucker!"

Spider ran over to his motorcycle, avoiding Jesse, and knelt down to check out the damage.

"I told you what I would do to you, Spider." Then Jesse turned to the big man.

"Get the rest of your guys out here. When I kick Spider's ass, I want you all to see it."

The big man did as Jesse asked. He watched as each of the other five Whores emerged from gang central. The fourth guy to come out onto the street was the man Jesse was hoping would be there. Sharon had described him perfectly. She said his name was Wallace, but that they called him Reaper. He was smaller than the rest of his gang brothers, but with a power lifter's build. He was thick everywhere a man could be thick. He had enormous hands that he balled up into brutal-looking fists. His hair was long and black and his eyes were a disturbing icy gray.

Jesse popped open the cylinder of his .38, held it up for the crowd to see, and turned it so that the spent shells and the last live round dropped out onto the sidewalk. The cartridges pinged and danced when they hit the concrete. Jesse snapped the cylinder shut, placed the weapon in his jacket pocket, and removed his jacket. He laid it down on the pavement and rolled up his sleeves.

"I just want you guys to know why I'm going to beat the shit out of Spider here. For one thing, he assaulted a woman named Sharon in front of me. Pretty stupid thing to do in front of a police chief," Jesse said.

"His old lady, his business," said another one of the gang.

"That's the rules," Spider said, puffing out his chest.

The rest of them nodded in agreement, Reaper less enthusiastically so.

Jesse wasn't finished. "Then he told Sharon he was going to kill her kids. What was it you called them, Spider? Little retarded bastards, right? And that in the wild, lions kill the offspring of—"

Before Jesse could finish, Reaper was on Spider. After one of Reaper's punches landed in Spider's midsection, Jesse understood why they called him Reaper. Spider's ribs cracked with the nauseating sound that only bone and cartilage make when breaking. No matter how many times you hear it, there's no getting used to it. But Reaper wasn't done with Spider, not by a long shot. He grabbed Spider's left arm and yanked it out of its socket. Spider wailed in pain.

The big man turned to Jesse and said, "Get outta here, man. This is our business. Tell Sharon she won't be hassled anymore. Tell her the Tsar gives his word."

Jesse picked up his jacket and left. He didn't look in his rearview mirror.

61

Lorraine proved tougher to shed than a deer tick after he told her what he was planning to do. She'd been a little weird since they'd got out of the shower. Vic decided that he must have given himself away, that she sensed something was up even before he explained about how he was going to Mexico and then on to Belize.

"Mike's going to have me killed, babe."

When Lorraine gasped, Vic knew he had her. He had to give her credit, though. She defended her husband.

"You're wrong, Vic. Mike wouldn't hurt you. He's always looked up to you since we were kids. He still gets those big eyes when he talks about you."

"Friends are friends. Business is business and I'm becoming a liability to his. Look at it this way, Lorraine, even if Mike would have trouble hurting me, Joe Breen would jump at the chance," he said, playing on Lorraine's uncontained animosity toward Joe. "And when I settle down and I know I'm safe, I'll get word to you. If you want to come make a life with me, I'll be there waiting."

Not a word of what he'd told Lorraine was true. He wasn't headed to Mexico or Belize. And the biggest lie of all was that he would ask her to come make a life with him. In fact, he was going to make Lorraine's life pretty tough for the next few weeks. Once he got far enough away from Paradise, he would call Mike Frazetta, confess his betrayal, and say his goodbyes. Once that call was made, he had no doubt Lorraine would repeat to Mike the lies about Mexico and Belize. Mike might not believe the lies. He would have to spend time checking them out, just in case. Any time and effort Mike spent following the lies would give Vic more of a cushion. He almost felt bad about lying to her, about using Lorraine this way. Almost. Sure, Mike had a temper on him and he might smack Lorraine around a little bit. That would be a pity, but this was Vic's ass on the line here and he meant to save it, no matter who got hurt in the process. **It's too late to worry about it now,** he thought, approaching Dee's room. As he moved down the hallway, he couldn't help but be excited at the prospect of finally nailing her.

For a year, he had lusted after her almost nonstop and had beaten himself up for not closing the deal that one time he had a chance. He guessed he understood now that Kayla had been the only obstacle for the both of them. Dee hadn't been able to bring herself to betray her friend. Until Dee had come along and in spite of his serial infidelity, Vic had always been careful never to sleep with any of Kayla's inner circle of friends. Not out of honor, but for self-preservation. As both Lorraine and Dee would soon discover, Vic had a highly developed instinct for self-preservation and very little in the way of honor.

As he rapped lightly on her door, Vic tried imagining how Dee would be dressed when she answered. Would she be coy, done up in something only slightly provocative? Would she make him work for it? Or would she be like Lorraine, dressed for sex, in garters, black seamed stockings, nosebleed stilettos, and a satiny bustier? No, that wouldn't be her style. Nude, he decided. She'd be waiting for him on the other side of the door nude. That was more her style. Maybe that's why she wasn't answering the door. She was stripping down, dabbing a drop of that crushed spice perfume behind her knees. He rapped on the door again, this time with a little more urgency. He smiled to himself, thinking that being with Dee would be the perfect farewell gift to himself. He just wished she would answer the door.

62

The kids were asleep in their car seats. Sharon rode up front with Jesse. He thought Sharon looked better than when she was working. She had showered and made herself up, done her hair. She had on a nice red-and-white floral-print dress that showed too much cleavage and was maybe a few inches too short. She smelled of raw patchouli, which, in small doses, Jesse didn't mind. Oddly, though, Sharon didn't seem as relieved as he thought she should be now that she was free of Spider forever. If anything, she was unsettled, fidgety, wringing her hands in her lap. She asked if she could smoke. He shook his head. She didn't seem real pleased about that, either.

"Did you get the kids something to eat?"

"Yeah, we had a nice breakfast and some lunch at Denny's." She reached into her bag and pulled out some crumpled bills. "Here's what's left. There's some change, too."

"Keep it."

"I don't want no charity."

"It's not charity. Buy Hector some flowers or something," he said.

"You sure?"

He nodded. She stuffed the bills back in her bag.

"Reaper acted like I thought he would," Jesse said. "Are both kids his?"

"Cassie's his," Sharon said, looking over her left shoulder at the little blond girl. "Johnny is another guy's. Asshole took off on me when he found out I was knocked up. But Reaper took to Johnny and Johnny loved Reaper. Both kids did. He was real good with them."

"Then why'd you break up with Reaper?"

"I didn't. Spider wanted me for his own."

"And that was okay with Reaper?"

"Club rules. Reaper was a probie then. You want in, whatever's yours is theirs. At least they didn't make me do all of them. I heard some gangs are like that. Spider was okay at first."

"But you weren't in the club. You didn't

have to play by their rules."

She laughed, but it had nothing to do with joy. "I needed somebody to look after me and my kids. What have I got? My father was on me twice a week since before I was thirteen. I ran away and didn't even finish ninth grade. I got a crappy job in a shithole diner in a shithole town. You do what you gotta do."

Jesse wished this was the first time he heard a story like Sharon's, but it wasn't. Not nearly. He had heard versions of this story from the day he got on the job in L.A. In Compton, in East L.A., the players and the gangs had different names. When he got to Paradise the names changed again. Sometimes the abused girls had rich fathers or Mob-connected fathers. When he was younger he used to have trouble believing the extent people would go just to belong and others just to escape. Sometimes they were the same thing. Not much surprised Jesse anymore.

"When we get back to my place, I'll get one of the neighbors to watch the kids for a few hours. We'll have some beers or something and I'll take care of you."

"No, you won't."

"Don't you think I'm pretty?" she said, wounded.

"Today especially, yes."

"But you still won't—"

"No."

"Don't you like sex?"

"**Like** is the wrong word."

"Then what's wrong? I'm real good."

"I don't doubt it," he said.

"Don't you like women?"

"Look, Sharon, I didn't do what I did because I wanted to sleep with you."

"Why, then?"

"Because it was right."

She snorted. "Right. What does that even mean?"

"Good question."

"But you know what's right?"

"Not always, but I almost always know what's wrong," he said.

"Like what?"

"Like a woman being passed around between a bunch of men like she had no say in things."

She snorted again but didn't say anything.

"What was that for?" he said.

"Women are always getting passed around between a bunch of men. That don't change, no matter what. I don't have much school, but it don't take a genius in history to see that. At least what Satan's Whores did was out in the open and nobody was pretending it was something else."

Jesse kept quiet the rest of the way until they got to Hector's apartment in Helton.

"This is your stop," Jesse said and clicked the door locks open.

Sharon didn't move immediately. It was like she was thinking of something to say.

"I want you to come in," she said. "Not because I owe it to you or nothing but because I like you."

He turned to look at her. "No, Sharon. I'm honored, but no."

She smiled at him. "Thank you, Jesse Stone. Between you and Hector, maybe there's some hope for people like me."

She leaned over and kissed Jesse on the cheek, then she slid out. Jesse got out, too, and unhitched the car seats after Sharon had brought her kids inside. He was walking back to get into the car when Sharon called after him.

He stopped and went back onto the sidewalk.

"I keep forgetting. Things have been so crazy between Spider and Hector and everything," she said.

"What is it?"

"When you came to Burt's that first time, we was talking about that older guy and his lawyer. Remember?"

"Sure."

"What I wanted to tell you was that there was somebody else that came in and sat with them for a few minutes. He made them real uncomfortable when he showed up. You could tell they all didn't like each other. I thought the guy with the pipe was going to blow a gasket. You waitress long enough, you notice stuff like that. I didn't hear it, but I think they even yelled at each other some."

"Can you describe him, the guy who came in?"

"He was about your age. Handsome, too. Carried himself like he was somebody. Do you know what I mean? His hair was turning gray, but silvery gray, not all washed-out or nothing. He had a nice smile that musta made his dentist pretty freakin' rich and he was dressed well, even though the sun was barely up."

"Vic," Jesse said to himself.

"What?"

"If you saw a photo of this guy, would you recognize him?"

"Sure I would."

Jesse took out his phone and tapped Vic's name into Google. He got a ton of hits, but the only site he was interested in was the one that showed photographs of Vic. Jesse turned the screen around to Sharon.

"This the guy?"

She nodded without hesitating a beat. "That's him."

"Perfect."

"Thanks." She hugged Jesse tight.

As he drove away, Jesse wanted to think that Sharon and her kids would be all right now that Spider had been dealt with. One thing police work and his relationship with Jenn had taught him was that people don't change easily, and not at all if they don't work at it. Sure, Sharon had it tough and had got mixed up with a lot of the wrong people, but not all of it had just happened to her. A lot of it had been because of the bad choices she'd made. Rescuing her from a bad situation wasn't going to alter her decision-making. He couldn't help but wonder what would happen the next time when he wouldn't be there to fix things. Somewhere deep down inside, he knew the answer.

63

Joe Breen was sitting in the front seat of his GTO across the street from the hotel. He was bored out of his mind and was really unhappy about it. He guessed that wasn't so unusual for him. He'd been a miserable, violent fuck his whole life. Life was a matter of survival. Any day you made it through without someone pissing on you was a good day. That was about it. He never gave life much thought beyond that. He never gave much thought to anything. All thinking ever did for Joe Breen was make him more miserable. But since the night he killed that girl, since the night he met Moira, he'd been doing a lot of thinking.

He wondered if there was life beyond Mike Frazetta. If there was a chance for a life with Moira. When he'd think about settling down with Moira, his first instinct was to mock himself. **You foolish fucker. She's likely back at your house,**

laughing up her sleeve at you. But she hadn't run. She hadn't cleaned him out. She genuinely seemed to want to take care of him. In the mornings when they'd get up, she would talk to him about how hard life was back in Ireland. How it was the place where she was from but that it was never much of a home to her. How she had always yearned for a man to build a home and life around. That was the startling thing: She had fallen even more deeply for him than he had for her. He had always hated that expression about pinching yourself to make sure you weren't dreaming. He hated it because he couldn't understand the concept. His life could never be confused with a dream. And though he hadn't yet pinched himself, he was tempted.

Dreaming of a life with Moira had its dark side. For when he thought of a happy life, of Moira's pale and lovely face, it came at a price. The price was the haunting image of Martina Penworth's nude, lifeless body tumbling out of Ben Salter's bed and onto the hardwood floor. The thud she made when she hit echoed in his ears. It twisted up his guts. Joe Breen had heard the sound of falling bodies many times. Some dead. Some not. When the dead hit a hard surface they made a sound like no other, for they were completely at the sway of gravity. They did not tense to self-protect. There was always that hollow thud. And no thud had gutted him like the sound the girl's body had made. He had never wanted redemption before. He never wanted forgiveness. Now, he thought, there would be no moving forward without it. That presented a major problem. Joe Breen hadn't the slightest notion of how to pay the bill for a commodity so precious as a young girl's life.

As the gnawing frustration of that notion had taken hold of him, Joe Breen saw Lorraine Frazetta coming out the main lobby of Vic Prado's hotel. Joe couldn't believe it. Mike had told him that Lorraine was back in Lowell, visiting her old aunt. He had no love for Lorraine. She none for him. Joe was sure Mike, with all his money and power, could have done better...much better. Maybe even if he'd been a regular working stiff, he could have done better. Lorraine was pretty enough, if you liked her type. But as much as he hated Lorraine, Joe never once thought she had cheated on or would cheat on Mike. Not because she was afraid of Mike, though that would have been reason enough. It was because she had found out back in high school what could happen if you cheated and got caught. She'd grown up poor in Lowell like the rest of them and learned you didn't risk the food on the table and the roof over your head without a really good reason.

Then Joe realized if there was anyone Lorraine would betray Mike for, it was Vic. For years Joe had suspected that Lorraine still carried a torch for Vic, regretted betraying him. Joe reached into his pocket for his cell phone and caught Lorraine as she hesitated under the hotel sign, gave the valet her parking ticket, got in the car, and drove off. He made sure to get a good shot of her license plate as she drove away.

When he was sure the coast was clear, Joe got out of the car and walked around the side of the hotel. He wasn't big on subtlety, but he wasn't as stupid as he looked or as people thought he was. Instead of trying to strong-arm the guy at the registration desk or pay him off, Joe went to where he was sure he would find some Mexicans smoking cigarettes during their breaks. Mexicans loved baseball, and he was sure one or more of them would have recognized Vic Prado. Once that happened, word would spread and they would notice every move he made inside the hotel.

He found just what he was looking for around back of the hotel, behind the hotel kitchen. Some of the Mexicans were dressed in kitchen whites and aprons. Some were dressed in black slacks, maroon golf shirts, and black shoes. There were some women there, too. Some were waitresses and some were dressed in polyester maids' outfits with white stockings and white shoes. Everyone but the kitchen help had little name tags on their chests.

Joe held up two twenty-dollar bills. That got their attention.

"Vic Prado," he said. "Room number?"

None of the hotel workers said anything. Joe didn't hesitate. He took out another twenty and a young man in a waiter's uniform stepped forward.

"Six-eighteen."

Joe handed him the money. "Thanks, Mex."

"Miguel. Not Mexican. I'm from Guatemala," he said, folding up the money and sticking it in his pocket.

Breen shook his head. "I don't care if you're from Mars." He took out two more twenties. "The woman in his room today… when did she get here and when did she leave?"

Same thing. No one answered until he added another bill.

A rotund woman with thick legs and a gap-toothed smile came to Joe.

"She come last night. Stay all night. She leave twenty minute…" She struggled for the word. She turned to a friend and said

something in Spanish. The friend
answered in kind. "She left twenty minutes ago." The housekeeper reached for
the money, but Joe pulled it back.

"And were they sleeping in separate
beds this morning, do you know?" he
said.

This really confused the housekeeper,
and she once again turned to her friend.
They had a minute-long exchange, but
this time it was the friend who spoke to
Breen.

"Rosa says she thinks the sheets will
need a lot of washing. The woman was
making a lot of moaning when Rosa tap
on the door to clean the room. She says
she wait until after this break."

Joe paid Rosa and gave the friend a
twenty. As Joe turned to go, a hotel-man-
agement type in a dark suit accompanied
by a security type approached him.

"Excuse me, sir," said the management
type. "This is an area restricted to hotel
personnel. I'll have to ask you to leave."

"No need, lad. I was going on my own."

Then the security guy made a really

dumb mistake. He blocked Joe Breen's path.

"You're not going anywhere until we find out why you were trespassing on hotel—".

In a blur, Joe gave the security type a backhand to the throat. The security guy grabbed his neck, made choking noises, and dropped to his knees. Joe gave a hard-guy look at the management type, who threw up his palms in surrender and backed away. No one followed Joe as he left. But instead of the buzz he usually felt when physicality was called for, Joe felt cold inside.

It was an unfamiliar feeling, as unfamiliar as the rest of the emotions he'd been experiencing lately. Deep down, though, he knew the cold he felt inside wasn't about this latest bit of violence. It was about Lorraine Frazetta. Until about a week ago, Joe would have delighted in trashing Lorraine's life. He could imagine watching as Mike confronted her with the video of her car pulling away from Vic's hotel. Could imagine the panic in her eyes.

Could imagine her fumbling for lies to tell. But as he got back in his car and pulled away, Joe felt no joy in the impending destruction of Lorraine's life. Mike's life would suffer, too. Joe told himself that it was really Mike he wanted to protect. That he was protecting himself, too, because he doubted Mike would thank him for bringing down his marriage. Joe knew it was a load of shite. The only person he didn't want to protect in this was Vic Prado. That was his only regret in choosing to do what he was about to do. Once he got out of Paradise, he put the gas pedal to the floor.

64

Dee finally pulled back the door. To Vic's disappointment, she wasn't nude. **So,** he thought, **she's going to make me work for it.** He could live with that. Lorraine had been no challenge at all. If he didn't need her to give him cover, she'd hardly have been worth the effort. Dee was a different story. Not only was she spectacular to look at, Vic knew she'd be good. That solitary kiss they shared back in Scottsdale had been electric, and that one feel of her under her tennis whites had stayed with him. There were times he couldn't quite believe his level of obsession with her. He had been with so many women in so many ways, yet the fantasy of Dee had persisted beyond all reason. Now she would be his bon-voyage party and gift rolled up in one hot and stormy package.

Vic stood in the hallway, Dee facing him on the other side of the threshold. He caught a whiff of that spicy perfume she wore and it set him off. **Patience be damned.** Given his plans to hit the road, he decided he wasn't in the mood to work for it. He reached out, grabbed Dee by the arm, pulling her out into the hallway. He held her arm behind her back, clutched her with his other arm, and pressed his lips hard against hers. As he kissed her, he marched her backward into the room. He reached back and slammed the door shut. But something was wrong. She stiffened in his arms. Her lips did not conform to his. She pushed back. And when he strengthened his hold on her, Dee clamped her hand over his, latched onto his thumb, and twisted it. He grunted in pain and let her go.

"What was that for?" he said, shaking the hurt out of his hand. "If you wanted to work up to it, you just could have said so."

She half smiled at him. The smile was accompanied by an unnerving tepid laugh. Still shaking his hand, Vic took a good look at her. Not only wasn't Dee nude, but she was clothed in a way he was unused to seeing her dress. Under a gray business jacket, she wore a white button-down blouse that fit so loosely it did nothing to accentuate her looks. Her matching gray pants and low black pumps were about as sexy as a catcher's mask.

"You going to a bankers' luncheon? You look like an accountant," he said.

"Funny you should say that, Vic. I used to be one."

Now **he** was laughing. "Get the hell out of here. You?"

"Me," she said, "really. In fact, technically, I still am an accountant, certified and everything."

"Cut it out, Dee. I never had an auditor that looked like you. Besides, why would a poor little rich girl need to be an accountant? What, your daddy needed someone he trusted to watch his money?"

She gave him that half-smile again as she reached over to the nightstand. Vic got a bad feeling when he saw the shape of the small black leather folder in her hand. When she flipped it open and held it out for him to read, Vic's bad feeling got considerably worse.

"Special Agent Diana Evans," Vic said as much to himself as to Dee.

"That's correct, Mr. Prado. I am an accountant, but my status with the FBI trumps that."

Vic noted that the vaguely Southern accent and come-and-get-me charm in Dee's voice had vanished. It had been replaced by a flat, cool voice with not an ounce of flirt in it.

He put his right hand over his heart. "Mr. Prado, is it? I'm hurt."

"Very funny, Vic. You'd have to have a heart for it to hurt."

"So, you're a liar," he said. "So what?"

"Undercover work requires lying some-times. I'm sure you have an encyclopedic knowledge of lying."

He stalled for time. "Yeah, maybe, but Kayla's going to be hurt. She really liked you. She trusted you."

Dee frowned. "Undercover work requires that sometimes, too. I'll explain it to her when I get the chance. She should be pretty familiar with hurt, given that she's been married to you for so long."

He shrugged. "So you mind if I ask you what all this intrigue and undercover bullshit is all about?"

"Harry Freeman," she said, as if those four syllables explained it all.

"Harry who?"

"Harry Freeman."

"Sorry," he said, "but I got nothing. Who's Harry Freeman?"

"Was."

"What?"

Her smile turned cold. "The question should be: Who was Harry Freeman? He's dead."

Vic said, "Too bad for him."

"And you."

"How's that, Dee—Diana? How is the death of some guy I don't know bad for me?"

"Murder," she said.

"Huh?"

"Harry was murdered."

"Same question."

"Harry was a college professor of mine who consulted for the Securities and Exchange Commission."

"Were you fucking him to get good grades? I bet you got all A-pluses."

She slapped Vic so hard across the face that she split his lip. When he saw that he was bleeding, he came at her. As he got close to her, she pressed the muzzle of a nine-millimeter into the soft part of his neck.

"Go ahead, Vic, give me an excuse."

He threw up his hands and backed away.

"Okay, all right, but you didn't have to slap me."

"Harry was my mentor. He guided me, took care of me. He never touched me," she said, her face distorted by grief and anger. "I'll tell you what he did do. He gave me your name and the names of your companies and told me to watch out for you. He said that something fishy was going on with the companies you were buying pieces of, that things didn't add up. He said he was about to go to the SEC and ask them to initiate an official investigation of your firms' practices. Two days later, he was murdered."

"What, somebody put a bullet in him?" Vic said. "Like on TV?"

"Something like that. He was beaten to death. The media reported it as a mugging that went wrong. How many muggings ever go that wrong? When I spoke to the investigating detective, he said he'd never seen a mugging like it. That, sure, sometimes muggings went wrong, but that when they did, people got shoved to the ground, even shot. But no mugger took the time to beat someone to death. Harry wasn't the type of man to fight back. He would have given the mugger anything he wanted. Pretty convenient for you, Harry getting killed that way. When he died, the investigation into your little financial empire died with him."

"Sorry to hear about your friend, but where's the connection to me? Sounds pretty thin."

"I don't care how it sounds to you. Maybe it's the kind of thing your pal Joe Breen might do. What do you think?"

But if she thought mentioning Breen's name was going to get a rise out of Prado, she was wrong.

"Joe Breen's not my friend," Vic said. "That miserable bastard doesn't have friends."

"So you admit you know him?"

"For a long time. We grew up in the same neighborhood."

"With Mike and Lorraine Frazetta," she said.

"Yeah. So what?" He shrugged. "I know Mike, Lorraine, and Joe Breen. I'm sure if I looked into your background I'd find some people you knew who you wouldn't be so proud of knowing."

She holstered the automatic and handed the surveillance photos to Vic. He looked at them without so much as blinking.

"I hate to keep repeating myself," he said, "but so what? I was visiting an old friend. Mike was my buddy in high school and Lorraine was my girlfriend. So the cops got pictures of me visiting them. Big deal."

"I got you, Vic," she said halfheartedly.

He threw the photos on the bed.

"You got nothing. You're desperate.

You're fishing." He smiled that white charming smile of his as he wiped the blood from his mouth. "You made yourself a part of my life and of Kayla's for a year and you came up empty. Let me explain something to you. You shouldn't mix your heart up in your business. It makes you blind. Worse, it makes you stupid. And revenge, it makes you even stupider and blinder than love. I'm leaving now. I'm willing to let this go without making a thing about it, but you come near me again and I'll sue you and the Bureau up the wazoo."

"This isn't over, Vic."

"Oh yes it is, darlin'," he said, mocking her. "It's more over than you know." He started for the door, then hesitated. "You should have let me have you. I wanted you so bad, it might have worked better than this. This…this was stupid. This was amateur hour. Good-bye." He blew her a kiss and left.

When the door shut, she slumped onto the bed. Vic was right. She'd been stupid and desperate. He was right about something else: She should have slept with him. That couldn't have been any worse a disaster than this. If there had been a white flag available or anyone to wave it at, she would have been waving it.

At the elevator, Vic pressed the down arrow. Dee or Diana or whatever the hell her name really was had done him a favor. The time had come to get gone. So he didn't even bother going back to his room. Instead, he texted his lawyer and had the doorman get him a cab.

65

When Jesse walked through the station-house door, Molly gave him a look that told him nothing good had come of the stuff he'd asked her to do.

"Give me a minute and then come into my office," he said as he passed her.

As he sat behind his desk, Jesse wanted nothing more than to pour himself six fingers of Black Label. It had been a hell of a shift so far, and he was only halfway through it. He put his .38 away, then reached for his glove instead of the bottle in his desk drawer. As he pounded the ball into the perfectly formed leather pocket of his old Rawlings, he tried to clear his head. Sharon hadn't called his cell phone, so he couldn't be sure that it was Vic Prado who'd met with Harlan Salter and Monty Bernstein. **What if it was? If it was, why? And could there be any connection between Vic, Martina Penworth's murder, and the Salter kid's abduction?** Those questions had kept their grip on him for the entire ride back from Helton to Paradise. Driving hadn't helped him make any sense of it. He put the glove down just as Molly knocked and came in.

"How did keeping your word go?" Molly said.

"It worked out in the short run. What have you got?"

She handed him a small slip of paper with a phone number on it. "That's the number in Taos you asked me to get. I'm not so sure you'll want to call it yet."

"Why's that?"

"Boston PD towed Kayla Prado's rental car late yesterday afternoon. It already had four tickets under the wiper for unpaid meters when they hooked it up and brought it to the impound lot."

Jesse said, "Not good, but I could explain that away. Maybe she was running late for the airport. Decided to take a cab instead of trying to get to Logan on her own. Maybe the car didn't start. Could be a hundred reasons."

"Do you believe any of that, Jesse?"

"No."

"She never made it to the airport. At least not to the flight she booked. She'd checked in online that morning but never showed at the gate. She hasn't tried to rebook."

"Damn."

"It gets worse, Jesse."

"How could it get worse? Did they find her bod—"

"Nothing like that, but it's still not good. After I alerted them about Kayla as a possible suicide candidate, Boston PD did some canvassing around the street her car was towed from." Molly hesitated, taking a deep breath. "It didn't take them long to find someone who'd spotted her. There's a witness who claims to have seen a woman fitting Kayla Prado's description involved in an incident on her block. She claims that the woman fitting Kayla's description fainted on the sidewalk and was helped into a car by a man."

"What man? What car?"

Molly handed Jesse several more sheets of paper. "It's all there. Boston PD faxed over the witness statement. You can read it later. The crib-notes version is that the witness couldn't describe the man beyond saying he was on the small side. He might or might not have been wearing glasses. The witness thinks the man had on a dark blue suit that might have been black. She says there wasn't much memorable about him. Strange because she described Kayla Prado perfectly and described the car as a white Honda or Nissan. She got a partial tag number, too."

"Between the description of the car and the partial, it should narrow things down."

"Yeah," Molly said, "to about two thousand cars, give or take. I've got the list on my computer if you want me to send it over. Even if we eliminate the cars from the western half of the state, it would take us a week to individually check out all these cars."

"Did you check with the hospitals? Maybe she really did just faint," Jesse said.

"Checked with most of the hospitals between here and Boston. Nothing. I've got a notice out to the rest of the hospitals in the state and the rest of New England."

"Maybe I should go talk to Vic. He needs to hear this, and there's a chance he might know something about what's going on."

Molly made a face that Jesse couldn't decipher.

"Put it into words, Crane."

"While you were over in Helton on that mysterious mission to keep your word, we had an interesting incident happen at the hotel. Some big guy went into a restricted area and assaulted Connor Cavanaugh. He—"

"Connor Cavanaugh?" Jesse said.

"Played fullback with Suit. Then linebacker at UMass. Had a training camp with the Pats. Now he's head of security at the hotel."

"Go on."

"When Cavanaugh and the hotel manager confront the trespasser, the guy gave Cavanaugh a chop to the throat and put him down. Suit took the report."

Jesse was losing patience. "Okay, Molly,

but what's this got to do with Kayla Prado or Vic?"

"I'm getting to that. This big guy was questioning the help about Vic and some woman he had with him in his room last night."

That got Jesse's full attention. He stood up and paced in front of the window.

"We have a description of the big guy and of this woman who stayed with Vic? Could it have been Kayla?"

"Yes. Yes. And no," she said. "Suit got a description of both the guy who attacked Cavanaugh and of the woman, but she wasn't Kayla. She had black hair, was attractive enough, but besides those two things the description doesn't match Kayla Prado."

"Okay. I think it's time I go have a talk with my old infield partner."

"You can try."

Jesse said, "What's that supposed to mean?"

"It means Suit thought he should warn Vic Prado after he took the report. According to Cavanaugh, this big guy was pretty menacing, so Suit thought he should give Vic a heads-up."

Jesse smiled. He had always been on Suit to show initiative, to act on his instincts. After all these years, Jesse was glad his lessons were paying off. Then he realized that Suit might have simply wanted Vic's autograph. Either way, it was the smart move.

"What happened when Suit spoke to Vic?"

"That's the point. Suit never got the chance. Vic wasn't in his room, and when Suit asked around, the doorman said he got a cab for Vic that afternoon."

"Did the doorman hear where Vic was headed?"

"No, but it wasn't local because the doorman heard the cabbie saying that a trip out that way wasn't on the meter, but a flat rate."

"All right," he said, retrieving his .38 and reloading it. "I'm going over to the hotel. Something's going on here."

"Something like what?"

"If I knew, I wouldn't have to go over

there."

Molly shook her head, smirking. "I wish I was smart like you. Then maybe they'd make **me** chief."

"Maybe."

"Should I ask you why you need to reload your weapon?"

"Probably not."

"Keeping your word took five bullets?"

"Four," he said. "One was just for show. Didn't I tell you not to ask?"

"You suggested it. That's different."

"From now on, when your chief makes a suggestion, take it as an order."

She stuck her tongue out at him.

"Very nice."

But their banter fell flat. They had both been cops too long to think there was an innocent explanation for what had happened to Kayla Prado. Jesse handed the slip of paper with Kayla's parents' phone number back to Molly.

"Call them up. Pretend to be a friend from Scottsdale. I want to make sure she really didn't get there. Try not to scare them."

Molly said, "They're probably already scared."

"You may be right. Do your best."

Jesse walked past her. She chased after him and caught him before he made it to the front door.

"Jesse!"

He stopped. "What?"

"I almost forgot. A woman called. Said her name was Sharon."

"Yeah."

"She said you were right. She looked online and that was the guy at Burt's. She also said to thank you again."

Jesse smiled for a brief moment, but not brief enough that Molly hadn't noticed.

"Is this another one of those things you'd suggest I not ask about?"

"You're finally catching on, Crane. Maybe they **will** make you chief someday," he said.

He left without another word.

Joe Breen waited for Lorraine Frazetta's car at a corner three turns away from his boss's house. No matter which direction she approached from, she would have to pass this corner. It was far enough away that even if the cops had eyes on the house, they wouldn't be here. And on the odd chance that they were following Lorraine, it wouldn't seem strange to the cops for Mike's right-hand man to have a chat with Mike's wife. Joe thought that was kind of funny because the only people it would seem strange to were the three of them. While Mike Frazetta didn't quite understand the depth of the animosity between his wife and Joe, he knew there was no love lost between them.

Joe watched the oncoming traffic in his sideview mirror and waited. He didn't think he'd missed her. Although she drove a sports car, she wasn't a fast driver. Nor was Lorraine the kind of woman to go directly home. She was always stopping for coffee or to shoe-shop or to buy some flowers for the house. Joe couldn't remember a time when Lorraine came back to the house empty-handed. She was always carrying something in with her that she didn't have on the way out. He figured it was one of the ways she coped with growing up poor. He found himself wishing he'd found a better way to deal with his own rotten childhood.

Just as he began to worry that this was the one time she would make an exception, Joe spotted Lorraine's black Corvette Grand Sport turning onto the block and heading his way. He got out of his GTO only when there was no chance she could back up to avoid him. He stood in the middle of the street, waving his palms at the pavement for her to slow down. When she came to a stop, he walked around to her window. But Lorraine wasn't happy about being ambushed this way and refused to roll down her darkly tinted window. He rapped his knuckles on the glass until she did.

"All right, all right!" she said, relenting. "What the fuck do you want?"

"To save your life."

"Get outta here!" She hit the switch to roll up the window.

"I know about you and Vic," he said, plenty loud enough for her to hear.

The window stopped going up, then came down halfway.

She put on a puzzled face. "I don't know what you're talking about."

"Don't you, now?"

Joe pulled his cell phone from his pocket, scrolled to what he was looking for, tapped the screen, and turned it to face Lorraine. She watched herself coming out the front door of Vic's hotel, hesitating, handing the valet her parking stub.

She shoved the phone back at Breen. "Enough, enough. Mike had you follow me?" Her face was calm. Her voice was brittle and thick with fear.

"Was Vic I was keeping an eye on, not you."

"That video is bullshit. It doesn't prove anything."

Joe shook his head. "Proves you're a liar. How's your old, feeble aunt in Lowell doing?"

"Vic called when I was heading to Lowell. He asked me to come visit. He was sick. His wife left him and he needed a friend."

"Easily enough checked out with phone records," he said. "But I don't think you'll want to push back too hard on that, Lorraine. I've talked to the staff at the hotel. They described you as if they had known you their whole lives. And apparently you've got quite the singing voice when you're properly inspired."

She sagged in her seat. "Okay, what do you want?"

"For you to follow me. We can't talk out here in the street much longer."

Twenty minutes later they were seated on a bench by the Frog Pond in Boston Common. Both of them feeling awkward as could be.

"So," she said, "how much do you want? I've got my own money that Mike's given me to—"

"Keep it. I've money enough."

"Then what? If you tell Mike, he'll kill me. He'll kill Vic."

"Maybe he would. I'm not at all sure. Was a time not long ago I would have done it with a smile on my face. For most of my life there were scarcely two people I disliked more than you two."

Lorraine said, "Something's changed?"

"It has."

"What?"

"That's my business alone, Lorraine. Be glad we're having this talk instead of me having it with Mike."

"Okay, Joe."

"Vic's going to take a runner, isn't he?"

The surprised look on Lorraine's face was answer enough.

She said, "How did you know?"

"I don't have use for the man, but he was always sharp. He could read the writing on the wall. Good athletes like Vic have the knack of slowing the world down and seeing what's coming around the bend."

"You mean Mike was going to—"

"No need for you to be concerned with

what Mike was or wasn't going to do," Joe said. "What you need to do is to tell me what he told you. The truth."

She didn't answer, clamping her lips tightly shut.

Joe didn't figure she would be eager to give Vic up, so he let her have a moment of bravery before explaining the facts of life.

"The choice is yours, Lorraine. I've got to tell Mike something. Either I tell him about the both of you or of Vic. Odds are Vic's already gone, so it's unlikely we'd be able to get to him now in any case. But if you don't give him up to me, I'll give you up to Mike. I'll have no choice. I'm saving your life here, but not at the cost of me own. Things between us have not changed that much."

"But how will you explain to Mike how you know about Vic leaving?" she said.

"You let that be my worry. Just know that if you tell me the truth now, you'll be safe. Mike will never hear a word of what I know of you and Vic," Joe said, feeling the grass beneath the bench for a pebble to toss in the pond.

"How can I be sure you won't ever use the video against me?"

He found a few pebbles between the blades of grass. He clicked them together, shaking them in his fist.

He said, "You have my word."

Lorraine wasn't buying. "What's your word worth."

"To anyone but Mike, not much. Like I say, things have changed." He lobbed a smooth pebble into the pond and watched the ripples. "The choice is yours." He threw in a second pebble so that another set of ripples echoed along the surface.

"He's going down to Mexico and then to Belize. He said he would send for me when he was settled."

Joe Breen turned to Lorraine and gave her the familiar cold stare many of his victims had seen before dying. "Is that the truth?"

Crying now, she said, "I don't know if it's the truth. I wanted it to be. But it is what he told me. I swear on my mother's life."

Joe scrolled down to the video of Lorraine once again, he tapped the screen until the option menu came up, and handed her the phone.

"All you need do is tap **erase**."

She didn't hesitate, then handed him back the phone.

"Go home to Mike, Lorraine, and don't say a word of any of this. Not of Vic and not of our talk. Not ever."

She stood and looked down at the man who just spared her, the man she had spent most of her life hating.

"Why, Joe?" she said, confusion and curiosity compelling her to ask.

Thinking of Moira and Martina Penworth, he tossed a third pebble in the pond and ignored Lorraine's question. It wasn't important for her to know the answer. It was only important for him to know.

67

Jesse was seated at the head of a conference table. Connor Cavanaugh was seated to his immediate right, and Warren Stroby, the hotel's assistant manager, was to his immediate left. Also seated at the table were Rosa the housekeeper; her translator, Maricela; Miguel the waiter; and Dave Stockton, the doorman. They'd been there for almost an hour and had gone over their stories three or four times. Of course, only Stroby, Cavanaugh, and Stockton had told the full truth. The others weighed the truth against losing their jobs. Taking money to divulge guest information wasn't exactly encouraged by management.

"Chief Stone, do you mind if I ask **you** a question?" Stroby said.

"Go ahead."

"I'm not a cop, but this all seems pretty straightforward to me. We've been here going over this again and again."

Jesse said, "You mentioned a question. Is there one in there?"

"Sorry." Stroby bowed his head. "To what end are we repeating ourselves?"

"Because I'm looking for something."

"What?" Stroby said.

"If I knew, I'd tell you. Part of police work is teasing information out of people. Often it's information they don't know they have. There are times it's information we don't even know we're looking for. That's what we're doing here."

Stroby didn't seem any more pleased than he was when he broached the subject.

"I'm sorry, Chief, but I can't afford to have all these employees away from their stations any longer. I'll have to ask you to let these folks return to their duties."

Jesse wanted to argue the point, but he knew the assistant manager was right. This wasn't a homicide investigation. He couldn't justify keeping all these people here indefinitely because he had a hunch. It wasn't even a hunch. It was more of a feeling, a feeling that all the things that had happened in Paradise lately were somehow connected.

"Okay, I'm going to speak to each one of you individually for a few minutes." Jesse spoke slowly so that Maricela could relay the information to Rosa. "After I'm done speaking to you, you can head back to your jobs."

Stroby still wasn't pleased, but he knew it was the best he was going to do.

About a half-hour later, Jesse still hadn't found what he was looking for. What he had found out from the doorman was that Vic Prado had left the hotel in a Paradise Taxi driven by a guy named Al Gleason. The last two people left in the conference room were Jesse and Connor Cavanaugh. Cavanaugh looked the part of a linebacker gone slightly to seed. He hadn't been very talkative in front of the others. It wasn't hard to figure. Ex-jocks, especially tough guys like Cavanaugh, don't respond well to getting taken down in public. Jesse knew the feeling, so he came at Cavanaugh sideways.

"Heard you played ball with Luther

Simpson," Jesse said. "Suit's a good man."

"Yep. We had a helluva high school team. Luther was tougher than he looked. If he wanted to work harder at it, I bet he could've made a pretty decent D-two program."

"Don't have to tell me. He's one of my best men. Rumor is you played for the Pats."

Cavanaugh's chest puffed out a little, his back straightened. He rode higher in his chair.

"Made it all the way through training camp to last cut," he said, suddenly very animated. "I got some tape of me from a nationally televised game against the Chargers. Made three special teams tackles. One...bang!" He punched his right fist into his left palm. "Took the punt returner five minutes to get up, I hit him so hard. After I got cut and no one picked me up, I went to one of those indie police academies down in the Carolinas and got my certification. I did some small-town policing for a few years and wound up back here."

"So, Connor, this asshole that sucker-punched you...can you tell me anything about him that you haven't already told me or the others haven't said?"

Unlike earlier, when the security man quickly blurted out one-word answers, he quietly considered Jesse's question.

Then he said, "I don't know if this means anything...I mean, it's kind of stupid."

"Let me worry about if it's stupid or not."

"The guy that coldcocked me is a big Celtics fan."

"Not exactly shocking around these parts," Jesse said.

Cavanaugh flushed red. "See, I told you it was stupid."

"No. No. How do you know he's a Celtics fan?" Jesse checked his notes and Suit's preliminary report. "Says here the guy that got you in the throat was wearing a black leather jacket over faded Levi's. So how do you know he was a—"

"Sneakers."

Jesse said, "What about his sneakers?"

"Celtic green with white stripes."

"Stripes?"

"Yeah," Cavanaugh said. "Three stripes. They were Adidas b-ball high-tops, old school–style."

Jesse had just found what he didn't know he was looking for. He sat in stunned silence as he went over the crime scene report of Martina Penworth's murder in his head.

"Connor, this is going to sound like a dumb question, but please try to concentrate. Only answer it if you're sure. No guessing, okay?"

"Sure, Chief."

"This Celtic fan, he have big feet or little feet?"

Cavanaugh didn't have to think about it. "Big, size twelve or thirteen."

"How can you be sure of that?"

Connor Cavanaugh smiled. "Remember Mr. P's Shoes on Skiff Street off Main, closed a few years ago?"

"Sure," Jesse said.

"Mr. P is my dad. Him and Mom retired to Sarasota. I worked in the store since I was a kid and all through college, too. I tell you he was a size twelve or thirteen, you can take it to the bank."

Jesse excused himself, got out his cell phone, and punched in Molly's number.

"I think we might finally have something on the Penworth homicide. I think the guy that attacked Connor Cavanaugh at the hotel today might be our man. Use the description in Suit's report."

"Anything else?"

"He wears size-twelve or -thirteen Celtic green Adidas basketball shoes just like the imprint forensics found at the Salter house. Call it in to Healy. I'm going to have Cavanaugh come down to look at mug shots."

"Which database?"

"All of them, but start him off with the Mass Department of Corrections and Boston."

"Connor will be here for a week, Jesse."

"Look, the guy we're looking for is Caucasian, blue-eyed, six-three, with brown hair, in his late thirties or early forties. That's got to eliminate a lot of candidates."

"This state's second-biggest crop is tough white boys."

"What can I say, Crane? Make a big pot of coffee and get a comfortable chair ready for him. We don't have much choice at this point."

He clicked off.

Jesse found Connor Cavanaugh again. "You have a passkey?"

"Sure do."

"Come on. I need a favor."

They found their way to the elevator. Jesse pressed the button for the sixth floor.

68

Cavanaugh wasn't pleased about having to go down to the station to look at mug shots after his shift. He was even less pleased about letting Jesse into Vic Prado's room even if Jesse was police chief. He had tried unsuccessfully to convince Jesse to get a warrant. Jesse wasn't completely unsympathetic, but he sensed he didn't have time to do things by the book. He suggested Cavanaugh simply give him the passkey.

"I'll let myself in," Jesse said. "This way, you're protected."

"Thanks, Chief, but I'd feel better if I was with you. Besides, we got cameras in every hallway. You'll be on video going in and out of the room with a key that'll get traced back to me no matter what."

"Suit yourself."

Cavanaugh needn't have worried. The bed was newly made, the floors vacuumed, the towels fresh—some still warm.

All they found in Vic's room was a few days' worth of Vic's clothes, a designer suitcase, some jewelry—including a World Series ring—and toiletries. Jesse held the World Series ring in his hand, slipped it on his ring finger. He had seen them on TV, met some coaches and guys in the minors who had them, but he'd never actually tried one on. Jesse lost himself for a moment, first rushing on fantasy, then crashing on the reality that but for a stupid exhibition game in Pueblo, he might have had one of these rings of his own. He couldn't imagine anyone ever walking away from a World Series ring as if it were a plastic toy from a Cracker Jack box. Yet Jesse sensed his old double-play partner was gone with the wind. He turned to Connor Cavanaugh.

Jesse said, "You've got video on all the movements in the hallway?"

"Lobby, bar, valet parking lot...elevators, too. You'd be amazed at what some guests get up to in the elevators." Cavanaugh winked at Jesse.

"I was a cop in L.A. for ten years. Trust

me, I wouldn't be amazed."

"I guess not."

"You mind me having a look at your video from today?"

"Sure, why not?"

They were down in the bowels of the hotel in a dank, windowless room about as welcoming as a bed of nails. The concrete-block walls were painted pistachio green. Two fluorescent light fixtures hung from the ceiling, one of the tubes displaying an irregular tic. There was a long metal table and a taped-up office chair. In contrast to the setting, there was a slick-looking bank of black-and-white monitors covering the entire wall directly before the table. Each monitor had a plastic black-and-white plaque at its base that indicated the area covered by the camera feeding that particular monitor. On the table itself was the computer that controlled the system. The odor of burnt coffee cut against the earthy mildew scent of the place. Jesse turned, noticing a coffee-maker on a beat-up hotel nightstand. The orange warming plate light was lit, but the liquid in the pot was black and thick as caulk.

"Help yourself," Cavanaugh said.

"No, thanks. I've had enough of that kind of coffee."

"We put in some long hours down here."

Jesse turned back to the monitors. "Pretty sophisticated."

"My idea. Before I got here, they used to have an old videotape system without much coverage. Now we cover almost everything. All the feeds are time- and date-stamped and compressed. It's digital, so we can access individual monitors or any combination if we need to. We can speed right through sections without having to slog through hours of tape."

"Any video on the guy with the green sneakers?"

Cavanaugh shrugged. "Not anything worth looking at. He didn't walk through the hotel. He was either very smart or very lucky."

"Can you give me what you got today on Vic's hallway from...let's say from nine this morning?"

Cavanaugh stepped in front of Jesse. He tapped on the keyboard. Told Jesse to sit.

"Here you go, Chief." Cavanaugh pointed at the computer screen. "That's Mr. Prado's room there. You can use the joystick, rollerball mouse, or the keyboard arrows to move forward or back. You see an image you want to capture as a still, hit this button. It will pause the video. Then I can print the image for you."

Jesse scrolled through the video, Rosa the housekeeper playing a starring role. A hotel guest or two made cameo appearances. Because of the speed at which he moved through the video, the movements of the people on screen reminded Jesse of old silent Westerns. The flickering light above him added to the strobing effect. Then, when Jesse spotted Vic's door opening, he slowed the action to normal speed, then slower than normal. Out stepped an attractive woman about his own age. The woman didn't seem to want to leave. Instead, she stood by the open door, turned back, facing into the room.

Vic appeared, partially in shadow. Clutched the woman tightly to him. Kissed her long and hard on the mouth. They stared at each other. Neither seeming to speak. The door closed. The woman hesitated again, turned to go, took a few tentative steps toward the elevator, stopped, looked behind her, wiped her eyes, and left.

Jesse said to Cavanaugh, "Can you get me a still of the woman's face?"

"Sure. I'll clean it up and enlarge it for you."

A minute later, the printer kicked on and out came a clear shot of Lorraine Frazetta.

"Do you know if she valet-parked her car?"

"We can check," Cavanaugh said, leaning over Jesse's shoulder, tapping at the keyboard again. "There you go, she's handing her ticket to the valet. Here he comes driving it up to the front entrance. Nice car."

Before Jesse asked, Cavanaugh printed out a still of the Corvette, clearly showing its tag number. He called the number in to

Molly.

"Also, try to track down Al Gleason from Paradise Taxi. I need to speak to him."

Jesse asked Cavanaugh to get him back to the video on Vic's hall. When the video showed Vic leaving his room and stopping by the elevator, Jesse asked Cavanaugh if he could follow Vic's progress. The security man leaned over Jesse's shoulder once again.

"Okay, here he is in the elevator," Cavanaugh said. "He pressed the button for three."

More keyboard tapping.

"Here he is getting off the elevator at three. He's turning. Hold on."

More tapping.

"Here he is again. He's stopping by room 323. You can take it from here, Chief."

Jesse let the video run forward. When he did, he got a knot in his gut. He hadn't felt this way since the day he found out Jenn had been cheating on him with some smarmy Hollywood producer. Jesse stood up from the chair and, in a monotone voice that barely seemed to belong to him, thanked Cavanaugh for his help.

Cavanaugh stared at the frozen image on the screen of Vic Prado kissing the woman in room 323.

"Hey, Chief Stone, don't you want me to print a still of this for you?"

Jesse didn't answer. He kept walking down the hall. When the elevator doors closed, he pressed the button for the third floor.

69

Jesse held himself stiffly as he walked right past Molly and the heavyset man sitting next to her desk. All Jesse could see was Vic Prado kissing Dee. It played over and over and over again in his head. He walked into his office, slamming the door behind him. He looked at his glove, shook his head, and pulled open the drawer with the bottle inside. Not many things got to him like this, but he did have his blind spots, and when things came at him from those dark places, they tended to crush him. He was feeling pretty damn crushed at the moment. The trick, he told himself, was not to let anyone else see the damage. He told himself that's what the drinking was for, to camouflage the wounds. He took his time with the drink, trying to focus on it, the liquor's flavor, the amber color, the spreading warmth, instead of what had driven him to it. But it was no good. It did nothing to erase the image of Dee locked in Vic Prado's embrace, his lips pressing against hers. Jesse didn't pride himself on his imagination, but it didn't take much imagination to figure out what happened next. He poured another drink.

By the time Jesse had made it up to Dee's room from the hotel basement, she was gone. When he asked after her at the front desk, the young woman stationed there told him that Dee had checked out.

Dave Stockton had gotten her a cab, and no, he didn't know where it had taken her. Jesse thought he had a pretty good idea of where she'd gone. Not where she had gone, exactly, but who she had gone to meet up with. **How convenient for them,** he thought, **Kayla disappearing.** It had taken all he had to hold himself together. He was no longer in the frame of mind to hold himself together.

Molly knocked. She didn't bother waiting for him to answer.

He slammed his hand on his desk. "Damn it, Molly! Did I tell you to come in here?"

"Watch it, Jesse. You don't want to knock over your drink."

He grabbed the scotch and poured it into the soil of a philodendron that was already on its last legs.

"What is it?"

"I got Al Gleason outside."

"Who?"

"Al Gleason! The cabdriver."

It took a few seconds for it to register. Molly noticed.

"Jesse, are you all right? You're acting—"

"Send him in," Jesse said.

"In a minute. I spoke to Kayla's dad. She never made it to Taos."

"Is he worried?"

"Not worried, concerned, but he says she's pulled stuff like this before. She's called and said she wants time to think and then doesn't show. She calls a few days later and apologizes for not showing up. Mostly the father grumbled about how Vic ruined Kayla's life."

"You didn't mention the abduction."

"For crissakes, Jesse, give me a little

credit."

"Sorry. Anything on the white car?"

"Nothing yet."

"Send Gleason in," Jesse said, sitting back down behind his desk.

Gleason smelled like old cigar smoke and coffee. He wore a dirty tweed cap and a windbreaker that fit him ten years and thirty pounds ago.

Jesse introduced himself.

"We've met. We play you four times a year in softball. You're a pretty good ballplayer," Gleason said.

"Thanks. I'll have that etched on my headstone."

"Huh?"

"Never mind. You had a fare today, a guy about my age. You took him from the hotel—"

"Vic Prado. Yeah, I drove him from the hotel to a gas station north of Lowell on the New Hampshire border."

"You guys talk much?"

"Nah. After he gave me the address, he kept his head down and his mouth shut, but I could tell he knew I knew who he was even with that black eye of his."

Jesse said, "How's that?"

"Chief, you drive a cab as long as me, you can tell. I saw it in his eyes when I looked in the rearview. You know when fares want to talk and you know when they don't. He didn't."

"You sound sure of yourself."

Gleason laughed and his belly jiggled. "Yeah, well, he tipped me a hundred bucks on top of the fare. I didn't figure it was for my good looks. That's keep-your-mouth-shut money, pure and simple."

"So why aren't you keeping your mouth shut?"

"I got to earn a living, you know. The cops can screw up my license." Gleason slapped his belly. "Believe it or not, Chief, I got other mouths to feed and not many marketable skills beyond my charm and driving a cab."

"If you two didn't talk on the ride up, what did Prado do to entertain himself?"

"Texted a lot."

"And when you got to this gas station, what happened?" Jesse said.

Gleason made a face. "Nothing. He settled up. Gave me the hush money and got out of the cab. I asked him if he wanted to wait for his ride in my cab. He didn't look happy about that and told me to go. So I went."

"You're sure he was waiting for a ride?"

"No, but what the hell else was he going to do out in the middle of nowheres?"

"Good question."

"Did he have any luggage?"

"Nope. Just the shirt on his back and the pants on his backside."

"Did you give Officer Crane the address where you dropped off Prado?" Jesse said.

"I did."

Jesse extended his right arm. They shook hands.

"Thanks for coming in."

"Always happy to help the police."

"Do me a favor, Al, ask Officer Crane to come in here, please."

"Sure thing. I'll enjoy watching her walk," Gleason said, a lecherous smile on his face. "She's got the best ass I ever seen on a cop."

Jesse gave the cabbie a look that would have given Medusa a run for her money.

"Sorry. Yeah, sure."

Jesse was feeling more like himself until the door closed behind the cabbie. The second it did, that image of Vic and Dee rushed back into his head. And there it got jumbled up with images of Jenn and Elliot Krueger, of Kayla at twenty-one and the young Vic Prado. He had lots of luck with women whom he didn't love, but none with those he did.

This time Molly's presence felt like a lifeline.

"If you ever decide to take another lover," Jesse said, "I think Al the cabbie just volunteered."

"Ick! I need to take a shower now."

"Not yet. I want you to call the gas station where—"

"Done. Gas station owner, a Turkish guy, says a van came and picked Vic up about fifteen minutes after he was dropped off by Gleason. And before you ask, no, he didn't get a plate number. He didn't know what state issued the plates. There were no markings on the van. He didn't look at the driver and didn't recognize Vic. I guess baseball's not so popular in Ankara."

"Dead end."

"Looks that way, but I got a hit on the plate number you called in. That Vette is registered to a Lorraine Frazetta of—"

"Frazetta as in Mike Frazetta as in Boston Mob Frazetta?"

"Give the chief a Kewpie doll," Molly said. "She's Mike Frazetta's wife."

"And Vic Prado's lover."

"So he was sleeping with a Mob boss's wife. Do you think that's why he ran?"

"I don't know. With what's going on lately, I feel like I know less and less as more and more happens. I know everything fits together somehow, but how?"

Molly tilted her head. "Everything? You think the guy with the green shoes is connected to Vic Prado's skipping town and Kayla's disappearance?"

"Everything, as in everything that's happened in Paradise since the day I left for the reunion. I feel like there's one thing that I'm not seeing and the harder I concentrate on it, the further away it gets."

"Have you talked to Kayla's friend, the one who—"

"She's gone. Let's drop that subject."

"Okay, Jesse, you're chief, but you're also my friend and for some odd reason I love you. What's going on with you?"

"I'll be okay."

"You always say that."

"Isn't it always true?" he said.

Molly shook her head. "No. And I don't want to have to come to your house tomorrow morning with Suit and scrape you off the floor."

"I had a bad moment before. Forget it."

"Forgotten. When's Connor Cavanaugh coming in?"

Jesse looked at his watch. "His shift's over soon. I told him to come straight over and that we'd get him dinner."

"How about breakfast?"

"Lunch, too, if it takes him that long. And if he can't find the guy, we'll get the other hotel employees in to have a look. We're going to play our one card. Now get out of here."

She hesitated.

"What?" Jesse said, noticing Molly hadn't moved.

She didn't answer.

He reached into his bottom drawer and took out the bottle of Black Label. He held it out to her. "Here, go water the rest of the plants."

70

He was hungry and cold, pacing the dock and rubbing his arms for warmth. The dusk air in that part of eastern New Hampshire was crisper than he would have expected this late in spring. As he gazed at the boarded-up summer home behind him, he regretted not having stopped to buy a hooded sweatshirt or something to eat. It occurred to him only after the van had dropped him off an hour ago that he hadn't eaten all day. He supposed he could have asked the van driver—a man who could be trusted, his lawyer assured him—to pull over and buy him some supplies, but he hadn't been thinking straight. He was so close to getting out of the mess Joe Breen had created, and he was consumed by the enormity of the step he was about to take. Making contingencies to walk away from one's life, Vic realized, was much easier than the act of walking away itself.

For the last sixty minutes, the only sounds he'd heard were the noises in his head and the slapping of lake water against the dock pilings. Before he could see it, he noticed a distant buzzing that grew louder and louder in the dying light. Then he saw it, the mustard-yellow seaplane, its pontoons slung beneath it like clumsy silver clown shoes. It flew in a descending arc over the surrounding pines before touching down on the rippled surface of the water. It took an eternity for the little plane to make its way to the dock, but as it floated nearer to him, Vic's old life seemed to retreat. Not even the acrid stench of spent gas on hot metal from the plane's motor could ruin his mood. The pilot flung the door open and called for him to throw him a tie line. He hesitated, then reached down and tossed the pilot a thick nylon rope.

That was ten minutes ago. Now Vic sat in the Piper Super Cub, eating a ham-and-cheese sandwich, a blanket over his shoulders. Both supplied by the pilot. The pilot, who'd gone to stretch his legs a little and let out some water before taking off again.

Never had a sandwich tasted so good. It took Vic back to his days in the minors when he got only a few bucks a day for meal money. He and Jesse used to exist on bologna and white bread so they could save up their meal money. For some reason he felt that turning his back on those days with Jesse and Kayla in Albuquerque would be a greater loss than his memories of the World Series. He wondered if the reunion wasn't more about that than anything else. That he knew his notion of a plea deal worked out by Jesse and his connections was always a pipe dream. He had just wanted to give those days a proper sendoff. Because of Joe Breen, Vic would never know the truth. There was only one thing to do now, to run, and he was doing it. The plane bobbed in the water, gently rocking him into a state of serenity. He guessed he was okay with making a new life for himself.

Then the electronic strains of "Take Me Out to the Ball Game" smashed the serenity of the moment into fragments large and small. That ridiculous song echoed through the trees, mocking him. He was tempted to throw the phone into the lake, which he intended to do, in any case, before the plane took off. But something, maybe that sense of timing he possessed that had allowed him to be such a fine ballplayer, made him look at the screen.

"Kayla!"

"Vic, Vic, help me."

She spoke slowly, slurring one word into the next.

"Are you drunk? Are you—"

"He's going to kill me, Vic."

"Who's going to kill you? Kay, what's wrong? What's going—"

A man's voice interrupted Vic's flurry of questions.

"Mr. Prado, if you want to save your wife from a very slow and painful death, please shut up and listen carefully."

The man's voice was nasal and high-pitched, a difficult voice to take seriously. And Vic, like many people before him, made the mistake of doing just that.

"Listen to me, you little motherfu—"

Now Kayla's screams echoed through the phone and into the trees. She sounded as if she were being burned alive.

"All right. All right! I'm listening. Just stop doing what you're doing to her."

Kayla's screams faded quickly into sobbing.

"That's more like it," the voice said. "What I did to her was very painful, but she will recover. The human body is quite resilient. That can be good or bad, and that is dependent on what you do next."

"I'm listening."

"After I've given you instructions, do exactly as I've said. Do not deviate. Do not hesitate. Do not alert anyone else, most especially the police. Do not try to trick me. I assure you I will know. Even if I think you've lied to me, I will cause your wife more pain than you can possibly imagine. Is that understood?"

"Yes."

When the voice was almost done giving instructions, Vic interrupted.

"I'm sorry for speaking, but I'm very far away from there."

"Are you stalling?"

"No, I swear. I swear I'm telling you the truth. I'm almost out of the country."

"That is not my concern. The clock is ticking, and when I'm satisfied you've had enough time, it will be very unpleasant for Kayla. Nothing would please me more."

Vic's phone went dead.

He pulled it away from his ear and stared at it. His mind was a jumble of panicked thoughts. Had Mike Frazetta found out that he meant to run? Had he found out about him and Lorraine? Had Mike meant to kill him all along, and was Kayla his insurance policy? Or was this something else altogether? That last possibility frightened him most of all. Vic supposed the who and the why didn't much matter in the end. He held the phone out over the lake through the open door of the plane. To be safe, all he needed to do was to let the phone slip out of his hand. In a few days he would have that new life. Kayla's pain, regardless of how intense, would be over by then. What did he owe her, anyway? She hadn't exactly been a model wife. She'd left him, hadn't she? Was he supposed to just walk into a trap and have this guy murder him, too? Vic was no fool. He knew that Kayla wasn't getting out of this alive, whether he showed up or not.

Vic was so lost inside his own head, he didn't hear the pilot return.

"Okay, we're good to go," the pilot said.

Vic was so startled by the sound of the pilot's voice, he nearly dropped his phone into the lake.

"You all right, mister? Relax. I've done these sorts of flights hundreds of times. We're going to be flying pretty low, so hold on tight."

But what Vic said was, "There's been a change of plans."

71

Harlan Salter IV was looking through the papers that would allow his son to be transferred to Tufts Medical Center. Monty Bernstein wasn't happy about it, but he hadn't been happy about nearly anything Salter had done since this whole mess began.

"Harlan, I want to again advise against doing this. Chief Stone would be within his rights to arrest Ben if you attempt to move him out of this jurisdiction. We both know Ben had nothing to do with the girl's murder, but he's still the only suspect they have and certainly the only viable material witness."

Salter stuck the stem of his unlit pipe into his lawyer's sternum. "You do that too frequently for my taste, Counselor."

"What's that?"

"Advise against things," Salter said. "I thought your people were supposed to be pushier, not so worried about making

waves. They certainly are that way in my
business. I admire proactive people,
Bernstein. I admire bravery and risk-taking.
You're not too keen on risk-taking."

Monty Bernstein was no fan of Harlan
Salter to begin with, and after his "your
people" remark, Salter had descended
several levels on Monty's popularity scale.

"When it's necessary, I take some pretty
heavy risks."

"Sure you do, but it's your clients that
pay the price when those risks don't turn
out."

"I'm good at my job. That's why I'm
standing here."

"Next time, you won't be."

"I am now, though, and my advice is to
let Ben stay put."

"Well, I've had contact with another
more cooperative lawyer who's had some
high-profile doctors draft a memo saying
that my son needs the kind of care he can
only receive at a major medical facility. It
should be arriving by messenger soon.
Let Stone try and make something of this.
Time that small-town bully got his bluff

called. And Bernstein—"

Before Salter finished his sentence, his cell phone rang. He stepped away from his lawyer. When he returned, he had what passed for a broad grin on his face.

"Good news?" Monty said.

"Excellent news. Mr. Vic Prado is about to get his comeuppance. Apparently the gentleman you procured for me has used Prado's wife to ensure he shows up to his own execution."

As broad as the grin on Salter's face was, it was matched by the frown on Monty Bernstein's.

"I dread saying this to you yet again, but I feel I have to as your—"

"Don't bother, Bernstein. Why not record yourself saying, 'I would advise against it,' and carry the recorder in your pocket? It would save a lot of wear and tear on your vocal cords."

"Still, I would plead with you to reconsider this course of action."

Salter shook his head in disgust.

"And I was going to ask you to accompany me to watch my pound of flesh extracted from Prado's hide."

Monty said, "No, thanks."

"I didn't make the offer, Counselor. I said I was **going** to ask, but that was before I decided that I no longer require your services. Consider yourself fired."

"Gladly. You are as unpleasant a man as I have ever met. And here's some pro bono advice. Don't go through with this. Right now you're free and clear. You've got total control of your firm back. It wasn't your daughter who was killed. Your son will be fine in a couple of months. Do this and it's murder one."

"Farewell, Mr. Bernstein. I'm certain I do not have to remind you to send me the bill for your services. In any case, I will pay it promptly."

With that, Salter turned his back on his former lawyer and began filling out the hospital transfer papers.

72

Mike Frazetta was seated before his huge flat screen, watching **High Plains Drifter**. One of Frazetta's favorite scenes, an exchange between the town preacher and Clint Eastwood's Stranger, was playing. Frazetta sat mute as Eastwood's character spoke.

"All these people, are they your sisters and brothers?" Eastwood's character asks the indignant preacher about the dispossessed residents of the town.

"They most certainly are," says the preacher.

Frazetta leaned forward, balling and unballing his fists in anticipation of Eastwood's reply.

"Then you won't mind if they come over and stay at your place, will ya?"

He clapped his hands together.

"I love that line," he said as Joe Breen came into the room. He turned to gaze at Joe. "What's wrong? I can tell something's wrong by that look on your puss."

"Vic."

"What about him?"

"He's gone."

That got Frazetta's attention. He stood up and spun around, his face twisted in anger.

"What do you mean, he's gone? Gone where? Gone how?"

"Mexico, then to Belize," Joe said. "How, I don't know, but he's out of here."

"Fuck! I thought I told you to keep an eye on him."

"I staked out his hotel. He must've slipped out the back or something."

"Then how do you know he split?"

"A source."

"What good is a source. I seen some of your sources, Joe. People will tell you all kinds of shit because they're afraid of you or they want to get greased or they need a favor."

"Not this source. This girl's as reliable as they come, Mike. I trust her like you trust Lorraine. You can make book on it."

"What, you trust a hooker?"

"I suppose she's an escort of a sort," Joe said. "Let's leave it at that. Whatever label you choose to give her, I'll vouch that she's telling the truth of what she knows. But why are you so troubled? We're rid of Vic. Isn't that what you wanted all along? Any stink is on him. We're insulated."

"It's not him I'm worried about," Mike said. "He could rot in Belize eating bananas and mangoes, for all I care. I was planning on him going for a long one-way ride no matter what. It's his documentation. It's his computer. It's anything he's got that links us to him other than us growing up together. He's the only person who can tie us to that SEC guy's murder."

"I think we'll be okay."

"Not for nothing, Joe, but thinking is my department. Listen, I want you to head out to Scottsdale. Pull Vic's house apart—stick by stick, if you have to. Find his computer, his papers, and bring them back. Go have a talk with his lawyer."

"A talk or 'a talk'?"

"If the normal kind of talking don't work, do your kind of talking."

"What if Vic's wife is—"

"Since when do I have to tell you what to do every step of the way? What's up with you lately? If the wife gets in the way, send her to summer camp like the Salter kid's girlfriend."

Joe's stomach twisted in a knot at that, but he didn't say anything.

"I'll arrange for you to fly out there on a private jet. We don't want records of you on a commercial flight. Use the alias you bought your house with, okay? You still got all the fake paper I got for you?"

"I got it."

"Go pack some stuff and head out to Logan. And, Joe, one more thing."

"What?"

"Dress your age, for crissakes already. Lose the faded jeans and sneaks. Wear a suit and some decent shoes. I'll arrange for somebody to fix you up with a piece when you land. Okay, get out of here."

When Joe Breen left, Mike Frazetta didn't call his connection at the airport or his contact in Phoenix. He sat back down, pressed rewind, then play. He sat forward.

ROBERT B. PARKER'S BLIND SPOT

Lorraine was pacing by the front door as Joe came out of the study.

"Don't worry," Joe said. "I've kept my word."

"I've hated you for such a long time. I feel all twisted up inside now. I don't know what I'm supposed to feel about you anymore."

"I did what I did for me, not for you. Stop fretting over it."

She stroked his cheek. "Bless you, anyway, Joe."

He smiled with his mouth closed tight. "It'll take more than your blessing to make up the ground I mean to make up. I'll be on my way."

He brushed past Lorraine Frazetta, down the front steps, and hoped like hell Moira was home. He wasn't any good at leaving notes.

73

Jesse wished Molly **had** taken the bottle and watered the other half-dead plants or dumped it down the drain. Molly was long gone, but he was still in his office, listening to Johnnie Walker singing his muted siren's song from the bottom desk drawer. It wasn't so much about Dee and Vic anymore, but about boredom and frustration. Alcoholics have an endless stream of reasons, rationales, and excuses for their thirsts. The funny thing is that they make the excuses to themselves, whether anyone else cares or is there to listen. Jesse was no different.

Connor Cavanaugh had been there for three hours, left-clicking, going over hundreds and hundreds of mug shots without any luck. He and Jesse had shared a large pepperoni-and-sausage pizza for dinner, though Jesse preferred mushroom and green pepper. He figured he owed it to Cavanaugh to let the hotel security man pick the toppings. For the first two hours he had gone out to check on Cavanaugh every fifteen minutes. He stopped when he noticed that it served only to frustrate the both of them. Jesse wasn't an action junkie like a lot of other cops, but quiet times in a crisis could be rough. He considered going home, then thought better of it. Even on good nights, he had a rough time getting to sleep. No, it was best to stay at work.

He had run out of straightening to do. Had paced the floor. Had pounded the ball into his glove. Had cleaned his .38 and his rarely used nine-millimeter. Had read and reread the files and forensic reports on Martina Penworth and Ben Salter. Had found himself staring at the crime scene photos of Martina Penworth. She had been a very pretty girl, on the verge of beauty. The photograph had captured that in spite of the damage the bullets had done. It also captured something else. The dead are different. As a homicide detective and as chief, Jesse had lived much of his life among the dead, but it wasn't until Abby Taylor had been murdered that the nature of that difference coalesced for him.

Jesse remembered standing over Abby's lifeless body and noting how still she was. There was more to it than her stillness. He had slept with her less than an hour before she'd been murdered, yet the body before him was no more Abby Taylor than the car on which her leg was caught. Something was missing. Jesse didn't know if people had souls. In fact, he could swear that many of the people he'd encountered as a cop, such as the couple who had murdered Abby as a kick, were pretty much soulless. But after standing over Abby's body that night, he thought he understood the genesis of souls. He only regretted that it had taken Abby's death for him to see it. He preferred lessons learned at his own expense. He closed the files.

He was pacing again when he caught sight of a plastic evidence bag on top of a file cabinet. It took a second for Jesse to make sense of it. **Gabe Weathers's**

personal effects from the Helton PD. With all that had been going on, he'd forgotten to give it to Gabe's wife. **Gabe.** Jesse hadn't given much thought to Gabe in the last few days. He supposed that was a hangover from his ball-playing days. You didn't think about injured teammates. It was a matter of reality, not cruelty. It was about the task at hand. If you could help the team, great. If you couldn't help the team, regardless of the reason, you were forgotten. And as a ballplayer or a cop, it didn't serve you well to think about getting injured. To do both jobs you needed to be focused. Distraction of any kind was a bad thing. To be distracted by fear of injury was the worst kind of distraction.

Jesse picked up the bag and looked at it: wallet, badge, nine-millimeter (clip removed), clip (ammo removed), ammo, pen, notepad, spare change, small binoculars, camera. He carried the bag out front to the desk. It was late, but not too late to have Pete deliver Gabe's things to his family.

"Pretty quiet night. What's up, Jesse?"

"Call Pete in. I want him to run this stuff over to Gabe's wife."

Ed, the cop working the front desk, gave Jesse an odd look.

"What?" Jesse said.

"She's probably not home. Remember, she's been staying—"

"Right, right. We put her up across from the medical center. Forget it. I'll run it over to her tomorrow. I should go see Gabe." Jesse nodded at Cavanaugh. "How's he doing?"

"He's doing okay, I guess," Ed said. "Talk about some needle-in-a-haystack shit, that's it."

"If he fades or barks about it, let me know."

"Sure thing, Jesse."

Back at his desk, Jesse sat with Gabe's things in his lap. He realized that he didn't want to give Gabe's things to his wife in an evidence bag, so he removed the items one at a time and laid them out on his desk. For some reason, his eyes kept drifting toward the camera. He hadn't instructed Weathers to photograph Salter's activities, but Gabe was a thorough cop with big-city experience. That's why Jesse had chosen him instead of the younger candidates. To the annoyance of his fellow Paradise PD colleagues, Gabe took the initiative without being prodded. Jesse picked up the little Canon, pressed the on/off switch, and flipped it around so the viewing screen faced him. As he fumbled with the buttons, trying to figure out how to display the photos in the camera's memory, he hoped like hell Gabe wasn't the kind of guy who took nude shots of his wife or worse.

"Here goes nothing," Jesse said to himself.

When a photo of Burt's All-Star Grill, Salter's black Navigator parked out front, appeared on the screen, Jesse breathed a sigh of relief. When he scrolled a few photos ahead and saw a white Nissan Sentra, he burst out of his office.

"Eddie, wake Molly up and send Pete over to get her."

"What is it, Jesse?"

"Just do it."

Before Ed could call Peter Perkins, Peter called in to the station on the radio.

"Unit three, unit three calling dispatch. Over."

"Unit three, this is dispatch. What's up, Pete?" Ed said. "Over."

"Jesse still there?"

Jesse Stone grabbed the mic. "This is Jesse. What's up, Pete?"

"There's been a little trouble at the Scupper."

"What kind and how little?"

"Bar fight. Couple of punches thrown, then a roll around on the floor," Pete said. "The usual thing."

"You need me for this why?"

"One of the parties involved says he's a lawyer. Driver's license identifies him as Monty Bernstein. Claims he's a close personal acquaintance of yours. That's an exact quote, Jesse. Figured I should give you a heads-up before I dragged his ass down there."

"Good thinking. Keep him there. I'm coming over. I wanted to have a talk with him, anyway. When I get there, I want you to pick Molly Crane up at her house and bring her down to the station. I'll explain when I get there."

"Okay, Jesse. Roger that. Over."

"Over and out."

Jesse turned to Ed. "Get Molly up. There's a camera on my desk. Tell her I want every one of the photos blown up and parsed like a sentence in Catholic school. She'll understand."

74

The southwest area of town, the Swap, as residents called it, had boomed in the wake of WWII and was now the most run-down part of Paradise. The small slab houses, built with only expedience and profit in mind, were showing their age. The Swap had been the only part of Paradise considered working-class and for sixty-plus years the Scupper had been the place where fathers brought their sons for first drinks. Like the climate and the economy, that was all changing. The Swap was the one area in town where a young couple without much in the way of financial resources could buy a house. It's where Paradise's tiny Hispanic population had taken root. It was also home to whatever art and food scenes Paradise could muster.

Five years from now, Jesse thought as he pulled up behind Pete's cruiser, **the rents around here will be through the**

roof. He'd witnessed transitions like this before in L.A., the churning of neighborhoods from least to most desirable. But any way you looked at it, the Scupper was a dump.

As Jesse came through the front doors he got a full dose of stale beer and cigarette smell. Although smoking in bars had been banned years ago, it still went on in places like the Scupper. Smoking was possibly the one thing the old and newer patrons of the Scupper agreed on. The bouncer, Brian Kent, another one of Suit's ex-teammates, nodded hello to the chief and pointed his thumb at the first booth in the back. The place was pretty empty. The bartender asked Jesse if he wanted something to drink. Tempted as he was, Jesse waved him off.

Peter Perkins was sitting across the booth from Monty Bernstein. Bernstein's face looked undamaged, but the same could not be said of his sweater or his pride. The black, fine-wool sweater was torn in three places and covered with dust and beer. The cowed, slump-shouldered way the lawyer held himself told Jesse everything he needed to know about Bernstein's state of mind.

"What happened here, Pete?"

"Seems like Mr. Bernstein had a few vodkas too many and picked a fight with a guy twenty years too young for him," Pete said. "Neighborhood kid named O'Connell."

"Who threw the first punch?"

Perkins pointed across the table. "All the witnesses agree on that."

"O'Connell pressing charges?"

"Probably not. I had a talk with him. I sort of suggested that Mr. Bernstein might show him some love and cash when he sobered up. I got his address and phone number."

"Good thinking, Pete. Next time there's a vacancy for UN ambassador, I'm putting your name forward."

Pete grunted.

"Okay, Pete," Jesse said. "I can take it from here. Go get Molly and then get back out on patrol."

Jesse waited for Pete to leave before

speaking to the lawyer.

"Come on, Monty. Looks like you need some fresh air."

Monty Bernstein stood up and wobbled a bit getting his legs beneath him. As he walked out of the Scupper he kept his eyes down and his head straight. Jesse nodded to the bartender and the bouncer as they left. The night air was cool and damp, smelling vaguely of the ocean. Although the Scupper was located about as far away from the sea as you could get in Paradise, it still wasn't very far. Paradise was all about proximity to the ocean and all one ever need do was to sniff the air to be reminded of that.

"Walk or drive?" Jesse said to the still silent lawyer.

"Drive. With the windows down, please."

They got into Jesse's Explorer and pulled away from the curb, Monty leaning toward the open window. Jesse headed northeast and asked Bernstein to explain himself, but Monty answered the question with one of his own.

"You ever do anything you were so

ashamed of you couldn't live with it?"

"I've come close," Jesse said. "I used to think it was my fault that my marriage fell apart. Then there's my drinking. I did ruin my career with the L.A.P.D. with that. No debating that one."

"You said you've come close, but you never crossed the line?"

"Never. If I couldn't live with it, I wouldn't be here now."

"That's right. You're a cop," Monty said. "If things got too bad for you, you'd eat your gun."

When Jesse nodded, his expression somehow both serious and fragile, Monty understood even through his drunken haze that Jesse had come close to doing that, too.

"But don't you feel guilty about things sometimes?"

"Guilt," Jesse said. "I know about guilt. But we're not talking about me, are we, Monty?"

"No, I guess we're not."

Jesse didn't say anything to that, opting for the trick of silence to work on the lawyer.

"Pull over. Pull over, Jesse. I'm gonna be sick."

Jesse swung the wheel hard right. His Explorer screeched to a stop. He hopped out of the driver's seat, came around the SUV, yanked Monty out of his seat. Monty didn't need any help with the rest. He emptied himself of everything except what was weighing on his conscience. In the meantime, Jesse'd got a bottle of water and a few aspirins out of the Explorer.

"I'm okay, now," Monty said, getting to his feet.

Jesse handed him the water and the aspirins.

"You better now?" Jesse said as he pulled back into the light traffic.

"I guess."

"I'm going to ask you some questions that you're probably not going to answer, but I'm going to ask them anyway."

It was Monty's turn to be silent.

"I've got a witness that will testify that you and Harlan Salter met with Vic Prado at Burt's All-Star Grill in Helton. I've got photographic evidence that will back up that testimony. You want to tell me what was being discussed?"

"You know I can't answer that, Jesse."

But Jesse noticed that Monty's expression was twisted in pain as he spoke. When Jesse had pulled away from the Scupper, he didn't have a destination in mind, but he had one now.

75

Jesse drove as quickly as he dared. He didn't want to use the portable cherry top he carried in his car just in case. He didn't approve of using lights and sirens unless they were absolutely necessary. Besides, he didn't want to risk freaking Monty out any more than he already was.

"Officer Crane," Jesse said, "Molly, she was onto you and Salter. She told me the night Vic Prado came in to my office that she thought you and Salter knew Prado. She said that Salter looked pretty angry at the sight of Vic."

"Officer Crane's a pretty good-looking woman."

"Obviously a pretty good cop, too. Her instincts about the three of you knowing each other were right on. So, let me ask you this a different way, Counselor. Did the business dealings between Salter and Vic have anything to do with Martina Penworth's murder and the kid's abduction?"

Bernstein didn't answer, but the lines of his tortured expression etched themselves more deeply into his handsome face.

Jesse navigated the twisty road up to the big old brick Victorian, the Explorer's tires spitting out pieces of gravel as it moved across the driveway. He stopped the SUV right in front of the porch.

"What is this place?"

Jesse said, "Get out." It wasn't a suggestion.

When they were out of the car, Jesse told Monty to wait where he was. Jesse disappeared around the side of the house. Feeling weak and hungover, Bernstein sat down on the porch steps. The wind was much stronger here and the air smelled more intensely of the sea. He could hear the waves rolling ashore down the bluff. He thought he heard something else, too, something like the sound of breaking glass. But the wind noise and his fuzzy-headedness made it hard to know. When the front door opened, Jesse was standing on the other side of the threshold.

"Come on in, Monty," Jesse said.

He stood and went into the house. Jesse had turned on the lights and had started up the stairs without waiting for the lawyer.

"Where are we?" Monty said.

There was no answer. The lawyer finally caught up to Jesse at the open door to a second-floor bedroom. Jesse pointed to a crusted red splotch on the floor on the right side of the bed as they faced it.

"This is your employer's house, Monty, and right there's where Martina Penworth's body landed. You know she was only eighteen and she was murdered for no other reason than she was an inconvenience. I know you're a criminal defense attorney and I know you were once a prosecutor, but can you even conceive of someone being killed because they were an inconvenience?"

"He's no longer my employer." Bernstein spoke in a whisper.

"What?"

"Salter fired me tonight. He's gone."

"Then tell me what's going on. Get it off

your chest."

"You know I'm bound by attorney-client privilege even now."

"Keep staring at her blood, then tell me that again. You want to come to the station and look at the forensics and the autopsy photos?"

Bernstein burst out of the room, running down the stairs, tripping face-forward down the last three steps. He crawled through the front door. Jesse found him on his knees on the porch, dry-heaving, gasping for breath. Jesse sat down on the porch steps, waiting. A minute later, Bernstein sat down beside him.

"You deal in hypotheticals, Chief Stone," Monty said, addressing Jesse formally.

"When I have to."

"What if I were to tell you that a hypothetical former client of a hypothetical lawyer was blind with vengeance for an incident involving a hypothetical son and his hypothetical girlfriend?"

"I'm listening, Counselor."

"What if I were to tell you that part of this hypothetical lawyer's job was to help arrange for that vengeance and that said revenge was about to be carried out and that it involved an innocent woman?"

"Innocent woman as in Vic Prado's wife?"

"Hypothetically speaking."

"I'd say that hypothetical lawyer better find a way to speak up unless he wants the kind of blood on his hands that he'll never get off. Maybe it would motivate the lawyer to know that Kayla Prado had once been the Paradise police chief's girlfriend."

Monty Bernstein went deadly still for a moment, then said, "They call him Mr. Peepers."

76

Jesse had dropped Monty back at the Osprey Inn to sleep off his hangover and shame. Now he sat at his desk, staring at the image of Wally Cox on his monitor. Seeing the late actor's face made Jesse smile. Cox, with his weak mouth, bookish, unremarkable looks, and wire-rimmed glasses, had a face that screamed **nerd**. It was a face made for blending into the background, a face made to be forgotten. Jesse remembered seeing the late actor on reruns of **The Twilight Zone**, **Wagon Train**, **Hollywood Squares**, and twenty other shows, the names of which were lost to him. He'd never seen Cox in **Mister Peepers**, not even in reruns, but the name fit. Only according to Monty Bernstein, the man he referred to as Mr. Peepers was anything but a harmless nerd.

"Watch out for this guy, Jesse," Monty said before he left the Explorer. "He's known to take a particular delight in slow death. He likes punishment. That's what my hypothetical client wanted. Be careful."

Molly came into his office without knocking, but he kept his eyes on the screen.

"Did you get those photos from Gabe's camera uploaded?"

"I did. I'll enlarge them and run the plates on all the cars in the photographs as soon as—"

"You were right, Molly, about Salter and Prado knowing each other. Maybe I'll start listening to you."

"That would be a nice change of pace."

"Do you remember the actor Wally Cox?"

"The name sounds familiar," she said.

"He was the voice of the cartoon character Underdog. 'Never fear, Underdog is here.'"

"Sure, I saw reruns of those when I was little, but it doesn't help me with his looks."

"Monty Bernstein says he's been told that the guy who snatched Kayla looks like Wally Cox. They call him Mr. Peepers."

"I can't remember what Wally Cox looked like," she said.

He laughed. "Underdog on a Wanted poster. Look him up on Google."

"I can't exactly call in a description of Wally Cox to the Boston PD. Do we have anything else?"

"A disconnected phone number," he said. "You saw the white Sentra in Gabe's photos?"

"You think it's Mr. Peepers's?"

"It better be. Did you send Cavanaugh home?"

"He's taking a nap in one of the cells."

"Good."

It wasn't five minutes before Molly was back in the office.

"Dead end on the Sentra," she said, holding up a photo of the car. "The plate's a match with the partial we had, but it's registered to a Sheila Brodsky, seventy-three, of Twelve Cottage Street in Sharon. I checked the list. The car hasn't been reported missing or stolen."

"Call the Sharon PD and have them send a cruiser over there."

"You think she's—"

"It's too early to think anything. Just call the Sharon PD. What else?"

"We had better luck with this," Molly said, laying a photo in front of Jesse. "That pearl Caddy CTS Coupe is registered to MAF Imports Inc."

Jesse shrugged.

Molly wagged her finger at him. "Remind me again why they pay you the big bucks? You want to take a stab at what MAF stands for?"

"It's been a long day, Crane."

"MAF. Michael Anthony Frazetta."

"If I didn't think you'd shoot me, I'd kiss you, Moll."

"If you drag me down here again off shift, I might shoot you anyway."

"So we know Salter and Prado are mixed up together somehow and that Vic is sleeping with Mike Frazetta's wife. Now we've got a car outside Burt's owned by Mike Frazetta. And if my gut is right, we also have Mr. Peepers watching everyone else." Jesse stopped talking and his eyes got a faraway look in them.

"What is it, Jesse?"

"It was Mr. Peepers who shot out Gabe's rear tire."

"Why?"

He grabbed the photo of the Sentra out of Molly's hand. "This! Monty says this guy is a ghost. No one even knows who he is. There are no pictures of him. He must have seen Gabe taking pictures in his rearview as he drove past. Guys like this are allergic to being photographed."

"But how can you know it was him?" Molly said.

"Because I saw him. I looked right at him when I was going to my car at Gabe's accident scene."

"What did he look like?"

"I don't really remember. There wasn't anything about him that stuck in my head, but it was him. The staties who pulled Gabe from the car told me they had to chase some creepy little guy away from the wreck, that he was sniffing around, looking for a souvenir. He wanted Gabe's camera."

"But he's just a shadow in the picture.

You can't even tell if it's a man or a woman driving the Sentra. He might as well be Sheila Brodsky."

They both laughed. Maybe too loudly.

"Mr. Peepers wouldn't know that," Jesse said. "He would do anything to make sure he wasn't on camera. One photo of him and he would be finished. With all the face-recognition software out there these days, there'd be no shadow dark enough to hide him. Think of where he snatched Kayla from in Boston. Two blocks in either direction and he's on CCTV. Molly, give me a minute. I have a call to make."

Jesse was already punching in the number of the Helton PD before Molly Crane was out the door.

77

Chief Ralph Carney of the Helton PD wasn't any more pleased by Jesse Stone's call than Molly had been about being called in to work. It went downhill from there, especially after Jesse asked if there had been a recent incident at Helton police headquarters. One near their evidence or property rooms.

"How the fuck did you know that?" Carney said. "Did someone in my department tell you about it? Was it that psycho Bynam?"

"No one told me anything, Chief. It was an educated guess."

"Bullshit! I know your type, Stone. If someone in this department told you, you wouldn't rat them out."

Jesse had little patience for this kind of paranoia, but he couldn't risk alienating Carney.

"I give you my word, Chief. It was a guess."

"I don't know how you'd guess that. We even snowed the local paper into writing it up as a friendly prank gone wrong."

"You tell me what happened," Jesse said, "and I'll tell you how I knew."

"A few days ago, the officer stationed at the evidence desk smelled smoke, looked out into the hallway, and saw a cloud of it. He pulled the fire alarm and the building was evacuated. After the fire department cleared us to reenter, we found the door to the evidence room pried open and the CCTV cameras had been spray-painted black. Wasn't even a real fire. It was an old Army-surplus smoke canister."

"Anything missing?"

"That's the weird thing. Nothing was missing that we could tell."

"Happened the night of my guy's accident, right?"

After Jesse upheld his end of the bargain, he got off the phone and went out to check with Molly on the Sentra.

"Just got off the phone with the Sharon PD," she said.

"And."

"Good news, bad news. Sheila Brodsky's alive. She's on a world cruise, but her garage was broken into. Her car's gone."

"Well," Jesse said, "there's no doubt about Mr. Peepers anymore. He tried breaking in—scratch that—he broke into the Helton PD evidence locker, looking for the camera."

"Why didn't he try that here?"

"Maybe he did and we didn't know it or maybe he didn't know it was here. Or if he did, he might have been gambling we wouldn't know what we had. If I hadn't been climbing the walls before, he would have been right. I would have just given the camera back to Gabe's wife with the rest of his things."

"What now, Jesse?"

"First thing, we report the car stolen. Probably won't get us anywhere, but it's worth a shot."

Molly said, "Did that. The Sharon PD is putting it in the system as we speak. I guess we can have the Sharon PD talk to Sheila Brodsky's neighbors and relatives and see if there's any connection that would lead us back to Mr. Peepers. How did he know she would be gone?"

Jesse shook his head. "We don't have that kind of time, and I'm betting Kayla doesn't, either. She's bait, and Vic's been gone since this afternoon. If Vic ran, Kayla's dead. If Vic does the right thing and shows, Kayla's dead anyway. For her, it's a lose-lose proposition."

"Then what?"

"I don't know, Molly. I don't know. I'm going to stretch my legs a little and think. Wake Cavanaugh up. Pump him full of coffee and get him back looking at the mug shots. No matter what happens with Kayla and Vic, we still owe justice to Martina Penworth and her parents."

78

Walking wasn't helping. Sometimes there are no good solutions, no rabbits to pull out of the magician's hat. Sometimes there are no hats. And Jesse Stone was no magician. Kayla was going to die, and from what Monty had told him, it wasn't going to be quick or easy. **Kayla.** He remembered the first time he'd seen her. Even the memory made his heart beat a little faster.

It was his first game in Albuquerque. He was in the on-deck circle, taking lazy swings with a weighted bat, his belly full of butterflies. Vic Prado was in the batter's box. Jesse should have been focused on timing the pitcher, following the sequence of pitches, checking the size of the ump's strike zone, eyeing where the other team's players were positioned. Instead, all Jesse could see was the stunning black-haired girl in the second row behind the dugout. And just before Jesse strode to the plate, she smiled at him and gave him a slight wave of her hand. Jesse doubled up the alley in left, driving Vic home from first base. As Jesse stood on second base, he looked for the black-haired girl. She was staring right at him. When he got back to the dugout between innings, he passed her a note. After dinner, after their first kiss, after waking up together, Jesse envisioned a future awash in Dodger blue and black-haired sons. The future, as Jesse discovered on the rock-hard infield in Pueblo, pays little heed to human visions.

He supposed he didn't much care about what happened to Vic. Whether Julio Blanco was full of shit or not, Vic had taken more from Jesse than his baseball career and his black-haired sons. And it hadn't stopped with Kayla. Dee was just the latest thing Vic had robbed from him. How many times had he come in contact with people who coveted only what those closest to them had? He tried counting up how many murderers he had arrested who had killed out of jealousy or because they could not possess the thing or the person they desired. Jesse quickly ran out of fingers and toes.

He found himself heading toward the ocean. For a guy born in Tucson, Jesse's life had largely played out within several miles of the Atlantic and Pacific. He found himself drawn to the ocean at the oddest times. He didn't fool himself that he would find answers in the vast blackness or in the sound of the waves. Nor was he seeking solace. But as he turned toward the water, Jesse became aware of glowing headlamps in the mist. He could see their reflection in the darkened store windows ahead of him as he walked. He purposely turned at the next corner and at the next corner again. The lights seemed to follow him as he went. As he turned the next corner, he dipped into the shadows of a doorway and pulled his freshly cleaned .38 from his hip. He waited for the car to catch up to him, to turn the corner, to pass him. When it did, Jesse had the advantage.

The car slammed on its brakes, its red taillights glowing pink in the light rain.

Jesse had led the car down a dead end and the driver had no choice but to risk reversing down the narrow cobblestone street or to K-turn. As the car pulled to the right to prepare to swing around, Jesse moved nearer, his back close to the store-fronts. When the driver nosed the car left and stopped to put it in reverse, Jesse came out of the shadows, gun held down at his side.

"Stop right there!" he said, raising his revolver so the driver could see it clearly. "Roll your window completely down and put your hands on the steering wheel. Do it slowly and do it now!"

The driver did as ordered. But when Jesse got close enough to get a good look at the driver, he holstered his .38.

"Dee?"

"I got as far as New York," she said.

"Move over. I'm driving."

79

The Gray Gull didn't have much to offer in the way of fine food. The sandwiches usually weren't fatal. The best thing about the place was its view of the water, and the mist was ruining even that. But the Gull was nearly empty, and it offered a more comfortable place to get out of the wet than the front seat of Dee's rented car. Jesse hadn't said a word since he'd got behind the wheel. That hadn't changed. He was desperate not to react. Not to show he was a mess inside.

Dee wasn't her gorgeous self. She looked old somehow, and defeated. He was familiar with that look. He'd seen it on the faces of many suspects who were sure they were never going to get caught. It was the face of someone who glimpsed a very different future than the one they'd dreamed of or hoped for. He had seen it in the mirror a few times himself.

"You mind if I get something to drink?"

she said, her hands unsteady. "I think I need a drink. You?"

He shook his head.

Dee walked up to the bar and came back to the table with a glass full of clear liquid on the rocks that, but for the smell of vodka, might've been water. Jesse kept quiet.

"I thought I would never see you again"— she raised her glass to him and sipped— "but I decided I had to come back to explain."

He shrugged.

"Well, I never thought you were effusive. I kind of like that about you, but you could say something."

"What happened to your Southern accent?"

She laughed. A reflex. No smile remained in its wake.

"My accent was put on," she said.

"And your affection?"

"Nothing phony about that. I was falling in love with you, Jesse. I am falling in love with you."

"I wasn't talking about me," he said. "I

was talking about Vic Prado."

Her jaw dropped and she took a big swallow of vodka.

"What are you talking about?"

"There was an incident at your hotel today. Some big guy roughed up the head of security and I went over there and had a look at some closed-circuit footage."

"What's that got to do with me?"

Jesse ignored the question. "I think this big guy is the guy who killed Martina Penworth, the girl who was—"

"The murdered girl?"

"Her. This guy was asking about Vic and a woman who'd spent the night in his room."

"It wasn't me," she said. "I swear."

"I know it wasn't you, Dee, but I asked to see all the video of Vic's movements within the hotel. That **was** you that answered the door to room 323?"

She was at the vodka again.

"It wasn't what you think," she said. "You don't understand."

"Then explain it to me."

"He kissed me. I didn't kiss him back."

Jesse was unconvinced.

"I've got to give Vic a lot of credit," he said. "He spends the night with Lorraine Frazetta and then he hops downstairs for—"

Dee cut him off. "Vic was fucking Mike Frazetta's wife?"

"How do you know who Mike Frazetta is?"

Dee reached into her bag, put a creased brown envelope on the table, and slid it across to Jesse.

She said, "That's Mike and Lorraine Frazetta. The nasty-looking guy is Frazetta's muscle, Joe Breen."

While he looked at the surveillance photos inside, she spread open a black leather credential case and held it next to her face. She whistled to get Jesse's attention. He looked up.

"I guess it's time we were properly introduced. I'm Special Agent Diana Evans of the Federal Bureau of Investigation, but probably not for much longer."

She explained about Harry Freeman's murder and about the lie she'd been living for the past year.

"It was crazy," she said. "I can see that now, to risk everything the way I did. I've pretty much thrown away my career. But Harry was the reason I got into law enforcement. Lord knows my parents didn't encourage me. All they ever wanted me to do was to be pretty and marry money. Harry treated me like a person, not as a pair of tits and lips. I'm not saying I don't like looking like I do. It's opened a lot of doors for me. It's made a lot of things easier for me, but it also makes people take me less seriously. After Harry was murdered, I couldn't get anyone at the Bureau to pursue it. All they'd say to me was that I was too close to the situation or that it was a local police matter. That not even the folks at the SEC were suspicious. The more I kept at it, the less they listened to me, though I had one of my supervising agents say he'd think about it if I'd fuck him. That was a pretty risky thing for him to do, to make that deal. He risked his career to proposition me like that. I guess he must've been pretty desperate to have me. You know, the funny thing is I almost said yes. I felt like it was all I had to trade, and Harry was worth it to me. Same thing with Vic. I almost—"

"What did you say?"

"I've been talking for twenty minutes, Jesse. Which part?"

"About trading."

"I said—"

"Never mind. Can you drive me back to the station?"

"Of course. What is it?"

"I need to talk to some people about a trade."

80

When Molly looked up to see them standing in front of her, she had a puzzled look
on her face.

Jesse held up his palms. "Don't even
ask."

"You're the boss," Molly said. "I just work
here."

Jesse pointed at Cavanaugh. "Anything?"

"I did what you told me. I pumped him
full of fresh coffee. When he yells 'Bingo!'
I'll come get you."

"Anything else from the Sharon PD?"

She shook her head. "I'm worried about
her, Jesse. I was thinking. We're pretty
sure it's a kidnapping, right? Why
don't we alert the FBI? They might have
something on Mr. Peepers we don't know
about, and they have resources not even
Healy has."

"Good idea. Di—Dee can advise you on
who to—"

"Worried about who?" Diana wanted to know.

Jesse said, "Kayla. Molly, fill her in."

"What?"

His palms were up again. "She'll explain. And Molly, until I come out there," he said, pointing at his office door, "no phone calls, no interruptions."

She saluted him. "Yes, fearless leader."

Jesse barely noticed. His head was already someplace else.

While the Boston-area underworld didn't publish its hierarchy on the sports page of the **Globe**, it was generally believed that Gino Fish was at or near the top of the food chain. A guy like Mike Frazetta, as ambitious and powerful as he seemed to be, wasn't nearly in the same league as Fish. Gino wasn't an easy man to see, and he was an even more difficult man to get on the phone, but Jesse Stone and Gino Fish had had dealings before. It wasn't as if they were pals, but they did share a healthy respect for each other. And, like most dealings between cops and crimi-nals, their relationship was a thing born of mutual self-interest.

It took two preliminary phone calls for Jesse to reach Gino, the second to Vinnie Morris, Fish's right hand. Vinnie was to shooting what Ted Williams had been to hitting a baseball, yet he was dangerous for more than his guns and everyone knew it. To come at Gino Fish you'd have to go through Vinnie, and not many rivals had been stupid or bold enough to try. Those that had were dead. Vinnie and Jesse also shared a mutual respect, but when Jesse explained to Vinnie why he needed to speak to his boss, he was surprised by Morris's answer.

"Be careful, Stone. Don't fuck with this guy."

"He can't be that good."

"He's better than that," Vinnie said. "He's the type of guy keeps me up nights."

"Thanks for the heads-up."

"Professional courtesy. Hang up and wait for the call."

There was a rapping on the pebbled glass of his office door. Molly stuck her head in.

Jesse jumped to his feet. He didn't scream very often, especially not at Molly, but Gino Fish wasn't the type of man you told to hold on for just a second, not at a time like this. Maybe not ever.

"Didn't I tell you not to—"

"I know. I'm sorry, Jesse, but this couldn't wait. You want to come out or have us come in."

He was already up, so he walked outside. When he did, all eyes were on him: Molly's, Ed's, Diana's, Connor Cavanaugh's, and a pair of eyes he didn't expect to see.

"Suit," Jesse said, "what are you doing in now? Your shift doesn't start for a few more hours."

"Yeah, I know, Jesse. Eddie called, said things were happening down here, so I thought I could come and help. You're always after me to show initiative."

"Thanks, Suit, but I don't think Molly got me out of my office because you came in to lend a hand. For her sake, I hope not."

Then Connor Cavanaugh, dark purple bags under his squinted eyes, held up one of the surveillance photos that Diana had showed Jesse.

"This is the guy, Chief. This is the guy who punched me in the throat."

Diana spoke first. "Joe Breen is Mike Frazetta's muscle."

"He's in the system," Molly said. "Bad boy. Did a bid for assault with a deadly weapon. Last known address is in Boston."

Jesse walked over to Connor Cavanaugh and stared him in the eyes. "You sure? If you're not a hundred percent sure, now is the time to tell me."

"As sure as I can be, Chief. That's the prick that was at the hotel. I'll pick him out of a photo array, a lineup, whatever. I'll swear to it in court. He's the one."

Jesse shook his hand and thanked him. Told him to go home and get some sleep. Then he turned to Ed.

"Ed, print a picture of Breen up and put it in a photo array. Go over to the hospital and see if the Salter kid can pick him out. Then go over to the hotel and see if anyone else recognizes him. Find the caretaker at the old Salter place, Ethan Farley, and see if he recognizes him. Go! Molly, put Breen's name out there, but for now, just as wanted for assault. We don't want to tip our hand about the homicide. I'll discuss it with Healy when I get a chance."

When the phone rang, the stationhouse got very quiet.

81

This thing Vinnie tells me you want...I can't do this for you, Stone" was what Gino Fish said.

"And here I thought you liked me."

"I like you just fine, for a cop. We've done fine by each other in the past, but this... doing this, it cuts against my nature."

"I'm not asking for you to give him to me, Gino. I only want five minutes with him, face time or on the phone."

"Why, what's so important to you?"

"That's my business, Gino."

"Not if you don't want me to hang up the phone on you, it isn't."

"Fair enough. He's going to hurt a woman that used to mean a lot to me."

"You loved her?"

"It was a long time ago. We were young. I'm not sure I knew what love was then. Not so sure now, either."

"Tell me about it." Fish grunted. "Still, she must've done someone wrong for this guy to get hired to deal with her. He's a specialist."

"She's not the target. She's the bait, and you know what happens to bait."

"It gets eaten by the bigger fish," Gino said with a hint of irony. "You're asking a lot to have me put myself in between this guy and his profession."

"I know I am."

"In the past, Stone, we did business because what benefited you benefited me. I don't see how that works here. I'm not getting anything on my side of the balance sheet."

"I don't suppose doing the right thing counts," Jesse said.

"Not this time. You got to understand my position. I did not hire this guy, so for me to put myself between him and his employer puts me on his employer's shit list. Worse than that, it might put me on **his** shit list. You understand?"

"The employer's no threat to you. I can promise you that, Gino."

"What about the other half of that equation?"

"No guarantees, sorry, but I've got something I know he wants very much. Something he was willing to break into a police headquarters to get. I think he'd be pretty grateful you arranged for the opportunity for him to get what he wants."

There was silence on the other end of the phone. Then, "Maybe, but this guy, I hear bad things about him, Stone. He even gives Vinnie the shakes, and nobody gives Vinnie the shakes. I wouldn't want this guy after me if this turns out to be a thing you made up just to save the woman. And I wouldn't want to be you if I find out that's what's going on here, that this is a line of bullshit, because that I would take very personally. You know how Vinnie gets when I take things personally."

"I know that."

"But we're back to that sticking point, Stone. Everybody is getting something out of this except me. The woman stays alive. You get the woman. This guy gets whatever it is you have. What's in it for me beyond feeling all warm and fuzzy inside."

"I'll owe you a favor."

Silence again.

"Gino..."

"I'm here. Listen, Stone, the kind of favor I would ask from you for this, it would be big."

"I understand."

"I don't think you do, Chief. It would be the kind of favor a guy like you doesn't like doing. It's also the kind of thing I won't let go of if you refuse. That's another thing I take very personally. If you say you understand now, there's no going back. There's no unmashing the potatoes."

Jesse didn't hesitate. "I understand."

"If I can get hold of this guy—and I'm not promising you I can—what do I tell him to give him incentive to talk to you? And be smart, Chief, don't make it a threat. The only thing that will incentivize him to do is to kill you very slowly and as painfully as possible."

"No threats, Gino. Just tell him I said that I hope he looks better in real life than in photos. Tell him to say cheese from now on. He'll understand."

"Okay, I got your numbers. Let me see what I can do."

A half-hour later, Gino Fish called with instructions, an address, and a time. He reminded Jesse about their deal and warned him not to do anything stupid. For the first time in the many years they'd known each other, Gino Fish sounded a little scared for himself and worried for Jesse.

82

No one wants to advertise his deal with the devil. Jesse Stone was no exception. He hadn't told anyone where he was headed or what he had in mind. Less chance of someone doing the wrong thing or playing the hero if nobody knew what he was up to. What he'd told them was that he was going home to shower and shave, to get on some fresh clothes, and that he'd be back in an hour or two. It all sounded reasonable enough, and he figured they'd all be preoccupied with tracking down Joe Breen.

When his Explorer came through the other end of the woods, through the abandoned security shack, past the eight-foot-high stone walls, and around the traffic circle, Jesse realized just how alone he would be. Masthead Manor was one of those McMansion developments of faux-Victorians and fancy, brick-faced colonials that the financial collapse had rendered ghost towns. Only a few of the thirty or so units had been completed. The rest lay in various states of construction. Some lacked only their façades, whole sections of Tyvek house wraps flapping in the wind like ragged-toothed sails. Others were nothing more than concrete foundations and a few sheets of plywood decking. Time at Masthead Manor seemed to have stopped mid–hammer swing. In the dim predawn light and gray mist, it felt to Jesse like a movie set for the end of the world.

Masthead Manor was laid out in six circular streets. The homes with the largest lots, backyards to the woods, were on Connecticut Circle, the outermost street. Jesse imagined it would look like a crop circle or a cornfield maze from the air. As instructed, he parked his Explorer in the unpaved driveway of 4 Connecticut Circle. The house itself was nothing more than a foundation and one floor of framed walls. He walked through the lots to 1 Rhode Island Circle, the innermost and, unsurprisingly, smallest of the six streets.

Surrounded by vast stands of old-growth pines, the development—a forty-five-minute drive west-northwest from Boston—was so isolated that not even the local teenagers had happened onto it. There wasn't one bit of graffiti anywhere, nor had any of the windows been broken or shot out.

The three homes on Rhode Island Circle had been completed, though their lots were nothing more than dirt mounds. One Rhode Island was a big colonial. Jesse noticed that the windows of this house, unlike any other in the development, had been boarded over. He wasn't sure he liked that, but there wasn't much to like about any of it. He found the most level path to the front door. He didn't hesitate. It was too late for second thoughts. The room was dark in spite of the light leaking through the front door.

"Close the door behind you, Chief Stone, and take two steps straight ahead. And, Chief, I will be able to see everything you do very clearly. Remember that."

The voice was high-pitched, with no

discernible regional accent. Not only couldn't Jesse identify an accent, he couldn't see the man giving him the instructions. But he did as he was told, closing the door and taking the steps. The room was now black and momentarily silent. The silence was broken by a grating metal noise followed by a sharp click.

"Do you recognize that sound, Chief?"

"M-4?"

"Fair guess. It's an MP-5, and if you deviate in the slightest from my instructions I will empty the clip into you before you can have another thought."

"No need to threaten me, Mr. Peepers. I've been warned about you."

"Use that name again and I will shoot out your kneecaps. And that would be just for starters."

"Understood. I'm not here to do anything but give you what you want and get Kayla out of here."

"Then this should be fairly simple. Place the item in question at your feet and take two more steps ahead."

Jesse took the camera out of his pocket,

placed it by his feet, and stepped. He felt something touch his forehead, and he fought not to react.

"You are a cool customer, aren't you, Chief Stone. Most people would have jumped at that touch."

"I'm not most people."

There was a strained, nasally laugh in the darkness. "Everyone thinks that about themselves. That they aren't like most other people. You would be very disappointed to discover that you are exactly like most people in any manner that counts."

"Is that a bad thing?"

Peepers paid the question no mind. "That was a string you felt. There is a flashlight attached to the end of it. Pull the string up until you have the flashlight in your palm. Do not aim it at my voice. Doing so—"

"My kneecaps. I remember. Besides, I saw your face even before I stumbled onto the camera. You were at the accident scene in Helton. I walked right in front of your car."

"So you did. Shine the light on the floor at the camera."

Jesse shined the light at the camera, but Mr. Peepers did not react.

"We both know it's not the camera you want," Jesse said. "It's the camera chip and the photos I printed out that you want."

There was a short burst of gunfire. Jesse fell to the floor, reflexively covering his head, for all the good it would have done him. But the camera was the only casualty.

"Now you are going to tell me you don't have the chip or photos on you. Would that be about it?"

"That's about it," Jesse said. "You aren't a stupid man. I'm not, either. I didn't figure Kayla would be with you. You tell me where she is, I tell you where the chip and photos are."

"And I should trust you because…"

"You've spoken to Gino Fish. If he didn't vouch for me, we wouldn't be standing here. Kayla would be dead and you would be gone. My word counts for something."

"Mrs. Prado is in the basement of the house next door to your left. She's unconscious but alive and relatively unharmed. A shame, really. I would have enjoyed destroying her one little piece at a time."

"Why?"

"Why what?"

"Why do you enjoy it?"

"Do you ask a praying mantis why?"

Jesse stopped before he made Mr. Peepers angry again.

"But she's okay," he said.

"My word counts for something, too, Chief. You will find a bonus in the basement as well."

"You killed Harlan Salter?"

There was that nasally laugh again. "You'll see. Now, Chief, the chip and photos."

"Front seat of my SUV. Door's open."

"Unoriginal," Peepers said.

"I'm just a cop. We're not known for our creativity."

"Go to the door and throw your car keys, cell phone, and weapon away from the house."

"I'm unarmed and I left my cell phone in Paradise," he said. "Those were your instructions."

"Your keys, then. Shut the door when you've finished. When you've done that, strip. All your clothes off."

Jesse considered barking about that last part, but he did as he was told. Only when he was unhitching his belt did he realize Mr. Peepers had already gone.

83

Jesse threw on his shirt and jacket, buckled his belt, and yanked the flashlight off its string. He ran to the house next door. As he ran he heard a car engine turn over, its tires rolling over rocks and dirt. He didn't bother looking for it. He wanted nothing more to do with Mr. Peepers, and he hoped Peepers wanted nothing more to do with him. He realized the killer wouldn't be pleased that Jesse had fudged the truth a little about the quality of the photographs, but at least Peepers would know there weren't any photos of him, good or bad, out there. The front door to the Victorian was open. When Jesse found the access to the basement, he used the flashlight to navigate the darkened steps.

The house was vast, as was the basement, and it was about thirty seconds before he found Kayla—nude and unconscious, but breathing—in a room lighted by a dozen portable lanterns. She was faceup on a stainless-steel table. There was a nasty burn mark the size of a man's fist on the inside of her left thigh. He folded up his shirt and placed it under Kayla's head. He put his jacket over her to keep her warm. While tucking the jacket around her, he heard muted groaning. He looked around the room and found a closet door. There on the concrete floor in a puddle of blood was the nude, barely conscious Vic Prado. His face was wrecked, his lips exploded. His arms were bent at unnatural angles. And it took Jesse a second to realize that the annoying little stones scraping under his boots were Vic's teeth. But before he could bend down to lift Vic up, there was gunfire.

Jesse was sprinting in the opposite direction through the lots he had taken to get to 1 Rhode Island Circle. Through the framing of two unfinished houses, he saw his Explorer, the front door flung open. As he got closer and his sight lines changed, he noticed the front end of another vehicle. It wasn't a white Nissan Sentra but a black Chevy Silverado. His heart jumped into his throat and his guts twisted in a knot because he recognized the pickup as Suit Simpson's. He didn't want to believe it, but he had very little choice. From half a street away, Jesse saw what he prayed he would never see: Suit Simpson facedown on the ground next to the open door of his truck.

"Fuck! Fuck!" Jesse screamed as he ran, tears streaming down his face.

Jesse loved Suit like a little brother and had always feared something like this might happen. In spite of what Jesse told him, Suit would never have made it as a big-city cop. Jesse didn't know what he would do if Suit was dead. Then he saw movement. Suit was clawing at the ground. Jesse remembered that he'd ordered his people to wear their vests since DeAngelo had been murdered at the mall by those psychos the Lincolns. That made him breathe a little easier until he reached Suit and saw all the blood.

He pushed Suit's nine-millimeter out of the way and flipped Suit onto his back.

There was a line of blood across his abdomen.

"What are you doing here, Suit?" Jesse said, stripping off Suit's jacket and pressing his palms down hard on the wounds.

"I think I winged him, Jesse."

"That's not what I asked you."

"Initiative, Jesse. You're always after me to take the initiative."

"If you live, I'm going to kill you."

Jesse patted Suit's pockets for his cell phone. Found it. Dialed 911.

"Officer down! Officer down! Multiple gunshot wounds. Multiple victims."

When he was done giving the location, he went back to stanching the wounds. Suddenly, Suit's chest was heaving and he was gasping for breath.

"I...I knew you were...lying...Jesse. You didn't e-even spot me following...you. I figured...you might need...back—"

"Did I ask you for backup?"

"I heard the...gunfire jus-just as I... pulled up, but...I didn't know where it—"

"Shut up, Suit. That's an order."

"Then I saw the...white Sen...tra and

I—I clipped him."

"You said that. Now shut up! Help is coming."

"Okay, Jesse."

Then Suit Simpson went quiet.

84

Joe Breen should have left Scottsdale for parts unknown after Mike called him and warned him he was burnt. That Mike used a phone at all should have let Joe know how bad things were.

"My guy in the Boston PD says your picture's all over the freakin' place. They're looking for you on some stupid assault charge in Paradise, but my guy says it don't smell right. They must've figured out you did the girl. You tell me where you land at and I'll wire you money."

But Joe Breen hadn't run. Running wasn't in his nature, but that wasn't the issue. It wasn't even that his split kit—a hundred grand in cash, a fake passport, driver's license, a knife, and a Glock—was in a self-storage locker in Newton. It was Moira. He couldn't walk out on her without an explanation or without asking her to come with him. Art was something you could do anywhere, and so was love.

He knew he had some time, that it would take the cops a while to find his house because he hadn't bought it in his name. So instead of heading north, south, or west from Scottsdale, Joe Breen headed back to Boston.

"Moira, Moira!" he called to her as he came through the front door. "Come on, we've got to talk."

But there was no answer.

"Come on, Moira. I know you've no classes this late."

When there was still no answer, he went looking for her in the kitchen. If she'd left a note about shopping, it would be there. As he approached the kitchen, something told him to slow down. Whether it was an unfamiliar smell or the nature of the quiet, he couldn't say. He looked at the decorative mirror another art-school girl had made for him that hung on the wall facing the kitchen. What he saw in the glass was Moira, the left arm of a nerdy-looking bastard wrapped around her throat, and the muzzle of a Sig Sauer pressed to her temple. He could have turned and been out of the house in a few seconds, but if he hadn't run from Scottsdale, he wouldn't run now. He put his arms in the air and stepped slowly into the kitchen. Moira's eyes were wide with fear, and when he appeared in the kitchen, tears began running down her cheeks. She shook her head as much as she dared.

"Run, Joe! Run!" Her voice was choked and cracked.

Mr. Peepers said, "He won't run."

"You're right. I won't. You'd be Salter's man, then."

"Something like that," Peepers said.

"Then you're here to extract payment."

"Same answer."

Now there was an added look of confusion in Moira's expression.

She said, "What are you talking about?"

Neither man responded.

"Well, the girl hasn't run a tab," Joe said. "She's done nothing wrong."

"Wrong place, wrong time. Keeps the wrong company. She's done a lot of wrong," Peepers said. "Easy way or the hard way? The harder it is for you, the easier for her."

"Let's talk deal."

Mr. Peepers smiled. He liked this part. When they bargained. It always started with bargaining. Eventually they'd get to begging. Then praying for death. He liked that part best of all.

"I'm listening."

"To start, there's a key to my locker in Newton. A hundred grand. But money won't be enough for you. No," Joe said. "You enjoy your work. So name your price."

"Would you slit your own throat to save her?"

"In a way, I've already slit me own throat."

Peepers didn't like that answer and squeezed harder on Moira's neck so that she was choking.

"Stop it," Joe said. "Yes, I'd slit me own throat gladly if you'll let her walk out of here."

"Too easy." Peepers relaxed his hold on her neck.

"Let me put it to you like this, then," Joe said. "I'm good at this myself, you know, and I've got a lot to answer for. I can force you to make it quick for the both of us. If I rushed you now, from this close, you'd have to put one in my head or risk me getting to you. Believe me, I'll take a lot of killing, certainly more than one nine-millimeter. I think you know that. More than one shot up here and you risk my neighbors hearing the shots. You'd have to do her quick or drag her out of here. Or you can let her go and take your time with me. You let her go. Once I know she's safe, you can have your way with me."

"How do I know you won't run?"

Joe said, "Name it."

Mr. Peepers nodded at the knife block on the kitchen counter. "Take the chef's knife and cut your Achilles tendon."

"Which one?"

"Both."

Moira let out a muffled scream. Peepers squeezed her neck again.

"Moira, don't fight him," Joe said. "I've got to answer for my sins. I've killed people for insults and money. I've killed people on the word of others. You'll be the better without me. Please let me do this for you."

Joe put his arms down, slowly removed the chef's knife from the block, and placed a folded dish towel in his mouth. He sat down on a kitchen chair, rolled up his left pants leg, and rolled down his sock. He put the blade to the taut skin at the back of his leg.

"No deal," Peepers said. "The second she gets through the door, she'll scream her head off, and the cops will be here in two minutes. We can't have that. Cut the tendon and I promise to do her quickly. You'll have to watch it, but it's all I'm offering. Clock's running. Tick. Tick. Tick."

Joe leapt forward out of the chair. Almost before his body straightened he felt the burn and tear of the bullet, but his momentum carried him into Moira and Peepers. Peepers's choke hold on Moira's neck released as he reflexively threw that arm behind him. Moira was knocked to the side as they all landed. Peepers let out a grunt, the tear in his shoulder from where the cop had hit him opening up.

REED FARREL COLEMAN

Blood soaked through the dressing, then his shirt and jacket. But he was good at his job and kept firing the Sig into Joe's body.

"Run!" Joe screamed. "Run!"

He heard her feet on the tile floor, and just before he took his last breath he realized that redemption sounded like a slamming kitchen door.

85

Diana Evans left her bags by the front desk and walked into Jesse Stone's office. She had stayed in Paradise for the last ten days and had made the ride to visit Suit Simpson with Jesse every day until Suit was taken off the critical list. And she had stayed long enough for Vic Prado to confess his litany of sins to several law enforcement agencies, including the Boston PD, the FBI, and the SEC. Of course he blamed his involvement on Mike Frazetta and Joe Breen. Mike Frazetta blamed Vic. No one quite believed either of them.

"You hear Vic's confession?" she said.

"Some of it."

"Their scheme was pretty smart. Pyramiding funds from one private firm to pay off investors at the next and skimming a small percentage. Madoff's mistake was that he did it too boldly. This was the same idea on a much smaller scale and spreading it around. It would have worked, too, as long as their inside connection at the SEC alerted them to firms with possible violations."

"In other words, forever," Jesse said.

She laughed, her smile lingering. Although it was a beautiful smile, the most alluring he had ever seen, Jesse had to admit that some of the neon had gone out of it. Whether that was in the smile itself or in his head, he couldn't say.

Diana nodded. "By the time the pyramid collapsed, Vic would have been dead or out of the country. Frazetta's name wasn't on any of the documentation, so he was insulated. Not now, not with Vic testifying against him. The insulation is gone."

"How about Harry Freeman?" Jesse said. "Vic or Frazetta cop to that?"

"No. They wouldn't, would they? With Breen dead, there's no link to them. At least you solved your murder. Have you spoken with the dead girl's parents?"

"A few days ago."

"What was that like?"

"Like living their girl's death all over

again," he said.

"Closure is overrated."

"Closure doesn't exist."

Diana nodded in agreement. "It's a myth. We humans like our myths. Do you believe Vic's story about the reunion? He says he hoped to talk to you about turning himself in and you working out a plea deal for him. Then, when Breen murdered the Penworth girl, it all blew up."

"Vic says a lot of things. It doesn't matter whether I believe him or not."

"Any news on Mr. Peepers?"

Jesse shrugged.

Diana said, "I guess he's gone with the wind. Breen's girlfriend described him the same way everyone else did."

"Nobody gets out alive, Diana. There are times I take comfort in that."

"Yeah, he'll die eventually or get himself killed. Your guy wounded him."

Jesse laughed. "Suit's in a hospital bed with his guts shot out and that's all he's talking about."

"Breen's girlfriend says he sacrificed himself for her although he could have run. I wonder why he did that."

"Love makes people do strange things," he said.

"Tell me about it."

"You going back to the Bureau?"

"I'm resigning. I probably would have gotten fired, anyway. Technically, I've been lying to them for more than a year now. I don't think I ever really belonged there, and now I'm sure I didn't. I'm heading back to D.C. to get things in order and then I'm going to New Mexico to be with Kayla for a while."

"Good. You know, I'm down two cops," he said. "I could use someone like you."

She leaned over and kissed him hard on the mouth. "I love you, Jesse Stone. Maybe someday I'll come back here and we can work on that. First I've got to work on me."

"I don't know. You seem more than okay to me."

She kissed him again. This time softly on the cheek.

"Good-bye, Jesse."

"You sure you don't want me to drive

you to the airport?"

"No, but don't. I'm not sure I could get on the plane if you were there, and I really need to get on that plane."

"Okay."

He stood and put his arms around her. He called her a taxi, and when it showed he walked her outside. He lingered until the cab's taillights were two tiny red dots in the distance.

When he forced himself to come back inside, Molly handed him a large brown envelope.

"Messenger brought it," she said.

"Anything else going on?"

"All quiet on the western front. Why'd you let her go, Jesse?"

"She needed me to."

"You're an idiot."

"What was that?" he said.

"You're an idiot, Chief."

"Better."

At his desk, he opened the envelope. Inside was an 8×10 color photograph of his ex-wife, Jenn. It was a candid shot of her in the sun at an outdoor café. Although he had finally and successfully broken the unhealthy ties between them, seeing her face made his heart jump a little. Jenn wasn't as stunning as Diana, and she was beginning to show some age, but Jesse didn't suppose a day would ever come when he wouldn't think her beautiful. When he flipped the photograph over, Jesse went cold. The note read:

Do you ask a praying mantis why?

Jesse reached for his phone and punched in Jenn's number.

Acknowledgments

I owe a huge debt of gratitude to Chris Pepe, David Hale Smith, Helen Brann, and the Estate of Robert B. Parker. Of course, none of this would have been possible without Mr. Parker's creation of Jesse Stone novels. Thank you also to Michael Brandman.

Thanks to Jim Born. He knows why. To Tom Schreck, Ace Atkins, S. J. Rozan, Peter Blauner, Hank Phillippi Ryan, Daniel Woodrell, and Peter Spiegelman for

\helping me through the process.

Special thanks to Otto Penzler for asking me to write an essay on Jesse Stone for **In Pursuit of Spenser** and to Judy Bobalik, who helped stoke my interest in the character. A nod also to Marjorie Tucker.

As always to Rosanne, Kaitlin, and Dylan. None of it would happen or mean a thing without them.